THE GREEN MAN

A Selection of Recent Titles by Kate Sedley
in the Roger the Chapman Mysteries series

THE BROTHERS OF GLASTONBURY
ST JOHN'S FERN
THE WEAVER'S INHERITANCE
THE WICKED WINTER
THE GOLDSMITH'S DAUGHTER *
THE LAMMAS FEAST *
NINE MEN DANCING *
THE MIDSUMMER ROSE *
THE BURGUNDIAN'S TALE *
THE PRODIGAL SON *
THE THREE KINGS OF COLOGNE *
THE GREEN MAN *

* available from Severn House

THE GREEN MAN

Kate Sedley

This first world edition published in Great Britain 2008 by
SEVERN HOUSE PUBLISHERS LTD of
9–15 High Street, Sutton, Surrey SM1 1DF.
This first world edition published in the USA 2008 by
SEVERN HOUSE PUBLISHERS INC of
595 Madison Avenue, New York, N.Y. 10022.

British Library Cataloguing in Publication Data

Sedley, Kate
  The Green Man. - (Roger the Chapman mysteries)
  1. Roger the Chapman (Fictitious character) - Fiction
  2. Peddlers and peddling - England - Fiction 3. Great
  Britain - History - Edward IV, 1461-1483 - Fiction
  4. Detective and mystery stories
  I. Title
  823.9'14[F]

  ISBN-13: 978-0-7278-6617-2 (cased)
  ISBN-13: 978-1-84751-052-5 (trade paper)

All Severn House titles are printed on acid-free paper.

Typeset by Palimpsest Book Production Ltd.,
Grangemouth, Stirlingshire, Scotland.
Printed and bound in Great Britain by
MPG Books Ltd., Bodmin, Cornwall.

One

It seemed a day like any other. Or as much like any other as days had been for the past nine months. For the autumn and winter just gone had been two of the worst seasons in living memory.

It had started the previous August with tearing gales and lashing rain, ruining the crops as they stood, unharvested, in the fields, and not letting up until late October. But when the wind and wet finally died away, it was only to give place to early frosts so severe that they turned the ground to iron; and by Christmas heavy falls of snow blanketed the countryside. Vegetables rotted in the earth, and those that were, with Herculean effort and broken spade-handles, eventually lifted into the light of day, were so blighted by disease, and so stunted, as to be barely worth the effort. On the other hand, people had to live – or try to – and any effort was better than starvation. For, of course, it goes without saying that famine, blood brother to storms and subsequent bad harvests, stalked the land from north to south, east to west. Meat, too, was scarce, cattle and sheep having succumbed to the biting cold, dying where they stood in the open fields as they struggled to survive. What hay and grain herdsmen had managed to lay their hands on, soon ran out or was commandeered for the troops mustering somewhere – or so we were told – in Yorkshire and Northumberland, ready to repel invasion by the Scots.

Our northern neighbours had been causing trouble along the marches for some two or three years now, and rumours of proposed retaliation had even become a common talking point in our south-western fastness, where what went on in the border country between England and Scotland was usually a matter of supreme indifference to us. Indeed, what transpired in France had more immediacy for Bristolians – although, admittedly, only a very little. Our preoccupation was always with Ireland, and the love-hate, friend-foe relationship that existed between us (you will note that after all those years living in the place I had at last begun to count myself a citizen) and the men of Waterford and the southern Irish coast.

However, as I have said, it was Scotland – a country generally as remote to your average southerner as the moon – that was one of the two main topics of conversation in the Green Lattis alehouse on that early May evening in the year of Our Lord, 1482. The other topic, it goes without saying, was what, if anything, our wives and goodies would have managed to scrounge, beg or borrow for our suppers; for as we had moved into the new year at the end of March, nothing much had changed. Food was as difficult to come by as ever.

My old friend, Jack Nym, was looking particularly gloomy. Goody Nym's meals were something to be avoided at the best of times and the scarcity of victuals had proved a godsend to her; an excuse to serve up nothing but mouldy bread and a few even mouldier vegetables. Kind-hearted neighbours shared their own meagre meals with the carter and his wife, taking pity on Jack's rumbling belly.

'What's your woman giving you for supper tonight, then?' he asked me, staring gloomily into his beaker of ale.

'Oh, Adela will have contrived something or another,' I answered with slightly more confidence than I actually felt.

But my wife was a good manager and a shrewd housewife who had her regular contacts among the stallholders of the city market. Always polite, always a prompt payer, they were willing to provide her with any extra titbits or savoury morsels that their own womenfolk had rejected. Nevertheless, the constant recurrence of a brown stew made from bones and bits of offal, flavoured with the herbs Adela had picked and dried the previous summer, was beginning to pall. For a good trencherman like myself, it was an affront to a hearty appetite.

'I'm losing weight,' I grumbled. 'I had to take my belt in another notch this morning.'

'Consider yourself lucky to have a belt,' remarked a stranger – a travelling mummer judging by the cap and bells he had just thrown down on the bench beside him – who had joined our table, squeezing on to the recently vacated stool next to Jack. (The inn was packed to suffocation with people, like myself, drowning their worries and sorrows.) He went on, 'In some parts o' the country, they're boiling 'em and eating the leather.'

'Pooh!' said Jack. 'D'you expect us to believe that? Go rattle yer bells in someone else's ears.'

The mummer took a long draught of ale and then slammed his beaker back on the table.

'Think I'm joking, do you? Mother o' God! You lot down here don't know you're born! Think you're hard done by? You know nothing! Nothing! It's twice, three times as bad in London and down into Kent. But further north! Dear God in Heaven! People are dying like flies in summer. In places, the ground's still so hard, they can't bury the dead. The charnel-houses are full and likely to remain so until the weather changes. This bit o' May sunshine and warmth you been gettin' these few days past ain't even reached as far as Gloucester yet. I was there yesterday with my friends.' And he jerked his head in the direction of a settle set against the wall where a couple of other mummers sat, gaily bedecked, but with faces as long as sin, glumly supping their ale. 'We did a bit of mumming on the abbey green, but folk didn't want to know.' He jiggled the purse at his belt, but there was no comforting, responsive chink. 'Empty!' he informed us. Our new acquaintance threw a few coins on the table. 'That's all our worldly wealth, my friends. It's the abbey dormitory for us tonight, and some black bread and broth from the monks' kitchen.' He glanced about him. 'Same story here by the looks o' things. Doom and gloom. Doom and more gloom. Have you had any riots yet?'

'Riots?' Jack and I asked, almost in one breath. 'Where has there been rioting? And who's been rioting?' I added.

'Everyone, everywhere,' was the comprehensive answer, accompanied by a shrug of the shoulders. 'There's a mort of unrest all over the country.'

It was my turn to shrug. 'Well, I suppose that isn't so surprising if conditions are as bad as you say.'

'It ain't only conditions brought about by the weather,' he

retorted. 'Wages are falling, especially in sheep farming country.' He took another swig of ale and wiped his mouth on his sleeve. 'It's this war between France and Burgundy that's half the trouble. More than half.'

I took a closer look at him. The mummer had a broken nose and bright, inquisitive eyes set in a small, shrewd face with, I suspected, an even shrewder brain behind it. Most of his calling had no interest in anything beyond shaking their bells, waggling their staves and earning enough by their antics to keep body and soul together. But this man was different: he evidently took a lively interest in what was going on around him, listened to what people said and had sense enough to add two and two and come up with the answer four.

Not so Jack Nym.

'Wha's it got to do with France and Burgundy?' he demanded truculently. He had all your average Englishman's contempt for anything that went on outside of his own borders.

Our companion looked down his nose, squinting into his empty beaker. 'War's going badly for Burgundy,' he said. 'People reckon we ought to be going to the aid of Duchess Mary and her husband. There's a lot o' bad feeling against King Edward that he won't send troops to assist the Hapsburg.'

'Why?' Jack's tone was more belligerent than ever. He was slightly drunk, and that always made him aggressive.

'Oh, for pity's sake, think man!' I exclaimed, irritated, before the mummer had a chance to reply. 'This country relies on Burgundy to buy vast quantities of our wool and woven goods. It's one of our best markets in the whole of Europe. Furthermore, our own Princess Margaret is its Dowager Duchess.'

Jack gave due consideration to this argument, then nodded in agreement. He was well aware from his experience as a carter that this was true. He switched sides.

'Then why don't the King do summat about it? Why don't he send men to aid Maximilian?'

'Because,' I reminded him, at the same time signalling to a passing pot-boy to refill our beakers and also that of the mummer, 'Edward receives a big, fat, annual pension from

King Louis – as do a number of his friends and cronies –
and my guess is that he can't afford to lose it. Which he
surely would if he intervened in the war on Burgundy's
behalf.'

'Still,' Jack objected, 'if not doing so is making him unpopular . . . if people are rioting, as our friend here says they
are, you'd think . . .'

'Money's money,' I pointed out. 'Especially when you
have all your wife's family to support. The Woodvilles are
a rapacious lot by all I've ever heard of them.'

The mummer nodded. 'By all anybody's ever heard o'
them,' he concurred. 'And then there's all the king's doxies
and by-blows making claims on him, as well.' He looked
across the table at me. 'I'm with you, friend. I don't reckon
King Edward'll be raising any troops. Leastways, not to send
to Burgundy.'

'But somewhere?' I queried. 'Where then?'

He grimaced. 'Scotland's my guess. There were fighting
up north, on and off, all last year.' He jerked his head backwards at his two dozy companions, now both half asleep,
one dribbling ale from the corner of his mouth, the other
just beginning to snore with an even, gentle rhythm. 'We
was way up last summer, over the border in fact, before the
start of this terrible weather drove us southwards in a hurry.
We was near Edinburgh when Lord Howard sailed the English
fleet up the River Forth and burned one o' their Scottish
towns to the ground. Blackness, I think they called it –
although it ain't easy to know what those heathenish bastards
call anything, the way they mangle the English tongue.
And o' course, that was another reason we had to leave
Scotland in double quick time. We Saxons – Sassenachs is
their word for it – weren't popular to begin with, but after
Lord Howard's little foray, as you might guess, we were
lucky to escape with our lives.'

'Is the Duke of Gloucester involved in any of this?' I
asked, my thoughts naturally turning towards that member
of the royal family I not only respected and knew well – I
didn't refer to this as it would surely have raised more questions and answers than I was prepared to be troubled with
– but whose birthday and age I also shared.

'Oh lord, yes!' The mummer was emphatic. 'As it so happened, both he and the king were at Nottingham when we passed through there last October. There was no official announcement, but all the townsfolk we spoke to said it was to do with the war in Scotland. In fact, it was only a few weeks later when we fell in with a travelling tinker who'd come from the Scottish marches who told us that Berwick has been put under siege.'

'Where's this Berwick?' Jack wanted to know. For once, I couldn't air my superior knowledge. I didn't know, either.

'Scotland,' our acquaintance informed us kindly with a condescending smile. (We were so obviously west country turnips with very little experience of the wider world.) 'Right on the border. Mind you, until about twenty years ago, it was English.'

'So how did them Scots buggers get hold of it?' Jack demanded, jutting his jaw pugnaciously. 'Some dopey garrison commander let them in?'

But on this head, the mummer was unable to satisfy our curiosity. So I'll set down here what I learned later; that two decades previously, the late King Henry and his wife, Margaret of Anjou, fleeing from the victorious Yorkist army, fetched up in Scotland and bartered Berwick for Scottish aid. Now, I presumed – correctly as it turned out – King Edward wanted it back; a sop to those of his many subjects who thought him a mercenary coward not to go to Burgundy's aid.

'Ah, well,' said Jack, scratching himself and disturbing his fleas, 'if it's that far away, there's nothing to worry us.'

'Nothing at all,' I agreed.

I really should have known better than to tempt fate. And I should certainly have known better than to treat us all to yet another beaker of ale. Money was scarce and getting scarcer as people saved what little they had for necessities instead of the frippery inessentials of a pedlar's pack. True, I continued to do a reasonable trade in needles, thread, laces and suchlike articles; but the items that really brought in the money – gloves, lengths of silk, the occasional copper or silver ring, picked up cheap and sold at a profit – now remained unsold week after week. As I have already mentioned, Adela was a clever housewife and had always been able to make one groat do the work of two when needed. And, indeed, during the past five years, since her marriage to me, this particular skill had been much in demand, but never so much as now when even early May had brought little relief to the sun-starved land. But a third beaker of ale, shared with convivial friends and strangers in the Green Lattis, made life appear a little rosier, a trifle more tolerable, than it had done before.

But all good things must come to an end. Our new-found acquaintance, the mummer, announced that he must be on his way, roused his two companions from their drunken slumber and asked for directions to St Augustine's Abbey. Jack thanked me for my generosity, but regretted that he was unable to stop any longer and return the compliment as his goody would be expecting him home for supper. (Goody Nym was never expecting him, and I doubted if she knew what supper was, but my sneer, indicating the belief that this was a blatant lie, was carefully ignored.) In a shorter time than it takes to tell, I found myself deserted, sitting alone at our table, ruefully counting the depleted contents of my purse and sobering rapidly.

A small, but determined hand clutched my sleeve and shook my arm. I turned in some astonishment to discover my seven-year-old daughter, Elizabeth, standing beside me.

'Bess?' I queried.

She gave me a leery glance which plainly proclaimed that she thought me as drunk as a wheelbarrow.

'Who else could it be?' she demanded impertinently. 'Do I look like another person?'

I might resent her manner, but I knew full well it was useless me trying to enact the Roman father. I could never sustain the role.

'Just tell me what you're doing here before I lose my temper,' I instructed her sharply.

'Mother sent me to fetch you,' she answered, totally impervious to the threat of paternal anger, and adding reproachfully, 'She guessed I might find you in the alehouse, and I have.'

I frowned. It was unlike Adela, however much she disapproved of my wasting money in such places at a time when it was sorely needed for other things, to send one of the children to winkle me out. She was a tolerant woman and an indulgent wife who would never put me in an awkward situation if she could possibly avoid it. (I noted a couple of grinning faces at a nearby table, and cursed under my breath.)

'So what does your mother want?' I asked, loudly enough for my fellow drinkers to understand that I was being called home for a specific purpose and not simply because my wife considered me to be malingering.

But my darling daughter refused to play my game.

'I don't know,' she replied, getting ready to leave, with or without me. 'She just said that I was to fetch you home if I found you.'

I settled myself more firmly on my stool.

'Something must have happened,' I argued sulkily. 'Otherwise, she wouldn't have sent you looking for me.'

Elizabeth sighed. She was a bright child and observed a great deal more than one imagined. She knew me in this recalcitrant schoolboy mood, and guessed that without further information I would dig in my heels and refuse to move. She pondered a moment or two, staring at me thoughtfully.

'Well, I don't know for certain,' she said at last, 'but it might have something to do with that funny little man who called at the house earlier this afternoon. About an hour or so ago.'

'What funny little man?' All my senses were suddenly alert to potential danger.

My daughter shrugged irritably. 'How do I know? I just caught a glimpse of him when Mother answered the door.' She creased her brow in an effort of recollection. 'I think I might have seen him before, though.'

'Where? When?' I had a sudden nasty feeling in the pit of my stomach.

'I can't remember. A long time ago.' Elizabeth ran out of patience and stamped her foot. 'Why don't you just come home, Father, and find out for yourself?'

It was the obvious solution, but my uneasiness was growing, although it would have been difficult for me to say quite why.

'Did your mother recognize this man?' I enquired, catching hold of Elizabeth's skirt to prevent her leaving.

'She must have done,' was the answer. 'She let him inside. He went into the parlour with her and I heard them talking. Mother said you weren't home and the man said he'd wait. He said it was urgent.'

'Is he still there?'

Elizabeth nodded. Her eyes brightened suddenly. 'Oh! And he brought us a lovely big piece of meat. I don't know what it is exactly, but it's roasting on the kitchen spit right now and it smells wonderful. And he also brought a great fat capon – for the end of the week, he said. Oh, do come on, Father! Just the thought of that meat is making my belly turn somersaults.'

'You run ahead, then,' I answered slowly, adding mendaciously, 'I haven't paid my shot yet. I'll follow you just as soon as I've done so. Tell your mother I'll only be a minute or two behind you.'

Elizabeth accepted this without demur, kissed my cheek affectionately in atonement for any offence she might have given – she knew from experience that any demonstration of submission could always win me round – and tripped gracefully out of the Green Lattis, looking forward to a roast meat supper and without a care in the world.

I, on the other hand, sat as though rooted to my rickety stool, staring unhappily into space and concocting various wild and impractical schemes for immediate flight. At the same time, I had no real idea why the advent of this stranger, and his urgent desire to speak to me, had filled me with such unease. Someone (Virgil?) had once remarked that he feared the Greeks when they came bearing gifts (or words to that effect). My sentiments exactly; and this 'Greek' had brought not just one, but two substantial offerings of flesh when most people would have been overjoyed with a very small pigeon. That in itself was sufficient to make any sane man suspicious.

But when I analysed my apparently unwarranted fear, there was something more. My daughter's description of 'a funny little man', whom she had a vague memory of having seen before, made me think at once of Timothy Plummer,

Spymaster General for (at different times) both King Edward
and his brother, Richard, Duke of Gloucester. His various
appearances in my life had never boded me any good, and
I feared that this one would prove to be no exception.

'You drinking, Roger?' the landlord called out as he passed,
pushing his way through the ever-increasing press of bodies.

Whoever else lost money in times of famine and economic
crisis, it was rarely the alehouses; at least not those in the
towns and cities. They provided comfort of a kind and a
temporary forgetfulness of men's problems. I was in the
wrong trade, but then, I had always known that. But I liked
the freedom it gave me, the sense of being in charge of my
own destiny, answerable to no man but myself. The previous
year, I had briefly given up that independence to work for,
and be paid by, my neighbour, Alderman Foster, now coming
to the end of his term as Mayor; but when the job was
finished, I had vowed to myself never to work at somebody
else's behest again.

'Another beaker of the same?' the landlord persisted. He
hated the waste of space non-drinking customers took up on
the stools and benches.

I shook my head resolutely and stood up. Before I had
taken two steps, another man, intent on drowning his sorrows,
had slipped into my seat.

Once outside the door, in the lee of All Saints' Church, I
paused to breathe in the cool late afternoon breezes. There
was a hint of rain in the air and a chill that, although not
untypical of early May, was nevertheless far more pronounced
than was customary, even for that unreliable month. I fought
down the urge to turn and run – anywhere so long as it was
away from Small Street and the man who was waiting there
for me.

Slowly, reluctantly, I forced myself to face the right direction.

I admonished myself angrily not to be so stupid; to stop
behaving like a child or an imbecile. After all, I wasn't even
sure that the 'strange little man' really was Timothy Plummer.
He might simply be someone who, having heard of my reputation as a solver of mysteries, had one of his own which
needed investigation. And that, of course, would explain the

gifts of meat as payment in advance for my services. After all, there was nothing more acceptable, or more of a bribe, in these dark and miserable times than something to fill an empty stomach.

I gave a deep sigh of relief. Of course that was it! I was allowing my imagination to run riot. And the longer I thought about things, the greater my folly in giving way to nervous fancies seemed to be.

If it were true, as the mummer had assured us it was, that King Edward and his brother were planning a summer invasion of Scotland, Timothy Plummer would be with one or the other of them, as indispensable as always. (Well, he liked to think so.) There would be absolutely no reason for him to be in the west country looking for me. It was true that I had been called upon, once or twice, to dabble my fingers in royal concerns, and had, on one occasion, gone to France in the wake of an invading army, but there had been a reason for that. I had already been engaged in an investigation that had left me little choice in the matter. But I had had nothing to do with Prince Richard or any member of his family for nearly two years. Surely, therefore, I was perfectly safe, and was letting myself fall prey to unfounded and childish fancies.

My mood lightened, and I was suddenly able to look forward to a supper of roast meat with an anticipation unmarred by ridiculous doubts and fears. The evening air all at once seemed less chilly, the clouds overhead less threatening. There was a spring in my step as I walked down Small Street, and I was even humming – in my own peculiarly tuneless fashion – a somewhat disreputable song vaguely remembered from my youth. I even began to feel carefree.

Fool! I should have known better.

As I pushed open the door of my house, the air was redolent with the delicious aroma of roasting pork with its sizzling fat, a smell I had been deprived of for what seemed like years.

'I'm home!' I shouted.

Two

'R oger, my old friend!'
The familiar voice, accompanied by an equally
familiar figure as Timothy Plummer emerged from our
parlour, made me jump nearly out of my skin. During the
short walk from the Green Lattis to home, I had so convinced
myself that my original suspicion had been at fault, that to
find it true was a greater shock than if it had never entered
my head in the first place.

'You!' I exclaimed, recoiling.

'Me, indeed!' he returned, arranging his narrow features
in a smile as false as a woman's promise to obey her
husband. He added reproachfully, 'You might sound pleased
to see me.'

'Well, I'm not!' My reply was uncompromising.

He sniffed the air suggestively. 'You'll note I've brought
my welcome with me.'

I pointed out that that in itself was unusual enough to
make me suspicious.

He tried to look hurt, but gave up the attempt after a short
struggle and grinned instead. Before he could say anything
else, however, Adela appeared from the kitchen clutching a
large ladle with which she had been basting the roast.

'What does he want, Roger?' she demanded truculently.
'Whatever it is, don't agree to it.'

Timothy clicked his tongue reprovingly, but offered no
comment; a fact that made me uneasier than ever. This was
his cue to wheedle, 'It's for Duke Richard, Roger. He needs
your services. You can't refuse him.' But he didn't. He merely
stared hard at me and said nothing, although with such an
air of authority in both look and silence that my heart began
to beat uncomfortably fast.

'Is he staying to supper?' my wife asked ungraciously, ignoring our unwanted guest by the simple expedient of turning her shoulder to him and addressing me.

I shrugged. 'I suppose he'll have to. He provided it, after all.'

Timothy bowed ironically.

'You'd better come and have it then. It's ready,' Adela snapped, and marched ahead of us into the kitchen.

The three children – my daughter, Elizabeth, my stepson, Nicholas, and Adela's and my son, Adam – were already seated around the table. The latter, who would be four the following month, was now considered old enough to sit on his little chair without the necessity of being tied to it; although the way in which he was wriggling around suggested that a few falls were in store for him before he mastered the art of behaving properly.

Adela had already removed the pork from the spit and put it on a plate which she placed in front of me. She handed me a knife as I took my seat at the head of the table, at the same time waving Timothy Plummer to a vacant stool between herself and Adam. She had boiled some vegetables to accompany the meat – cabbage and root vegetables and those little water parsnips known as skirretts – and she spooned a portion on to each plate as I handed them round, a proceeding accomplished in complete silence. Even our normally ebullient brood seemed cowed, as though aware that something unusual was going on. Finally, when everyone had been served, I said grace and picked up my knife, spearing a mouth-wateringly large chunk of pork on its tip; enough to preclude conversation for several minutes.

At last, however, I had emptied my mouth sufficiently to ask, 'So, why are you here, Master Plummer? What do you want with me?'

If he noticed the formality of my approach, he ignored it. He put down his knife, sucked his greasy fingers and beamed.

'Roger, my lad, this is your lucky day!' I knew at once that I was in serious trouble.

'You're going to Scotland.'

Scotland? Scotland! As well be invited to go on a trip to find the elusive Isle of Brazil or the lands of Prester John.

'No,' I said flatly.

'No!' echoed Adela with even greater emphasis.

'No!' yelled Adam at the top of his powerful lungs, giving us, for once, his unstinted support, even if he didn't understand why.

I paused in the act of chewing and took a deep breath.

'Tell the Duke,' I said, 'that much as I regret having to refuse any request of his, on this occasion I must decline. Scotland is too far afield. It's a journey that is bound to take months and I cannot abandon my wife and children to fend for themselves for so long. God in heaven, man! You must know what conditions have been like these past months. I haven't enough money to leave Adela safely provided for, for such a length of time.' I added bitterly, 'It's not like His Grace to be so unreasonable – unless, of course, he isn't aware of what's been going on in the country at large?'

'Of course Duke Richard's aware!' Timothy bit back, dropping all pretence at amiability. 'Especially living in the north, where matters are a great deal worse than they are down here, in the south, I can assure you. But that's beside the point. Mistress Chapman and your family will be provided for – well provided for, I promise you – during your absence.'

'No,' I said again, shaking my head slowly from side to side to make certain that he understood. 'I am not going to Scotland for any consideration whatsoever, and that is my final word. What? That heathenish country, where the barbarians can't even speak English like civilized human beings! No, I thank you. And you may tell His Grace of Gloucester so with my blessing.'

Timothy regarded me pityingly while he removed shreds of meat from between his teeth with the point of his knife. Then he heaved a dramatic sigh. (He really should have tried his hand as Judas Iscariot in one of the Easter Passion plays.)

'I'm afraid you don't quite understand, Roger.' He smiled gently. 'This isn't a request or an appeal to your friendship or better nature. This is a royal command, not just by the Duke, but by the King himself.'

I refused to believe it. 'You won't coerce me into whatever it is you want me to do by telling lies. I will not go to Scotland.'

For answer, Timothy reached into the pouch at his waist

and, with his free hand, withdrew a folded parchment with an important looking wax disc attached.

'The king's personal seal,' he said. 'This is my authority to take you back to London with me, when I return, and from there on to Northamptonshire, to the king's castle at Fotheringay. Do you want to read it? I believe you can read.'

He knew perfectly well that I could read, and write, too. Brother Hilarion had taught me to do both, and many other things besides, during my novitiate at Glastonbury Abbey. It was not that good old man's fault that I had rejected the cloistered life and decided on the freedom of the open road. But now that freedom was being eroded. I put up a fight, even though I knew in my heart it was useless.

'Northamptonshire? Make up your mind. I thought I was going to Scotland.'

Timothy pushed aside his empty plate. Adela had also stopped eating, but that, I could tell, was due to a sudden lack of appetite. I made a pretence of continuing my supper, but I, too, had ceased to be hungry. Only the children continued to mop up the meat and vegetable juices on their plates with hunks of barley bread.

'Fotheringay first, then on to Berwick and, finally, Scotland,' Timothy explained.

There was an even more pregnant pause before I said in a taut voice that didn't seem to be my own, 'Someone told me that Berwick is under siege.'

'So it is,' he answered crisply. 'It's all right, Roger. Don't look like that. You're not going to be asked to do any fighting.'

I laid my knife down very slowly and deliberately in order to disguise the fact that my hand was shaking. Adela stood up and began pouring ale for us all: some of it was spilled on the table. Timothy smiled understandingly. It was as much as I could do to stop myself from leaping up and rearranging those smugly sympathetic features.

'Perhaps,' I said carefully, 'you might like to explain what this is all about, before we go any further.'

The Spymaster General lifted his horn beaker to his lips. I could tell that he was savouring not just the ale, but the moment, as well.

'I'm very much afraid, Roger, that this is a predicament

for which you have only yourself to blame; a situation which
has arisen – as far as you are concerned – because of your
inability to keep that nose of yours out of affairs that aren't
your business.'

'I knew it!' my wife exclaimed furiously. 'I knew this
would happen one day!'

'Knew what would happen?' I shouted, as angry as she
was. For Adela to turn on me in front of a stranger was an
unaccustomed betrayal.

Timothy waited patiently for us both to calm down. In the
interval, I sent the children to play upstairs, and the thud of
their feet was soon to be heard overhead – rather like an
army on the march, I thought with renewed dismay.

'So?' I asked our unwelcome guest, once I had my voice
under control. 'Perhaps you would care to explain how I've
brought this on myself – whatever "this" is.'

Timothy sipped his ale thoughtfully for a moment or two
before replying, then picked his teeth again. At last, he asked
slowly, 'What do you know about the present situation north
of the border?'

I could see by his expression that he wasn't expecting
much of an answer. I intended to surprise him, thanks to my
friend, the mummer, whose appearance in the Green Lattis
this afternoon had been so peculiarly fortuitous.

'Well, I know, for instance that Lord Howard sailed up
the River Forth last summer and burned a Scottish town
called Blackness. I don't imagine the locals were too happy
about that, so I would assume that there has been some retaliation in the form of border raiding.'

Timothy's eyebrows shot up until they almost disappeared
into his receding hairline.

'My, my!' he remarked, demonstrating exaggerated surprise.
'Don't tell me that there is someone in this benighted city
who actually knows what's going on beyond its walls.' I
shrugged, but said nothing, waiting for him to continue. The
bastard was enjoying himself hugely. 'As a matter of fact,' he
went on, 'the Scots have been giving us trouble for the past
two years. More trouble than usual, that is,' he amended.
'Which is why His Grace of Gloucester was made Lord
Lieutenant of the North, and why he personally oversaw the

rebuilding and repair of Carlisle's walls the winter before the
one just gone. And why he and Percy of Northumberland have
been raising the border levies.'

'And why, I suppose, he and King Edward met at Nottingham
last autumn to discuss plans for a full-scale invasion,' I put
in, and once again had the pleasure of seeing Timothy both
astonished and disconcerted.

'Roger, you astound me,' he admitted with a rueful grin.
'You have had your ear to the ground.'

'This is a port and, moreover, the second city in the kingdom,'
I pointed out. 'It's always full of sailors and itinerants generally, all bringing news of the outside world.'

'Which is mostly ignored by your fellow citizens,' was the
immediate riposte, not without some justification. The denizens
of my adopted town were an inward-looking, self-sufficient
race, not much interested in other people's problems.

'Look!' I exclaimed irritably, conscious of the mounting
tension inside me. 'This is all very well, but it doesn't explain
what you are doing here and why I am being commanded
– if that's the truth – to go to Scotland.'

'Or why it's Roger's own fault,' Adela added.

'True.' Timothy scratched his chin and one or two other,
more gruesome parts of his anatomy (where, presumably,
the fleas were settling down to their own evening meal)
before helping himself, unbidden, to another beaker of ale
and leaning forward, his elbows planted squarely on the table.
He turned to me. 'What do you know of King James, third
of that name, of Scotland?'

'Nothing whatsoever,' I answered promptly, then hesitated.
'Ah!' A faint light began to illuminate the dimmer recesses
of my mind.

'Ah, indeed!' smirked Timothy. 'So? What have you remembered?'

'I know King James has – or, rather, had – two brothers,'
I answered slowly. 'He quarrelled with them both and had
them arrested. I think I was told . . . by someone . . . that the
younger . . .'

'John, Earl of Mar,' Timothy supplied, as I paused uncer-
tainly. His small, bright eyes, reminiscent of a ferret's, stared
at me across the rim of his beaker.

'Yes. Well . . . whatever his name was . . . he died in prison in suspicious circumstances. The elder, the Duke of Albany . . .'

'Aha! You have no difficulty in recollecting his name,' my unwanted guest leered at me from the other side of the table.

I continued doggedly, as if he had not spoken. 'The elder, the Duke of Albany managed to escape and fled to France.'

'Oh, France is where he eventually fetched up,' Timothy agreed, 'at the court of his dear cousin, King Louis; who, with his propensity for stirring up trouble whenever and wherever he can, was no doubt delighted to see him. Yes; three years ago, Albany fled from Scotland to France. At least, that was the official story. You and I know somewhat better, don't we, Roger?'

I nodded dumbly.

'We know,' the spymaster continued, 'that a few ardent supporters of the Lancastrian cause brought him to Bristol with a view, when the moment should prove propitious, of taking him to Brittany to replace that uninspiring figurehead, Henry Tudor. Both, after all, are descendants of John of Gaunt's bastard Beaufort line – the Tudor through his mother, Albany through his paternal grandmother – so one was as good as another. And at the time, as I recall, there were rumours concerning Henry Tudor's health, which was supposed to be failing. Unfortunately for the conspirators, things started to go wrong when a certain pedlar stumbled into their affairs . . .'

'Unwittingly,' I cut in angrily.

'Oh, I believe you,' Timothy laughed. 'Just as I believe that, once having got the scent of a mystery, you were unable to keep that long nose of yours out of what was going on.'

'I foiled the plot,' I muttered sulkily.

'Oh, undoubtedly. You also helped the central player, Albany, to get away to Ireland with the help of those disreputable slavers you call your friends.'

'I don't call them my friends,' I retorted. 'And they call no man friend!'

Timothy shrugged. 'Probably not. I'll take your word for that. But it doesn't alter the fact that you helped an enemy of this country to escape. Albany would have been a valuable hostage in our negotiations with Scotland.'

'I don't see that,' I argued. 'Not if King James wanted him dead. Besides which,' I added indignantly, 'a year later he was in London, capering around as King Edward's honoured guest. I saw him myself when I was there at Duke Richard's request to solve that business of the young Burgundian . . . And that's not the only favour I've done His Grace over the years.'

'The duke is aware of that fact.' Timothy stretched his arms above his head until the bones cracked. 'Which is why the whole affair of Albany's escape from Bristol was overlooked and hushed up. If the king had ever found out . . . well . . . that might have been a different tale altogether. However – and here, at last, we come to the nub of the matter – Albany has always remembered you kindly. He trusts you, Roger, as he seems to trust no other person, and he wants you with him on this invasion of Scotland.'

I had to wait a moment or two before replying as the children were, by now, rampaging up and down the stairs like stampeding cattle, but when the game took another direction and the noise faded, I asked tautly, 'Are you saying that the Duke of Albany is a party to this invasion of Scotland?'

'We're going to make him king,' Timothy smiled, at his blandest. 'King Alexander the fourth.'

'And what about his brother, King James the third?' I demanded. 'Is he going to stand idly by while the English depose him?'

'Probably not,' my guest conceded. 'But he is very unpopular amongst his nobles and in the country at large – or so I've been reliably informed by those who should know. Indeed, members of my own network of spies tell the same story. I believe even his Danish wife isn't over-fond of him.'

'And hasn't he any children?'

'Three sons, but all minors. The eldest is, I think, eight. But His Grace of Gloucester tells me that in the annals of Scottish history, there is something called the Declaration of Arbroath which states that an unsatisfactory ruler can be removed by the will of the people and someone else elected to fill his place. The Scots, it seems, do not place so much emphasis on the importance of primogeniture as we do in this country.'

I drew in a hissing breath. 'And you're telling me that the Duke of Albany wants me – me! – to accompany him on this harebrained adventure?'

'That is the request he has made of King Edward. And that is the request King Edward intends to grant him. And who are you to decide that it's a harebrained adventure? Some of the wisest heads in the land have decided it's a plan that should be pursued.'

'Then some of the "wisest heads in the land" have the brains of idiots,' I retorted vehemently. 'Do they seriously expect the Scots to allow the English to choose their king for them? It hasn't happened in the past, and it won't now.'

For a long moment, Timothy and I stared at one another across the table. Then he lowered his eyes and coughed, but I knew in that instant that he agreed with me, although he would never admit it.

'That's not for you nor me to say,' he answered in a flat voice, without any trace of emotion. 'The likes of us obey orders, Roger, my lad. We don't query what we're told to do.'

True enough! But I still raised objections.

'But why in the Virgin's name does Albany imagine that he needs me? He must surely have retainers of his own, supplied by either King Louis or King Edward.'

'As a matter of fact, he has his own small household, servants of his brother, Mar, who escaped from Scotland to France after the earl was murdered.'

'He was murdered then?' I asked swiftly. 'It's certain?'

The spymaster shrugged. 'Not certain, no. But there are always rumours, and the more colourful the better. The point is, Albany thinks Mar was killed on the orders of their brother. He's nervous. That, it seems, is the reason he wants you. Not just as a bodyguard, but because he's convinced you'll be able to sniff out any plots against his sacred person.'

'This is ridiculous!' I exploded. 'The man will be surrounded not only by his loyal Scotsmen and a whole army, but by the officers of two royal households as well. I am presuming that the king leads this expedition?'

'That is the intention,' Timothy agreed. But there was a note of reservation in his tone that made me look at him rather sharply. He saw it and once again shrugged. 'His Highness has been unwell for some time. His health may . . . just may preclude his taking part in the invasion. It will . . . It maybe His Grace of Gloucester and my lord Northumberland who will finally – it is hoped – win back Berwick.'

I gathered from these stumbling sentences, from the pauses and qualifications, that King Edward's health was a great deal worse than Timothy was admitting to. It was on the tip of my tongue to make further enquiries, and I would have done so, but for the realization that I was being sidetracked yet again.

'You still haven't explained why Albany wants me to accompany him. Whether the king leads the army or stays at home, there will still be more than enough men to provide the duke with protection from his enemies. Or,' I added, as a sudden thought struck me, 'does he not trust these wonderful new allies of his? Surely he doesn't suspect the English – his old enemy – of plotting to double-cross him?'

Timothy was betrayed into a laugh, but all he said was, 'Your tongue will land you in trouble one of these fine days, my lad.' Then he agreed, 'Oh, I daresay Albany's sufficiently uneasy to be wary of our intentions towards him once negotiations are opened with the Scots . . .'

'That's after we've trounced them in open battle, of course,' I sneered.

'Roger!' Adela cut in warningly, always frightened that I was going to overstep the bounds of other people's tolerance.

The spymaster nodded approvingly at her. 'Listen to your wife, my friend. It's never wise to be too free with your opinions.'

'All I said was . . .'

'I know what you said,' Timothy snarled, losing his patience. 'It's not necessarily what you say, but how you say it. However, to return to Albany and his fears. I gather from what Duke Richard let fall that he – Albany, that is, – is convinced that his life is in danger, not from the English but from one of his own household. From one of the loyal band of the Earl of Mar's retainers who joined him in France. He suspects one of them of being in the pay of his brother, King James.'

'Why doesn't he get rid of him, then?'

Timothy sighed. 'No doubt he would if he were sure which one of them it is. But he isn't. In the opinion of Duke Richard – and, I must say, in my own – it's nothing but a mare's nest. Albany is in a highly nervous state, jumping at shadows.'

Understandable, I thought, and was inclined to sympathize with the Scotsman until the full purport of this speech suddenly hit me.

'You mean,' I demanded hotly, 'that I'm being taken along simply to protect Albany from his own stupid fears? That is the sole reason for my being torn from my wife and family, simply because Albany doesn't trust his own entourage? If that's all that's troubling him, why doesn't someone provide him with a bodyguard from the levies? A nice, tough, burly foot soldier who'll slit throats first and ask questions afterwards.'

The spymaster peered anxiously into his beaker as though surprised to find it empty. Adela, to my great annoyance, refilled it for him. Timothy raised it in my direction.

'Try not to be as stupid as you look, old friend.' I was about to remind him furiously that he was drinking my ale, even if he had brought his own victuals, but he gave me no chance, hurrying on, 'That's just the sort of mindless violence we want to avoid. The chances are that no one amongst his household is trying to kill Albany, but if it should prove that one of them is, then we want the right man brought to justice.'

'I see.' I recharged my own beaker and took a long, hard swig. I could foresee a rather nasty snag. 'And if there is such a man, and if he succeeds in his object, but I fail to stop him, where does that leave me?'

Our companion swilled the ale thoughtfully around his mouth. 'It could affect your popularity,' he admitted cautiously, after a pause.

'Oh, undoubtedly,' I snapped back viciously. 'I'd probably have to flee the country and offer my services to King James for having rid him, albeit unwittingly, of this Clarence of the north.'

Timothy gave another spontaneous bark of laughter and once more advised me to watch what I said.

'But seriously, Roger,' he added, 'Duke Richard firmly believes that there is no such danger threatening Albany. He holds it as nothing but a nervous disorder of the mind. Nevertheless, he is ready and willing to pander to the duke's wishes, and if it will make him feel any safer to have you along as his personal protector, then Duke Richard has no intention of gainsaying him. I'm sorry, my friend, but however little you may relish the prospect, on this occasion you have no choice but to obey. It's an order this time, Roger, not a request. You must be ready to accompany me to London tomorrow – a mount has already been provided for you – and from thence to Fotheringay Castle for an assembly of all the commanders and their levies on the eleventh of June, Saint Barnabas's Day.'

'And if I refuse?' I knew it was only bluster, but I was desperate and there was no harm in trying.

'Then you will come under armed escort, as my prisoner.'

I glanced at Adela. She was looking sick and white with the thought of my going so far from her and the children and with the fear that I might never come back again. I stretched out a hand and squeezed one of hers, trying to speak bravely for her sake.

'I shall be all right, sweetheart. I'll be home again well before Christmas, you'll see.' I grinned feebly. 'The months will fly by without me to distract you. You know you always say that it's like having four children to look after when I'm around.'

'He'll be safe enough,' Timothy endorsed heartily. 'And both Duke Richard and my lord Albany have sent purses of money so that you'll want for nothing, Mistress, in Roger's absence.'

'Men!' my wife exclaimed scornfully. 'You all think money makes up for everything. Well, it doesn't make up for a cold, empty bed or for someone to fetch wood and bring in water. It doesn't make up for someone to talk to after a day of talking to no one but the children.'

I knew this latter statement was something of an exaggeration. If two days passed without Margaret Walker – my former mother-in-law and Adela's cousin – visiting our house, or my wife visiting hers, I knew nothing of the matter! But I made no comment, merely turning my own reproachful gaze on our guest, even though I knew it was in vain.

'I'm sorry,' Timothy said; and to do him justice, he did manage to sound genuinely regretful. 'But there's no help for it. Roger must go to Scotland, and that's an end to it, I'm afraid.'

Three

M y first sight of Fotheringay Castle filled me with fore-boding.

A great, grim pile rising out of the flat Northamptonshire landscape, it looked like some prehistoric creature crouched to spring and devour the unwary traveller. A heavy, brooding keep stood stark against the skyline. A double moat guarded three sides of this formidable fortress and a river, which I later learned to be the Nene, made up the fourth side of its defences. Within the massive walls was a huge courtyard, around which were grouped the living quarters, including the great hall, chapel and all the workshops necessary to make such a vast edifice self-supporting. In the event of a siege, it could probably have held out for months.

This, then, was the stronghold of the Yorkist branch of the Plantagenet tree, who now occupied the throne and to whom we all owed allegiance. Here, Richard, Duke of Gloucester, had been born nearly thirty years earlier, and here the bodies of his father, Richard, Duke of York, and one of his elder brothers, Edmund, Earl of Rutland – both killed at the bloody battle of Wakefield – had been re-interred with great pomp and ceremony a mere six years ago.

I have to record that nothing about it alleviated my feeling of deep misery and gloom.

I had left Bristol the day after Timothy's unwelcome appearance and accompanied him first to London where I was reunited – if I may call it that – with His Grace, Alexander Stewart, Duke of Albany. The duke was lodged in Westminster Palace in a suite of rooms that did justice to his importance as a future king of Scotland, and one, moreover, who would be grateful enough to do exactly as he was told by his English ally. (A Canterbury tale if ever I heard one. Who was fooling whom? It was impossible to tell.) To do my young lord justice, he seemed genuinely delighted to see me, and made it plain from the start that I was to be accorded preferential treatment and never to stir far from his side. I was to sleep in his bed and to sit at his table, unless, of course, he was dining with the king or any other of his exalted kinsmen and friends. Even then, I was to remain near at hand.

Daunted by the prospect of such close and continuous proximity, I consoled myself with the knowledge that it could not possibly last beyond the first few weeks, when the duke would begin to find my ubiquitous presence as irksome as I would no doubt find his. However, his initial dependence on me was bound to make me highly unpopular with the rest of his personal servants, particularly if they had any suspicion of the reason for my inclusion in Albany's house-hold. Fortunately, although the five of them tended to scowl and mutter whenever they saw me, I had no real idea of what they were saying, for each one talked in a broad Scots dialect that was unintelligible to my west country ears.

The eldest of the five, James Petrie, was the duke's body servant, assisting him with washing, dressing, undressing and all other intimate bodily functions. (I was very relieved to know that nothing of that sort was expected of me.) Although roughly of Albany's own age – the duke was, at this time, twenty-seven years old, two years younger than myself – he looked a great deal older, a tall, emaciated man with lines of care and worry cut deep into his face. His eyes were a fierce, dark blue beneath bushy eyebrows as black as his hair, a combination of colours often to be found in the Celts. He was naturally taciturn, so I was not plagued by his mutter-ings every time I hove into view, and, indeed, said little to Albany himself. He carried out his tasks quietly and effi-ciently and even gently, with the minimum of fuss; but whether or not he were fond of his new master it was impos-sible to say. I felt that he would have behaved in the same way to a stray dog had he decided to befriend one.

John Tullo was the groom, a weather-beaten man with a passion for horses that made him almost one of them. He would whisper sweet nothings into the ear of the most mettlesome brute that ever trotted on four legs, and these terrifying creatures would drop their heads into his unsavoury bosom and nuzzle him like love-sick girls. Of course, he despised me from the start, as soon as I admitted that horses frightened me to death and insisted on being mounted on only the most docile mare in Albany's stable. He roared with laughter and passed what were obviously ribald remarks every time he clapped his big brown eyes on me; eyes that were slightly protuberant and appeared to bore right inside me. I found his gaze extremely disconcerting.

Then there was the page, David Gray, always known as Davey, a slight, willowy creature who could, if the mood took him, speak English well enough to be understood, although he would affect not to comprehend my west country speech with its harsh 'r's and diphthonged vowels. He was a pretty boy with fair, wavy hair and violet-blue eyes, who accepted with good humour the obvious teasing of his fellow servants, and of Albany himself.

'My brother, Mar, was very fond of Davey,' Albany once remarked to me, with, I thought, a certain amount of significance.

Lastly, there were the two squires who, I gathered, had been devoted to their late master, the earl, and who had now extended that loyalty to his brother, Albany. They were both handsome youths of about the duke's own age, the slightly younger one, Donald Seton, having red hair and the freckled skin that so often accompanies it. His eyes were hazel, flecked with green, and he tended to avoid looking directly at people when he spoke to them.

His companion and close friend was Murdo MacGregor, taller by half a head than any other member of Albany's household, including James Petric, and who seemed to be the more important of the two. Indeed, this brown-haired, blue-eyed man, with his princely bearing and aloof attitude sometimes appeared to be more important than the duke himself. He ignored me.

'Don't mind Murdo,' Albany told me with a laugh. 'The motto of the MacGregors is *'Is rioghal mo dhream'*. 'My blood is royal'. And they all claim descent from the Clan Alpin, which is the oldest and most purely Celtic of all the highland clans. Furthermore, they hold rigidly by the ancient clan rule of defending what's theirs by the sword and not by sheepskin.'

'Sheepskin?' I queried, puzzled.

'Marriage charters, written agreements with their neighbours. The only way the MacGregors settle a dispute is with cold steel.'

Needless to say, after this introduction, I gave the elder squire as wide a berth as possible, and, as I have already mentioned, he didn't seek me out. That isn't to say that I didn't notice him watching me very closely on occasions. All of which explains my misery. I was lonely, homesick and ill at ease.

At the beginning of June, our great sprawling cavalcade of lords and their levies, with the king at its head, set off northwards from London for Northamptonshire where, at Fotheringay Castle, we were to rendezvous with the Duke of Gloucester and the Earl of Northumberland, travelling south. Before we reached our destination, news came of a successful foray into Scotland by Duke Richard and his forces, during which Dumfries had been taken and burned. His Grace had then coolly retired before an army could be raised against him and set out to meet his brother.

'This doesn't bother you?' I had the temerity to ask Albany, lying by his side in bed at some inn where we were billeted for the night. It was blowing a gale and pouring with rain, and I could not help thinking of the poor foot soldiers and archers trying to sleep in some sodden field.

To my surprise, my royal bedfellow, sharing my company in the fire-studded dark, failed to snub me. He merely hunched his shoulders under the quilt and answered laconically, 'You can't make a cake without breaking eggs.'

I couldn't let it go. 'But these are your people being burned out of their homes. Aren't you afraid such actions by your allies will turn them against you?'

There was a another shrug. 'It's more likely to turn them against my dear brother for not retaliating. They don't like him, anyway.'

'Why not?' I asked. A log on the hearth crackled and fell, spangling the room with fire. Outside the door, I heard someone stir. One of the squires was sleeping across the threshold.

Albany, who had been half turned away from me, rolled on to his back and stared up at the bed canopy overhead. He had pulled back the curtain on his side to give himself more air.

'Well, for a start,' he said, 'they don't like the way he stays cooped up in Edinburgh instead of travelling around the country, showing himself to his loving subjects. Then those same loving subjects don't like the way he's forced the price of everything up by issuing copper coinage – 'black' money the people call it – while at the same time he's enriching all his low-born favourites.'

'Ah, favourites,' I echoed. 'They're always a problem.'

'Especially when they're as disreputable as James's,' Albany added viciously.

'Such as?' I murmured, intrigued.

'Such as William Scheves, who was a shirt-maker for the court and is now Archbishop of St Andrews. Such as Thomas Cochrane, who is reported to have started life as a stonemason and is now one of my brother's chief advisers. Such as William Rogers, musician, James Hommyl, tailor, Torpichen a fencing master and Leonard somebody, or somebody Leonard, a shoe-maker; upstarts the lot of them. Bloody little nobodies, whose farty arses the old lords have to lick before they can get anywhere near the king.'

I digested this. 'Not a very lovable man, King James,' I ventured at last.

My companion gave a snort of laughter and turned his head on the pillow to look at me.

'No, not a very lovable man, as you so rightly remark. But perhaps I should warn you, Roger, not many of us Stewarts are. My grandfather, the first James, was murdered by his own nobles when my father, the second James, was seven years old. And we're unlucky, too. My father had a huge birthmark which earned him the nickname "Fiery Face" and he was killed when a cannon exploded while he was inspecting it. My brother James was eight when he succeeded to the throne, John and I a few years younger.'

I was silent for a moment or two, contemplating the often

unhappy lives of our rulers; but not for long. At least they could be unhappy in comfort, which was never the lot of the poor.

'Do you really believe that your brother, the Earl of Mar, was murdered?' I asked.

'I know he was,' Albany rapped back. 'He was imprisoned in Craigmillar Castle and Murdo and the others have told me that, shortly after they were all withdrawn from his service he was reported to have died. A chill was the official version.'

'And the unofficial?'

'One of his gaolers told the groom, Tullo, that John was held down in a tub of hot water while his wrists were slashed.' Albany gave a harsh laugh. 'There's some dignity in a Roman death, I suppose.'

'What was he accused of?'

'Treason and witchcraft.'

'Witchcraft? Was that true?'

'Of course not!' The reply came a little too swiftly and positively, but I let it pass.

'Why do you suspect one his servants of being in the pay of King James?' I wanted to know.

I had been itching to ask this question ever since our first meeting in London, but somehow had been unable to do so until this moment. It had proved difficult to get Albany to myself, and until tonight, he had fallen into bed and gone straight to sleep. But because of the bad weather, and on account of King Edward's failing health, the march had been shorter than on previous days and, as a consequence, all of us were less tired. Albany certainly seemed livelier than usual and therefore willing to talk.

But his answer when it finally came was unsatisfactory.

'I don't know anything for certain. It's just a feeling I have.'

Dear God in Heaven! I hated feelings. I wanted facts.

'There must be some reason why you feel this way,' I persisted.

The duke remained vague, muttering that it would be just like the king to suborn one of the earl's retainers, offering the man unlimited bribes in order to persuade him to betray his trust.

'James is a cunning bastard,' Albany continued with a sudden spurt of merriment. 'He's far shrewder than is generally thought. People – all his advisers and the population at large – thought he was mad to insist on marrying a Danish princess. I mean, it was a well-known fact that King Christian was practically penniless at the time and couldn't pay more than a fraction of Margarethe's dowry. But James simply said he'd take the Danish islands of Orkney and Shetland as a pledge of Denmark's good faith until the rest of the money could be handed over.' Again, my companion laughed.

'And King Christian agreed?'

'Of course! It seemed an easy way out of his difficulties. But on each occasion that he's offered to pay the remainder of the dowry, James has refused it, saying he'd rather keep the islands. You mark my words, Shetland and Orkney will never be returned to Denmark. They'll belong to Scotland now for the rest of time.'

'Even if . . . I mean, even when you become king?' But I could guess his answer. Politics is an unpleasant game.

'Naturally. Scotland's boundaries have been considerably increased. However, I don't expect to have the same success in the matter of the other dowry. King Edward's a bird of a different feather.'

I frowned into the darkness. The flames of the fire had by now almost turned to ashes.

'What dowry's that?' I asked.

Albany sniggered. 'You should keep your ear to the ground more, Roger. Eight years ago, when my eldest nephew, the Duke of Rothesay was barely one, he was betrothed to your little Princess Cicely. A formal betrothal ceremony was held at the Blackfriars, in Edinburgh. I was there. Pomp, ceremony, great solemnity! And Princess Cicely's dowry was set at twenty thousand English marks, of which five thousand marks were paid over the next three years with – I must admit it – great promptitude. But now that the marriage has fallen through, King Edward wants his money back. And so far, he hasn't received it.'

I pursed my lips. There was much to mull over here, but, although interesting, nothing that touched on my own problem. After a decent interval to allow for a change of

subject, and while I listened to the wind and rain rattling the
inn's many shutters, I asked again, 'But which of the late
earl's men do you think means you a mischief, my lord?
Surely you must have some idea?'

But a snore was the only answer.

The weather changed next day, becoming warmer, drowsy
with the scent of wayside flowers, and the amorphous mass
of men and horses was able to make better progress. A pale
sun caught at the tips of spears with pinpricks of light, and
we moved forward, a forest of stars in the afternoon haze.
People had come out and were working in the fields, and
those who had sheep were beginning the business of washing
and shearing them, preparatory to taking their wool to market.
But everywhere I looked, I was struck by the truth of my
friend the mummer's words. We had been luckier in the west
country than any of us had realized: famine and disease,
caused by the winter's terrible storms and the spring flood-
ings, had taken a greater toll in other parts of the country
than anything we had experienced. Children with emaciated
limbs, men and women as scrawny as their own scarecrows
stopped work and watched us pass in sullen silence, or else
mouthed insults and obscenities at us and shook their fists.
I remembered that when I had accompanied the army to
France, seven years earlier, people in every village that we
rode through, shouted, 'The king! The king!' and rang the
church bells and strewed our path with flowers. Today, the
only cries that reached our ears were demands to know why
England wasn't supporting Burgundy against King Louis.
The army commanders ignored them, pushing on with stony
faces, glancing to neither right nor left, and I doubted that
King Edward could even hear them, carried as he was in a
litter with the curtains drawn. His doctors had decreed him
too weak to mount a horse that day, and for several days
prior to that.

In the ordinary way of things, someone as insignificant as
myself would have seen little or nothing of the royal
entourage, but my instructions to remain closer to Albany
than a second skin had brought me into daily contact with
the king and his immediate circle. And the shock of my first

sighting of King Edward had increased as the days passed, rather than diminished. I recalled him as he was not so very many years ago; a great, golden giant of a man: 'the handsomest man in Europe' he had been called, and not without justification. His badge of the Sun in Splendour had described the man to perfection; huge, generous, radiating warmth. But now, he was fat, disease-ridden, his face the colour of unbaked dough, his marvellous energy dissipated by the pleasures of the flesh; too much food, too much wine, too many women. Perhaps I exaggerate a little – women still found him attractive, I was told – but he appeared to me to have deteriorated rapidly since my last glimpse of him, in London, two years earlier. (And as I write these words, an old man in his seventies, I cannot but recall that I have seen the youthful Edward live again in his grandson, our present king, Henry, as unlike his cheese-paring, miserly Tudor father as it is possible to be, but with the same tendency to excess in everything as his maternal grandsire. Will he go the same way as King Edward? Or will he be able to curb his insatiable appetites? Who can tell? Certainly not me. My life will be ended in a few more years.)

And so, after that digression, I have lost my thread, and serve me right. Where was I? Ah, yes! Approaching Fotheringay Castle in those early June days of the year 1482 when I was still a young man – well, comparatively young – of twenty-nine, although a little more than three months off my thirtieth birthday; an unhappy man, desperately missing his wife and children.

Fotheringay was as gloomy inside as it was out.

The Duke of Albany and his retinue were assigned a number of rooms on the ground floor, close to the king's own suite, which were, as I soon discovered, somewhat more luxurious than those of even such highly placed lords as Earl Rivers and Sir Edward Woodville, two of the king's brothers-in-law, the Marquis of Dorset, his elder stepson, Lord Hastings, his particular, life-long friend, Lord Stanley and many others. These flowers of the English court were definitely not pleased by Albany's preferential treatment, and made their annoyance plain, at least to us, his servants,

if not to the prince himself. Not that he was unaware of it,
but he was not in the least discomposed by their disap-
proval.

'After all, I am a future king of Scotland,' he said to me,
as we tumbled into bed that first night, adding with a grin,
'And you will see tomorrow, or whenever my lords of
Gloucester and Northumberland arrive from the north, that
I shall be given pride of place when His Highness receives
them.' His voice sharpened. 'And don't you move far from
my side, Roger! There's something about this place. I don't
like it. I have a premonition of danger.'

I sighed, not caring if he heard me. What use to me
were his feelings and premonitions? What I needed were
reasons for them. If I could have talked to any one of my
fellow servants – for there was little doubt in my mind
that the status of servant was what I had been reduced to
– it might have helped. But James Petrie, John Tullo, Davey
Gray and the two squires all seemed unable to speak in
anything but the broad Scots dialect whenever they found
themselves in my company. (I wondered how they had
fared in France.) The five of them made their contempt
for me, as a Sassenach, perfectly plain; yet, in spite of
derision and occasional insolence, they tolerated my presence with far less resentment than I would have expected
in the circumstances; a fact that made me wonder if they
knew of their master's suspicions concerning at least one
of their number.

I asked Albany.

'God's Nightgown, no!' he exclaimed. 'I want to flush the
bastard out, not put him on his guard.'

'So what explanation has Your Highness given them for
my inclusion in your retinue?'

He laughed. 'What else but that you are guarding my
sacred person from the possible machinations of the English?
They know the part you played in my escape from Bristol
to Ireland three years ago and that, as a consequence, I trust
you. And to tell you the truth, Roger,' he added, clapping
me on the shoulder, 'that's not just an All Fools' Day story.
These forebodings that possess me, warning me of danger,
might well apply to my English hosts and have nothing to

do with my brother's men. Or—' At that 'or' I heaved another sigh, deeper than before, but Albany ignored me. 'Or,' he continued, 'I could have enemies in both camps.'

'Or in neither,' I suggested.

He shook his head. 'I'm a sensitive soul, Roger. I don't have the "sight", I admit that. I cannot "see" things that are about to happen, but I can feel them. Oh, yes! Definitely I can feel them. And I have known for some weeks now that danger threatens me from some quarter or another. I racked my brains for someone disinterested enough to guard me without the possibility of his being in the pay of either my brother, King James, or King Edward, who might secretly have decided to make peace, after all, thus reducing me to an embarrassing encumbrance.' He gave me a radiant smile. 'And suddenly, I remembered you, my dear friend and saviour. I knew, at that juncture, that Cousin Edward would deny me nothing. So, here you are!'

'Just sitting on my arse and doing nothing.'

Albany put an arm about my shoulders and grinned at me. 'Don't sound so bitter! I'm paying you well, aren't I? What I mean is that I will be paying you well as soon as I get my hands on the allowance dear Edward has promised me. Meantime, you're better fed and clothed, I daresay, then you've ever been in your life before. And all you have to do in return is to watch my back.'

'Do all your family have this fatal charm?' I grunted. 'I'm persuaded Your Highness could turn a Mussulman Christian.'

He smiled broadly. 'Oh, we Stewarts are noted for our charm, but unfortunately not for our tact or superior understanding. We make enemies all too easily.'

Against my will, I smiled back. He had an ironic streak that appealed to my own. I found myself liking him in spite of the instinct that told me to resist the notion that, whatever he might call me, however much he might flatter me, he regarded me as a friend. Members of the nobility never made friends of people like me. They used us, then forgot us when we were no longer of value to them. There were no exceptions. I suspected that even the man I admired above all others, Richard, Duke of Gloucester, was completely oblivious to my existence until he had work for me to do.

Then my name would flit into his mind as a useful tool for
his purpose.

All the same, fool that I am, I have to admit that I was
more than somewhat flattered when, the following day, June
the eleventh, the Feast of Saint Barnabas, the duke caught
my eye and nodded as he entered Fotheringay's central courtyard. He and Henry Percy, Earl of Northumberland, arrived
midway through the afternoon to be received with all the
panoply of state that King Edward could muster. Banners
waved, trumpets sounded, choirboys sang, the assembled
company cheered itself hoarse and the king embraced his
only surviving brother with an affection that had him crying
tears of joy.

Normally, of course, I should have been on the very fringes
of such a gathering, unable to see or hear a thing that was
going on. But on this occasion, thanks to Albany, there I
was, right in the thick of it, a privileged auditor and spec-
tator. I was able to note how anxiously the duke scanned the
king's face, and the tightening of his rather thin lips as his
eyes rested on those lords ranged closest about the monarch,
members of his inner circle, bosom companions of his hedon-
istic life. (It was common knowledge that they passed their
various mistresses about amongst each other, and that Lord
Hastings and the Marquis of Dorset were at daggers drawn
over the favours of the delectable Dame Shore.)

It was as he freed himself from King Edward's embrace
that the duke noticed me and nodded. It was nothing more
than the barest of acknowledgements, but sufficient to make
one or two people glance my way in outraged surprise, and
for Albany to dig me, most unroyally, in the ribs and give a
little snort of laughter.

Later, as I watched Davey Gray and Donald Seton dressing
my lord for the evening's great feast, he coaxed me into
telling him what services I had performed for the duke of
Gloucester, and I could tell that he was impressed.

'You found the Lady Anne for him when Clarence had
hidden her away in London? No wonder Prince Richard trusts
you! And I see how right I was to trust you, too.' He lapsed
into broad Scots and spoke to Davey, who went to one of
the great chests standing against the wall of the chamber,

from which he produced an amber velvet tunic – somewhat rubbed, it's true, but perfectly whole and sound – and some yellow hose, together with a pair of piked yellow shoes.

'Put them on, Roger,' Albany commanded. 'I want you immediately behind my chair throughout the banquet.'

Four

It had rained a little in the early evening and we crossed the wet courtyard, where the cressets hissed at their drowned reflections in the puddles underfoot, and entered the light and warmth of Fotheringay's great hall, the torches flaring against the grey walls with a sound like torn parchment. Tonight, there was to be feasting and entertainment: tomorrow, the serious business – the demands, the conditions, the promises – would be hammered out, and the following day, the army would once again be on the march, heading for York.

'Then to Berwick to try to end the siege, and thence into Scotland,' Albany informed me as he was dressed for the banquet by Davey Gray and James Petrie in cloth of gold and royal purple. 'At least, that's what I'm told.' He eyed me up and down as I stood there, feeling extremely foolish, in my amber velvet tunic and yellow hose and shoes. He must have noted my expression because he started to grin.

'I feel like a Welsh daffodil,' I complained bitterly. 'And I shan't be able to move with these pikes. I shall trip over them as surely as God makes the sun and moon to shine.' Before he could answer, I asked, 'Why do we go to York? Why not straight to Berwick?'

James Petrie glanced sharply at me, as though reproving me for such familiarity, but I ignored him. If the future king of Scotland – although I'd believe that when I saw it – wanted me to dance attendance on him, then he would have to put up with my impertinence. He could dismiss me when he pleased: I should be only too happy to leave his service and return to Bristol.

But Albany showed no sign of being offended, grinning even more broadly as he shrugged on a houppelande of rich

purple damask trimmed with deep borders of ermine, the
candlelight coruscating over the shimmering folds in shades
of palest violet to deepest plum. He stooped to allow the
page to place a golden coronet set with precious gems on
his curly head, then straightened himself with a sigh of satisfaction. He knew that tonight he looked every inch a king.

'Why do we go to York?' he mused, echoing my question. Something like a sneer curled his lips. 'I think, my dear
Roger, that we go to York so that we may all be amazed by
the display of affection which will be accorded to His Grace
of Gloucester by its citizens. Prince Richard wishes to impress
on us how greatly he is loved in the heartlands of his power.'
He cast a last glance at his reflection in the long, polished
bronze mirror held up by James Petrie, beckoned to his two
squires who had been waiting patiently in the shadows and
nodded at me. 'Right, my daffodil, let's discover what delights
have been ordered for our amusement this night.'

I had always known that the life of a royal servant was not
all it was claimed to be, in spite of regular warmth, shelter
and pickings from the rich man's table. I had once sampled
it for a brief while and was aware that the sleeping quarters
were so cramped that you would be better off being a dog
or a horse in the royal kennels and stables. But until that
evening at Fotheringay, I had never experienced the sheer
agony of standing behind someone's chair while he gorged
himself silly and drank himself stupid while your own
stomach rumbled and ached with hunger.

Donald Seton and Murdo MacGregor had found themselves places at one of the lower tables, but Davey Gray and
I were expected to remain close to Albany throughout the
feast. And although it was not my place to wait on our royal
lord, as did the page, taking victuals from the servers and
presenting them on bended knee for his inspection, it was
even more trying to have nothing to do except be buffeted
by the lackeys who sped in a continuous procession from
kitchen to table and back again, until I lost count of the innu-
merable dishes that were piled upon the groaning boards. I
vaguely recall great sides of beef, legs of mutton, swan and
peacock, cooked and re-dressed in all their plumage, syllabubs,

tarts, pies, haunches of venison, wonderful subtleties of spun sugar, representing castles, animals and birds, the sun, moon, and stars. One course seemed to follow another almost without pause.

Many of the escutcheons of those present had been fashioned from marchpane and coloured with dyes such as saffron and parsley juice, alkanet and rose petals. I remember the White Rose and Fetterlock of King Edward; the White Boar and Red Bull of the Duke of Gloucester; Northumberland's White Crescent and Gold Shacklebolt; the White Escallops of Anthony Woodville and the argent and pink of his nephew, the Marquis of Dorset. There must have been many more, but I can't recollect them after all these years, and wouldn't weary you with them if I could. Half the nobility of England was present, all eager to fight under the banner of the king.

But looking at the king – and I was only a few feet from him, Albany, as guest of honour, being seated on his right hand – I doubted very much if any of them would have that distinction. Toying with his food, drinking far too much wine, he seemed to me to be too sick a man to lead an army into Scotland. My guess was that, on the morrow, he would relinquish overall command to my lord of Gloucester and return to London.

By the time that the main courses had finally been cleared from the tables and replaced with bowls of fruit, dishes of nuts and raisins, sugared violets and strawberries soaked in wine, I was feeling faint with hunger. I hissed at the page, 'When do we eat?' but he only shrugged and turned away, indicating patience. But I was beyond patience and, noting that Albany was deep in conversation with Lord Hastings, seated on his right hand, I abandoned my post and followed a line of servers to the kitchens.

There, the heat and noise were almost overpowering, cooks bellowing their orders above the general din, bellows-boys heating cauldrons of water over three or four great fires so that the scullions could begin the endless chore of washing the dirty dishes, more flagons of wine being dragged up and loaded on to salvers by the cellarer and his assistants and a sense of chaos prevailing over all. No one took any notice of me, which was just as well as far as I was concerned.

I had discovered six huge baskets, each one rising above my waist in height and crammed to the top with leftovers from the banquet. The broken meats – including whole joints – pastries, pies, tarts, most with hardly a bite taken out of them before being pushed aside for yet another dainty, would surely have fed the whole of Bristol for several days, and certainly kept me happy for as long as I needed to assuage my hunger. And just as I was feeling that my belly would explode if I crammed it with any more food, I espied, laid out on a side bench, a row of untouched jellies, striped red and yellow and green, beautifully gilded as so many of the rest of the victuals had been. (Early on in the feast, a dish of gilded meatballs had provoked much ribaldry at the high table, even the king shaking off his lethargy to join in the laughter.) I grabbed a spoon from a pile close at hand – clean or dirty, it was all the same to me – and attacked the jelly nearest to me.

It tasted delicious.

'Oi!' shouted an indignant voice. 'Ooever you are, leave our jellies alone! They're only for people oo work in the kitchen.'

I didn't even deign to glance round, merely holding up two fingers in the devil's sign. A man in a sackcloth apron, and brandishing an enormous carving knife, seized me by the shoulder.

'Didn't you 'ear what I said? Oo are you? Get off back where you belong. Yer master'll be looking for you, anyway. The mummings and suchlike are about to begin.'

I didn't feel I could argue with the knife, but managed to sneak a last spoonful of jelly before holding up my hands in submission.

'I'm going! I'm going! These are very good,' I added, wiping my sticky chin on one sleeve. 'You can tell the cook I said so. What mummings? Nobody tells me anything.'

The kitchener, a small man who had had time to assimilate my height and girth, grew less aggressive.

'Oh, jugglers, tumblers, lutists, singers, the usual sort o' thing. And a masque to finish.' He added lugubriously, 'There's always a masque. If you turn sharp right when you leave the kitchens and mount the flight o' steps at the end of the passageway, you'll find yerself in a room next the great 'all, where all them lot'll be waiting while the lackeys clear away the trestles and put the benches round the walls, ready fer the performance.' My companion sniggered. 'Such a prancing about and clearing o' throats and tuning up of instruments you've never witnessed in yer life! I peeped in on 'em just now. You never saw such antics. Laugh! I thought I should've died! Poncy fellows, the lot of 'em. Poxy, too, I shouldn't wonder.'

I thanked him for his information, but said I must be getting back to my master who would no doubt have missed me by this time.

'Well, tell 'im, ooever 'e is, t' feed you,' the kitchener grunted, eyeing with dissatisfaction the havoc I had caused to the first of the jellies.

I promised to do so and edged my way out of the steam and the noise into the comparative coolness and quiet of the corridor. I was about to return to the great hall following the same route by which I had come, using the stairs immediately opposite the kitchen entrance, when a slight noise to my left attracted my attention and made me pause.

'Who's there?' I demanded, peering into the gloom of the passageway, which seemed suddenly, eerily, deserted. I turned around and stared behind me. 'Is there anyone there?'

There was a rush of movement and I was thrown against the wall, an extra shove with an outstretched hand sending me sprawling on the bottom few treads of the stairs. I was vaguely aware of a strange, mask-like face before struggling to pick myself up.

'Stop!' I commanded, but I was badly winded and the word came out in a breathless croak.

I staggered forward a few steps, but of course there was no one there. Whoever had brought me down had vanished while I was getting to my feet. After a moment or two, when I was feeling a little more myself, I recalled hearing the rattle of a latch and the thud of a closing door, and came to the conclusion that my assailant was one of the mummers late for the start of the entertainment, and that I had been in his way. He had most probably been unaware of the force with which he had pushed me aside. I toyed with the idea of going

after him, but then realized that not only would I not recognize either him or the mask he was wearing, but I should be
laying myself open to ridicule. I was a big, strong man. Was
I going to complain because a mummer had accidentally
floored me?

Nevertheless, for no good reason that I could fathom,
the silly little incident had upset me and made me uneasy.
I stared for a few seconds longer into the gloom of the
passageway before brushing myself down and mounting
the staircase behind me. At the top, I shouldered open the
door into the great hall which had now been transformed
into a vast empty space, with all tables except the high
table, on its dais, folded and stacked away, and the benches
arranged around the room's perimeter ready for the audience to take its seat for the evening's entertainment. A
great number of the guests were still strolling about,
exchanging greetings with people they had been unable to
come at during the feast, and I noted with relief that my
lord Albany, attended by the faithful Davey Gray, had
crossed the hall to speak to Master Hobbes, King Edward's
personal physician. (As a matter of interest, I will mention
here that there were no less than nine other surgeons in
the royal retinue, not one of whom, it is needless to say,
was included for the benefit of the ordinary poor bastard
of a foot soldier.)

My relief was short-lived. Turning away from Master
Hobbes, Albany spotted me and came striding back to the
dais, a gathering frown marring his handsome face.

'Where the devil have you been?' he demanded wrath-
fully, mounting the three steps in a single bound and seizing
me by one arm. 'I ordered you to remain behind my chair
throughout all mealtimes. And you have the damned effron-
tery to disobey me.'

'Then you should have the grace to see that I'm fed, not
left standing while you gorge yourself half to death and I'm
nigh fainting with hunger . . . Your Highness!' I added as an
afterthought.

I heard the page draw in his breath and saw him tense his
slim form as he waited for the explosion of royal anger. But
this failed to materialize. Albany and I stared at one another,

eyeball to eyeball, for several seconds, then he dropped his hand from my arm and gave his charming smile.

'Roger, forgive me my thoughtlessness. Of course I should have made provisions for your sustenance. Have you managed to forage for yourself now?'

'I found my way to the kitchens,' I said. 'There was enough provender in the waste baskets alone to feed half the starving population of Northamptonshire for weeks, if not months.'

Albany laughed. He knew my opinions on the gulf that existed between rich and poor, and although he naturally didn't share them, he had let me have my say on several occasions, merely advising me not to be so open with anyone but himself. I wondered sometimes why he was so tolerant, but decided that he found me amusing and, moreover, had need of me.

'But don't wander off again without permission,' he said, resuming his seat at the king's right hand. 'I've told you, I want you in attendance day and night. Now, stand close. The mummings are about to begin.'

The jugglers came first, tossing a rainbow of coloured balls into the air and catching them again with amazing dexterity. And not only balls, but spoons, knives, beakers or anything else that took their fancy. The leader even begged the use of three of the precious Venetian glass goblets used by King Edward and his most important guests, throwing them, sparkling, into the candlelight while everyone gasped and held his breath. But they were returned to the high table undamaged, and the king took a velvet purse full of money from one of his attendants, tossing it to the man, to be shared out between him and the rest of the troupe.

Tumblers followed, rolling around the floor, balancing on one another's shoulders, contorting their lithe and agile bodies into a variety of shapes. It all looked very painful and risky, and once or twice I found my eyes watering in sympathy for the agony they must be enduring. But they seemed none the worse for it and departed from the hall to resounding applause.

Musicians and dancers came next, then a group of singers; but I have to admit that my attention wandered during these last two items. I have absolutely no ear for music of any kind and, personally, cannot sustain a tune for more than a couple of notes. But other people enjoyed it judging by the applause and the number of coins tossed to the performers, while the king handed out purses with a liberal hand. It was obvious that no expense was being spared, and if there were any Scottish spies lurking amongst the onlookers – as there no doubt were – word would get back to King James that his brother was being treated by the English as if he were already the reigning monarch.

There was a slight pause before the final entertainment, which, I gathered, was to be the masque, and I took the opportunity to glance around the hall searching for Murdo MacGregor and Donald Seton. But I was unable to locate them; hardly surprising considering the crush of people standing along the walls behind the row of benches. What was surprising, however, was the discovery, on looking over my shoulder, that Davey Gray had disappeared. He had been dancing the most assiduous attendance on his master all evening, only stepping a few paces from Albany's side when he needed to relieve himself behind one of the wall-hangings. But now there was no sign of him. I presumed that, at long last, he had been given permission to go and eat.

The Master of the Revels, who had been fussing about, instructing the lackeys where to place various candelabra and a number of artificial trees – whose leaves glowed with the green fire of emeralds – now approached the high table to announce the start of the masque. This, it seemed, was to take the form of a forest glade, where animals, nymphs and wood sprites cavorted and sang hymns to the great mother goddess, Earth, and her consort, the Green Man. And the moment that latter name was mentioned, I knew at once what mask it was that my assailant had been wearing. The glimpse had been fleeting, but I could see again in my mind's eye the sprouting foliage from the mouth and the leafy eyebrows and hair.

I waited impatiently for the masque to progress while the mummers in the animal heads leaped around pretending to be rabbits and foxes, hares and stags. Then the nymphs and wood sprites, naiads and fauns added their bit to the general jollification, harping and singing until it fairly set my teeth on edge. But finally and not a moment too soon as far as I was concerned – Mother Earth arrived in the form of a buxom, large-bosomed lady, trailing blue, brown and green draperies and attended by her consort, the Green Man.

I had not been mistaken. The mask was the same as the one that had loomed over me as I lay sprawled on the steps. Fleeting as the moment had been, I was ready to swear to it had anyone asked me. But there was something wrong. The mummer playing the part was a big, well-fleshed man, half a head taller than his equally robust dame, whilst the impression I had gained of the person who had knocked me down was of a short man, of no more than middling height, if that. After mulling the problem over for a minute or so, I reached the conclusion that there were either two players of the part in the mummers' troupe or that the mask had been borrowed. A few more seconds of cogitation led me to discard the former theory: with a Mother Earth of such generous proportions, it was unlikely that a small man would have been chosen to act as her partner. So someone else had borrowed the mask, but to what end?

The masque drew to its inevitable close. The pagan revellers, suddenly confronted by a woodland hermit were brought to acknowledge a greater force in nature than themselves and bowed down before the simple wooden cross which he took from around his neck and held up for them to worship. Then they advanced to the high table and made their obeisance to the king as representing God's Anointed on earth, after which, they skipped off to the loudest applause of the evening and carrying by far the heaviest purse. Without asking Albany's permission, I made my way to the corner of the dais, jumped down and followed them into an anteroom of the great hall.

Here, the chaos was very much as the kitchener had described it to me; shrill voices of self-congratulation drowning out others' less complimentary remarks; actors and mummers, in various states of undress, preening themselves on a job well done; the master of the troupe sitting quietly apart, counting out the contents of the king's purse into little piles of coins on top of a clothes' chest; several people posing and posturing in front of a mirror of polished steel that had been set up in one corner of the room for their use.

In spite of the press of bodies, it didn't take me long to locate my quarry. The 'Green Man', mask discarded, was struggling out of the leafy hose and tunic which had formed the rest of his costume. I wriggled my way through to his side.

He looked at me enquiringly.

'I come from His Grace, the Duke of Albany,' I lied. 'He wishes me to congratulate you on a part well performed.'

The man straightened himself to his full height. Ignoring the fact that he might appear ridiculous in nothing but his under-shift, he made a magnificent bow.

'His Grace is a man of taste and discernment,' he announced in a deep, sonorous voice, which attracted a few covert sniggers from his fellow players.

'For my own part,' I went on, braving his wrath, 'I thought you were a little late on your first entrance. Oh, not by much,' I hastened to add, as his chest swelled with indignation. 'But just by the merest fraction.'

'And what would a mean fellow like yourself know about it?'

'Mother Earth', now attired in a sober grey woollen gown, who had been listening jealously to our exchange, interrupted us to say, 'You were late, Clement. I noticed it myself. I was well into the centre of the floor before you condescended to make an appearance. You should have been beside me when we left this room and accompanied me all the way to the "glade". It wasn't good enough on such an important occasion.'

The man called Clement turned on her furiously. 'Well if you know who's stolen my best mask, you can save your reproaches for him.' He picked up the one he had been wearing and dangled it by its strings. 'This is only my second best. I was still hunting for the other right up to the moment of our entrance, and even so I had to go on without it. And it's still missing.'

The woman was immediately all concern.

'Oh, that's too bad!' she exclaimed. 'It's a beauty, that other one. I thought something didn't look right about you.

"Not enough foliage," I remember thinking to myself at one point, but there was so much else to be worrying about, I didn't give it more'n a passing thought. Come and speak to Matthew,' she added, nodding towards the man counting the money. 'If someone's playing a stupid prank, he'll soon give 'em short shrift.'

They went off together, arm in arm, animosity and professional jealousy forgotten. I went back to my post behind Albany's chair.

By the greatest of good luck, he and Lord Hastings had been so deep in a ribald assessment of 'Mother Earth's' physical charms that he had failed to notice my absence. Not so the page, who whispered in my ear, 'And where've you been?'

I spun round. 'So you're back, are you? And suddenly you can speak English. Well, understandable English.'

'Oh, I've always been able to speak English,' Davey replied in that cool, light tone of his. 'It's just that I don't always choose to. Where have you been?'

'I might ask you the same question.'

He smiled his sweet, effeminate smile. 'There's no mystery about that. His Grace sent me to the kitchens to get something to eat. Unlike yourself, I don't go wandering off on my own, but wait until I'm bidden. It's easy to see that you've never been in service to the nobility. Which raises the question why exactly are you here?'

There was a slightly contemptuous note in the young voice that flicked me on the raw. I longed to tell him the truth, but managed to bite my tongue. Instead, I retorted with equal contempt, 'You ought to listen more carefully, Davey, when your royal master speaks. He told you, I heard him, when I first joined the household in London, that I'm his personal bodyguard. It's my job to protect him from harm. He fears his brother's assassins.'

'He has good reason,' the page nodded, adding, 'Well, mind you do protect him, or it will be the worse for you.'

Before I could take exception to this threat, the king rose from his seat, announcing it was time for bed, and everyone else rose with him. Albany turned and beckoned to me at the same moment that his two squires emerged from a doorway at the back of the dais. Davey fetched a couple of torchbearers to light us all back to the royal chambers where James Petrie was waiting to assist his master to undress, while I took the opportunity to divest myself of the hated yellow shoes, hose and amber tunic, stripping down to my shirt and climbing in beside Albany in the massive four-poster bed. The page dragged his own truckle-bed from underneath it, assured himself that the 'all-night' of bread and ale had been placed on the table next to his master, pulled the curtains around us and bade us goodnight. Donald Seton and Murdo MacGregor likewise made themselves scarce, leaving the bedchamber for the ante-room where they both slept.

Albany was in buoyant mood and disposed to talk. He was delighted with his reception by the English nobles and by the way in which King Edward had embraced him before the feast, hailing him with all the familiarity of a fellow monarch. I think that for a moment even his natural cynicism had evaporated, and he was allowing himself to believe that he would indeed be crowned as King Alexander IV.

'I've come to the conclusion, Roger,' he said, linking his hands behind his head and staring up at the canopy above us, 'that maybe I've nothing to fear from the English, after all.' This was the wine talking, and I had no doubt that he would sing a different song in the morning. 'No,' he went on, 'the danger lies, as I always thought it did, with my dear brother.' He turned his head on the pillow. 'You've not discovered anything yet?'

I hesitated, then answered slowly, 'I'm not sure.'

He was alert on the instant, heaving himself up onto one elbow and peering anxiously at me through the darkness.

'Out with it, man! What is it?'

'A silly incident, Your Grace. Nothing more.'

'Tell me!'

So, somewhat reluctantly, fearing what I felt would be his quite justifiable ridicule, I told him about the man in the Green Man mask.

'I thought it would prove to be one of the mummers late for his entrance,' I said. 'But that turned out not to be the case.' And I proceeded to describe my meeting with 'Mother Earth' and her 'consort'. 'So Your Grace can see,' I concluded, 'that I was right to call it a silly incident and not to wish to worry you with it. It's nothing, in my opinion, but a stupid jest being played by one of the mummers' troupe on another of their number. Your Highness has nothing to fear. You may sleep easily in your bed.'

Five

To my surprise, Albany seemed to be genuinely concerned by my story and interrogated me closely regarding the details. Did I think the attack had been deliberate? Where had I been standing exactly when the man had pushed past me? From which direction in the castle had he come? Was I sure that I had had no glimpse of his face? Was it certain that he had not been one of the mummers' troupe?

I did my best to answer these and other questions, but my knowledge of the castle was as limited as his, never having set foot in it – never, indeed, having set foot anywhere north of Hereford – before the previous day. I had to admit to myself that repetition of the incident had convinced me how very trivial it had really been, and that I had built a mountain out of a molehill. What did it really amount to, when all was said and done? A man wearing a mummer's mask – at a time when mummers' masks abounded in the castle – had given me an ill-natured shove because I was in his way. That was all there was to it.

Or was it?

Later, when my bedfellow had fallen into what appeared to be an uneasy slumber, judging, at any rate, by his tossing and turnings, I found myself lying wakeful in the darkness. The mummer playing the Green Man had either mislaid or had his best mask stolen. But why? For what reason? Was there a sinister motive? And, if so, what was it? Did it really have anything to do with me? On reflection, wasn't it far more likely to have been taken as a prank by another member of the group who had a grudge against the leading player? That was a much more plausible explanation. Clement, as 'Mother Earth' had named him, had struck me at once as a man with a large opinion of himself, and therefore one who had probably made many enemies amongst the troupe's younger generation. Moreover, it was just the sort of silly trick a boy would play, and there was no doubt that the figure I had seen so briefly had been shortish and lacking in bulk.

With this finally settled in my mind, I heaved a sigh of relief and turned over, presenting my backside to my unquiet companion. Beyond the drawn bed-curtains, Davey gave the occasional gurgle and snort as he wriggled around on his truckle-bed, but other than that all was quiet except for the occasional shout of 'All's well!' from the watchmen guarding the castle walls. The closed chamber door shut out all sounds from the ante-room where the two squires were presumably sleeping the sleep of the just.

I was slipping across the borderline of sleep, having lain awake for quite some time, when something roused me. I had no idea what it was, but it brought me sitting upright in the bed, every faculty alert, my ears straining, my eyes trying desperately to pierce the stuffy, all-embracing gloom. Then I was on my feet, the flagstones striking chill on my bare soles, and out into the room at large, where the page still slept peacefully at the foot of the four-poster, his young limbs sprawled anyhow, his mouth open, saliva dribbling down his chin.

I had grabbed my cudgel from the floor and now gripped it firmly as I stared around the chamber. I thought something moved behind me and whirled about, but no one was there, only a corner of the room, thick with shadows. I suddenly realized that I could hear Murdo and Donald snoring, where before all had been quiet, and I glanced in the direction of the chamber door. A line of less dense blackness showed that it must be standing slightly ajar. My heart beating unpleasantly fast, I tiptoed towards it, swinging the weighted end of my cudgel backwards and forwards, ready to strike whoever was lurking behind it . . .

It was abruptly pushed wide open and Donald Seton stood yawning and stretching in the doorway, his eyes still clogged with sleep.

'Is something amiss?' he muttered. 'I thought I heard someone moving.'

'You must have the hearing of a rabbit, then,' I snapped,

but keeping my voice as low as possible. 'What are you doing up and about at this dead hour of the morning?'

'I needed the piss-pot,' he answered shortly. 'What's your excuse?'

I hesitated, not being at all sure what had roused me. I countered with another question.

'Why was the door to the ante-room open?'

He frowned, puzzled.

'I just opened it. You saw me. I thought I heard a noise.'

I shook my head. 'It was ajar before you appeared. I was just coming to investigate.'

The squire glanced over his shoulder to where his companion was still snoring peacefully.

'Couldn't have been,' he whispered positively. 'No one's been through here, I'm ready to swear. And the other door into the passageway is closed. You can see for yourself.' Gently he pushed the inner door yet wider.

I crossed the ante-chamber, soft-footed, to verify the truth of this statement. The door was indeed closed and latched, but it wasn't bolted, an omission I hastened to point out.

Donald Seton shrugged.

'Why bolt it?' he asked. His lips twitched in a small, mocking grin which I could see with eyes now grown accustomed to the darkness. 'We're amongst friends, after all. Or aren't we? Perhaps His Grace is right to fear the Sassenachs.'

I bit back the retort hovering on the tip of my tongue; that the duke seemed more fearful of his late brother's servants than he did of his English hosts. That would have been to put one of them on his guard – always provided, of course, that Albany's suspicions had any sort of foundation.

Our voices, although pitched low, had finally aroused Murdo, who struggled up on his pallet to demand what, in the name of Saint Mungo, was going on.

'I needed the piss-pot, only to find our friend the pedlar up and prowling about.'

'Why?'

'Ask him!'

'Before I answer any of your questions,' I hissed angrily, 'what I want to know is why, ever since we left London and before, you two and Davey have pretended that you couldn't

speak anything but the raw Scots' tongue, when all the time
you can speak English perfectly well.' I considered this statement. 'Well enough, at least, for me to understand you,' I
amended.

'We've had nothing to say to you before,' was Murdo's
laconic answer; which I supposed, in its own way, was true.
I had hardly sought their company. But their deception irked
me, nonetheless.

'So what's the answer to my question?' Murdo insisted.

'Something woke me – I don't know what – and then I
discovered that the door between the main bedchamber and
this one was ajar. Master Seton will vouch for that.'

'Donald?'

'It's true. It was open, but I didn't open it. And I'll swear
nobody could have come through here without rousing one
of us.'

'Impossible,' his fellow squire agreed.

But it wasn't impossible, not the way those two had been
snoring. I reckoned more than one assassin could have walked
into my lord's chamber without disturbing either of his
guardians in the room without. I wondered uneasily about
that unbolted outer door. Was it just carelessness, an ingenu-
ous belief that their master was indeed safe amongst his
English friends? Or was it an alibi to cover their own tracks
if they really did intend Albany harm?

Murdo rapped out something unintelligible and lay down
again, pulling the blanket over his head.

Donald nodded. 'He said let's get back to bed before we
catch our deaths of cold.' He seized the chamber-pot and
unrinated into it, a long, steaming, healthy-looking stream.
'That's better. Now, get back to sleep, chapman, and settle
down. You've been dreaming. Your belly's overfull and you've
been riding the night mare.'

Copying his friend's example he, too, lay down and pulled
the blankets up around his ears. As he did so, something
floated to the ground. Unnoticed, I stooped and picked it up,
carrying it back with me into the main chamber where the
object of my concern was peacefully sleeping, oblivious to
the whisperings and shufflings in the ante-room. His earlier
restlessness had abated, and Albany now lay quietly, one

cheek pillowed in his hand, like an innocent child. Cautiously, I found the tinder-box and lit a candle, well away from where its light could shine on the bed, and held my prize towards the flame.

What lay in my palm was a silken leaf, green and veined with golden thread. A leaf come loose from a mummer's costume – or a mummer's mask.

The Green Man!

It was long before I slept. Dawn was rimming the shutters before I finally closed my eyes.

The night's events had convinced me that Albany's suspicions concerning his Scottish servants, however nebulous, were nevertheless founded on reason. They were not the figment of his overripe imagination that I had at first thought them. The explanation given to his immediate retainers for my constant presence – for my presence at all – had been that he feared treachery by the English. Yet his two squires were unimpressed enough by this threat to leave unlocked a door that, if they took their royal master's fear even half-seriously, should have been carefully bolted. Moreover, while they had pretended to an ignorance of English, except as it was spoken in Scotland, I had presumed, as I was meant to presume, that their understanding of the tongue was equally feeble. I wondered what unguarded remarks I had made to Albany, and he to me, that the squires and Davey Gray, at least, had found perfectly intelligible.

But was the duke so ignorant of these men that he did not know this? Perhaps. When he addressed any of them it was in broad Scots, and they answered him in the same language. I had noticed that he kept them all at a distance, having no more converse with them than he was bound to. He certainly did not treat them with the camaraderie that he used towards me. And yet . . .

And yet the five of them had joined him during his exile in France, fleeing the wrath of King James after the Earl of Mar's murder. If it had been murder . . .

But it was at that particular point that my tired brain refused to be teased any longer and, with the sun rising on another day, I at last fell asleep. Not for long, of course. All too soon the trumpets were blaring in the camp beyond Fotheringay's grim walls, servers were hurrying up from the kitchens with jugs of hot shaving water and the whole castle wakened to life. Through a fog of sleep, I remembered that today we set out for York either under the command of the King or under that of His Grace the Duke of Gloucester.

To no one's surprise, it turned out to be the duke who would lead us – eventually – into Scotland. As soon as King Edward entered the great hall after breakfast, it was obvious to all but the meanest intelligence that he was in no fit state of health to head a military expedition. His face had taken on an even greyer tinge than it had worn the previous evening and he was supported on both sides, leaning heavily on the arms of Lord Hastings and his elder stepson, the Marquis of Dorset. There was a sheen of sweat across his forehead; and the way in which he dropped thankfully into his chair at the head of the council table proclaimed that his legs were in imminent danger of collapsing under him.

His first words, therefore, were to announce that he was passing over command of the army to his dearly beloved brother, the Duke of Gloucester, whom we were all to obey as we would himself. Prince Richard, rising from his seat, knelt to kiss the king's hand and promised faithfully to carry out the royal commands.

'Berwick shall be yours again, my liege, if we die in the attempt.'

A cheer went up at these words from the assembled nobility. All very well, I thought to myself, but it will be the poor bloody foot soldiers who do most of the dying. Then a sense of justice made me revise this opinion. I knew Richard of Gloucester by repute to be a valiant soldier, not afraid to put himself in the thick of any fight should his presence be needed. As a young man he had fought valiantly for his eldest brother at the battle of Barnet, when Edward returned to England eleven years previously to reclaim his crown. In the vanguard of his men, he had helped to carry the day. And a month or so later, his actions on the bloody field of Tewkesbury had again brought the Yorkist faction victory and preserved his brother's throne . . .

My wandering thoughts were interrupted by the general

surge of movement as the council disbanded. The king had risen to his feet and was embracing his brother, tears of weakness glistening on his sunken cheeks. He held the duke tightly as though loath to let him go, and it seemed to me that no one who saw them could help but be struck by the contrast between them; one, once so handsome and athletic and strong, now a sad wreck of a man, worn out by a life of excess; the other, so fragile in youth that his life had more than once been despaired of, now a creature as healthy and lithe as a whippet, his skin tanned by wind and sun, his dark eyes alive and eager in his thin, sallow face.

The king next turned to Albany, his embrace more perfunctory than the one he had bestowed on my lord Gloucester, but warm enough and sufficiently prolonged to impress those watching with a sense of the duke's importance. But although he addressed him fondly as 'Cousin' it was plain – to me at any rate – that true affection was lacking, as he adjured Albany not to forget, once he was crowned, the urgent matter of the Princess Cicely's dowry.

'Our coffers are not so full, my dear fellow, that we can afford to forgo its return.'

Albany smiled thinly; a smile that failed to reach his eyes.

'I never imagined for a second that Your Highness had any intention of relinquishing his claim. Once my brother is deposed –' the words 'and dead' weren't uttered, but I think we could all hear them, echoing in the air – 'I shall, of course, be Your Highness's liege man of life and limb.'

There was a snort of laughter, hastily suppressed. Heads half-turned, searching for the culprit, but every face was smooth and stern: there was no telling who had let his natural scepticism get the better of his credulity. But whoever it was, was being more honest than the rest. The king frowned and pretended not to have heard.

The company began to disperse. Duke Richard issued his orders that we were to be on the march by noon. There were some miles to be covered before nightfall on the first stage of our journey to York.

I returned with Albany to our apartments where James Petrie was overseeing the packing of the duke's chests and jewel caskets with the help of two of the castle's lackeys, acting under his mimed directions; for they, like me, were unable to understand his broad Scots dialect. I wondered if he, too, spoke better English than he let on, but had no means at present of finding out. His gaunt, seamed face was even more careworn than usual and he elbowed me out of his way with what I guessed to be a muttered curse as I attempted to collect together my own meagre belongings and stow them in my satchel.

Donald Seton appeared to say that the baggage waggons were waiting and that my lord's gear must be taken out immediately if it was not to be left behind in the rush.

'And John Tullo's below in the courtyard, my lord, with the bay. He thought you'd wish to ride him today. The animal's a bit restive, he says, from lack of exercise. He will be leading the other two.'

Albany nodded curtly, seated on the bed and watching almost absent-mindedly while the rest of us busied ourselves about his affairs. He had been thoughtful and inclined, most uncharacteristically, to be silent ever since we returned from the great hall.

'Is everything ready?' he asked abruptly as the squire turned to leave the room.

Donald looked faintly surprised at the question and, if the truth were told, a little offended.

'Of course, Your Grace,' he answered stiffly.

I noticed that he had given up all pretence at not being able to speak English, and also that Albany accepted this without question.

'You've deceived me, my lord,' I said as Donald left the chamber. I folded a clean shirt and stuffed it into my satchel on top of a spare pair of hose. 'You and your henchmen.'

At first, I didn't think that he had heard me, but then he raised his eyebrows in a haughty look. The friendliness had suddenly evaporated.

'In what way?'

'You all led me to believe that your squires and page could speak only Scots and were unable to understand English.'

He regarded me coldly.

'I don't think we ever gave you to understand that, Roger. That was your own assumption.' He glanced across at his serving-man who was snarling something unintelligible at the two lackeys as they staggered out of the chamber, bearing the weight of one of the duke's three great chests. 'Although it's true that James and John Tullo are most certainly not fluent in the English.'

'But my lord,' I protested angrily, 'did it never occur to you that Murdo or Donald or Davey might have overheard your suspicions of them? And what they know, they can easily communicate to the other two.'

The duke's face relaxed and he gave a little laugh. He slid off the bed and clapped me on the back.

'No one's overheard us,' he assured me. 'I've taken good care of that. Think back, my friend. There's been no one about. And now who's being incautious?' He nodded at James Petrie, just disappearing through the door to the ante-room. 'If you're so suspicious, say nothing until we are alone.' He added sharply, 'Do you have anything to tell me? I had a feeling there was some disturbance during the night, but I may have dreamed it. I was too exhausted to do more than nod straight off to sleep again.'

I hesitated. 'There was something, my lord, but it will keep. It might be of importance, but then, it might not. The trumpets are blowing. Your Highness had better make his way to the courtyard. It surely won't do for you to be late. My lord of Gloucester will be waiting on your arrival. He can hardly set off without you.'

Albany grinned, his good humour restored by my flattery. I could never make out quite how cynical the man was about the chances of his becoming king of Scotland. Sometimes, he seemed to view those chances with amused detachment, looking upon this whole expedition as nothing more than an adventure; an opportunity to make life as difficult as possible for his hated elder brother. But then there were other times when he lapped up compliments and references to his future kingship as greedily and as eagerly as a child cramming its mouth with sweetmeats.

Fotheringay's huge courtyard was crowded and exceedingly noisy, the babel of sound contained within the surrounding walls, like a cup filled and overflowing with water. Horses neighed. Trumpets blared. The Duke of

Gloucester and most of the nobles were already mounted, gentling their steeds and glancing around anxiously for Albany's arrival. A slight cheer went up as he finally emerged into the watery sunlight, a greeting he acknowledged with an ironical bow.

My lord of Gloucester was plainly unamused by such tardiness, but merely said, 'Welcome, Cousin,' with a dryness of tone that might have conveyed annoyance to anyone with a less thick skin than my temporary master. Albany laughed.

John Tullo led up the bay and stood ready to assist the duke into the saddle. The two squires were slightly to the rear, waiting to mount their own horses, while I and the patient beast, who had already borne me so many weary miles, eyed one another with mutual suspicion. As far as I could see, Davey Gray and James Petrie were nowhere in view, the latter, in any case, always riding with the baggage waggons. What Davey did was a bit of mystery. Sometimes he attended upon the duke, but a great deal of the time he went missing. I wondered where he was during these absences, and might have suspected him of gaining experience of life amongst the horde of camp followers who straggled in the wake of the army, except that he so obviously had little interest in women.

Albany waved John Tullo aside and vaulted, unaided, into the saddle, displaying at one and the same time his superb physical fitness and his splendid horsemanship. But as he did so, the bay, who had been fidgeting only a very little, suddenly reared, whinnying furiously and slashing the air in front of him with vicious, flailing hooves.

There was a flurry of movement, as those in the vicinity wrenched their own steeds out of the way, and cries of alarm as it seemed certain that Albany must be thrown, and thrown badly. John Tullo leaped for the horse's head, but it was the duke's own unrivalled skill that finally brought the bay under control, and his voice, whispering soft endearments in its ear, that quietened the outraged animal.

The groom, white-faced and trembling, muttered something that only Albany and the squires understood. The duke gave an uncertain laugh.

'Fresh, indeed, John,' was his answer, before turning to my

lord of Gloucester and saying with bravado, 'My groom warned me, Cousin, that the animal was restive after the inactivity of the past few days, but even he hadn't counted on quite how restive.' He made a sweeping gesture to include the other nobles, now crowding around him again in an admiring group, impressed, in spite of themselves, by his remarkable horse-manship. 'There was no need for anxiety, my lords. None whatsoever. There was not a moment when I did not have the animal under control. You were in no danger, I assure you.'

There was a polite, if somewhat dubious murmur.

Lord Stanley said diplomatically, 'The anxiety was not for ourselves, Your Grace, but for Your Grace's own person. You might have been very seriously injured, had you been thrown.'

Northumberland nodded agreement.

'Very seriously injured,' he concurred, adding infelici-tously, 'If not killed.'

I saw the Duke of Gloucester's sudden frown and quick glance round, the first swiftly smoothed away with a pleasant smile and the second curbed in mid-movement.

'I'm sure there was no danger of that, my lord. Our Cousin of Scotland is noted as an equestrian of great style and flair. And now, gentlemen, we must set forward if the army is to be even halfway to Leicester by nightfall.' There was a general murmur of assent. Duke Richard turned once again to Albany. 'You are recovered, Cousin?'

'Recovered?' Albany's tone was disdainful. 'What is there to recover from, my lord? As you can see, the animal is perfectly well-behaved now. He has always had a little play-fulness in his disposition.'

But playfulness, I thought to myself as I mounted my own placid steed, was not the word I would have used. The bay had been seriously put out by something. He had most defin-itely been harmed in some way; a dig, a prod, a cut, maybe, with the tip of somebody's knife. I had seen the whites of his eyes as he reared. And I had seen the whites of Albany's, too. There had been a moment, albeit fleeting, when he had been terrified.

I was not surprised, therefore, as we rode out through the great gates of Fotheringay, when he turned his head and said curtly, 'Stay close, Roger.'

'Yes, my lord.'

I took up my position a pace or two behind the rump of his horse, not caring who I jostled out of my path as I did so. I tried to picture to myself the scene as John Tullo had led up the bay for the duke to mount. The two squires had definitely been there, and either one of them could have made the animal rear. Any movement in that crush would have passed unnoticed, and I had been too busy contemplating the unwelcome ride ahead of me to pay Murdo and Donald any particular attention. It was inexcusable: I knew full well that after the events of the previous night, I should have been alert and on my guard against mischief. I was failing in my duty; and if any harm were to befall Albany, it would be the worse for me. I owed it to myself, as well as to the duke, to be more vigilant.

It was as the brilliant cavalcade streamed across the flat Northamptonshire plain, banners bravely waving and flapping taut in a freshening breeze, that I had a sudden, clear vision of that tableau in the courtyard. I could see again the two squires and the tension on Donald Seton's face as John Tullo had led the bay forward for Albany to mount. I wondered that it had not struck me at the time that the man was as taut as a fiddle string. Had he been waiting for something to happen? Or had he simply been afraid that some mischief was brewing? I tried to recall the look on his companion's face, but Murdo's expression rarely, if ever, gave anything away.

I let my imaginary gaze roam over the rest of the crowd, but saw nothing except a blur of bodies. And then, suddenly, just as I was giving up on what I felt certain was a fruitless exercise, a face stood out from the throng; a delicate face with fair, wavy hair escaping from beneath a green cap worn at a rakish angle; large eyes that, close to, would prove to be violet-blue. A pretty, womanish face.

Davey!

Six

It took us almost another week to reach the city of York, with a number of nightly stops along the way, while the mounted advance guard, of which I was one, waited for the sluggishly moving army to catch us up and pitch camp. The first night, we slept at Leicester, where the abbey reluctantly provided bed and board for the Dukes of Gloucester and Albany and other such nobles as could be accommodated, without actually turning the monks into the fields to find what comfort they could on the hard ground.

Because of Albany's insistence on my continued presence in his bed at night and at his side during the day, I was assured at all times of the best lodgings to be had; better even than that accorded to many of the minor nobility, who were obliged to take shelter in the various local houses or hostelries available to them. Some, indeed, were forced, on occasions, to have their tents removed from the baggage waggons and pitched alongside the common soldiery, bivouacking in the open countryside. Squires, body servants and the like were lucky to find room wherever they could.

I expected that the continuing favour shown to me by Albany would arouse resentment amongst his immediate household, and was vaguely surprised when the five of them persisted in treating me with the same contemptuous tolerance that they had displayed since I was first introduced into their midst in London. None of them liked me – or seemed not to, at any rate – and all avoided my company when they could; but there was no actual animosity, no overt hostility, not the slightest indication that they had the least suspicion why Albany had asked for me to be his personal bodyguard when he had the five of them to take care of him.

I put this point to the duke that first night after we left

Fotheringay, when we rested at Leicester Abbey. But he shrugged the question aside, anxious to discuss the incident with the bay.

'Pegasus would never have reared like that unless provoked. Did you see anyone touch him, Roger?'

The mattress we were sharing was a hard one, promising a poor night's rest, and I was tired out after half a day's riding; a bad augury for the long days in the saddle which lay ahead. Moreover, I could not rid myself of the growing belief that Albany had no real need of my protection and that I had been wrenched from my home and family without good reason.

'No,' I snapped – but then thought better of my ill temper (or of showing it, at least). After all, I was as much the servant of his grace, the Duke of Gloucester, as of Albany, so I added in a more conciliatory tone, 'I saw nothing, my lord. Murdo and Donald were behind you and Davey was in the crowd. I saw him. But not near enough, now I come to think of it, to do the horse a mischief. John Tullo, of course, was at the bay's head. Why, my lord? Do you truly think that one of them tried to unseat you?'

'You saw what happened. I could have been thrown. At best, I could have been made to look a fool in front of all those arrogant English fools, sniggering up their sleeves. At worst, I could have been killed. And I tell you, Pegasus doesn't play tricks of that sort. Not with me. Someone goaded him on purpose.'

'It might have been an accident,' I protested. 'There was a great press of people all round. The noise alone could have frightened him.'

Albany scornfully dismissed this suggestion. 'For the love of Mary, he's used to it! Pegasus is a French horse, given to me by Cousin Louis. If you've never heard a flock of Frenchmen all screeching at once, you don't know what noise is. I told you I'm in danger, Roger, and I meant it. One of those five has sold himself to my brother James and doesn't intend that I shall be king.'

He was managing to convince me again. Slowly, but ineluctably, I was being drawn once more into the net of his suspicions. Perhaps I had never really escaped it: it was just homesickness that made me pretend I had.

So I told him of the previous night's incident and of the green silk 'leaf' I had found in the ante-room. Now, he was seriously alarmed, and so far forgot what was due to his position as to jump out of bed himself to test the bolt on the door. But, of course, there wasn't one. Abbeys, as a general rule, don't have locks and bolts. They are the houses of God and, as such, are free of access, one brother to another. The cell we were occupying had been made as comfortable as possible, but it gave on to a badly lit passageway without the luxury of an ante-room or a guard of any sort.

Albany was in no doubt as to what must be done.

'You must sleep outside, across the doorway, Roger. It's warm tonight. Wrap yourself in your cloak. You won't be cold.'

He was right. I wasn't cold, but it was damnably uncomfortable, in spite of a pillow for my head, and I tossed and turned, dozed and woke all night, angry and resentful. I wondered, in those brief intervals, when I managed to gain a few moments relief from my bodily aches and pains, why mention of the Green Man affected Albany with such profound unease. I had noticed it when I first broached the subject to him. Did it hold some special significance for him? And who was the man in the mask, anyway? My original thought had been that it could be neither of the squires, but further consideration changed my mind. Either one of them could have planted the 'leaf' for me to find with a view to exonerating himself. Whatever had roused me the previous night – and I was still uncertain what that had been – could have been caused by Donald or Murdo creeping into the duke's chamber, reaching through the bed curtains and touching my arm, perhaps, before scurrying back to the ante-room and feigning slumber. Something of the sort . . .

But here I must have fallen into my final sleep of total exhaustion and was only wakened again by the abbey bells tolling for Prime, and by the general hurry and scuffle of men scrambling to get dressed and be on the march again as soon as possible. We were, in fact, saddled up and on the move while the mist still lay thick upon the ground, and had left Leicester behind us, a dark smudge on the horizon, before it dissolved like smoke trails blown on the wind.

We rode northwards for Nottingham, a mere distance, or so
I was told, of between twenty and thirty miles, and where our
mounted vanguard would wait for the rest of the army to catch
us up while my lord of Gloucester held a council of war. And
it was indeed barely mid-afternoon when we rode across the
hills encircling the town and ascended to the massive fortress
that is Nottingham Castle, towering above the surrounding
houses on its dark up-thrust of rock.

Nottingham is a royal castle, so there was no makeshift
accommodation here. My lord of Albany was accorded every
deference and given a bedchamber, two ante-rooms and his
own private garderobe in keeping with his status as a future
king.

'Well, at least we can shit in private, if only for a night,'
he remarked jocularly as one of his many chests of clothing
was carried into the bedchamber by two of the castle's
lackeys. 'I do so hate baring my arse to the public gaze.
Make the most of it, Roger. When we finally get to Berwick
– if we ever do – and join the siege, it'll be a different story.
We'll be lucky if it's a hole in the ground with the whole of
the army looking on. You're not a fighting man, I believe.'

'Your Grace knows full well that I'm a pedlar,' I answered
drily, unpacking my few modest belongings from a saddle-
bag, which I had humped indoors myself, through various
dark and dingy passageways smelling of dirt and damp to
this large and airy chamber strewn with fresh rushes and
flowers. 'I assume your lordship doesn't wish me to accompany you to the council meeting this afternoon?'

The duke grimaced sourly. 'I doubt your presence would
be welcomed. But I want you close to me at the feast this
evening, mind that! So to prevent a repetition of the night
before last, you'd better spend the time I'm in council getting
yourself fed in the kitchens. I can hear your belly rumbling
from here.'

'I'm not surprised,' I grumbled. 'A handful of dried oats
was all I got for breakfast, and another one for dinner when
we stopped on the road.'

Albany laughed. 'And a big fellow like you needs some
feeding, eh?' There was a rap on the outer door. 'Ah! No
doubt this is my summons to the council-of-war.' He shrugged.

'I thought everything had been decided before we left Fotheringay. Why do Englishmen like to talk so much?' Davey appeared in the inner chamber, but before he could say anything, Albany nodded. 'All right. Tell whoever it is I'm coming.' He glanced back over his shoulder. 'Remember what I said, Roger. Get yourself fed.'

I didn't need telling a third time.

Davey went with me into the bowels of the castle where one of the many kitchens had been cleared to make room for trestles and benches, and which was already full of a chattering, munching throng of servants and hangers-on belonging to the nobles who were now in conclave somewhere above us.

'There are Murdo and Donald and Jamie,' the page said, steering me towards a table set right against the far wall. 'They've saved places for us.'

I wasn't at all sure that I wanted to eat in the company of the Scotsmen, but before I could demur, Davey had seized me by the elbow and was propelling me across the room. And after looking about me in vain for another empty seat, I allowed him to do so without protest.

I found myself seated between Davey and Murdo MacGregor. For a time, while I filled my empty belly with hot mutton and barley broth and a hunk of black bread – served with a bad-tempered thump and splash by one of the castle scullions – the four of them ignored me. In truth, they were also too busy eating to say much, but they did, every now and then, mutter to one another in their own broad Scots tongue. I let them get on with it.

Eventually, however, the edge of everyone's appetite was blunted and the noise of wagging tongues increased. I had scraped my bowl clean and was sitting, picking scraps of mutton from between my teeth, staring into the distance at the chattering throng, seeing, but not seeing, when I was suddenly addressed by Donald Seton in English.

'I'm told, Chapman, that you were once a novice at Glastonbury Abbey. Before you took up peddling, that is.'

I blinked, jerked out of my reverie.

'Who told you that?' I asked.

He shrugged. 'I forget, but it doesn't really matter. Is it true?'

I nodded. 'What of it? I've never made any secret of the fact. Why should I? I left before I took my vows. I discovered that the contemplative life was not for me. Nor the celibate life, either.'

He laughed. 'All right! No need to take that defensive tone! I'm not blaming you. A religious house is no place for an able, red-blooded man, as I can see you are.' Murdo nodded in agreement, but I didn't much care for the cynical grin that accompanied the nod. Donald went on, 'What interests me – us –' he made a little gesture that included his fellow squire – 'is Glastonbury itself.' He hesitated for a moment, glancing first at Murdo, then at Davey, as though uncertain whether or not to continue, before returning his gaze to me. The pause was prolonged before he added, with seeming inconsequence, 'They say you have the "sight".'

'Who are these mysterious "they"?' I demanded irritably. 'Who have you been talking to?'

'Do you have the "sight"?' Murdo interposed, ignoring my questions.

'Not as my mother had it, no. But I do sometimes have dreams. They don't, however, foretell the future, but they do, on occasions, guide me along the right path.'

'You say your mother had the "sight"?' It was Davey's turn to speak. 'You inherited your gift from a woman?'

'My mother was generally acknowledged to be a woman,' I replied with heavy sarcasm. 'And I don't claim that what I have is a gift. It's merely my mind clearing itself by way of dreams.'

'It's a gift,' Davey repeated obstinately, 'inherited through a female.' He nodded at the other two. 'I was right. He belongs to the old world as well as this one.'

'What old world?' I demanded, playing innocent.

But by the pricking of my thumbs, I had already guessed the answer. He meant the pre-Christian world; the world of faerie; the pagan world of our ancestors, who worshipped the gods of the trees, the goddesses of the lake, the inhabitants of the hollow hills. I felt the sweat suddenly stand out on my brow. I glanced anxiously around me to make sure that we could not possibly be overheard.

But all our neighbours were too busy talking themselves hoarse to pay any attention to us. We might as well have been alone, in the middle of a field or on an island. Nevertheless, this was dangerously heretical talk and I made an effort to change the subject. Before I could even form a thought, however, let alone actually say anything, Donald forestalled me.

'This is why we are interested in your time at Glastonbury. They say entrance to the Otherworld lies beneath the Tor. Do you know of anyone who has ever found it?'

One of my faults – one of my many, should I say? – is that I can never forbear airing my knowledge (when I have any to air, that is). It was the same now. Although I knew full well that we were on perilously forbidden ground, I couldn't help saying, 'Beneath the Tor is supposed to be the home of Gwyn-ap-Nud, son of Nud, the Wind God, and lord of the Wild Hunt. Also occasionally known as Avallach, the Fisher King.' I took a deep breath. 'Look, such talk is not only dangerous but foolish, so just let's . . .'

'Have you ever been there?' Donald interrupted ruthlessly.

'Or your mother, perhaps?' Davey added. 'Has she? In the old times it would have been the goddess of the lake who ruled. It would be her handmaidens, even today, who have the power which is handed down from generation to generation to enter the Otherworld.'

'This is becoming nonsensical,' I snarled. 'My mother died many years ago, but in any case, I never asked her such a foolish question. Mind you,' I couldn't restrain myself from adding, 'there is a legend that a holy man, named Collen, once found his way inside the hill, guided by a beautiful girl.'

'Like Thomas the Rhymer,' Davey said eagerly, and the others nodded, even James Petrie, who had so far contributed nothing except a puzzled frown as he tried to follow a conversation that was largely unintelligible to him. But he obviously recognized the name of this Thomas the Rhymer. He said something in rapid Scots to the other three.

I asked, 'Who's Thomas the Rhymer?' and then immediately regretted the question. I was only prolonging a discussion that would be better terminated as soon as possible. Indeed,

I half rose to my feet, preparatory to lifting one leg over the bench, but curiosity got the better of me and I sat down again.

Davey slid me a sidelong glance of triumph. 'In Scotland, the Eildon Hills are said to conceal the entrance to the Otherworld. Thomas was led inside by the Queen of Elfland, herself. The Otherworld, unlike our Christian one, acknowledges women to be the equal of men and accords them equal importance.'

'Why was he called the Rhymer?' I asked rather stupidly.

Murdo gave a superior smile, while Donald looked down his nose. Davey gave a little crow of laughter.

'Because he made rhymes, of course,' he said. 'I should have thought that was obvious.'

This time I did get up and stepped over the bench. The crowd in the kitchen was beginning to thin out as servants and retainers finished eating and went in search of their masters. The noise had decreased accordingly: kitcheners and scullions were busy removing empty bowls and dishes, sweeping the remains of broken meats and bread into their aprons, stretching across the shoulders of those diners still seated.

'You and your companions would do well to watch your tongues, Master Davey,' I told him. 'They'll wag once too often.' With this parting dart, I was about to stride away when I recollected my unanswered question. 'Who has been talking to you about me?'

Murdo chuckled deep in his throat. 'An old friend of yours. My lord of Gloucester's Spymaster General. One, Timothy Plummer.'

I was astonished. I hadn't clapped eyes on Timothy since we parted company in London after he had handed me over to Albany.

'I didn't know he was travelling with the duke,' I said.

Donald gave a short laugh as he, too, finally stood up, yawning and rubbing his belly.

'I don't suppose we know half the people who are travelling in Gloucester's train, what with the chaplains, the doctors, the musicians, the lawyers . . . You'd be lucky to catch a glimpse of your little friend.'

'How did you, then?'

'Quite by chance, I overheard him talking to my lord.'

'Albany? But why were they discussing me?'

'How in Hades should I know? Should I go barging in demanding information of my betters? All I know is that I came upon them talking together just before my lord went into the council chamber. I couldn't help hearing something of what Master Plummer was saying, although I didn't know who he was then. My lord informed me of his identity.'

'And what exactly was Timothy Plummer saying about me?' I enquired indignantly.

Donald shrugged. 'Simply that; that you had once been intended for the church and had entered the monastery at Glastonbury. I think it must have been in response to some information my lord was seeking. But what, I have no idea.'

'Then I shall ask him.'

In the event, however, I held my tongue, at least for the time being. The council of war had plainly rattled Albany and he was in the foulest mood I had ever seen him in. I saw the two squires exchange white-eyed glances and, together with the page, they made themselves scarce, giving their master a wide berth and leaving me to bear the brunt of his ill-temper. I was uncertain what had caused it, but from various remarks he let drop, and from the way he proceeded to vilify some of the other council members, I came to the conclusion that there were those who regarded the attempt to replace King James with his brother on the Scottish throne as a grave mistake; a stumbling block to any negotiations to regain the Princess Cicely's dowry and to win back Berwick.

'They're fools!' Albany stormed, pacing up and down his chamber. 'The only way the English will get back either is by making me king. I've already sworn fealty to Edward.'

'Berwick is already under siege,' I dared to point out. 'It might yet be won back by force.'

'It's been under siege for months,' sneered Albany. 'Why can't the idiots see that I'm their only hope.'

'Duke Richard . . .' I began.

Albany swung round to face me.

'Duke Richard will do what he considers most advantageous for this country,' he snapped, adding, 'I don't trust that man.'

I was genuinely shocked, so much so that I was moved to expostulate.

'His Grace of Gloucester is considered a man of the greatest probity,' I said, and I could hear the anger trembling in my voice. I took a deep breath and continued more moderately, 'He is a very religious man. His word is considered his bond. His loyalty to King Edward has been the cornerstone of his life, unlike his brother, the late Duke of Clarence.'

I was suddenly aware of Albany's ironic glance, and recollected that I had heard him described on more than one occasion as a 'Scottish Clarence'. He had undoubtedly heard the phrase, too, and I waited for the vials of his wrath to break over my head. But one thing I have to say in Albany's favour; he had a sense of humour and was never so set up in self-conceit that he couldn't take a joke at his own expense. He laughed and shrugged.

'All that may be true,' he admitted. 'In fact, it is true. *Loyaute me lie* is Gloucester's motto. But I have often thought him a man who has carefully weighed up the alternatives in life, and then acted in what he considers to be his best self-interest. But also,' Albany added thoughtfully, 'I think him a man who could lose that self-control if ever he allowed his emotions to get the better of him. He hates the Queen and all her family with a depth of loathing that has bitten deep into his soul, but, for his brother's sake, he suppresses it so rigorously that he is almost unaware of it. One day, maybe, it will take him by surprise. That's why I say I don't trust him. Any man who exerts such command over his feelings won't let himself acknowledge just what his real feelings are. Such men, in my estimation, are dangerous.'

'Your Grace seems to know a great deal about my lord Gloucester,' I sneered, forgetting my place in my anger. 'I wouldn't have thought him a man to take anyone so far into his confidence.' I didn't add, 'especially you,' but it was implicit in my tone.

Albany's eyes flashed dangerously. He had been sitting on the bed, but now he slid off and came to stand close to me. He was nearly as tall as I was and could look at me face to face.

'Be careful, Roger,' he said quietly. 'It's true that I owe you something for your help three years ago. It's also true that I need your help now. But don't think that entitles you to speak to me as you please. Remember, I am a future king.'

But this reminded him of his original grievance and he resumed his pacing up and down the bedchamber floor, fulminating for the next ten minutes against those English lords who had hinted that he might be more of a liability than an asset in treating with the Scots.

'Earl Rivers had the gall to suggest that when James is either dead or deposed, my eldest nephew, Rothesay, might be the better alternative to be placed on the throne. A boy of nine! I ask you! No kingdom prospers when the ruler is a child, and so my lord of Gloucester was quick to point out to him.' He glanced at me and I raised my eyebrows, although saying nothing. The stormy look left Albany's face and he grinned reluctantly. 'Yes, all right. He did back me in that. But I still don't altogether trust him. And now, go and find James Petrie for me. I need to change. Cousin Richard has arranged a hunting expedition in Sherwood Forest for the rest of this afternoon, to sharpen our appetites for the feast this evening.'

'I'm not hunting with you,' I said, appalled.

'Dear, sweet Virgin, of course you're not!' he exclaimed, and burst out laughing. 'Your horsemanship's abysmal. Donald and Murdo will accompany me. If the traitor is either of them, I shall be safe with so many other people around.'

I found this hard to reconcile with what little I knew of hunting, particularly in a forest where it seemed to me that the chances of meeting with an accident were naturally high, and which offered the potential assassin opportunities not to be found elsewhere. However, it appeared that my services were not required, so, having despatched James Petrie to my lord's chamber, I was left with time on my hands.

I went in search of Timothy Plummer.

I eventually ran him to earth in the council chamber, seated at the head of the table in what had obviously been my lord of Gloucester's chair, and talking low and earnestly to a couple of nondescript-looking men whom I guessed, judging by their shifty expression and the way in which they blended effortlessly into the background, to be two of his spies.

He was plainly none too pleased to see me and sent the men away as soon as he saw me.

'What are you doing here?' he demanded abruptly. 'Why aren't you with Albany?'

'Hunting? Really, Timothy, you should know better than that. Even the duke knew better than that. But he was willing to dispense with my invaluable protection in order to pursue the pleasures of the chase.' I hitched one knee over a corner of the table and sat on it, an inch or two from Timothy's chair. 'Is this the way wars are always conducted?' I asked disgustedly. 'With pauses for feasting and hunting and general jollification? It's a miracle any actual fighting gets done at all.'

He took a lofty tone. 'You know nothing about anything, my lad, that has to do with your betters. You just stick to what you've been hired to do. Watch Albany's back and keep your eyes on that precious pack of Scots he's got around him. He seems pretty certain that one of them means him a mischief. Do you have any idea which one?'

I said I hadn't, but then went on to tell him about events at Fotheringay and the strange business of the man in the Green Man mask. I even produced the silk leaf from my pouch and laid it on the table in front of him. Timothy seemed unimpressed, flicking it back to me with a careless finger.

'Well, it appears to lend credence to Albany's fears, at any rate. So just make sure that nothing happens to him.' The Spymaster scraped back his chair from the table and rose. 'We're holding you responsible for his safety, Roger. Try to remember that. You don't want to find yourself hanging from the end of a rope.'

Seven

As we continued northwards, it became ever more obvious that the devastation in these northern shires, occasioned by the recent, terrible weather, was greater by far than anything we had experienced in the south. Although an uncertain June had brought bouts of tremulous sunshine, much of the soil was still waterlogged, and such shoots as had dared to thrust their way above ground, were pallid and weak. The people working the land were grey-faced and despondent, barely lifting dull eyes from the toil of grubbing in the earth to watch our brave cavalcade pass by. Facing the prospect of yet another bad harvest, they had no time to waste on the vagaries of their lords and masters. It was all one to them if Berwick were an English or a Scottish town, and was of small importance beside the fear of death, disease and empty bellies. It's true that as we moved into sheep country, there were a few raised fists, and a few raised voices, also, demanding to know why England had not gone to Burgundy's aid in her war with France. But, generally speaking, apathy and despair held the bulk of the population silent.

I stayed close to Albany, riding behind the two squires, watching carefully for any hostile move on the part of either one of them; or on the part of Davey Gray, James Petrie or the groom. However, as the days went painfully by, nothing happened except that I became ever more weary and saddle-sore, while the conviction grew in me that the threat from his late brother's retainers was merely a figment of Albany's over-fertile imagination.

Eventually, I told him so and demanded to be released from his employ.

'My lord, I beg you to tell Duke Richard that you have been mistaken and no longer have need of my services.'

It was the evening of the 17th day of June, and the entire army was encamped outside the walls of York in readiness for the Duke of Gloucester's triumphal entry into the city the following morning. This was the heartland of Prince Richard's vast northern palatinate, and he would have been less than human had he not wanted us all to see how revered and beloved he was by those whom he regarded as his own special people. Albany, already short-tempered at the prospect – realizing, perhaps, that he would never command such devotion – was in no mood to grant my request or even to consider it.

'Do you think I'm a fool?' he barked. 'A hysterical woman who jumps at shadows? Besides, it's not just these five, one of whom *may* – all right! I admit it – *may* have been suborned by my brother, James. But there are those, too, in the English camp who wish me ill and doubt my good intentions once the Scottish crown is set on my head. No! I will not release you, Roger. You are the only person I trust wholeheartedly; the only person who has proved himself my friend – and that at some risk to himself. Now, please don't raise this subject again, or I shall be forced to advise my cousin Gloucester that you are unwilling to obey his orders.'

Albany had gone very red in the face, and I found myself wondering, in a detached kind of way, if he might not die of an apoplexy and so relieve me of the necessity of looking after him. He was obviously working himself up for another such outburst, accompanied by the further possibility of a seizure, when, just at that moment, James Petrie's tall, emaciated figure entered the crimson silk pavilion, anxious – or so I gathered from Albany's reply – to know what clothes his royal master would be wearing on the morrow. His agitation made it plain that Scotland's honour must be upheld amidst this horde of Sassenachs.

'The purple velvet and ermine of course,' Albany snapped. Then, with a shrug of impatience, repeated the words in the broad Scots dialect that I found so hard to follow, in spite of some recognizably English words being embedded in it, like jewels amongst the dross.

James Petrie nodded, apparently satisfied, before adding something else that made Albany yelp in protest.

'Daybreak?' He turned to me, aghast. 'Jamie says we're entering the city at daybreak! Dear, sweet God in heaven!'

His henchman smiled grimly.

While the duke was still voicing his disgust, in both English and Scots, with some choice French phrases thrown in for good measure, I escaped from the pavilion and went to cool both my head and my temper amongst the other splendid silken tents, topped by their gaily waving pennants. I had strolled some distance, fascinated by all the bustle of a great encampment – the comings and goings, the toing and froing, the many and varied orders shouted and then almost immediately rescinded – when it occurred to me that I had left Albany alone with one of the men he ostensibly distrusted. Yet he had made no move to detain me; just as, four days ago, he had gone hunting in Sherwood Forest, quite content to leave me behind. There was something odd about it all. It was making me very uneasy.

The Aldermen were resplendent in scarlet. There were also dignitaries in crimson, who, someone said, were the Twenty-four – although the twenty-four what I never discovered. Craftsmen and other citizens sweated in their Sunday best as the common folk crammed the narrow alleyways in a wildly cheering throng. Every house was decorated with some token or another; a bunch of flowers, a tapestry hung out of an upper window, knots of ribbon in the duke's colours of blue and murrey. Women vied to get themselves noticed, flaunting more flesh than was seemly. (Well, not as far as I was concerned. I like the female form, but some, no doubt, objected.)

My lord of Gloucester himself, his face alight with pleasure and happiness, was presented with gifts of a fine milk loaf, ten gallons of wine and a great many very large fish, all of which seemed to be of the extremely pungent varieties. Albany, as guest of honour and future king of Scotland, received a similar offering, but not quite so generous, a fact he acknowledged with a small, ironic quirk of his eyebrow. And afterwards, there were pageants, songs and speeches by the score, and all before the sun had properly gilded the sky above the eastern horizon. For my own part, I groaned inwardly. I could feel in my bones that it was going to be a long, hard day.

Judging by the slightly jaundiced eye that Albany rolled in my direction, he thought so, too. But honour had been satisfied, and vanity appeased, by references to his anticipated kingly status and by the reverence accorded him – although any fool with half a brain would know that these blunt and honest Yorkshiremen were merely buttering him up to please their prince. That Richard of Gloucester was adored – almost worshipped – in these parts was plain to all; the love and warmth radiated towards him everywhere he went was almost palpable. It was doubtful if the king himself, had he been present, could have commanded one tenth of such affection. But not everyone was happy at this demonstration of un-bridled loyalty: I noticed my lord of Northumberland, for one, looking as sour as a green apple.

Albany and his immediate entourage, myself included, spent the night at the Augustinian Friary, a favourite lodging, so I was told, of Prince Richard himself when he stayed in York. Tonight, he graciously ceded his place to his guest and withdrew to the Archbishop's Palace, with orders to his generals that they were to be on the march again at dawn the following day.

'Such energy,' Albany complained in that half-mocking tone I was coming to recognize so well.

He was, I reflected, a difficult man to know, who revealed far less of himself than I had thought in the beginning. My original impression of Albany – both during our brief acquain-tanceship in Bristol and earlier this year, in London – had been of a shallow man, motivated by vanity and petulance, envy and overweening ambition. He was not the first man, nor, doubtless, would he be the last, to resent having been born a younger son, and to aim at his brother's crown. But he was less of a George of Clarence than those who so dubbed him (behind his back, it goes without saying) would admit. Over the past weeks, I had come to realize that Albany was not so trivial as popular opinion made him out to be. There was an unfathomable side to his nature that he took great pains to keep hidden; a side of which I had had the barest glimpse just once or twice when his guard had slipped, but so elusive that I could not pin it down. A circumstance that caused me a good deal of apprehension.

'So, what do you think of the great northern city?' he asked me as we lay side by side beneath the roof of the friary's guest-house, on a deeply filled goose-feather mattress in a bed with richly embroidered hangings. 'This must be your first sight of it, as it is mine.'

'A very rich city,' I said. 'Rich by any standards, north or south. The castle's a bit of a ruin, but otherwise the buildings are well maintained with plenty of gilding and good paintwork. And the mayoral banquet tonight,' I added with a certain amount of bitterness, 'sported enough dishes to feed the five thousand.'

Albany chuckled. 'Plenty of rich leftovers, though, or so I should imagine.'

I snorted derisively. I didn't suppose that he had ever eaten leftovers, rich or otherwise, in his life, not even when he was on the run from his elder brother's court or in hiding.

'Leftovers,' I pointed out with an aggrieved air, 'are either cold when they're meant to be hot or tepid when they should be cold, and the saucers are usually wiped clean.'

That made my companion laugh outright.

'Ye're getting too particular, man! Too used to good living. You'll have to get accustomed to common fare again when you eventually go home to your Jenny.'

'Adela,' I snapped.

He turned his head towards me on the pillow and grinned.

'I like you, Roger,' he said. 'When I become king, I've a good mind to keep you with me as a lucky talisman.'

'You couldn't,' I retorted sharply. 'I shouldn't stay.'

'You might have no choice,' was the soft response; so soft that it was like the breath of doom sighing between the bed curtains and gently brushing my cheek and making my blood run cold. I could have sworn that I saw the embroidered hangings stir.

I was seized by a sudden fear of never getting home again; of never seeing my wife and family again; after the fear of death, the most primeval fear of all.

My terror must have communicated itself to Albany for he grasped one of my wrists and shook it.

'I don't mean a lot of what I say, you know. I was jesting.'
He gave a sudden groan and sat up, his knees doubled up
to his chest.

'What's wrong?' I asked.

'Bellyache!' He groaned once more, clasping his hands
around his knees. 'I knew I shouldn't have had second
helpings of everything, especially the peacock. There was
something evil about that bird . . . Ah! . . . And I thought the
pike tasted a bit queer, but you couldn't really tell. The galen-
tyne sauce disguised it . . . And I had three servings of curd
flan and pears in white wine syrup . . . Eeeh! . . . For God's
sake, where's the night-stool, Roger?'

'Over here, on my side of the chamber.' I pushed back the
curtains and sprang out of bed, hoping desperately that Albany
could control his bowels and vomit until he was clear of my
side of the sheets. I lifted the lid of the night-stool invit-
ingly.

The duke, who was now heaving most pathetically, flung
himself on his knees beside it and I held his head down over
the pot, waiting for the inevitable. But although the retching
continued, nothing happened, and after several minutes,
Albany jerked upright and sank back on his heels, tears
streaming down his cheeks, but with nothing else to show
for this sudden spasm.

'I–I don't think I am going to be sick after all,' he
announced, wiping his face with the hem of his night-shift
and giving me a splendid view of his powerful physical attributes. (In his time, he had probably made a lot of women
extremely happy.) 'The nausea seems to be getting less . . .
Yes . . . Yes . . . Praise be! I'm definitely beginning to feel
better.'

'If Your Highness is certain . . .' I murmured doubtfully,
unsure whether or not to replace the night-stool's lid.

'I'm certain,' Albany replied, getting to his feet. He gave
an apologetic smile. 'At least, I think I am.'

'Perhaps Your Grace had better wait a moment or so
longer,' I suggested, 'just to avoid a nasty surprise.'

Although the June day had been mild, a fire had nevertheless been lit on the hearth in our bedchamber, and now one of
the logs gave a dying spurt of flame as if caught by a sudden

draught of air. I remembered the other small draught I had experienced earlier, but which I had attributed to my imagination. I stepped quickly around the bed, but the stout oaken door was firmly shut. I lifted the latch and pulled it open, expecting to see Davey or one of the squires sleeping across the threshold, but saw only a blanket in an abandoned heap.

I became aware of the duke at my elbow.

'What's wrong?' His voice sounded shrill. 'And where's Davey? He was supposed to be on watch tonight.'

At that moment, the page appeared round a bend in the narrow passageway that led to the main door of the guesthouse.

'Where have you been?' the duke demanded angrily.

'Your grace . . . my lord . . .' Davey stammered. 'I'm sorry, but I had to use the privy in the yard. It's my belly, my lord. I was feeling sick.'

Albany was grudingly sympathetic.

'You, too? Roger here will tell you that I've been suffering likewise.'

'And were you sick?' I asked the page. 'And how long have you been out there?'

He shook his head, as though dazed.

'I don't know. Some little while. And yes, I was sick,' he added resentfully. 'Why? Has something happened?'

Albany, still clutching his belly, turned to look at me with raised eyebrows.

I was forced to admit that, as far as I knew, nothing actually had. 'I just thought that perhaps someone had entered the bedchamber,' I explained. 'Draughts,' I muttered not very intelligibly.

'Draughts?'

'Yes, my lord. I was just being careful.'

Albany shrugged, wished Davey goodnight and turned back towards the bed.

'We'd best get some sleep if we're to be up at dawn,' he advised, pulling back the hangings on his side of the bed, which had so far remained undisturbed.

I heard, almost with incredulity, the long, shuddering intake of breath that became a half-strangled cry of terror, and moved swiftly to his side.

'My lord? What is it? What's the matter?'

Albany, bereft of speech, could only point with a shaking finger. Sticking out of the bedclothes, its blade invisible, was the haft of a black-handled knife.

We fell into an uneasy slumber eventually, but not before we had both partaken liberally of the wine in our 'all-night' jugs and sat, huddled in conference, around the dying embers of the fire.

'You see!' the duke accused me in trembling accents. 'I have not been imagining the danger that I'm in. Someone has made an attempt on my life and only by the greatest of good fortune – my feeling sick and needing the night-stool – have I avoided being done to death while I slept. And you have been trying to persuade me that I don't need your protection.'

I was too shaken myself to think of pointing out that I, too, could have been asleep and therefore unable to avert the tragedy. My only thought was that Davey's absence from his post had been all too opportune. I said nothing, but the same idea shortly occurred to Albany, who promptly stormed into the passageway, kicking his dozing page awake with a violence that made the poor boy jerk upright, shivering and whimpering with fright.

'My–my lord?' He blinked in astonishment at his master, but was still more horrified when confronted by an accusation of having deliberately deserted his post in order to leave the way clear.

'No! No, my lord! I was sick. I told you! Something I ate at supper.'

His tearful protestations sounded sincere enough, and his white face gave credence to his claim of feeling ill, corroborated as it was by the duke's own bout of nausea. But it would have taken a shrewder man than myself to say for certain whether Davey's tale were true or merely a skilful piece of play-acting. The fact remained, however, that whoever had made this attempt on the duke's life could have had no foreknowledge of the page's possible absence from outside the door unless he were in league with Davey himself . . .

Then I recollected that the boy normally slept on a truckle-bed or pallet inside the bedchamber, and only lack of a bolt on the door had, on this occasion, banished him to the passage. Davey's absence might therefore have led the killer to suppose that such was the case tonight, and he had stolen in to accomplish the fell deed as quickly and quietly as possible.

Yet surely, I thought, as I tossed and turned sleeplessly beside the duke when we had finally decided that nothing further could be gained by continuing our deliberations until morning (and having decided, also, that our assassin was unlikely to chance his luck a second time that night) the man must have heard the noise of Albany's suffering as he retched and strained at the stool. There had been no candle burning: the light of the dying fire had been sufficient for our needs, but the hangings had been drawn back on my side of the bed and it could easily have been seen by the killer. On the other hand, a man intent on murder might well not have noticed the glow until too late. He would, of necessity, only have pulled back the bed-curtains as little possible before plunging his knife into what he imagined was the duke's sleeping form. Realizing his mistake, and that the occupants of the room were both wide awake, he would have withdrawn with all speed to try again another day.

I rolled on to my back and stared sightlessly at the canopy above me. Something was bothering me and would not let me rest, but in the end, I fell into an uneasy slumber without resolving what it was that troubled me. And the next thing I knew, it was morning.

A careful study of the knife in daylight gave no clues as to its owner. Indeed, it was plainly a kitchen knife – one of those sharp, broad-bladed implements used primarily for cutting up meat – and could have been procured by anyone who had access to the friary's kitchens. And who was to say that it necessarily belonged to the friary? It could have been stolen at Fotheringay, Leicester, Nottingham or at any other of the stops we had made during the past week on our journey northwards. No, there was nothing to be learned from the intended murder weapon. Nor was there any certainty that the murderer himself was one of Albany's servants, for the

Austin friars had offered hospitality to the retainers of many
other lords who could not be accommodated under the same
roofs as their masters; and upon enquiry I discovered that
there had been very few spare corners anywhere in the buildings that night.

The duke himself seemed to have recovered the tone of
his mind with surprising speed. He was almost inclined to
make light of the incident except for his insistence that I was
necessary to his safety and must never again consider leaving
him until we reached Scotland and he was crowned king.
My suggestion that last night's happening should be reported
to the Duke of Gloucester, so that extra measures might be
put in place for his protection, was brushed aside.

'And lay myself – in whom the honour of Scotland is
invested – open to the ridicule of Sassenachs?' Albany
demanded indignantly. 'Never!'

'It was a determined, a genuine, attempt on your life, my
lord,' I argued, amazed at his attitude. 'Neither Prince Richard
nor any other English noble will think you ridiculous for
making a fuss over such a matter. Do you really believe that
if such a thing had happened to any one of them the whole
city would not now be in an uproar in an attempt to find the
would-be assassin?'

But Albany remained adamant, even going so far as to
swear both Davey and myself to silence on the subject.

'We'll never catch this murdering bastard if we put him
too much on his guard,' he said, as we once more rode northwards just after dawn, leaving the rose-tinted walls of York
behind us.

I considered him to be over-sanguine if he thought the
page would keep a still tongue in his head. I wondered if
Albany were truly unaware of the close bond of comradeship that existed between the late Earl of Mar's former
servants, or if he simply ignored it as an inconvenient fact.
For my own part, I had no doubt whatsoever that both the
squires, James Petrie and John Tullo would be in full possession of the story before many hours had passed. Indeed, it
seemed to me, glancing at the faces of Donald Seton and
Murdo MacGregor, as they rode alongside me, immediately
behind their master, that they already knew. There was a sly

expression in the former's green-flecked eyes, and a wry twist to the latter's usually stern-set mouth that convinced me Davey had wasted very little time in informing his fellows of the night's events.

As for what I thought myself, I was in a quandary, my head reeling from a lack of sleep and a growing sense of unreality. The suspicion kept obtruding that the previous night's attempt on Albany's life had been staged for my benefit, in order to keep me from defecting, as I had threatened to do. I could not choose but remember that the duke, although pleading sickness, had not actually thrown up into the night-stool. There had been a great deal of retching, but no actual vomiting. His claim to be ill, however, had removed him providentially from his side of the bed, and had, moreover, occupied my full attention. And that was another thing, the killer had, apparently, known in advance on which side of the bed Albany was sleeping. Had he been forced to part the bed curtains wide enough to ascertain this fact, he must have seen that Albany wasn't there; could not have helped seeing, in fact, his quarry's kneeling figure beside the night-stool and myself bending over him. Furthermore, Davey's absence had been so opportune . . .

And yet the whole notion was so absurd as to be laughable. It was foolish beyond permission. There was no possible reason why Albany should go to such lengths to keep an unwilling man in his service. It argued some sinister motive for which there was no justification. No; his desire for my presence must surely be what he had always claimed it was. I was somebody in whom he could trust; somebody who, for no better reason than that I liked him, had once broken the law to help him evade his pursuers by arranging his passage to Ireland. It was no use my complaining. As Timothy Plummer had pointed out to me, I had brought my present situation on myself.

So I might as well get on with things and see what transpired.

We reached Berwick at last, sometime in the early weeks of July, all twenty thousand of us, together with siege machines, baggage waggons and the hangers-on that, or so I was told, all armies gather to themselves as they progress. The town was already under siege, and had been since the preceding October. But now we had arrived to wrest this border town back from the Scots and establish it as a part of England once and for all. Such was the Duke of Gloucester's avowed intention.

As we approached, I could just make out through the gloom the scorched and flattened earth outside the town and the battered fortifications beyond. As preparations began for the pitching of tents and the lighting of camp fires, dark clouds began to gather. Dragons, mountains, castles stood carved in ebony against the rays of the dying sun. Thunder muttered across the hills, and a flock of crows swooped and cawed their way overhead as they flew to roost. The surrounding countryside stretched black and purple in the fading evening light. Heavy drops of rain began to fall.

There was a flurry of horse's hooves as my lord of Gloucester rode alongside. He clapped Albany on the back.

'Not an auspicious beginning, cousin,' he said, laughing, and pulling his cloak tighter about him as protection against the elements. 'But I'm sure you don't believe in such auguries. You're within spitting distance of your native soil. We'll be across the border in no time at all. You'll see! You're almost home now.'

'There might be a case for arguing that I am home already,' Albany answered dryly. He noted Gloucester's swift, side-long glance and added, 'Oh, don't worry, coz. If you can retake Berwick, it's yours as far as I'm concerned. It's always been a troublesome place and not one worth fighting over. When I'm king, I shan't go back on my word.'

Prince Richard smiled, a little grimly I thought. 'I'm glad to hear it.' He suddenly noticed me and the long, thin mouth relaxed somewhat. 'Roger!' he acknowledged before turning once more to Albany. 'My intelligence is that your brother is on the march. It seems there's a sizeable army moving south from Edinburgh.'

Eight

The town of Berwick fell quickly. The English were masters of the shattered streets and eyeless houses in a matter of days after our arrival, but the citadel continued to hold out, the wild skirling of the Scottish pipes hurling defiance from the battlements. Many of the citizens had taken refuge inside its walls, adding no doubt to the fortress's congestion and its shortage of food and water. Albany, returning to his pavilion from a council of war in the Duke of Gloucester's tent, railed bitterly against his countrymen's obstinacy.

'The fools know they can't win, so why don't they just give in sooner rather than later?'

It was not a question to which he expected an answer – indeed, there was a note of pride underlying his irritation – but, scrambling up off my straw mattress, bored and restless with inactivity, I suggested, somewhat impertinently, that the defenders could be waiting for the arrival of King James and his army. 'Except that Your Highness's brother seems to be taking his time in getting here.'

For a moment, Albany looked as if he might be about to remind me of my status as slightly lower than a worm – one of which was squirming across the ground towards me as I spoke – but then he thought better of it and laughed.

'James is incapable of bestirring himself for anyone or anything. No doubt dalliance with his favourites is consuming a great deal of his time and energy.'

'Would he have brought them with him?'

'Brought them with him?' the duke snorted. 'Of course he's brought them with him. He never stirs without 'em! One of 'em's doubtless in charge of the army – probably that louse, Tam Cochrane – while good men like our uncles, Atholl and Buchan, are thrust aside and humiliated.'

I said nothing. There was nothing I could say. The names were unfamiliar to me, as were my surroundings. With each succeeding day, I felt myself to be in an alien world where strangeness was beginning to be the norm; where home and family and the soft green contours of my native west country were fading into a kind of dream glimpsed now and then in the long, dark watches of the night, but gone by morning. There were even times when I wondered if I had perhaps indeed strayed into that world of faerie beneath Glastonbury Tor, or into the elfland that Donald Seton had mentioned as existing under the Eildon Hills.

The call of a trumpet jagged the afternoon silence, and was answered by the keening wail of the pipes. Immediately all was bustle and confusion as men suddenly sprang into action. Murdo and Donald appeared as if by magic, ready to arm their master.

'A sortie from the citadel,' the former said in answer to Albany's barked question, while the latter pushed me unceremoniously aside with a well-aimed kick.

'Out of the way, Roger, my lad! This is soldier's work. Not for hangers-on like you.'

I didn't rise to the bait, but took myself off to a vantage point a little way outside the town where I could view the action in safety. It was a place I had discovered some days earlier; a small knoll where the delicate blue of the harebell and the deep, sweet pink of the clustering ling tinted the summer grasses; a little haven that had somehow escaped the general surrounding devastation.

Ten minutes later, I was watching the Duke of Gloucester, with Albany and Lord Stanley at his heels, closely followed by Earl Rivers and half a dozen other of his captains, engage in hand-to-hand fighting with a hundred or so of the enemy who had suddenly erupted from the citadel's main gate. Hordes of screaming citizens lined the walls above them, indiscriminately hurling missiles at friend and foe alike. I couldn't help laughing when an earthenware chamber-pot, with all its contents, landed upside down on a man-at-arms' head; but it was laughter quickly silenced when the man, blinded, was ripped open from waist to neck by an enemy dirk.

A voice screamed above the general din, 'The hay-cart! They're firing the hay-cart!'

The cart stood close to the ballista, its contents waiting to be woven into fire-balls to be hurled over the citadel's walls. In the panic of the moment, it had been left unguarded, and suddenly its contents were aflame. Even I, hanger-on that I was, could now see that the sally had been a mere diversion to keep the English occupied around the main gate, while another party of Scots crept out by a postern door and set fire to the hay-cart, which they were in the process of pushing towards the huddle of dwellings nearest the centre of the town. A rainbow of sparks whirled and tumbled in the afternoon light. Smoke billowed and wreathed in choking clouds.

I could just make out my lord Gloucester, Albany and the rest, spluttering and coughing, smoke-blackened and sweating, laying about them with their swords as they struggled to overpower their opponents before the citadel gates were slammed shut in their faces. But it was no good. The heat of the burning buildings distracted and confused them, and the width of the barbican drawbridge made it impossible for more than two men to go abreast. The great wooden leaves creaked defiantly together, the last Scotsman disappeared, like a wraith, through the final crack and the whirr and clatter of the iron bar could be heard, even above the general din, as it was laboriously levered into place.

A chance to end the siege of Berwick by capturing the citadel had been lost thanks to the stupid error of leaving the hay-cart unguarded. I decided I wouldn't care to be in the shoes of whoever was responsible for that.

No one was in a happy mood that evening; but then, as far as the common soldiery was concerned, that was nothing new. Albany was dining in the Duke of Gloucester's pavilion along with the other commanders, while they no doubt apportioned blame for the afternoon's fiasco, and I was left to line up beside the cooks' great cauldrons of what passed for stew with the rest of the unwashed masses. For some reason best known to themselves, the cooks had elected to build their fires and set out their trestles within shouting distance of the hospital tents, so while we chewed on bits of gristle and choked on pieces of turnip that were so raw they cracked our teeth, we were entertained by the cries, groans and screams of the wounded and dying.

A little man, a Londoner by birth I reckoned, seated on the ground beside me, spat out several choice morsels of the caterer's art and, lumping all army cooks and commanders together, blasted them to hell.

'A bloody good chance to end this siege once and for all,' he grumbled, 'and what 'appens? Our lords and masters allows 'emselves to be diddled by a party o' kilted savages. Disgraceful I calls it.'

A second man gave a throaty chuckle. 'You ain't surprised, surely, Dickon? Don' you know by now that if anythink can be cocked up, it will be? Tha's the first rule o' warfare.'

There was a general murmur of agreement in the fire-studded dark and a general shifting of bodies. After a while, people began getting up and wandering away from the heat of the flames and the sound of their fellow men in agony. With full bellies, they sloped off to find their own or some-body else's woman amongst the camp followers at the rear of the baggage waggons, and I found myself isolated in a little pool of shadow thrown by one of the cannon used earlier in the siege, but at present abandoned in favour of more old-fashioned weapons. It reminded me of Albany's story of how his father, King James II, had been blown up and killed by a piece of his own beloved artillery . . .

'Chapman!'

The apparently disembodied voice came out of the dark-ness, making me jump. I scrambled to my feet, staring wildly about me.

'Chapman!' The hoarse whisper came again, like the scraping of a fiddle bow across catgut. 'Chapman, I say!'

'Who are you? What do you want?'

I had, by this time, located the source of the sound as coming from the opposite side of the cannon, and moved purposefully to round it.

'Stop!' ordered the voice with such urgency that, against all my natural inclinations, I obeyed. 'Don't come any closer. Stay where you are on the other side of the gun. You'll regret it if you don't. I have a knife and I shan't hesitate to use it.'

The man, whoever he was, sounded desperate enough to carry out this threat, so I retreated. The nearest fire was nothing now but a carpet of red-hot ashes. It was a clear night, the sky above swimming with stars, but moonless, the distance curtained by the shadowy outline of the town. The cannon stood in a pool of blackness.

I repeated my earlier questions. 'Who are you? What do you want?'

A head was raised cautiously into view, but not an ordinary head. It was over-large and, as my sight adjusted to the darkness, I could see that it trembled with what seemed to be leaves. From the mouth drooped branches of foliage and where the eyes should have been were two glittering slits. In other words, the fellow was wearing a mask; the mask of the Green Man.

The realization gave me courage.

'For heaven's sake, take that stupid thing off and let me see your face,' I begged. 'If you have something to tell me, say it openly like a man.'

'Hold your tongue,' rasped the voice, 'and listen to me. It's for your own good and I haven't much time. Watch your back, Chapman. You're in danger.'

'Danger? In what way?'

'I don't know exactly. If I did, I'd tell you. But I repeat, watch your back!'

I could feel little worms of fear beginning to crawl over my skin, but I answered jauntily enough, 'Are you certain you have this right? Surely it's my master, the Duke of Albany, who is threatened, not me. I have been hired to protect him.'

'Albany?' was the grim retort. 'Maybe he is in danger. There are plenty of people who'd no doubt like to see him dead, his brother, King James, amongst them. But I do know you're in jeopardy, as well. It's no good asking me how I know this because I'm not allowed to tell. Just do as I say and be on your guard and maybe nothing will come of it.'

'That's not much use,' I grumbled, adding violently, 'I wish you'd take that damned Green Man mask off and we could discuss this face to face, man to man. Incidentally, was that you at Fotheringay who threw me against the wall and sent me sprawling to the ground?'

'Yes. There was someone, I couldn't see who, standing on the stairs above you. Whether or not he meant you harm, I'd no idea, but he could have done.' Suddenly the Green Man flung out an arm. 'Look behind you, Chapman!'

I whirled round, my right hand flying to the knife stuck in my belt, all my senses straining to meet whatever danger was threatening, and to meet it head on . . .

But there was nothing and nobody there, just a slight breeze stirring the darkness. The noises of the camp had grown muted; even the cries of the wounded had diminished and I realized it must be later than I thought. Albany would doubtless have returned to his pavilion and be looking for me. I turned back to address my companion . . .

He had vanished. I walked round the cannon several times, but there was no trace of him. He had deliberately misdirected my attention, and I had fallen into the trap like any green schoolboy. 'Over there!' we used to shout to unpopular school fellows. And while they were looking 'over there', the rest of us used to run away and hide.

Angered by my own stupidity, I made my way back to Albany's tent and only just in time. A minute or so later, he walked in.

I lay tossing and turning on my straw mattress, listening to Albany's snores which were loud enough to waken the dead. It was obvious that he had drunk too much of the Duke of Gloucester's best wine, and it had taken the combined efforts of Davey and myself to strip him and get him to bed. If, I reflected sourly, the other commanders were all in the same state of inebriety, a surprise night attack by King James and his army could not only retake the town of Berwick, but drive us back as far as the River Tyne, if not farther. I wondered how distant the Scots' army was.

But this was the least of my worries. My first concern was to work out the identity of the Green Man and the second to try to fathom his intentions. There had surely been something familiar in his voice, some intonation I had heard before, but although I went over and over his words in my mind, I could not pin it down. One moment I thought I had it, the next it had eluded me and, like a will-o'-the-wisp, was gone. And what was the purpose of his warning? Was he right? Was I really in danger, or was he, for some unknown reason, attempting to unsettle me and so make me less on my guard where Albany was concerned? And should I tell the duke what had happened, or did this unknown danger emanate from him? Yet why should he wish me ill? To listen to his protestations, I was his only friend, the one person he could trust. On the other hand, could I trust him?

It struck me suddenly that perhaps this was what the Green Man wanted; to sow seeds of discord between Albany and myself. My discontent with my present lot was probably no secret in general, and was most certainly known to each one of the five Scots. If I could be frightened into actually carrying out my threat to desert and make my way back home, relying on the Duke of Gloucester's eventual clemency towards one who had rendered him several important services, then Albany would be deprived of a vital protection and left vulnerable to whatever mischief was being hatched against him.

As I tried desperately to calm my tumultuous thoughts, I recalled that only recently I had doubted if the duke was in any actual danger and had suspected him of some ulterior motive in keeping me by his side. Had I been right? Now, I didn't think so. The more I went over my conversation – if you could call it that – with the Green Man, the more I was persuaded that someone was trying to scare me off, which seemed to imply that Albany really was in peril of his life. Whoever it was, would discover that I was not so easily intimidated.

The morning found me in the same frame of mind. Indeed, the first moment I was alone with Albany, I confided in him the details of my previous night's encounter with the Green Man. We had made our way to the grassy knoll from where I had observed yesterday's debacle and the spectacular failure of the English to take the citadel when offered a heaven-sent opportunity to do so. Below us lay the war-torn town; above, the bowl of the summer sky hung newly scoured and shining. The distant hills were burnished by the morning sun, and on their lower slopes I could just make out cattle and a few thin goats quietly cropping the grass. A little stream, possibly a tributary of the Tweed, washed the glittering mosses and gurgled over sun-bleached stones, fringed by crumpled,

gently waving fronds of bracken. A lovely day; too lovely
for the sights and sounds of war and the discussion of death
and destruction.

Albany listened to me in silence before letting rip with a
string of oaths that could only command my respect and
admiration.

'Who is this bastard creeping about in a damned Green
Man mask?' he finished on a quieter note, but his handsome
face still suffused with colour. He was shaking, too, and not
altogether from anger. He was frightened. 'Someone's trying
to scare you away from me, Roger.'

'That had occurred to me, my lord,' I admitted. 'Otherwise,
I probably wouldn't have told you.'

'Why not?' he sounded alarmed. 'You can't possibly
imagine that I mean you harm? What reason do I have? Well?
Tell me! I asked to have you with me. This fellow, whoever
he is, is trying to make you jumpy. It's as plain as the nose
on your face. While you're worrying about yourself, your
attention is not on me.' His voice had become shrill. He
heard it and took himself in hand. 'If the scoundrel bothers
you again, I shall complain to Duke Richard,' he added on
a calmer note. 'He'll soon root the fellow out and have him
whipped at the cart's tail.' He glanced at me curiously. 'You
have no idea, yourself, who it might be?'

'None at all, my lord.' True enough; with the coming of
the light I could no longer recapture that faint inflection of
the voice that had brought momentary recognition.

Albany hesitated. 'I meant . . . You have the sight, have
you not?'

I was reminded of the discussion with the squires and
Davey and wondered at this constant harping on my ability
to 'see'.

'No, my lord, I do not,' I answered firmly, determined to
put this mistaken notion to rest once and for all. 'It was my
mother who had the "sight", not me. All I have ever experienced are certain dreams that come to me occasionally and
help me interpret things that I already know, but have failed
to connect to one another in the proper and necessary way.
Sometimes they may even jog my memory about things I
have forgotten. But this is not "sight" as you mean it.'

'Nevertheless, your mother had it. You have inherited your powers through the female line.'

'I repeat, my lord, I have no powers. I cannot see into the future. If you imagine that I can foretell your destiny, you are mistaken and I am of no use to you.'

It had suddenly occurred to me that perhaps this was the reason Albany had insisted on my company and kept me by him, expecting some revelation concerning his ultimate fate – a revelation that would never come.

He read my thoughts and laughed. 'I keep you with me for my protection, Roger. Because you are big and strong and, at the risk of repeating myself yet again, I trust you. I genuinely believe myself to be in mortal danger, either from one or more of Mars's servants, who travelled to France after his death specifically to seek me out, or from someone within the English camp who thinks that King Edward's attempt to put me on the Scottish throne is a mistake.'

'Do you think it a mistake?' I asked bluntly, risking his displeasure, or perhaps his scorn.

But he made no immediate answer. Overhead, a lark soared away eastwards towards the distant shimmer of a line of hills. Albany followed the bird's progress until it flew out of sight.

'I know my countrymen,' he answered at last. 'They won't readily accept a king foisted on them by the Sassenachs, who have tried that game more than once in the past, and been thwarted. It will take more than my brother's unpopularity and King Edward's will to place the Scottish crown upon my head and keep it there.'

I was surprised by this sudden pessimism from one whom I had previously considered too confident for his own good, and said so.

Once again, Albany laughed.

'Oh, I intend to take my own precautions for securing the crown, Roger.' He slapped me on the back, unexpectedly jovial. 'Don't ask me what they are –' the question had indeed been on the tip of my tongue – 'because I shan't tell you.' He raised his arms above his head and stretched until his bones cracked. 'This damn siege!' He was petulant again. 'We stay here like so many sitting ducks while James and his army get closer and closer, when the sensible thing to do is to abandon this God-benighted town – when I'm king I shall hand it back to the English, anyway – and march to meet him.'

We descended the knoll and walked back towards Berwick, across the scorched and blackened earth, to the encampment outside its walls. Here, Murdo met us with the intelligence that the Duke of Gloucester was holding yet another council of war in his tent and desired his dear cousin of Scotland's immediate attendance.

Albany swore.

'More damn talking. Why don't we get on and *do* something?' he roared and strode off in the direction of the royal pavilion, the squire at his heels.

I knew what Albany meant and had a sneaking sympathy with his impatience. The continuing siege of the citadel was under the direction of Lord Stanley and Earl Rivers who, with a handful of gunners, kept up a desultory bombardment of its battlements without producing any result other than occasional abuse and defiance hurled from its walls. Occasionally, women would appear and start emptying their chamber-pots on the besiegers' heads; or they would throw rotting meat and cabbage stalks at their tormentors along with some pretty foul language that men, in their innocence, always like to believe the female sex could not possibly know. (My experience is that women are less easily shocked, and have more fortitude of mind, than husbands, fathers and brothers give them credit for.) But these latter occasions were growing less frequent as food supplies dwindled inside the citadel and starvation began to take its toll.

But although, as I say, I shared Albany's impatience, my faith in the Duke of Gloucester's military ability remained unshaken. Here was a man who, at eleven years old, had been Admiral of England, Ireland and Aquitaine, while I, born on the same day, had still been trying to kick an inflated pig's bladder between two upright sticks stuck in the ground (unsuccessfully, I regret to say). And eight years later, at nineteen, he had helped his brother, Edward, to regain his throne at the battles of Barnet and Tewkesbury, where he

had fought with the skill and precision of a man twice his
age. My trust was in Prince Richard.

This did not mean, however, that I was not suffering from
all the prickles of boredom that afflict those with too little
to do and too much time in which to do it. The result was
not only bad temper but a fatigue that had more to do with
the mind than the body. I would lie down at night on my
pallet feeling worn to the bone, only to find sleep elusive. I
would doze and wake, doze and wake throughout the night,
but at the same time, I had trained myself to lie as still as
possible so as not to disturb the duke, who, on his camp bed
with its swansdown mattress, passed his nights in comparative comfort and who resented being aroused by my tossing
and turning.

But that afternoon, after his return from the council of
war, Albany re-entered the pavilion in a particularly restless
mood, and, when night fell, spurned his bed in order to sit
up and read in an attempt to tire himself out. He had pulled
his camp stool and table close to the brazier which gave the
tent both light and warmth. Lozenges of incense gave off a
sickly sweet smell that at first irritated my nose, but then
had a soporific effect, lulling me into slumber.

A slight commotion as the tent flap was opened and Davey
announced, 'My lord of Gloucester!' brought me, however,
wide awake. I lay perfectly still, unnoticed in my pool of
shadow.

'Cousin!' Albany rose to his feet, although with a lack of
urgency that plainly indicated this was merely a social gesture
from one prince to another.

'Cousin.' Gloucester's deep voice acknowledged the cour-
tesy. 'I'm sorry to disturb you. I've interrupted your reading.'
I sensed rather than saw that he was turning over the folios
spread out on the table, and his next words confirmed it.
'Let me see. Richard Rolle. "Meditations on the Passions."
Saint Thomas Aquinas. Thomas à Kempis. "Imitation of
Christ." You favour the mystics, cousin?'

'As you do, yourself, I believe.'

'True.'

Davey reappeared with a second camp stool, then discreetly
made himself scarce again. I lay doggo, hardly daring to

breathe in case I attracted attention to my own presence. That nosiness, so frequently deplored by my nearest and dearest, had me agog with anticipation as to what I might overhear.

'What can I do for Your Grace?' Albany enquired, evidently sensing that this visit had a purpose and was not simply the desire on Gloucester's part for a friendly chat.

There was a momentary hesitation before the duke said abruptly, 'You have three nephews.'

Albany waited for a second or two, obviously expecting his companion to continue. But when nothing more was said, Albany replied, 'Yes. The eldest, the Duke of Rothesay is nine, his two brothers six and three.'

'What . . . What do you plan to . . . to do with them when you become king?'

'Why . . . nothing.' Albany sounded startled, as well he might. It was not the question either of us had been expecting.

'Nothing? Won't they prove a menace to you?'

'A menace?' Suddenly Albany seemed to grasp the meaning behind the query. 'Ah! You mean as my brother's rightful heirs? No, no! Scotland, like other Celtic countries, has always adhered to the law of tanistry, not to the rule of primogeniture, as you do in England.'

(At that moment, I had no idea what the law of tanistry was, but I discovered its meaning later. The heir (the tanist) of a Celtic prince or chieftain is not necessarily his eldest son, but can be elected from a whole circle of his male kinfolk, thus ensuring that the strongest or the wisest or the most talented member of the royal family is chosen as leader of the nation. Of course, it doesn't always work that way; people make foolish mistakes or they grow lazy and accept the next in line as a matter of course, as had happened with the present Scottish king. I imagine that one danger tanistry is intended to obviate is the child ruler with all the attendant jockeying for power amongst the nobles. 'Woe to thee, O Land, when thy king is a child.')

The Duke of Gloucester made no immediate answer, but sat drumming his fingers on the table top, lost in thought. Then he rose abruptly.

'Thank you, Cousin. You've . . . er . . . you've relieved my mind of a worry about . . . ah . . . about the position of your . . . your nephews.'

He spoke almost at random as though he were thinking of something else altogether and I guessed Albany must be as puzzled by this little episode as I was. Indeed, I heard him clear his throat preparatory to making some remark or other, but before he could say anything, the tent-flap was once again flung back, but this time with some force, and Timothy Plummer made an unceremonious entrance.

'Your Grace! My lord Albany! Forgive me butting in like this, but you must both come at once. A messenger – a scout – has just ridden in to camp with the most momentous news!'

Nine

Within a few hours, the entire camp, from the highest to the lowest, knew that the Scots were in full retreat, taking their king with them – as a captive!

Albany was jubilant and could scarcely contain his excitement.

'All of them, Cochrane, Scheves, Rogers and the rest, hanged from Lauder Bridge like common criminals and James forced to watch! And now he's the prisoner of my half-uncles!' The duke so far forgot himself as to fling his arms around me and kiss me on both cheeks as if I had been a prince of the blood instead of a menial hired to do his bidding. He was almost incoherent in his joy, and inclined to lapse into broad Scots with every other word, but, gradually, I pieced together what had happened.

The advancing Scots' army had reached the little town of Lauder, a mere thirty miles or so distant from Berwick, when the Earls of Atholl and Buchan – two of the three sons of Joan Beaufort by her second marriage and descendants of that fiery old warhorse, John of Gaunt – together with the impetuous young Archibald, Earl of Angus, had finally become so incensed by the arrogant behaviour of the king's favourites that they had led a wholly unexpected and, seemingly, totally unplanned *coup d'etat*, rousing the other nobles to mutiny, seizing the king's minions and hanging them from the parapet of the bridge which spanned the Leader Water. It was believed – or, at least, Albany had been told – that this drastic measure had been provoked by the appearance of the hated Thomas Cochrane, in a suit of gilded armour with a gold chain worth five hundred crowns or more around his neck, to announce that King James had appointed him Head of Artillery. The Earl of Angus had apparently snatched off the chain with the remark that a rope would suit the favourite better and matters had just developed from there.

The Scots' army was now in such a state of disarray that its leaders had decided to withdraw to Edinburgh, leaving the road into Scotland open to the English; and at a council of war the following morning, the Duke of Gloucester chose to leave Lord Stanley and part of his troops to reduce Berwick's citadel by starving out the garrison – now without any hope of being relieved by their fellow countrymen – and to march the rest of the army straight on to the capital.

'We shall be there by nightfall,' Albany declared exultantly.

This statement proved to be optimistic. Striking camp and getting an army on the move, even one reduced in numbers, was a protracted task, taking at least a day, but finally I found my self in the saddle once again and moving northwards into a rugged terrain, the like of which was totally alien to me. To begin with, the warm – well, warmish – July weather we had been experiencing for the past few days, gave way to rain and a howling storm. Clouds raced before a screaming wind and were torn to shreds in the teeth of a gale. Occasionally, a pallid sun would peer wanly through the broken rack, but at other times, day became night with thickets and stunted trees looming up briefly, before disappearing once more into the gloom. The rain-wet roofs of distant huts gleamed, corpse-like, then were swallowed again by the mist. Monstrous boughs of oak whipped at our faces. I thought that I had never been in such a God-forsaken place.

The second day, however, was a little better. The weather improved temporarily, and the accommodation which had been commandeered for the night for Gloucester, Albany and their respective households had proved dry and comfortable, if far from luxurious. The shrill whistling of the wind in the roof, like the wailing of lost souls in the upper air, had at first been a deterrent to sleep, but 1 had been so weary and homesick that nothing could have kept me awake for long. In the morning, while James Petrie brought hot water for his master to wash and shave in, I joined the queue at the outdoor pump and experienced for the first time the snow-broth chill of the crystal-clear water of the north.

A score of other southerners were also cursing its icy numbing of their skin, while they hacked off the night's stubble as best they could and, like me, cut their chins to pieces. The Scots among us, including Donald Seton and Murdo MacGregor, laughed openly at our discomfiture and derided what they were pleased to call our womanish Sassenach ways. But no one was in a mood to challenge them, and I slipped back into the cottage – one of a cluster in some village whose name I have long since forgotten (if I ever knew it) – and ascended the narrow, twisting staircase to the tiny room under the eaves where Albany and I had passed the night, side by side on a lumpy mattress that I strongly suspected was stuffed with turnips.

James Petrie was still there and had been joined by Davey. The serving man was his usual taciturn self, the bushy eyebrows drawn together in their perpetual frown. But the page was saying something to the duke in the Scots tongue, which I still had not mastered sufficiently to understand more than the odd word here and there. I did think, as I reached the half-open door at the head of the stairs, that I made out the words 'not needful now', but I wouldn't have sworn to it. Albany's reply, however, seemed to confirm that I had understood aright.

'Better safe than sorry,' he answered tersely in English, before raising his eyes to see me standing in the doorway. 'Roger!' His greeting, I thought, was something over-hearty, as though he might be genuinely pleased to see me, but the peal of derisive laughter which followed it at once put me in my place. 'Good God, man! What have you done to your face? Your chin looks as if you've been suffering death by a thousand cuts, which, they tell me, is a form of punishment dealt out by the Great Cham of Tartary. Is your hand still shaking after all that wine you drank at supper last night?'

I was incensed.

'I got precious little wine,' I snapped, 'not after your lordship had finished with the bottle, and Murdo and Donald had drunk their share.'

This was true. The duke and his squires had been in riotous mood at the prospect of being almost home and at the bloodless victory that seemed to be handing Albany the crown without one further blow being struck. Yet if Albany's suspicions really were correct, then one of the five Scots surrounding him must now find himself on the horns of a dilemma; whether or not to proceed with his murderous mission for a king now held captive by his own nobles, or to abandon this waning star and throw in his lot with the rising sun. Of course, there was always the consideration that Fortune was a fickle jade and not to be trusted, so maybe both the duke and I had reason to be still on our guard. (I had not totally dismissed the warning of the 'Green Man' and continued to be watchful on my own account however much Albany might try to persuade me that it was someone trying to deflect my attention from himself.)

A messenger arrived from one of the other cottages to say that the Duke of Gloucester would be ready to move on in half an hour, and the pleasantries concerning my cut chin were instantly forgotten in the hustle to be ready in time. Trumpets were already sounding in the camp beyond the village, from the sodden tract of open countryside where the poor devils of the main army had spent a miserable night, so we ate a hurried breakfast of oatmeal cakes and honey and drank cold water from an earthenware jar. We were in the saddle almost as soon as my lord of Gloucester himself, and ahead of some of the other nobles, who emerged from their billets looking bleary-eyed and bad-tempered and wishing themselves at home in England amongst their goose-feather mattresses and linen sheets. Furthermore, with the expedition petering out in this unsatisfactory fashion, there would be no glory and, worse still, no money to be made from ransomed prisoners to swell dwindling domestic coffers. Only Albany seemed – understandably – to be in high spirits as we moved forward along what Davey condescendingly informed me was an old Pictish road, in places not much more than a deer track curling, snake-like, beside a bubbling stream. Beyond the rush and spill of water, a pine forest rose, thunderous in the early morning light, and I pitied the foot soldiers as the advance guard hacked its way through scrubland and brakes of gorse.

It occurred to me, as I rode in Albany's wake, that in all

the upheaval of the last two days, I had forgotten that strange little conversation between him and the Duke of Gloucester on that last evening outside Berwick. At least, the strangeness had been all on the latter's side. What, I wondered, had been in Prince Richard's mind that he had enquired so closely about the probable fate of Albany's nephews once Albany was king? In all probability, nothing; and yet I had to own to a totally unjustified feeling of unease in which the memory of King Edward as I had seen him at Fotheringay – a very ill man by the look of things – played a part. I recalled that for a fleeting second I had considered Edward of Rouen not merely sick, but dying. I had then dismissed the notion as he had roused himself to some display of his old vigorous self; but now I recollected the effort he had been forced to make to do so . . .

I caught myself up short. What was I saying? That Edward, the fourth of that name, was a dying man? That his heir was a twelve-year-old boy who might be king in the very near future? That Prince Richard . . . ?

I took a deep, shaken breath and slammed my mind shut against the half-formed thought. It was an idea not to be entertained for a single moment. This man with whom I shared my birthday I knew to be an honourable, upright man and a loyal friend once a person had won his trust. And in all the vicissitudes of King Edward's colourful life, Gloucester had been the brother who remained at his side, who had never betrayed him, who loved him with an unwavering devotion. And yet . . .

And yet – the thought would insist on intruding – it was common knowledge that he hated the Queen's family with a passion that had only increased since the execution of his brother, George of Clarence. And the Prince of Wales was more Woodville than Plantagenet if the rumours were true.

In fairness, how could the boy not be? Unlike his younger brother, the Duke of York, Prince Edward had been brought up in his own household at Ludlow, on the Welsh marches, under the tutelage of his maternal uncle, Earl Rivers, now riding a little ahead of me and conversing in his free and easy manner with his brother, Edward. A very popular man was the earl, but a Woodville to his fingertips, wedded to the interests of his sister, the queen, and to those of all the rest of the large Woodville clan, whose members were notoriously devoted to one another . . .

'You're daydreaming, Roger! Keep alert, man!'

Albany's voice cut across my reverie, recalling me to my duty, but for once, I was grateful for the reprimand rather than resentful; glad to abandon the path down which my thoughts had been leading me and return to the world of sanity and common sense. The Duke of Gloucester's enquiries concerning the possible fate of Albany's nephews had been for some perfectly proper purpose unknown to me.

'My lord.'

'You're supposed to be guarding me,' the duke complained fretfully, his sunny mood of an hour ago having apparently turned sour in the meantime.

I should have liked to point out that the necessity he felt for my protection was as variable as a woman's mind when she's trying to decide what ribbon to buy to re-trim her Sunday gown. But I held my tongue. I realized that I needed Albany as much as he needed me, for I was now in a strange and foreign country, hundreds of miles from home, where language and customs were totally alien to me and where Albany was my only friend. Or, at least, the only person who cared what happened to me. It's true that I was surrounded by fellow Englishmen, but not one of them (the Duke of Gloucester was far too preoccupied to spare me even a passing thought) cared a jot for my welfare or what might be my fate.

A mile or so further on, the advance party drew to a halt so that the riders could water their horses. I led my cob to the edge of the chattering stream and knelt down amongst the quivering rushes that bordered it, cupping my hands in order to drink, myself. The ice-cold water felt like silk, easing my parched throat and, when I had splashed it over my face, the smarting of the cuts on my lacerated chin. The day was turning warm (or warmer than it had been). Somewhere overhead a bird voiced its enchantment and the track stretching ahead of us glittered whitely under the morning sun, burnishing the tall tree trunks on the opposite bank. It sparked suddenly among the branches, dazzling my eyes . . .

For a second or two, I was blinded and while I stood blinking, trying to clear my sight, someone thrust something into my hand. I whirled about, but there were too many people and animals around for me to distinguish anyone clearly. I grabbed the nearest person, one of the Marquis of Dorset's men judging by his silver and pink livery.

'Did you see who gave me this?' I demanded, waving my closed fist and still not sure as yet what 'this' was.

The fellow gave me a haughty stare, as befitted a retainer of the king's stepson accosted by a nobody like myself. He did not deign to reply, so I asked one or two other people, but no one had seen anything. And they all plainly considered me mad to think that they might have done so. No one was interested.

Frustrated and angry, I eventually opened my hand to discover what it was that I'd been given, and found it to be a scrap of parchment with the single word 'Beware' written on it. I stared at it for a moment or two before tossing it into the water and watching it float away downstream. I almost plunged after it to grab it back, but decided to let it go. Someone was trying to make a fool of me.

Our lords and masters were now up in the saddle again and ready to move. I mounted the cob and thought savagely that once I was free of this whole mad adventure I would never willingly undertake a journey on horseback again. I was saddle-sore and weary, aching in places I hadn't even known existed in my previous life. For that, more and more, was how I felt; as if I had died without knowing it, and for my sins been sent to hell.

Davey came to find me.

'My lord's asking for you. He says to keep up.'

'What's he afraid of? That I'll run away?'

'Perhaps.'

'Tell me why he should care.'

The page shrugged. 'He must have told you that himself.'

'But do you know?'

Davey looked round at me and I thought I saw a momentary awareness at the back of his eyes. But it vanished on the instant, leaving those violet-blue orbs as blank and expressionless as two pebbles.

Again, that worm of unease gnawed at my guts; and again, I dismissed it as nonsense.

I forced my way through the press of squires and body servants to Albany's side to find him in heated altercation with Earl Rivers. Well, perhaps not heated: Anthony Woodville was too gentlemanly a man to raise his voice, but his tone and expression were both politely adamant.

'His Grace says no, my lord. You must be at his side when he enters Edinburgh.'

'And so I shall be,' Albany answered hotly. 'Roslin lies only a few miles west of here and a mere seven or so miles south of the capital. It would take me and my household half a day, maybe less, to ride there and back. I wish to pray at the chapel for God's blessing on my enterprise. Is that so much to ask?'

'Is there a chapel there?' The earl looked faintly interested. 'I've never heard of it.'

'Probably not.' Albany sounded defensive for some reason or another. 'It was built less than forty years ago by a distant kinsman of a very dear friend of mine; by the last Sinclair Earl of Orkney.'

Earl Rivers, who had the reputation of being an extremely devout man (rumour had it that he even wore a penitential hair shirt beneath his splendid clothes) still shook his head regretfully.

'I'm sorry, my lord, but His Grace of Gloucester is not to be moved on this. No one, above all, not yourself, is to leave his train. You of all people must know that we are within striking distance of Edinburgh, and although Prince Richard assumes that no resistance will be offered – not in the present circumstances – he cannot be certain, and will take no chances. Moreover, your safety is essential. He dare not risk your capture while on this expedition to . . . to Roslin, was that the name? And he does not wish, at this juncture, to spare an armed escort to go with you. Besides –' the king's brother-in-law raised slightly satirical eyebrows – 'there must be plenty of other shrines at which you can offer up prayers for the success of this venture. Scotland is surely not so pagan a country that it is devoid of chapels and churches?'

'Of course not.' Albany tried to look affronted, although

there were times when I suspected him of being unorthodox in many of his religious views. (I had endeavoured, on several occasions, to draw him out on the subject by voicing a few of my own doubts and fears, but he had always refused to play my game, frustrating me with a quip or some light rejoinder.) 'It's just,' he continued, 'that I have a special fondness for the chapel at Roslin. I feel that to beg God's blessing there, will . . .' He broke off, looking flustered.

'Bring you good luck?' the earl finished for him, and permitted himself a small, cynical smile.

'Oh well!' Albany said hastily. 'If my Cousin Gloucester refuses his permission, so be it. There will be time enough for a visit once we are settled in Edinburgh. And when I am king . . .' He broke off, shrugging.

'Of course.' Anthony Woodville inclined his handsome head. 'I will inform His Grace of your compliance with his wishes.'

'I'll do it myself,' Albany snapped. 'There's no need for your lordship to constitute himself my errand boy. Roger! Davey!' And the duke drove the bay horse, Pegasus, forward, pricked by a cruel spur.

The page and I followed as best we could and the two squires followed us. It was only then that I realized all three had been listening intently to the conversation between Albany and Earl Rivers; and seemed, judging by the discontented expressions on their faces, to be as disappointed by the thwarting of their visit to the chapel as their master himself. And for the hundredth time, I marvelled at Albany's perversity; at his willingness to place himself in a position where he could so easily be at the mercy of the suspected assassin amongst them. But then again, there was safety in numbers, and I would have been with him.

For what that was worth.

It was the last day of July and we reached Edinburgh towards evening.

The sun was just beginning to set, the clouds thinning to vapour trails and mackerel shoals in the rapidly cooling sky. And there, perched high above us – so high it looked impossible to reach – was the castle, like some giant eagle's eyrie on its impregnable rock.

I sat astride my horse, mouth open, staring upwards, just as the soldiers, ordered to set up camp in the valley below, were also gaping.

Albany smote me on the back.

'A sight, eh, Roger?'

'How–how do you get up there?' I managed at last.

'Oh, it's not impossible, nor so difficult as it looks. It's true that the north and south faces of the rock are well nigh vertical and almost impossible to scale, and the same, to a lesser extent, goes for the western side. But we shall approach from the east, through the town, where the ascent is gentler.'

He spoke with the confidence of a native, as he had every right to do having spent a great part of his life in the city. And no doubt he had advised the Duke of Gloucester and his captains to that effect, for the sun was setting ahead of us, going down in ribbons of flame as we prepared to lodge for the night at the monastery outside the city walls, beyond the eastern gate. This, Davey informed me, having constituted himself my guide, was the Abbey of the Holy Rood, founded by King David I and granted to the Augustinian Canons in the twelfth century.

'On a day which should have been devoted to fasting and prayer, the king decided instead to go hunting, but was knocked from his horse by the maddened stag he was pursuing. While he lay unconscious and close to death, the king saw a vision of the stag with a cross between its antlers and heard a heavenly voice telling him to build a religious house on the spot where the accident had happened. He promised and his life was spared. As well he did,' the page ended flippantly, 'as we are thus provided with our night's lodging before entering the city tomorrow.'

Albany, whom neither of us had heard approach, cuffed Davey smartly over one ear.

'Enough of that kind of talk,' he said sharply. 'You're entering the House of God. Remember it!'

Davey stammered an apology and slid away to attend to his duties, while Murdo MacGregor came to conduct his master to his room in the guest house, where the Duke of

Gloucester was already lodged together with members of his immediate household. The abbey's accommodation was restricted and the rest of the nobles had been obliged to have tents and pavilions raised in the lee of the great crag which rose behind it. And yet again on this fantastic journey, I found myself, thanks to Albany, housed in better state – within the comfort of four walls and lying on a goose-feather mattress – than my superiors. It would be something to remember in old age, I thought, and to tell my children (if they were the slightest bit interested) when I was a grey-beard, sitting in the chimney corner. If, that is, my children were well-enough-to-do to possess chimneys.

But this sudden recollection of my family, so carefully suppressed for so long, hit me like a blow across the heart and made me want to turn tail and run. But run where? I was hundreds of miles from home and everything familiar, in a hostile land of beetling crags and crowding forests of twisted birch and towering pine. We had ridden through one such wood only an hour or so previously, where the pillared trunks had closed about us, and where dense undergrowth of scrub and stunted bushes had thinned in places to reveal the dark, slinking shapes of wolves. Carpets of cranberry and last winter's leaves had deadened the noise of the horses' hooves; had, indeed, deadened all noise as men and riders were engulfed by the flood-tide of green. The road had cut, like some gloomy cathedral aisle, straight through the heart of the trees, and I had found myself whispering, as though fearing to desecrate a holy place – or some pagan shrine! This was a countryside as inimical to me as the Waste Land of the Arthurian legends. To set myself adrift in it would be to court madness or death.

I became aware of Albany watching me as though he knew what I was thinking. He was being undressed by James Petrie, who must have entered the cell-like room without my real-izing it.

The duke gave his sudden short bark of laughter.

'You were in another of your reveries, Roger.' He eyed me narrowly. 'Or was it more than that?'

I began to get ready for bed myself, which I did by the simple process of stripping down to my shirt, peeing in the chamber-pot and then waiting respectfully for Albany to get between the rough linen sheets before following suit.

'I don't know what Your Highness means.'

The duke, clad in a soft woollen nightshift, waved at James Petrie to be gone, but listened for the click of the latch as the door closed behind his henchman before speaking again.

'You were out of your body, Roger, I'll swear to it. What were you seeing?'

'In the sense you mean, nothing, my lord!' I spoke with suppressed violence. What could I say to convince him that I did not have, had never had, the 'sight'? 'If I was lost in thought, I crave Your Grace's pardon, but I was thinking – seeing, if you like, but only in my mind's eye – my own people, my own patch of ground.'

It seemed for a moment or two as if he might take issue with me on the subject, as he had done earlier, but then he shrugged and turned away to use the chamber-pot before climbing into bed.

Thankfully, I got in, also.

But Albany was not yet disposed to sleep in spite of a long, hard and wearisome day in the saddle. He sat up, hugging his knees.

'You don't care for this country of mine,' he said accusingly.

'I find it strange, my lord. Wild, untamed. Even, if you'll forgive my plain speaking, somewhat barbarous.'

To my relief, he was not offended. In fact, the description seemed to please him. He smiled.

'Full of hobgoblins and witches, eh? You hear echoes of a much older religion?'

I hastened to disclaim. 'I didn't mean to imply that Scotland was not a Christian country, Your Grace.'

'No, of course not.' His tone was suave, but he gave me a sharp, sidelong, bright-eyed look. 'But then, in your own western part of England, you have many pagan beliefs, do you not? The Old Ones in their hollow hills; the Druids; Mithraism, the worship of the Bull; the Great Goddess, Mother of the Earth . . .'

'These heresies did exist once,' I admitted.

'But no longer?'

There was an urgent rap on the bedchamber door. I heaved a sigh of relief as the latch was lifted even before Albany had time to call 'Come in!'

'What the devil—?' he was demanding furiously, as Donald Seton fell on one knee beside the bed, but checked as he looked into the squire's white face. 'What is it? What's happened?'

Ten

A torrent of words followed, only a few of which I understood, but I could tell from Albany's face that something
serious – or, at least, something which touched him nearly
– had happened. As the squire finished speaking, the duke
fired a number of rapid questions at him, using the same
Scots tongue as his servitor, and, eventually, when they had
been answered, he lay back against his pillows, biting his
thumb.

He reverted to English. 'He's in the castle dungeons, you
say?' Donald nodded. 'And likely to be brought to trial?'
Another nod. 'How did you learn this?'

'From one of the lay brothers here. It's common knowledge.' The squire, taking his cue from his master, also lapsed
into language I was able to comprehend.

'Do you know any details of the murder? Does Master
Sinclair protest his innocence?'

The squire shook his head. 'No. Quite the contrary.
Apparently he admits openly to the crime, but claims it was
done in self-defence.'

Albany drew in his breath.

'Let me understand this properly,' he said, his fingers
plucking restlessly at the hem of the sheet. 'Rab Sinclair
confesses to stabbing his wife – his unarmed wife – but says
it was done in self-defence? This informant of yours, this
lay brother, is sure of his facts?'

'He swears to it. It only happened the day before yesterday,
on Monday afternoon. Master Sinclair made no effort to
escape and was arrested almost at once with the knife still
in his hand.'

The duke swung his legs out of bed and demanded his
bed-gown.

'I must see my Cousin Gloucester,' he said. 'I must find out if my uncles and the Council mean to open negotiations with us or whether they intend to make us lay siege to the city. If the latter, it might be weeks before we are inside the walls, and by then Rab could well have been hanged.'

He hunched himself into the furred velvet gown that Donald fetched for him and disappeared through the bedchamber door. The squire made no move to follow him, so I seized my opportunity to ask questions in my turn. Whether or not I would receive any answers was another matter.

'I've gathered the gist of the story,' I said. 'But who is this Master Sinclair?'

Donald looked round at me in surprise, as though he had forgotten my existence, or, more likely, been unaware of it so anxious had he been to impart his information to Albany.

'Oh, it's you, is it? Of course! I should have thought. You're still guarding His Grace.'

The words could have had a sting to them, but somehow they didn't. They were uttered in a flat, dry tone that was almost one of indifference.

'Yes, I'm still here,' I snapped back, 'although what good I'm doing continues to be a mystery to me. I'm hoping that once my lord and the rest of you are safely inside the city, I shall be allowed to return to my home. Now that King James is a prisoner of his nobles, surely there can be no impediment to the duke assuming the crown?'

The squire laughed. 'I wouldn't be too certain of that, chapman. No Scot worth his salt is going to let himself be manipulated, or have his king chosen for him by a Sassenach. Your countrymen have tried it before, several times during the course of the centuries, and, eventually, have always been worsted at their own game. No; if anything, I would guess that my lord's chances of the crown are slimmer now than they would have been had King James and his army been beaten fairly and squarely in battle.'

'Then—'

'Oh, have no fear! His Grace will take his own measures to ensure his coronation.' And again, Donald Seton laughed.

'What are they?' I demanded.

The squire raised his eyebrows. 'Do you really think he confides in me?'

I had to admit to myself that it seemed unlikely, but the man had spoken with such authority that my suspicions were aroused. Moreover, his words echoed something that Albany himself had once said to me. But I decided to let the matter drop, knowing that even if I pursued it, I should get no satisfaction. I returned instead to my original question.

'Who is this Master Sinclair who is in the castle dungeons on a charge of murdering his wife?'

My companion hesitated for a second, then shrugged.

'No reason why you shouldn't be told, I suppose. Master Sinclair is a close friend of the duke and was one of my lord's most faithful servants before he – my lord, that is – was forced to flee the country after the murder of my former master.'

'The Earl of Mar?' I queried, and he nodded. 'Then why,' I went on, 'did this most faithful servant not join you, Davey and the others when you escaped to France to offer your services to my lord Albany?'

Donald snorted. 'What a damnably curious, long-nosed fellow you are.'

'So people tell me,' I answered coolly. 'Nevertheless, I should like an answer.'

The squire hunched a shoulder. 'Well, for one thing, he had no notice of our intention. We kept that a secret between the five of us. We had no wish to be arrested and executed on a charge of high treason or, more likely, clapped in the dungeons of Craigmillar Castle and murdered like poor Mar. And for another thing, Master Sinclair is – or rather was – a married man who doted on his young wife. I doubt very much he'd have left her, even for my lord's sake.'

'And yet now he's killed her without, it would seem, any provocation on her part?'

The squire frowned. 'According to my source of information—'

'The lay brother.'

'The lay brother, yes. According to him, Master Sinclair is pleading self-defence.'

'Strange . . .' A thought occurred to me. 'Is this man the

one my lord was referring to when speaking to Earl Rivers yesterday? The one whose distant kinsman built the chapel at . . . oh, I forget the name.'

'Roslin. Yes, this is the man.' Donald's tone was suddenly curt, as though he had had enough of my questioning, and he made for the bedchamber door, no doubt feeling that only by his absence could he stem the flow of my insatiable curiosity.

And there is no doubt, either, that he was right. Unfortunately for him, he nearly collided with Albany in the doorway as the duke came back into the room, an expression of dissatisfaction marring his handsome looks. The squire's retreat was necessarily checked.

'What news, my lord? Good or bad?'

Albany shed his bed-gown and chewed a thumbnail for a moment or so before replying.

'I'm not sure. The arrival of a messenger from my uncles and other members of the Council coincided with my own. Indeed, he was shown into Gloucester's bedchamber a second or so before I was.'

'And, my lord?' Donald prompted when the duke broke off, staring absent-mindedly into space.

'What?' The duke gave a start as if recalled from a long way away. 'Oh, yes. The Council is offering to negotiate. I gather that a part, at least, of the Princess Cicely's dowry is on offer, to be repaid immediately, with a promise of further instalments later on.' He chewed his nail again. 'There will be no siege, no conquest. My Cousin Gloucester, together with certain chosen lords – myself included, naturally – will be admitted peacefully to the city tomorrow morning to be received in state at the castle, where we shall be housed. The English army will remain encamped in the valley, to be victualled at the Scots' expense until such time as they withdraw from Scottish soil. Gloucester has agreed, of course. He'd be a fool not to.'

Albany again appeared to be distracted by his own thoughts, and this time it was my turn to recall him to himself.

'But surely, this is no bad thing, my lord. Negotiations are better any day than the death and destruction of war. Think how many lives will be saved.'

For my own part, I could scarcely conceal my relief and joy that the end of this madcap adventure must now be in sight. A week, perhaps less, could well see me on the long road home in the wake of the retreating English army.

I wasn't certain that the duke had been attending to my words, but he suddenly spun round to face me, his eyes narrowing.

'And where do you think these negotiations will leave me, Roger? Not crowned king of Scotland, you may be sure. I shall be one of the bargaining counters. Let me guess. On behalf of King Edward, Cousin Gloucester will not press my claim to the throne, while the Council, acting in my brother's name, will leave Berwick to its fate, allowing it to become once again an English town, one of the main aims of this expedition. I am no longer necessary to your countrymen, you see.'

I could see, now that it was pointed out to me, and I was able to understand his bitterness. I could see, too, that, whether it had been planned or not, the killing of King James's favourites and the taking of the king himself into custody had been a shrewd move on the part of the Scots nobles. Furthermore, their offer of a peaceful settlement had rendered Albany valueless to the English.

Donald cleared his throat. 'My lord!' He put out a hand as if to grasp his master's wrist before thinking better of it. 'My lord!' he repeated with an urgency I failed to under-stand. Albany, still looking a little dazed, also failed to grasp his meaning judging by the questioning glance he turned in the squire's direction. Donald muttered something in the Scots tongue and the duke's face lightened momentarily.

'Ah, yes!' He took a deep breath like a drowning man coming up for air and spoke more cheerfully. 'Of course!' But then he hesitated, obviously thinking better of what he had said, and shook his head. 'That must wait,' he continued. 'First, Rab Sinclair must be cleared of this charge against him. I can't and won't attend to my own affairs before I see him freed.'

'But, my lord, what can be done?' the squire protested. 'He's plainly guilty. He was arrested with the knife still in his hand, the body still warm.'

'If Rab says it was in self-defence, however improbable that may seem, then I for one believe him. His claim must be investigated, and –' he turned to me, throwing out his arms in a triumphant gesture – 'here is the very man to do it!' Donald eyed me sceptically, but Albany continued enthusiastically, 'Yes, yes! He has a reputation for being able to solve mysteries and problems. He has even done so for Cousin Gloucester and other people of note.'

He smote me on the back with such vigour that I lost my balance, toppled over on to the bed and decided that, while there, I might as well climb between the sheets again.

'Your Grace is pleased to joke about it,' I ventured, praying to God and the Virgin that he would agree.

My luck was out, as I had feared it would be.

'No joke, Roger.' Albany got into bed beside me. 'What foresight on my part to insist on bringing you along. It's almost as if I had had a premonition.'

'I thought I was brought to guard you from your enemies,' I snapped, glancing meaningfully at Donald Seton.

'Oh, that mainly,' Albany agreed, adding hurriedly, 'From those English lords and their hired assassins who desired my death. But I think that now, until I put my own plan into execution and once more become a threat to them, they will consider King Edward's intention to have me crowned king of Scotland as unlikely to be fulfilled.' He nodded dismissal to the squire. 'All right, Donald, you may go. Tell the others what has happened and be ready to accompany me into Edinburgh tomorrow morning, whenever the embassy arrives from the castle and His Grace of Gloucester decides to enter the town. Now, for God's sake, let's all get some sleep.'

I don't know that I slept much, there were too many thoughts crowding my mind, but I can vouch for it that, whatever cares and prospects of potential disappointment were troubling Albany, he slumbered peacefully until daybreak. (I can also vouch for the fact that the monks had fed their noble guests garlic at supper, for the smells which rose from beneath the bedclothes from time to time were of an indescribable pungency.)

I lay awake for at least an hour, staring at the four walls

of the austere, cell-like guest-room of Holy Rood Abbey, wondering what this plan of the duke's was that would ensure his coronation despite the wreckage of his and his English allies' schemes to seize the Scottish throne in the wake of military conquest and the possible death or capture of his brother. I also lay awake cursing my fate at being pitch-forked into a murder mystery that Albany would expect me to solve by exonerating his friend, even though it seemed to be a straightforward case of a husband killing his wife in a fit of – what? Jealousy? Betrayal? Or just a fit of pique because the meat had been undercooked at dinner? (Not such a ridiculous idea as you might think.) I had a few choice words to say to God on the subject, just to let Him know what I thought of the situation, but, as always, He ignored me and let me get on with venting my spleen without vouch-safing any reply. He knew that I knew He would give me His help when it was required.

Having given God this piece of my mind I felt better and commended my soul, and the souls of all those whom I loved, to His care throughout the hours of darkness. After that, I was at last able to sleep until the sounding of trumpets from the camp and the voices of the monks at their devotions – it was the hour of Prime – finally roused me.

Breakfast was a handful of oats, some black bread and a cold sausage in the monks' kitchen in the company of other low-life like myself, while our masters were, by the smell of things, feasting on bacon collops, honey cakes and the best of the abbey's home-brewed ale. There was, too, another faint aroma lingering on the air which Murdo MacGregor condescended to inform me was that of the famous 'water of life', the 'usquebaugh' (whisky we called it in England: we never were any good at getting our tongues round foreign words) that had first come over with the Scots from Ireland and been made here ever since. It was, he said, very good for warming the body, and the monks partook liberally of it to keep themselves warm during the office of Matins and Lauds. I sympathized. I knew from experience that the small hours of the morning can chill one to the marrow in an icy church, with the cold of the flagstones striking up through the bones and sinews.

Long before the abbey bells began to toll the office of Tierce, and before a pale sun was halfway to its zenith, my lord Gloucester, with Albany by his side and a cluster of his chosen nobles at his back, was mounted on his favourite horse, White Surrey, waiting in the Canongate – a borough independent of town or abbey – for the Scots deputation from the castle. I guessed he was none too pleased at the delay, but kept his features schooled to indifference, unlike Earl Rivers and his nephew, the Marquis of Dorset, who grumbled openly about bad manners, and others who were voicing their doubts about the good faith of the Scots. Albany said nothing, torn, no doubt, between resentment at these slurs cast at his countrymen and a rising hope that maybe members of the Scottish Council had changed their minds after all and that a siege would be the order of the day.

But, finally, as the clamour of the bells died away and the chanting of the monks began, trumpets sounded from beyond the city walls and, minutes later, the gates were opened to let a cavalcade of men and horses stream out to welcome in the Duke of Gloucester and his entourage. Heading this company were three men whom Davey Gray immediately identified as Albany's three half-uncles; the Earls of Atholl and Buchan, two of the chief architects of the coup at Lauder Bridge, and their brother, the Bishop of Moray.

Diplomatic pleasantries, palpably insincere, were duly exchanged, although I noticed that no one on the Scots' side actually addressed a word to Albany or responded to his greetings. All he received were glances of contempt and acute dislike, and it struck me then that however much a reigning monarch might be reviled, a usurper – or, in this case, a potential usurper – was hated even more. (I recalled that as a child I had heard old men talk about Henry of Bolingbroke's seizure of the throne from his cousin, King Richard, in the first years of the century, and how his great popularity with the masses had oozed away, turning to resentment after he had assumed the crown.)

At long last, we entered the city, the Duke of Gloucester riding shoulder to shoulder with the Earls of Atholl and Buchan, Albany behind them, side by side with his other uncle, the bishop, who remained tight-lipped and stared straight ahead between his horse's ears. His nephew's attempts to engage him in conversation were totally ignored, and after a while, Albany shrugged and gave up trying. But the expression on his face augured no good for his relatives if ever he did become king. For a minute or two, I speculated on how he thought he could achieve this end, what possible plan he could have up his elegant sleeve, but then I forgot about it as I looked around me, taking in details of my surroundings.

Albany had told me that this eastern approach to the castle was up a gentler incline than the stark rock faces of the north, south and west, but even so, it was a steady climb. What fascinated me most, however, was the medley – one might almost have said the muddle – of different kinds of dwelling. It soon became obvious that, originally, the community had been largely rural, owners of smallholdings and farmsteads, and a few of these spreads still remained, hens and pigs and even the occasional goat, wandering across the road as a snare to unwary horsemen. But new, two-storey wooden houses were springing up everywhere, although it was soon apparent that not every occupant was as yet prepared to abandon pastoral ways. Here and there, cattle and other livestock peered from ground-storey windows, while the goodman and his dame lived on the upper floor, reached by an outside staircase. In the midst of these dwellings, a fine, large church was under construction, the hammering of the masons and carpenters almost deafening us as we passed. I later learned that it was dedicated to Saint Giles, that preceptor and confessor of Charlemagne, and was rising on the site of the old Norman church, destroyed by the army of the last King Richard when English forces had ransacked the city nearly a hundred years earlier.

The people watching our cavalcade pass by were silent and sullen, refusing to raise so much as a cheer, even for their own lords and masters who, for the most part, ignored them. I could see that the Duke of Gloucester was ill at ease, used as he was to the cheering, adulatory crowds of York and London. The English generally were tense, and Earl Rivers more than once fingered the jewelled haft of the dagger he wore at his belt as though he expected treachery from his hosts. But we reached the castle in safety with only one incident when an onlooker scooped up a handful of mud from the roadway and, with a muttered curse, flung it at the Bishop of Moray. Men-at-arms immediately moved to restrain the offender, one of them felling him to the ground with a single blow. They were big men, these Scots, even though many of them were pale and gaunt with hunger, the ravages of the past winter having taken their toll on a yet greater scale here than in the northern shires of England. (And that, believe me, was saying a very great deal.)

As we crossed a rugged forecourt, I was surprised to see fewer defences than I had anticipated; but Davey, who had manoeuvred his mount alongside my cob in order to constitute himself my guide, told me that all of them had been demolished by the Scots themselves at the beginning of the previous century, after an English occupation of the fortress in the reign of the first Edward.

'But why?' I asked.

The page chuckled. 'So that when you Sassenachs overran us again, you were unable to defend the castle, and so it was easily retaken. Rebuilding was only started after King David II was released from his English captivity. He built that great tower yonder and this defensive wall.'

As a Wessex man, born and bred, and with forebears equally native to the west country, the wars between England and Scotland had barely touched my consciousness, except as something that happened a very long way away. Wales, Ireland and even France were all nearer than this distant northern land, and once again I was nearly physically sick with the longing for home that engulfed me.

In the forecourt, the cavalcade drew to a halt and everyone dismounted. Grooms came to lead the horses to the stables while we humans were led up a steep flight of stone stairs by the portcullis gate to the very summit of the rock, where all the main buildings of the castle seemed to be crowded inside a curtain wall. The chief of these was a great hall, built of timber, which, as I soon discovered was used for sleeping, eating and recreation by all household servants and retainers, including those of visiting dignitaries, and consequently was hot, smelly and noisy eighteen or nineteen hours a day.

The royal apartments lay on the south-eastern point of the rock; a series of chambers built, so Davey informed me, by Albany's grandfather, the first King James, the one who had eventually been murdered by his nobles, and whose ghost was said to haunt the place, even though he had not been killed there. Arrangements had been made to house my lord of Gloucester in the royal bedchamber – no one knew where King James was being held: it was thought probably in Craigmillar Castle – his squire and other household officers using the ante-room. Earl Rivers and his nephew, the Marquis of Dorset, were lodged in the Constable's tower, while the remainder of the English lords were left to shift for themselves and find what accommodation they could, either in the castle itself or in the town.

At this point, obviously growing bored with my company and his self-appointed task as my guide and mentor, Davey abruptly disappeared, presumably in search of Murdo or Donald or even old friends and acquaintances, some of whom he must have had in the castle. Where Albany was I had no idea, but guessed him to be closeted with his uncles and the Duke of Gloucester. Not for the first time, he seemed able to do without my protection when it suited him, although I doubted if anyone was really interested in his demise any more. I couldn't help feeling that his importance as a political pawn to both sides was diminishing by the minute. The Scots nobles had their king securely under lock and key, but had no intention of deposing him in favour of his brother, while the English, provided their terms were met – Berwick ceded and Princess Cicely's dowry refunded – were quite willing to negotiate with King James and his spokesmen. My part was played, and I experienced a surge of anger that I was still being treated as though my presence were essential to Albany's well-being.

The anger receded, giving place to an even greater panic than I had known earlier. A gnawing fear that I would never get home again suddenly grew into an overwhelming conviction that this was not merely some nightmare that would eventually be vanquished by common sense, but the brutal reality. I broke into a sweat, even though the day was chilly, and discovered that I was trembling. I needed help, and urgently.

I found it close at hand.

Davey had pointed out to me a small, square stone building, probably one of the oldest on the site, as the chapel of Saint Margaret of Scotland, the second wife of King Malcolm III and a lady of whom I had learned much from Brother Hilarion during my days as a novice at Glastonbury. Although she might never have lived in the west country, and although her mother had been a Magyar princess, on her father's side, Margaret was descended from all the Wessex kings from Cerdic, through Alfred to her great-grandfather, Ethelred Unraed, who had tried to keep England free of the Danes with payments of gold. For by that time, the descendants of the Cerdingas were rulers of all England, not just of Wessex, and Saint Margaret had been of their line, brought to Scotland with her brother, the Atheling, and sister for safety after the Norman Conquest.

I pushed open the chapel door and went in.

Inside it was very cold and dark, a smell of dampness lingering on the air. But there was a light burning on the altar and I stumbled towards it, falling on my knees and lifting my eyes to the effigy of the saint which stood in a niche behind the guttering candles. I lit a fresh one at a flame of one of the three already burning there, then clasped my hands and sent up a silent prayer to be returned safely to my home and family. I don't know exactly what I said now, after all these years, but I remember that I prayed with an intensity so great that I almost cracked my finger bones. I recollect vaguely that I also asked for the intercession of that other son of Somerset, Saint Dunstan, sometime Abbot of Glastonbury and, later, Archbishop of Canterbury, and also of Saint Patrick, born and bred in the west before being sold into slavery in Ireland. With such a trio of saints on my side, how could I fail to return home to Adela and the children?

Slowly but surely the panic drained out of me, leaving me with a feeling akin to emptiness, like a vessel that has been cleaned and scoured. And gradually, in its turn, calmness and sanity returned. I was not alone any more. I was sure, although I had had no sign, that my prayers would be answered.

The chapel door creaked open and I turned my head. A man's form was framed in the doorway.

'What, by all that's holy, are you doing in here, Roger?' Albany demanded. He sounded annoyed. 'Murdo and Donald have been searching everywhere for you.'

Eleven

I turned my head.

A shaft of pale sunlight – too pale for early August, though I guessed that to be normal this far north – inched its way across the threshold elongating Albany's shadow and making him appear both taller than he was and somehow menacing. Motes danced along its length, whirling and spinning. Somewhere I could hear a cat mewling and a faint smell of cooking wafted from the castle kitchens, borne on a freshening breeze.

'Do you want me, my lord?' I asked, surprised. I moved towards him across the dusty floor. 'I thought you would be closeted with the duke and your uncles, working out terms of the peace. I presume there is going to be peace?'

'All that can wait,' Albany answered tersely, adding on a bitter note, 'Whatever they decide, I doubt it will concern me. At least, not yet.' He grinned, baring his teeth like a hunting dog scenting his prey. Not for the first time I speculated about this plan of his that would secure him the throne of Scotland in the face of what was obviously turning into a combined opposition of friends – well, former friends – and foes alike. There was nothing to be gleaned from his expression as he moved out of the sunlight and glanced around him, a little contemptuously I thought, at the meagre proportions of the chapel. 'You still haven't said what you're doing here. Is our sainted Queen Margaret of such interest to you?'

I explained her descent from the kings of Wessex, including Alfred, and her relationship of half-great-niece to the Confessor himself, and then told him bluntly that I had sought her protection to see me safely home again to the west country. I added that I had also offered up prayers to those other two sons of the Somerset soil, Saint Dunstan and Saint Patrick.

To my astonishment the information seemed to disturb him.

'Nonsense!' he exclaimed sharply. 'What I mean is,' he amended hurriedly, 'that the saints have too much else to do, are far too busy, to attend to the likes of us.'

I knew he really meant 'the likes of you', but was too tender of my feelings to say so. (I've never yet encountered a high-born person of either sex who did not think him- or herself worthy of the special attention of every saint known to man.) But I let it go with a smile and a shrug.

'Besides,' Albany went on with a nervous laugh, 'I don't want the saints' intervention on your behalf, at least not yet awhile. I've work for you to do. That's why Murdo and Donald and I have been searching for you.'

'Work, my lord?'

He snorted. 'Oh, don't put on that innocent, I-don't-know-what-you-mean face with me, Roger. You were present when Donald brought me the news that my servant and friend, Rab Sinclair, has been arrested and is awaiting trial for the murder of his wife. I've already said that I want you to prove him innocent.'

I sighed. 'My lord, as I understand it, Master Sinclair was caught literally red-handed, still holding the knife, in the presence of his wife's body. It would need a miracle, a total suspension of belief, for anyone to prove your friend innocent.'

Albany looked mulish. 'He swears he's innocent. That's good enough for me.'

'Have you seen him?'

'Not yet. He's immured in one of the prison cells. But I have permission to visit him. You will accompany me.'

'So you don't yet know what his story is?'

'No.'

'He doesn't deny, I take it, that he did indeed kill his wife?'

'No, of course not. How could he?'

'So what is his defence?'

'I've already told you!' Albany sounded irritated. 'I haven't yet seen him. I'm waiting for you to accompany me. Now!'

The considerate prince and master had disappeared. In his place was an arrogant man used, even in exile, to having his orders and whims obeyed. It reinforced my belief that, however much one may delude oneself, it is impossible ever to know real friendship between commoner and king. (Or, in this particular case, not quite a king, but one who had not altogether given up hope.)

There was no point in postponing the evil day any longer, so I stood back with a courteous gesture – well, I thought it was courteous, but the duke looked highly suspicious of my sudden politeness – and begged him to lead the way.

The prison cells of Edinburgh castle were as noisome as any other prison cells anywhere, probably, in the world. The smell was, as always, the worst thing; an odour compounded of shit and urine and rotting food mixed with sweat and that peculiarly sour stench of bodily fear. We had no difficulty in passing the guards; a scrawled line from one of Albany's half-uncles opened all doors. My own feeling, which I naturally kept to myself, was that each side of the Council table, Scots and English, were glad to be rid of him on any pretext: he had become an embarrassment to them both. The case of Rab Sinclair had proved a godsend; it was rather like tossing a dog a bone or giving a child a toy to play with while the adults made the important decisions. I didn't suppose for a minute that Albany saw it that way, or that any such suspicion crossed his mind, so intent was he on helping his old servant, even to the extent of neglecting his own affairs. Reluctantly, I was forced to admire him for that.

There was the sound of trickling water somewhere in the cell and the walls were furred with lichen and moss whose seeds must have entered one way or another, though it was impossible to tell exactly where. There was no glimmer of daylight to be seen. The gaoler, a grim man with greasy black hair and a wall eye, had provided me with a lantern whose feeble glow nevertheless gave sufficient illumination to make out the figure of a man hunched up in one corner of a bed – if you could have called it that – his manacled feet fastened by a chain to a rusty ring fixed in the wall. As we approached, the wavering beam illuminated a handsome face not yet grown haggard by incarceration, but showing signs of worry and fatigue.

He glanced up and, with a cry of joy, struggled to his feet.

'My lord! My dearest lord! You're here! You're actually here, in Edinburgh!' He seized Albany's hand and tried to kiss it, but the duke gently pushed him back on to the bed and sat down beside him. I was left standing, holding the lantern, like the lackey they thought I was. The man went on joyfully, 'I didn't expect you, not without some fighting. I knew, of course, that the Sassenachs were within sight of the city walls, but like everyone else, I suppose, I imagined that there would be resistance.' He added eagerly, 'Have the Council already affirmed you as king?'

'No, not yet.' Albany spoke tersely, but then, as his friend would have spoken again, silenced him by continuing, 'No more of that for now. Your concerns are more pressing. We need to prove you innocent of this charge against you before you are brought to the humiliation of a trial. And here –' he nodded towards me – 'is someone who is going to help us.'

I would have demurred, but was interrupted by the prisoner.

'Who is he? How can he possibly help us?'

The tone was arrogant, dismissive even, making it plain that no low-born commoner could possibly be of use to a Sinclair except in a menial capacity. 'And why are we talking English? Is he English?' was a question uttered with the utmost suspicion. 'I thought it was Murdo – he's tall enough – but I see now that it isn't.'

'No, no! His name is Roger and yes, he's English. He's been my bodyguard, assigned to me by the Duke of Gloucester, ever since we left London.'

Master Sinclair was obviously puzzled, a frown creasing his high, wide forehead.

'Your bodyguard? But surely Donald and Murdo and the others . . .'

Albany broke in tetchily, 'Leave that for now. I'll explain later. As I said, your affairs are more pressing than mine, and Roger, here, has a reputation as a solver of mysteries. A fine reputation,' he insisted as the other man would once

again have interrupted with a question. 'He has solved problems for my Cousin Gloucester himself. Now, what higher
recommendation could there be than that?' He eased his
buttocks where the edge of the two boards that comprised
the bed's base cut into him. 'So, my dear friend, tell us the
story. From what we have heard, there seems no doubt that
you were found with Aline's body. Rumour goes that you
were discovered with the knife in your hand.'

His companion shuddered. 'Rumour doesn't lie.'

I decided it was time that I took a part in the conversation. I was tired of being ignored and treated as though I
were in truth nothing more than a lantern-bearer.

'Rumour also goes that you claim to be innocent, Master
Sinclair. In the circumstances, how is that possible?'

He glanced at me in surprise as though a cockroach had
crawled out of the wall and spoken, then looked a query at
the duke.

Albany said impatiently, 'You must trust Roger, Rab. He's
no ordinary serving man.'

'I'm not even a serving man,' I informed him shortly. 'I'm
a chapman by trade and my own master.'

'A pedlar?' Master Sinclair visibly reeled.

Albany gripped his friend's wrist and gave it a shake.

'You have to trust us both, Rab. Now, for the sake of sweet
heaven and all its saints, tell us why you are innocent. Did
someone else kill Aline, is that it? Did you stumble across
her body and pick up the knife?'

Master Sinclair shook his head. 'No. I killed her.' He drew
a deep breath, gave me another leery glance and from then
on, addressed himself exclusively to the duke. 'It was self-
defence,' he said. 'I thought she was going to kill me.'

'Aline?' Albany was frankly incredulous. 'Rab, she adored
you. You adored one another. And she was one of the gentlest
creatures alive.'

Master Sinclair made a wry mouth. 'That's what everyone
thought. It's what I thought myself. Oh, you're right about
one thing. I adored her. From the first moment I saw her I
thought her the most perfect woman I'd ever met. But there!'
he heaved a deep sigh. 'Better men than I have been deceived
by a beautiful face.'

The other man grimaced. 'Surely that's not difficult to fathom, my lord. It might have been greed for my fortune, but it wasn't that . . .'

'I should hope not,' Albany interrupted. 'You were the most generous husband alive. I have never seen another woman so bedecked with tokens of her husband's affection than Aline was. You gave her everything her heart desired.'

Again came that rueful twist of the lips. 'Not everything, my lord. You forget, I am twelve years older than she is – was – and therefore perhaps not always as virile as she would have wished.'

'Pooh! What nonsense! Why, I've known you satisfy eight or nine whores in the Golden Horn in a single evening. Come, come, man! In our younger days, you were known as the biggest ram in Edinburgh. You can't have changed that much. I've only been away three years.'

'Long enough, my lord. Three years can take their toll on even the most virile of us. But no, I must admit I wasn't conscious of neglecting Aline. Not in that way. Not in any way, if it comes to that. If anything, I would have said I was even more attentive since giving up my wilder habits and settling down as a sober married man.'

Albany picked his nose reflectively, then wiped his finger on his purple velvet sleeve.

'Are you saying,' he asked, but on a note of disbelief, 'that there was another man? That Aline had taken a lover?' Master Sinclair nodded his head. 'Then who was he, for heaven's sake?'

'Now that I'm afraid I do not know.'

I decided it was time to make my voice heard again, so I asked the obvious question before Albany had time to do so.

'Then how do you know that what you're claiming is the truth?'

'Besides,' the duke chimed in, suddenly shifting and scratching as something nasty in the bed's scanty straw mattress bit him, 'if it's the truth, and Aline was indeed cuckolding you with someone else, no jury in the country would convict you. For Christ's sweet sake, Rab, if this is

what you really think, you must have some idea of who
it was.'

The man beside him gave a sob. 'That's the trouble, I
don't. She never mentioned him by name.'

'Mentioned him?' Albany was incredulous. 'Do you mean
to say that Aline – Aline of all women – was brazen enough
to boast to you that she was bedding with a lover? No, no,
my dear friend! I find that very hard to believe.'

Rab Sinclair moved impatiently, jangling the chain that
shackled him to the wall.

'No, of course she didn't! What woman in her right senses
would?' He saw Albany's eyebrows lift in hauteur and immediately apologized. 'Forgive me, my dear lord, for speaking
so sharply. A very few days in this place makes a man forget
his manners.' The duke nodded understandingly and signed
to him to continue, which he did after a moment to draw
breath. 'No, no! Aline gave me no indication by either look
or word or deed that she loved me any the less. Looking
back, I can acknowledge that it was the most perfect performance. I suspected nothing – nothing, that is, until, quite by
chance, I discovered the book.'

'What book?' Albany and I asked almost in chorus.

'Some leaves of parchment with a couple of holes skew-
ered through each page and the lot bound together with
ribbon. Scarlet ribbon,' Master Sinclair added, as though the
colour had some relevance (which I suppose it might have
done in his eyes).

'So? What of this . . . this book, as you call it?' Albany
was growing a trifle impatient as more and more uninvited
guests decided to sample the royal blood. I could feel them
hopping over my own skin as I tried to shift the little beasts
with a vigorous scratch. Master Sinclair seemed indifferent
to the creatures' bite.

He went on, 'The leaves were covered in Aline's writing,
which I recognized at once. She had a very small and delicate hand, as though a spider had walked across the page.'

'And?' I asked with an impatience that outstripped
Albany's, as Rab Sinclair seemed inclined to dwell with a
lingering fondness on his wife's fine script. My belly was
reminding me it must be well past ten o'clock and that it

was empty. It was a thought that also seemed to have occurred to the duke as he patted his stomach, belched up some wind and remarked that it was a long time since breakfast at the abbey.

Master Sinclair apologized once more; to Albany, of course, not to me. So I urged again, 'What had Mistress Sinclair written? Are we permitted to know?'

'Naturally you're permitted to know! It's the whole point of the story.' I had at last managed to capture his attention and he had actually turned his head and spoken directly to me.

'Well?'

By this time my legs were aching and, my eyes having become adjusted to the gloom, I noticed a small, three-legged stool in another corner of the cell, so I dragged it forward and sat myself down. It was low for my height and my knees were uncomfortably close to my chin, but at least it removed the weight from my feet. Albany regarded me thoughtfully, but made no remark, silencing his friend, who was goggling at me as though I had taken leave of my senses, with a quick motion of his hand.

'Roger is privileged,' he murmured in explanation. 'Pray proceed, Rab. What secrets did this folio of Aline's contain? Are we to understand that it mentioned this lover of hers?'

'Oh, it mentioned him all right, on every page.' The tone was acid. 'Their meetings, their kisses, their . . . their couplings. Yes, you may well look amazed, my lord. You would have said, as I would, that Aline was the most modest woman alive. Do you know that I have never been permitted to see her naked, not once in all the years we were married? Even in bed she insisted on never removing her night rail. And the bedchamber always had to be as dark as pitch.'

'Unbelievable,' commented Albany, and looked as though he meant it. 'Did you never exert your rights as a husband and compel her to obey your wishes?'

Rab Sinclair hung his head, somewhat shamefaced.

'I couldn't,' he said. 'I loved her too much to risk upsetting her. Don't misunderstand me, my lord. She never repulsed me, never said no. She did her duty, always. She never pleaded headaches or any of the other womanly excuses

– except, of course, when she had the flux – and I had always assumed that she got as much pleasure from the act of love as I did. Women aren't passionate creatures, like men. It would be unseemly if they were. Not the sort of women one marries, that is. Whores, naturally, are different.' He paused for a moment, plainly looking back at a misspent youth with considerable pleasure, before continuing, 'So, you can imagine, my lord, the horror and sense of betrayal with which I read, actually read in her very own words, detailed descriptions of her lovemaking with another man.'

'So how did Mistress Sinclair refer to this other man?' I asked, interested now in spite of myself and my hunger. 'She must have called him something.'

Albany nodded in agreement.

'She simply called him by an initial. J.' Rab Sinclair spread his hands in a despairing gesture. 'J. How many James and Johns are there, do you suppose, in this city alone?'

'How did you come across this "book"? This diary?' I asked, leaning forward and resting my elbows on my knees. 'Surely Mistress Sinclair was not so careless as to leave it where you could find it?'

'No, of course not.' He spared me a fleeting glance before turning back to the duke. 'Aline had gone for a day or two to visit her old aunt, who lives in Roslin. I don't know if you recollect the woman, my lord? Margaret Sinclair, the sister of Aline's grandfather and the only living kin that she and her brother had left since the death of their parents. Anyway, be that as it may, my wife had gone to visit her because word had reached us that the old lady had been ill.'

'You didn't accompany Mistress Sinclair?' I broke in to enquire, and got a dirty look for my pains. (I was beginning to get the impression that Rab didn't like me. In his eyes, I was a low-born interloper poking my long nose into his affairs; but as it was his master, the duke, who had introduced me into their counsels, he was forced to conceal his antagonism as best he could.)

'No, there was no need of my presence. Her brother, John, escorted her.' He suddenly seemed a little bewildered. 'Where was I? What was it you wanted to know?'

'How you came to discover this confession of Aline's,'

Albany prompted gently. 'You say she'd gone to see her great-aunt for a day or two, so obviously she wasn't in the house when you stumbled across it.'

Rab Sinclair pushed a hand through his thick, dark hair.

'It wasn't I who found it,' he said. 'It was Maria Beton, my housekeeper. She was cleaning out our bedchamber the day after Aline left. She said it was a good chance to do so, because, when she was at home, Aline spent so much time up there, in that little window embrasure overlooking the street, that she could never find the time to clean it properly. It's not,' he interrupted himself indignantly, 'that I hadn't made provision for a solar for Aline when we wed. There's a little room on the ground floor at the back, overlooking a scrap of garden, which I said could be hers. But she preferred the front of the house, where there's more to see.'

'Understandable,' I murmured, and was treated to another glance of distaste.

Albany frowned at me. 'Go on, Rab,' he urged. 'And as quickly as you can, man! It's past dinnertime and my Cousin Gloucester will be wondering where I am.'

I endorsed this sentiment with a firm nod and the determination not to distract Master Sinclair with any more questions unless it was absolutely necessary. I did feel, however, that a little prompting wouldn't come amiss, our informant, judging by his vague expression, being not quite sure at which point he had arrived in his story.

'Your housekeeper found the book while cleaning out your and Mistress Sinclair's bedchamber. Whereabouts exactly did she discover it? It must have been well hidden not to have come to either your, or her, attention earlier.'

There I was again, not two minutes after making my resolution breaking it almost at once. I just could not curb my natural curiosity.

'Maria – Mistress Beton, that is – had long wanted to turn out a corner cupboard that Aline had brought with her as a bride and which she normally kept locked. Oh, I had seen inside it many times, and as far as I knew it contained nothing more than a few childhood keepsakes, the gown she wore on our wedding day (and which, for some reason, she had not wished to store in her general coffer with the rest of her clothes) and a cedarwood box holding a few bits of jewellery belonging to her mother. That was all.'

'Why did Mistress Beton wish to turn it out?' I'm not sure who asked the question, myself or Albany, but it was probably in both our minds.

Rab Sinclair looked surprised.

'Dust. Spiders lurking along the shelves. Maria Beton,' he added heatedly, 'is a very house-proud woman. It bothered her to think that the cupboard had never been properly cleaned. And when she discovered that my wife had left the key to it behind, she thought it a splendid opportunity to do so at last.'

'And the parchment leaves – the diary, I suppose, if one may call it that – was inside?'

'Yes. Concealed in the folds of the wedding gown.' Rab Sinclair shivered. 'When Maria shook out the folds of the skirt, in case the moths had got into it, the parchment leaves fell out. We could both see at once that the pages were covered in Aline's writing, so naturally Maria handed it to me.'

'So you read it?'

'Wouldn't you have done?'

Albany chuckled. 'He has you there, Roger.'

I was forced to admit he had. If I had discovered a diary in Adela's handwriting, I would have been unable to resist the temptation to read what she had to say. Besides, wives have no business to conceal things from their husbands: the luxury of secrets is a man's prerogative, not a woman's.

'So you found out that Aline had a lover.'

The duke began rubbing his cramped thighs preparatory to standing up. He told me to shout for the gaoler, but before I could do so, Master Sinclair exclaimed urgently, 'But not only that!'

Albany's waning attention was rearrested. He had half-risen from the bed, but at these words, sat down again.

'What else then?'

'My lord!' His friend leaned forward, grabbing unceremoniously at a velvet sleeve. 'My lord, a whole page – more – was devoted to the different ways she and her lover had thought up to kill me. Poison; an arranged accident; stabbing, making it look as if an intruder had broken in at night; drowning; and other ways I can't remember for the moment. It was obvious that they were planning to murder me, my lord!'

This put a different complexion on the matter. I asked the one question that mattered. 'Where is the book now?'

'I don't know.'

'What do you mean, you don't know?' Albany seized his friends by both hands and shook them. 'You still have the book? You kept it, of course? You confronted Aline with it when she returned home?'

'Not at once. I was too shocked. I didn't really believe what I'd seen. I . . . I put it back in the cupboard, under the folds of the wedding gown where Maria had found it. I was so shaken, I was ill for several days. Mistress Beton will confirm what I say.'

'Did you tell her what you had discovered?'

'No. How could I? It was too horrible.'

Albany asked angrily, 'Didn't you have the sense to show her the diary?' But Rab Sinclair just shook his head.

'I was too ashamed. And I still wasn't sure that it wasn't some kind of horrible joke.'

'But when Mistress Sinclair came back from Roslin, surely you tackled her about it eventually? What did she say?'

'She denied everything. She became quite hysterical. She said I was making it up. She challenged me to produce the . . . the diary.'

'So? Did you?' Again, I don't know whether it was the duke or myself who spoke, but I feel sure that the same question was on both our lips.

Rab Sinclair shook his head.

'No. When I went upstairs to fetch it and confront her with it, it had gone.'

Twelve

Someone had to ask the stupid question, so I saved Albany the embarrassment and framed it myself.

'What do you mean, gone? Are you certain?'

Rab Sinclair turned on me savagely. 'Of course I'm certain,' he snarled. I thought he was going to strike me.

The duke again clasped his friend's arm.

'Robert! Rab! Calm yourself. Roger just needs to make sure. Did you search the cupboard thoroughly?'

Master Sinclair controlled his temper with an effort.

'I had everything out of it. I shook out the wedding gown. I scraped with my nails along the back and sides of each shelf to ensure that there was no crack between it and the cupboard wall where the diary could have lodged.' He raised his hands in a despairing gesture. 'Mind you, I don't need anyone to tell me that that was a waste of time. The parchment sheets were too big, and the knots of ribbon that bound them too thick, to permit of such a thing happening. I merely mention it to demonstrate how desperate I was. No,' he finished on a quieter note, 'it had vanished.'

'But who might have taken it?' I asked. 'Do you suspect your housekeeper, this . . . this Maria Beton?'

'Of course not!' His anger flared again as he leaped to his servant's defence, before once more controlling his emotions. 'Why should she? She had no idea of the diary's contents.'

'Normal curiosity,' I suggested. 'Mistress Beton must have seen that when you read them they upset you. Surely it would only be human nature to want to find out what the diary said. Had you locked the cupboard again after you replaced it?'

Master Sinclair shifted uncomfortably.

'Yes,' he admitted at last. 'But I left the key where Maria

had found it, on a neighbouring shelf. All right! Perhaps, with hindsight, it was a foolish thing to do, but I was so upset at the time that I couldn't think properly. Besides,' he added defiantly, 'I trust Maria totally. She is a distant kinswoman of Aline's and has been with us since we were married.'

'Nevertheless, the diary vanished,' Albany pointed out grimly. 'And according to you, she was the sole person, apart from yourself, with the slightest knowledge of its existence and where it was hidden. As Roger says, her curiosity to know what was in it – what had disturbed you so greatly – must have been extreme. And the key was there to her hand, where you had left it.'

'But why would she steal it?'

The duke gave vent to a splutter of laughter. 'My dear friend, don't be so naïve! To blackmail Aline, of course. Once she had mastered the contents, Mistress Beton could have held them over Aline's head and wrung from her anything she wanted.'

Master Sinclair, who seemed to have shrunk back into his corner while we talked, suddenly sat forward, flapping his hands.

'No! No, she couldn't. Maria can't read.'

Albany and I were both stricken to silence by this information. Our chief suspect – the obvious and, as far as we were concerned, the only one – had been snatched from us.

'Well,' I said grudgingly, 'that necessarily puts a different complexion on the matter.' I thought for a moment or two, while Albany looked equally nonplussed. At last, I said, 'Leave that for now. Let's go back to Mistress Sinclair's denial of any knowledge of the diary after her return from her aunt's. When you failed to produce it, what happened then?'

'She maintained her total ignorance of any such object. She became even more hysterical, accusing me – me! – of having a mistress and of fabricating this tissue of lies – that was what she called it – in order to divorce her.'

'Did she say who this mistress of yours was supposed to be?'

'No, how could she? For she knew as well as I did that

there is no one; that I have always been faithful to her and her alone. I swear on our Saviour's suffering on the Cross that this is the truth.'

I didn't much care for Robert Sinclair, but I reckoned it would take great courage to swear such a tremendous oath if he were lying. The fear of eternal damnation, of roasting for ever in the fires of Hell, would surely deter him as it would us all.

Albany evidently thought the same, for he sprang to his feet and went to put an arm about the other man's shoulders, once more exhorting him to be calm. 'We believe you, Rab. We believe you.'

'Master Sinclair,' I broke in, 'where was your wife's brother while all this was taking place? You told me he had accompanied his sister to their aunt's house at . . . at . . .'

'Roslin.' Albany supplied me yet again with the name.

'Roslin,' I repeated, trying to commit it to memory. 'So,' I continued, 'he had presumably brought her home.'

'Yes. But naturally I said nothing to Aline until Johnnie had left to go to his own house in the Grassmarket. It was their parents' home. He still lives there.'

I nodded. 'So, after he left you confronted your wife with your knowledge of the diary. What happened next?'

'I told you. She denied the accusation frantically. She pretended to be hysterical . . .'

'Pretended?'

'All right,' was the snapped response. 'Perhaps she really was frightened by the realization that I had discovered the diary and was aware of its contents. But by the time she had challenged me to produce it, and by the time I had searched for the thing upstairs and been forced to admit that I couldn't find it, she was perfectly calm. Moreover, she had had the opportunity to think. She must have known that, from then on, I should be on my guard. Any hope she had cherished of planning my murder to look like an accident was gone. She had to do something quickly. I can't imagine what was in her mind, or how she hoped to explain my death afterwards, but she ran into the kitchen and grabbed a knife that Maria uses for cutting meat. I had followed her, and when she turned round and came at me, clutching it in her hand,

I knew she meant to use it. I struggled with her furiously and finally got possession of the handle, but as I did so, she must have slipped and fallen forward on to the point of the knife. The blade entered her heart. She died immediately.'

'In other words, an accident,' Albany proclaimed triumphantly.

Master Sinclair bowed his head. 'An accident. But without the diary to prove the cause of our quarrel, how can I prove it? There were no witnesses. Maria had been in the garden, picking herbs to savour the meat for our dinner. And it was the purest misfortune that our neighbour, Mistress Callender, entered the house at that particular moment to welcome Aline home after her absence. The screech she set up was loud enough to waken the dead. Then she ran into the street, screaming.' Rab shook his head as if still bewildered by the turn of events. 'After that, the house suddenly seemed full of people . . . there was a lot of noise . . . shouting . . . I was arrested and brought here, to the castle, and charged with murder. No one will believe that Aline attacked me first. Everyone knew her for what she appeared to be; a loving, sweet-natured, devoted wife. And without that diary, there's no proof to the contrary. I shall be hanged for certain.'

'Not if I can help it,' Albany asserted, adding with a confidence I was far from feeling. 'Our friend here is going to find the proof for you. He's going to find out who stole that diary and why, aren't you, Roger?' I gave a half-hearted sort of gurgle that could have meant anything and which the duke ignored. 'But I want it done quickly,' he went on. 'I've my own affairs to attend to and I shall need your help –' this was an unwelcome surprise to me – 'so bring all your wits to bear on this mystery. Any assistance you want, you shall have. Just ask Murdo and he will ensure that you get it.'

The cell door creaked open and the wall-eyed gaoler grunted, 'A message for your Grace.' And, with the help of his toe, he booted in a small boy as unprepossessing as he was himself and bearing a strong family resemblance. His son, I decided, who added to the general coffer by running errands and delivering messages for anyone within the castle precincts. His mother was probably the castle washerwoman. 'Well, go on then,' the gaoler added, as the boy hesitated, glancing awkwardly between me and Albany. 'Tell His Highness what you've come to say.' He spoke in the broad Scots' tongue, but, with a certain amount of guesswork, I was beginning to follow simple sentences and phrases.

The boy gabbled something which, however, I was unable to understand except for a word which I guessed to be a rendition of 'Gloucester'. Albany confirmed this when he announced that his absence at dinner had been marked, and that his presence was now urgently required at a meeting of the Council with Duke Richard. He clapped me on the shoulder with a great show of camaraderie and I knew what was coming. When royalty start to get familiar, it can only mean that they want something. And woe betide you if you fail to deliver.

I was right.

'Roger, I'm putting this entirely in your hands,' Albany said. 'For the next few days, my place will be at the council table.' He didn't add 'guarding my interests' but I knew that was what he meant. 'I must leave you here now with my good friend, Rab Sinclair. Rab, my man, give Roger your full cooperation and he'll have you free of this coil in no time.'

Again I made a gesture of protest, and again it was ignored. Albany swung on his heel, tossed a coin to the expectant boy and was shown out by the obsequious turnkey. I was left in the evil-smelling cell, extremely hungry with no immediate prospect of a meal, and facing a hostile gentleman who regarded me as way beneath him in God's scheme of things. It did fleetingly cross my mind that now, while Albany was suddenly absorbed by his own affairs, might be a good time to effect my escape from the castle and start on the long journey home, but common sense prevailed. I had very little money in my purse, all my bodily needs having been provided for ever since I left Bristol – where was that? Somewhere on the far side of the moon? – and no means of earning a living, my pack having been left behind me. And I was, moreover, in a country not my own, where even the language of the inhabitants was strange to me. I was likely to get lost very quickly, a prey to all the vagabonds and outlaws that no doubt roamed this thickly wooded region. (And what was not forest seemed to be made up of treacherous bogs and wild, open tracts of moorland where it would be easy to lose my way and go round and around in circles, ending up where I had started.)

But if I were honest, I had to admit that there was another reason that prevented me making a bid for freedom. All my natural curiosity was aroused by any mystery or conundrum: I never could resist ferreting around for the truth of any puzzle. So I sat down on the stool again, drawing it closer to the prisoner, ignored my belly's insistent grumbling and proceeded to question Rab Sinclair, freed from Albany's inhibiting presence.

'This all happened three days ago, on Monday, I believe?'

'How do you know that?' The tone was aggressive and the eyes glittered angrily beneath their heavy lids.

'I heard Donald Seton tell the duke so last night when he brought His Grace the news of your arrest and imprisonment.'

Master Sinclair gave a sudden crack of laughter. 'Donald Seton, eh? I heard my lord mention the MacGregor. Who else is with him? Davey Gray? Tullo? Petrie?' I nodded and he laughed again. 'Mar's people. At least, the ones who were with him when he died so mysteriously in Craigmillar Castle.'

'So I've been told. They fled to France after the earl's death to offer their services to his brother. Is it of any significance?'

'No, no!' The disclaimer was a little too vehement, but I let it go. It was none of my business. My job was to discover and retrieve, if possible, the missing diary of the dead Aline Sinclair. And the sooner I achieved that aim, the sooner I could persuade Albany that my usefulness was at an end; that his life was no longer in jeopardy. He would either be king (and his wretched elder brother, the imprisoned James III, deposed, probably murdered) or, if not, he would no longer be considered a threat who needed to be eliminated.

'Were you and your wife kin to one another?' I enquired of Rab. 'I ask because you mentioned that her great-aunt, her grandfather's sister, was also called Sinclair.'

He gave me a quick, sideways glance from beneath those heavy eyelids.

'You don't miss much,' he said, almost as if he resented that I had my wits about me. 'Yes, Aline was a cousin in the second or third degree, I can't remember which. Is it important?'

I shrugged. 'Perhaps. Most likely not. But it isn't always possible to say what might prove to be of importance.' I regarded him straitly. 'Who do you think has the diary? Is it not possible that your housekeeper, this Maria Beton, stole it, even though she's unable to read? As I said before, unless she's a fool, she must have noted your reaction when you read it and worked out for herself that it contained something very damning. Why should she not have taken it to someone, a friend maybe, who could inform her of its contents?'

He shook his head vehemently.

'No! I told you just now, she's – I mean she was –' tears started to his eyes – 'devoted to Aline. She's some sort of distant kinswoman. When we got married, Mistress Buchanan, Aline's mother, suggested her as a housekeeper on account of her trustworthiness and her fondness for my wife. Mine had been, up to then, a bachelor household with just myself and my man servant. It was necessary for Aline to have another woman to keep her company, apart from her personal maid.'

'Wait!' I interrupted when he would have gone on speaking. 'You mention a man servant and a maid . . .'

It was his turn to cut in. 'The maid, Gudrun, a silly young piece, had accompanied Aline to Roslin and had been left behind on account, I think my wife mentioned, of some belly-ache caused by eating too many plums – or some such thing. I really can't remember. Events happened so fast after John's departure that other matters have slipped my mind.' And he leaned forward, clutching his head in his hands, the picture of abject misery and despair.

I ruthlessly ignored this bid for my sympathy and continued, 'This man servant of yours! Presumably he remained at home with you and Mistress Beton?'

'Jared? Yes, he was at home.' The voice was muffled as it issued between the long, elegant fingers muzzling Rab Sinclair's mouth. 'There was no need for him to go to Roslin. Aline had her brother.'

Her brother, John. Now here was another J, the man servant, Jared. As my companion had pointed out, J was a very common letter. I cursed under my breath.

At that point, the gaoler reappeared, carrying a bowl of something highly unsavoury and a hunk of black bread, both of which he plonked down on the bed beside the prisoner with such force that some of the bowl's contents slopped over on to the blanket.

'Dinner,' he grunted. Well, I took it to be what he said.

Master Sinclair removed his hands from his face and peered into the bowl, a look of pure revulsion contorting his features. I didn't blame him. Hungry as I was, there was no way I could have swallowed even the smallest spoonful of such a grey and greasy-looking broth. A rapid exchange in the Scots tongue, too fast for me to be able to distinguish more than three or four words, resulted in money changing hands, the coins being produced by Rab from a purse looped on to his belt. These the gaoler pocketed with a satisfied grin and departed, returning almost immediately with a tray – obviously already prepared – on which reposed white bread of the finest quality, a wing of fowl, a hunk of goat's cheese and some fruit. My mouth watered and my belly rumbled louder than ever.

The gaoler gave me a sadistic leer and was preparing to take his leave for the second time, when he was detained by Rab Sinclair speaking to him again. And again I was unable to follow the gist of their conversation; although I did understand it to be a favour that Rab was asking, partly by the intonation of his voice and also by the way the gaoler rubbed his chin considering before finally nodding his head.

When the cell door at last closed behind him, I at once resumed my questioning, afraid, judging by the ravenous way in which the prisoner was attacking his dinner, that his mouth would soon be too full for him to answer.

'This man servant of yours, this Jared, could he have stolen the diary?'

'Why should he?' My companion spoke thickly, having already made a determined onslaught on at least half the cheese. 'He didn't know anything about it. Wasn't present when it was found, and I said nothing.'

'But Mistress Beton could have told him,' I pointed out. 'They could have been In it together.'

Rab Sinclair bit into the wing of fowl and savoured it with relish, at the same time shaking his head.

'Maria wouldn't have done that,' he stated positively, as soon as he could speak. 'She and Jared don't like one another. Never have, never will. They never exchange more than a word or two, and that only when necessary. He always resented the authority she took upon herself as housekeeper. Until my marriage, he had things pretty much all his own way.'

I watched enviously as another mouthful of flesh was slowly chewed and swallowed before asking, 'You don't think, then, that her curiosity could have overcome her dislike, and that she might have confided in him?'

My companion spluttered with laughter, spraying me with fragments of bird. 'No, I don't! I tell you, those two can't stand the sight of one another.'

I sighed. I was getting nowhere.

'Well, do you have any idea who might have taken the diary, and why? You've dismissed the notion that Mistress Beton could be behind the theft, in spite of the obvious reasoning that she might have taken it to someone who would be able to read it for her, with a view to threatening either you or your wife with its contents later on. Think about it, Master! If what you say is true, she was the only person with any knowledge of the book's existence, and the only one who saw your dismay on reading it. I imagine she's no fool. She can add two beans to three and make five.'

'It's wasn't her,' Rab Sinclair reiterated obstinately. 'As for who it was, I don't know any more than you. But the one thing I do know is that it has disappeared. Also that it has to be found if I'm not to choke to death at the end of a rope.' He eyed me malevolently as he dug his teeth into an apple and crunched on it loudly. 'So you'd better start looking for it if you want to keep in my lord Albany's good graces. From all that I hear he may soon be king, so, if you fail, it's possible you could also find yourself dancing on air.' He gave a sudden deep-throated, gloating chuckle. 'You may not know it – in fact you most likely don't – but my lord is a great believer in Jedburgh Justice: hang first and ask questions afterwards.'

I forbore to point out that it was no matter to me whether Albany was crowned King of Scotland or not. By the time that happened – if it happened – I would be on my way home. Nor was it a priority with me to keep in the duke's good graces. But I would pursue my enquiries out of pure curiosity and because I hated to see the innocent punished for the guilty. And if Master Sinclair were indeed speaking the truth, then the accident that killed his wife was nothing more than her just deserts. Not only had she been cuckolding a man who had treated her well and, above all, given her his love, but she had also attempted to murder him.

I got to my feet.

'Where are you going?' Rab Sinclair paused in the act of biting into a second apple. 'What are you going to do?' He was suddenly filled with panic.

'Well, I shan't get any further just sitting here, shall I? I must see and talk with people for myself. Your housekeeper, your brother-in-law, your man servant for a start. Maybe also your neighbour. Mistress Callender, did you call her? So I shall need directions to find your house, also Master Buchanan's in the . . . where exactly did you say it's located?'

'The Grassmarket. Anyone will tell you where that is. As for my house, get Murdo or one of the others to take you there. They all know where I live.'

'Can't you tell me?'

He shrugged. 'Many of those houses look alike. It'll be easier if someone shows you the way.'

I could see by the obstinate set of his mouth that I would get nothing more out of him.

'Very well,' I agreed. 'Although it may still be dinnertime.' It struck me that if that were indeed the case, I might be able to grab some food for myself, so I made no further demur and shouted for the gaoler.

It was a relief to be out in the fresh air again, free from the fetid atmosphere of the cells. I filled my lungs with it, drawing in great, deep breaths and letting my head clear, shaking my whole body to rid myself of the dirt and grime, much as a dog will shake itself free of water. I didn't immediately go in search of Murdo, Donald and the others, but stretched my cramped limbs by walking from one end of that towering crag to the other. In one direction I could see below me the smoke of houses, billowing grey wreaths in the windy sunshine of that early August morning, the trees in the orchards looking no bigger than dandelion heads. In another, away in the distance, I could just make out – with the white foam flecking its blue and with the occasional flash of a white sail – the wide expanse of what Davey had told me was the River Forth as it broadened out towards the open sea. Clouds were scudding inland, and I felt I had only to lift my hands in order to touch them. Edinburgh Castle rock, I decided, was the nearest to heaven that I was likely to come in this life. (And as for the next, I decided not to speculate, but hoped that when the time came, my sins would be forgiven me.)

On this pious hope, I made my way to the great hall where my luck held, for although the trestles were being dismantled and moved to stand against the walls until suppertime, the baskets of broken meats which had been cleared from the tables had not yet been carried into the kitchens. I was able to help myself to bread, cheese and several hunks of beef. Excellent beef, too: someone had once told me that the Scots bred good cattle in spite of a largely barren landscape.

'Stuffing your face again, chapman?' asked a mocking voice, and I turned to find Donald Seton at my elbow.

'Ah! Just the man I was looking for,' I said, grasping his wrist and seizing another lump of meat to chew on as I led him outside. 'I need you to show me Master Sinclair's dwelling.' And in answer to his raised eyebrows, I told him how I had so far spent my morning.

He regarded me meditatively for a moment or two, then nodded.

'Follow me.'

He didn't, as I had half-expected, make further enquiries as to what exactly had been said or what I intended to do. In his place, I would have been unable to curb my curiosity, especially when it concerned someone I knew. But Donald displayed no such interest. I had thought, just for a fleeting second, that he had looked at me rather pityingly, but I was used to people underrating my ability to winkle out the truth, even when a problem seemed insoluble.

We left the castle, reversing the route by which we had entered earlier that same morning; descending the steep stairs by the Portcullis Gate, past the Constable's Tower to the rugged forecourt that gave on to the town outside.

Donald led me down the main street a little way and then pointed to a house on the right-hand side as we stood with the castle at our backs. It was one of the newer timber-built dwellings, but differing from its neighbours in that it had no outside staircase. The first storey window, like many others, hung out over the street and, I reflected, it must have been there that Aline Sinclair had sat in preference to the solar so lovingly provided for her by her husband, at the back of the house. Watching for the lover whose name began with J? Writing her secret diary and plotting the death of that same husband? I suddenly felt cold, and it had nothing to do with the general chill of the day.

'I'll be leaving you then.'

Donald's voice broke in on my reflections and made me jump.

'Oh . . . Yes. Very well, then,' I said. 'If His Grace asks for me, you'll tell him where I am?'

'I'll tell him.'

The squire gave me a brief nod before striding away, uphill towards the castle. I looked after his retreating form for a minute or two, vaguely disturbed, but not knowing why. Then I gave myself a little shake, crossed the street and knocked loudly on the door of Master Sinclair's house.

Thirteen

B efore I had time to knock twice, however, the door flew
open and the gaoler's son emerged, helped on his way
by a pat on the back from the woman who was holding the
inner latch. They both started at the sight of me, the boy
glancing up with a shifty, white-eyed look of uneasy surprise,
his companion giving me a haughty stare of enquiry.

She said something, plainly a question, at which the lad
turned and muttered in the same tongue. Then he slid from
under the woman's hand and raced off in the direction of
the castle as fast as his legs would carry him, not even pausing
to look back over his shoulder.

'Mistress Beton?' I asked.

I wasn't sure that I would get a comprehensible reply, but
after only a second's hesitation, while she sized me up from
head to toe in a somewhat unnerving manner, the housekeeper
nodded.

'You must be the Sassenach young Archie was just telling
me about.' She spoke perfectly clear, if heavily accented
English, but in the correct, slightly stilted way of someone
speaking a foreign tongue. 'My lord duke has sent you to
try to find Mistress Sinclair's diary. I am right?'

'Yes,' I agreed in some relief.

Whatever Master Sinclair's purpose had been in sending
the gaoler's son ahead of me – and I recalled how he had
appeared to be asking a favour of the gaoler himself – it had
certainly saved me a long and involved explanation. Perhaps
that had indeed been his object, but somehow I doubted it,
and couldn't help wondering what message the boy had really
brought to Mistress Beton.

The housekeeper held the door wide and beckoned me
inside with a brief motion of her head.

'Come with me, if you please.'

There was no deference in her tone, and I guessed that quite apart from what the boy had told her, she had summed up my social standing as no better, if as good, as her own. Women are cleverer than men at that sort of thing. (Adela and Margaret Walker could always distinguish at fifty paces or more if a female was a gentlewoman or not, and whether she merited a curtsey or a mere nod of the head.)

I followed Mistress Beton along a narrow, stone-flagged passageway, where an open door to our right showed the interior of what was a comfortable, well-furnished parlour, to a smaller chamber at the back of the house. This, too, showed signs of luxury with painted beams and ceilings, cushions piled up at one end of a high-backed settle, two colourful tapestries hung on a north-facing wall and windows of oiled parchment, one of which stood wide, revealing a little garden. This latter was a mere patch of ground, maybe three or four yards in both directions, but it was neatly kept and pleasant to look at, with two beds of herbs and an apple tree in one corner, spreading its leafy branches against one of the enclosing walls. This, I decided had to be the solar mentioned by Master Sinclair and made by him for his wife – who had spurned it in favour of the overhanging window in their bedchamber.

'Please to sit down, Master.'

Mistress Beton indicated one end of the settle – the bare end, naturally – then sat down at the other, nestling into the bank of cushions with something of a sigh. She made no attempt to offer me anything to drink, which, if whisky was all she had in the house (as was probable) was just as well. It was a liquid neither my stomach nor my brain could take. She regarded me expectantly, but made no effort to break the silence, sitting with her hands folded quietly in her lap.

It was my first chance to view her properly, and I saw a tall woman, too tall for her sex, almost the same height as myself. But there was nothing scrawny about her, either, as you sometimes find with people who have outgrown their strength in youth. She was deep-breasted and well-fleshed and would probably, if she ever married, give a man pleasure in bed – provided, that was, that the lights were

out. For the most striking thing about her was her plain-
ness of feature.

It would be too unkind to say that Maria Beton was ugly,
but, having conceded as much, it would be no more than the
truth to state she was one of the least attractive women I had
ever seen in my life. She had a broad, square face in which
sat an equally broad nose flanked by smallish eyes of an indeterminate hue and fringed with sandy lashes. Eyebrows of
the same colour were almost invisible. I was unable to guess
how old she was, although I learned later that she was my
own age – or the age I should be in two months' time – thirty.

She flushed under my scrutiny, but still said nothing, simply
waiting expectantly. I cleared my throat awkwardly, realizing
how rudely I had been staring.

'Mistress Beton, you were with Master Sinclair, I understand, when the diary first came to light. Indeed, I believe
you were the person who found it.'

She nodded. 'If you have seen and talked with Master
Sinclair in prison, as Archie informed me that you have, then
you will know this for the truth.'

'But you had no idea what was in it.'

'Not then. I know now, of course. I have had speech with
Robert. He has told me.'

'Robert?' Then I realized she meant Rab Sinclair. 'You
call him by his baptismal name, Mistress?'

She seemed somewhat confounded by my surprise.

'You may not have been told,' she answered with dignity,
'that I am . . . I mean that I was kin to Mistress Sinclair.
Aline was my cousin in the third degree. Therefore I am also
kin to her husband.'

'Nevertheless, you are his housekeeper.'

The naturally high colour of her cheeks deepened almost
to crimson.

'You are a Sassenach,' she said contemptuously. 'You do
not understand these things. But if it upsets your notions of
propriety, I will refer to him as Master Sinclair.'

Her fluency in the English tongue was greater than I had
at first thought it. But I was becoming sidetracked.

'After you had discovered the diary and given it to your
mas— to Master Sinclair to read, what was his reaction?'

'He seemed extremely distressed. Disturbed beyond all measure. A man who had received a desperate blow.'

'You didn't ask him what was wrong?'

'No.'

'Why not?'

'If he had wanted me to know, he would have told me. I do not pry into other people's affairs. Their business is their own.'

I set my trap. 'You didn't, later, read it yourself?'

She turned her limpid gaze on me. 'I am unable to read, Master. I was never schooled in my letters.'

Why did I feel that the answer came a little too pat? I shrugged the question aside.

'But you do know now?'

'I have told you. I have had speech with Rob . . . With Master Sinclair.' She smiled slightly as she said it.

'You have seen him since his arrest?'

'Of course. I have visited him at the castle. Yesterday,' she added.

'And that's when he told you the truth?' She inclined her head in assent. 'Were you shocked by his revelations?'

There was a long pause, so long that I began to wonder if she had understood my question. But just as I was about to repeat it in a simpler form, she said, 'No. I was not even surprised.'

I was startled. 'You mean you knew about your mistress's lover?'

'No. But I knew my cousin.' She emphasized the last word, making it plain that she deeply resented any assumption of her menial position in the household. I raised my eyebrows and she went on, 'Aline was not the innocent she pretended to be. Even as a child, she had only to put on that sweet, pretty face of hers and everyone would believe every word she said. She could . . . I do not know the English phrase.'

'Get away with murder?' I suggested drily. 'But in this instance, it was not she who did the killing.'

'Not for the want of trying,' was the fierce response. 'She had already plotted and planned to kill her husband, and indeed tried to do so. Robert says that it was only by God's grace that she failed.'

'Is he telling the truth do you think?'

She rose majestically to her feet, drawing herself to her full height and expanding that magnificent bosom.

'Will you please to go now?'

I didn't answer immediately. At full stretch, her head, in its white linen coif and cap, was a mere inch or so lower than the solar's ceiling beams; and I was suddenly aware that both ends of each beam were decorated with painted carvings – birds, insects, flowers, masks. This in itself was not unusual, and was frequently to be found in houses where money and time were no object. But the particular carving that met my eye, picked out in green and gold, was the head of the Green Man. There were the branches wreathing out of his mouth, up around his head to form his leafy hair and down around his chin to make his beard. It reminded me of the warnings of my mysterious friend, which I had managed to forget for the past few days, and gave me a nasty jolt.

With an effort, I withdrew my gaze and set myself to the task of placating Mistress Beton, whom I had managed to offend. It was obvious that her sympathies lay with Master Sinclair and not her late cousin.

I had risen with her, and now invited her to sit down again.

'My only object, Mistress, is to uncover the truth, I promise you. But to do that, I must ask questions. I must know why you believe what Master Sinclair tells you. On your own admission, you never saw the contents of the diary and could not have understood them even had you done so. Why should he not be lying to you?'

She allowed herself, somewhat grudgingly, to be mollified and resumed her seat at the other end of the settle, but this time with a stiff back as though ready to jump to her feet again if I re-offended.

'I do not think Robert is lying because I saw with my own eyes how shocked – how horrified – he was when he read what Aline had written. I shall never forget the look on his face and the way his hands trembled. He was a man who had received a . . . a death blow. But more than that, as I have already told you, I knew my cousin. I knew her far, far better than other people; better than her brother, better than her parents. They were fools. They accepted

Aline as she was on the surface, not as she really was under-neath.'

'You have known her a long time?'

'All my life. She was much younger than I was, but we played together as children and always I was aware that the girl others saw was not the person who subjected me to petty humiliations; the girl who played unpleasant tricks on others and then made it look as though the fault were mine. I was punished many times for leading her into mischief, when the truth was exactly the opposite, when I had been trying to rescue her from the results of her own folly. Oh no, it did not surprise me at all to learn that she was unfaithful and was scheming to murder her own husband.'

'But until you learned all this from Master Sinclair yesterday, you had no firm knowledge that your cousin had taken a lover? You have no inkling of who he might have been?'

'Inkling?'

'Idea. Suspicion. I find it difficult to believe that some-thing had not come to your attention.'

Mistress Beton gave me a hostile stare.

'It was not my business to poke and pry,' she protested. 'And with such a loving, adoring husband as Robert, I felt sure even Aline must be satisfied. Her smallest wish was like a royal command to him. She was indulged, petted, pampered. Why would she need or want another man?' She shrugged. 'It is true that she very often went out alone and stayed out for several hours at a time, but this I could understand. Too much adoration can occasionally become . . .'

'Overwhelming?'

'Yes.' She nodded. 'That is the word I was looking for. But surely not for long.'

I guessed that Maria Beton had been envious of her cousin. To be – what was it she had said? – indulged petted and pampered was not a condition that had ever come her way. And yet too much affection could be a burden, as I had learned from a case I had investigated in Bristol only last year. But it did not warrant pre-planned, cold-blooded murder. Nothing did. I got back to the matter in hand.

'Mistress Beton,' I said earnestly, 'do you have any idea

who could have removed the diary before your cousin's return home? How many days elapsed between Master Sinclair finding it and Monday?'

Again the housekeeper frowned and queried a word. 'Elapsed?'

'Passed.'

'Ah!' The frown deepened as she concentrated. 'Let me see. Aline and John left for Roslin on Thursday. That would be a week ago today.' I nodded. She went on, 'I decided to turn out that cupboard the following morning when I noticed, while making the bed, that Aline had left the key on the shelf where she kept her pots of unguents and ointments for her skin. She was very proud of her beautiful white skin.'

Afraid of being sidetracked by further female jealousies, I interrupted quickly, 'And that was when you found the diary?'

'Yes, hidden under the skirt of her wedding dress which Aline kept folded on one of the shelves.'

'What was it like? The diary, I mean.'

'Oh, two or three leaves of parchment tied together with red ribbon threaded through holes pierced at the edges.'

This description tallied with Master Sinclair's. I sucked my teeth thoughtfully.

'So this was Friday?' She murmured agreement. 'What happened to it when your employer had read it? Do you know?'

Yet again I had ruffled her feathers.

'Robert is not my employer. I keep house for him as a favour, as a kinswoman, and because Aline is not – was not – domesticated and regarded cleaning and cooking as beneath her. As for your question, when Robert had finished reading the diary, he replaced it on the shelf, under the wedding dress, where I had found it. Then he closed and locked the cupboard before I had a chance to finish dusting it and told me to leave him alone. He sat down on the edge of the bed looking, as I said just now, as if he had received his death blow.'

'You naturally asked him what was the matter?'

She inclined her head. 'Naturally. But he refused to say. I could not force him to confide in me, so I did as he asked and went away.'

'Consumed with curiosity.'

A faint smile, the first she had given, lifted the corners of her mouth and lightened the heavy features.

'Of course.' That was honest at any rate.

'Did you return to the bedchamber later to see what you could discover?'

The small eyes glinted at me beneath their sandy lashes.

'For what purpose? As Robert and I have both told you, I cannot read.'

I grinned a little sheepishly in acknowledgement of the second trap I had set for her.

'Mistress,' I resumed, 'you say that this all took place on the Friday.'

'Friday morning,' she agreed.

'Very well then.' I leaned forward, my elbows on my knees. 'Between that time and Monday, when Mistress Sinclair returned home, who called at the house? More importantly, who went upstairs? In short, who could have removed the diary from the cupboard in the bedchamber? Who would have known it was there?'

If I had hoped to fluster her, I was disappointed. And if she was concealing any guilty knowledge she hid it admirably.

'Unfortunately, I can remember no one.' She added with a touch of irritation, 'I have already been questioned on this matter and have given the same answer.'

'But the diary is missing. Somebody must have taken it,' I argued.

She shrugged. 'This is true. But I cannot tell you or anyone else what I do not know. As far as I am concerned, no one called at the house on either Saturday or Sunday. I was busy and Robert told me to deny him to any callers.'

'He was still in a state of shock?'

'He certainly did not wish to burden himself with visitors.'

I digested this, then said, 'Let me understand this clearly, Mistress. You are saying that no one at all, neither male nor female, knocked on your door throughout the whole of Saturday and Sunday?'

Maria Beton inclined her head for a second time. In spite of her plebeian looks, she had a regal air about her.

'That is what I am saying, yes. Mistress Callender came in on Friday afternoon with a recipe for quince jelly she had promised to give me, but after her, no one.'

'Mistress Callender?' I queried sharply. 'The goodwife from next door?' Foolishly, I had overlooked the rest of Friday. 'Did you at any time during her visit leave her alone?'

My companion regarded me in astonishment.

'My good man,' she expostulated, 'you surely cannot suspect our neighbour! That is foolishness! How could she possibly know of Aline's diary when no one else was aware of it?'

She was right. I was clutching at straws. Nevertheless, I persisted. 'I repeat, did you leave her alone?'

Maria Beton made a despairing gesture, as one humouring an idiot. 'I left her in the kitchen for perhaps five minutes while I picked some herbs for her from the garden. She wanted to try my recipe for braised venison, but had no fennel. We have plenty. But please! Do not go bothering Mistress Callender. You must see that she can know nothing.'

She seemed so disturbed by the fact that I might upset her neighbour that I let it go. All the same, I secretly determined to call on the goodwife when I left Master Sinclair's. But before doing that, I had a request to make.

'May I be permitted to see upstairs?' I asked. 'The bedchamber where the diary was found.' I saw a refusal hovering on her lips and added swiftly, 'Who knows but that another pair of eyes might discover something? I know you will tell me that you have searched the chamber thoroughly, but it may be that you have overlooked some clue.'

'How is that possible?' Her tone was contemptuous. 'Robert put the diary back in the cupboard. Indeed, I saw him do it myself, and also lock the door afterwards.' Then, suddenly, she altered her tone. 'But yes, why not? As you have said, two pairs of eyes may be better than one.'

She rose and signed to me to follow her. We left the solar and returned to the passage before mounting a narrow, twisting stair to an equally narrow landing with three doors leading from it. I could see why most people had preferred to have an outer staircase; the space was very cramped. Mistress Beton opened the door immediately ahead of us and ushered me into the front bedchamber with its bow window overhanging the street.

It was larger than I had expected, containing a canopied bed with hangings portraying the story of David and Bathsheba and covered with a gold and green quilt, a large clothes chest ranged along one wall, a rosewood bedside table with an inlaid marble top, a shelf supporting, as Maria Beton had said, various small pots, and, next to it, the cupboard, a lofty piece of furniture almost touching the ceiling. The housekeeper walked forward, took a key from the shelf and unlocked the door to it, flinging it wide.

'There you are! You may search it for yourself.'

I did not immediately accept her invitation, instead strolling over to the window and peering into the street below. I recognized the way our cavalcade had ridden earlier that same morning, but which was now alive with the usual business of the day; stalls set up at cach side of the road, the good-wives out marketing, baskets hooked over their arms, refuse being loaded on to carts but being replaced as fast as the inhabitants could drop even more filth in the gutters and, above all, important-looking messengers forcing a path through the crowds as they rode to and from the castle, laying about the local population with their batons. The shutters were standing open, so I was not only able to smell the pungent odours rising from the cobbles – the night's bodily voidings thrown from windows, rotting meat and vegetation – but also to hear the insults and imprecations that followed these self-important gentlemen as they went about their masters' business. (I couldn't understand exactly what was said, but the tone of voice and accompanying gestures needed no interpretation.)

I noticed that there was a narrow seat running round all three sides of the window, upholstered in dark green velvet. It was here, then, that Aline Sinclair had sat in preference to the downstairs solar, presumably watching for her lover. But when he had finally appeared, this man whose name began with J, walking either up or down the street, glancing towards the window where sat his murderously inclined young sweetheart, what happened next? As neither Rab nor Mistress Beton had previously known of his existence, he could not have been admitted to the house unless Aline was alone. I turned to my companion who still stood beside the open cupboard door.

'Was your mist . . . I mean your cousin often by herself in the house?' I asked.

'Of course there were occasions, yes.'

'Frequently?'

She shrugged. 'Often enough, I suppose. Robert had his own interests to attend to. I had food to buy. Robert likes his food,' she added with another slight smile. 'He is a fussy eater.'

I thought briefly of the conditions in the cells of Edinburgh Castle and grimaced.

'Where did you do your shopping? At these stalls?' And I gestured down towards the street.

She came across to my side then and peered out of the window, a little moue of distaste distorting her features.

'Sometimes, but not always. There are better stalls to be found in the Grassmarket.'

'Where's that?'

'A street or so away. Why are you asking me all these questions? Why do you wish to know these things?'

'I am trying to discover what opportunities Mistress Sinclair had to entertain a lover. Did you never feel sometimes, when you came home, that someone else had been in the house during your absence? That maybe, on occasions, that there was someone else present? Someone who perhaps was smuggled out later when you were busy in the kitchen or the garden?'

'No, never,' she answered, but then hesitated. 'At least, I have never thought about it until now. But . . . Yes, since you have put it into my mind, perhaps there were times when . . .'

'When?'

'When, as you say, a feeling that maybe something was not quite . . . quite right suggested itself to me. A creak of the stair . . . the closing of a door . . . Aline acting a little strangely.' She broke off, hand to her mouth, lost momentarily in contemplation of the past. But then, suddenly, she lifted her head and met my eyes squarely. 'But nothing to rouse my suspicions. Not at the time.'

I nodded, satisfied. I had established that there had been opportunities for Aline to entertain a lover. I moved back to the cupboard, Mistress Beton following me.

Rab Sinclair's description of its contents had been accurate enough. Although there were a number of shelves, all of the upper and lower ones were empty. There remained just three, at eye-level, on which reposed various objects. The first of these was a cedarwood box, containing, as I had been told, a few items of jewellery. On the next shelf down rested, rather endearingly, a collection of childhood toys, including a wooden doll, still dressed in all her finery of a gold brocade gown and white lawn coif, a whipping top and a box of coloured counters, each carved in the likeness of a letter of the alphabet. And, finally, on the third shelf reposed the wedding dress of white Damascus silk.

I lifted it and shook out its folds, hoping against hope that something might fall to the floor; three or four sheets of parchment tied together with red ribbon. But, of course, nothing did. I felt with my hand all round the shelf. I examined all the lower shelves and stood on a stool, fetched by Maria Beton from another chamber, to make certain that the diary had not been replaced by mistake on an upper one. It wasn't there. My companion flicked me a pitying glance; an I-told-you-so look.

But I hadn't finished yet. I turned towards the bed.

It was then that I saw the coverlet properly in all its glory of green and gold, a pattern of leaves and branches. And the central medallion from which all this verdure sprang, was the head of the Green Man.

Fourteen

I must have started or taken a step backwards because Mistress Beton asked sharply, 'What's the matter?'

'Matter? Why . . . n-nothing,' I stammered, feeling extremely foolish. 'Nothing.'

She followed the direction of my gaze and laughed, but without displaying any sign of real amusement.

'Oh, that medallion,' she said. 'Those eyes staring up at you! They are very lifelike, are they not? The embroidery is remarkable. In fact the whole coverlet is extraordinarily well done.' She came to stand beside me, stooping to smooth the quilt with one admiring hand.

'The Green Man,' I murmured. 'A strange conceit for a bed-covering.'

'Not for the St Clairs. Or Sinclairs, as the name goes nowadays.' She glanced sideways at me. 'The chapel at Roslin, built by the last Earl of Orkney forty years ago, is almost a shrine to the Green Man, there are so many heads carved into the wood and stonework. You have not been there?'

I shook my head. 'No. Although my lord of Albany was very anxious to make a detour to visit it as we approached Edinburgh the day before yesterday, but the Duke of Gloucester forbade it.' I looked round at the housekeeper as I spoke and realized, by the sudden lowering of her sandy lashes and the slight flush that stained her cheeks, that she had been regarding me with an intensity which, had I noticed it earlier, I might have found unnerving. However, I gave no sign of having marked anything untoward and asked, 'Does the Green Man have any special significance for the Sinclair family? I caught sight of a beam end, downstairs in the solar, which also showed his head.'

'Special significance?' she repeated, then paused a fraction of a second too long to make her subsequent denial truly convincing. 'No. I do not think so. The Green Man is, of course, a symbol of fertility, of renewal, but that is all.'

'Who embroidered this coverlet?' I enquired. 'Mistress Sinclair?'

'Aline?' Maria Beton was scornful. 'She was not a skilful enough needlewoman. No, it was made many years ago by her grandmother's mother. Or maybe, perhaps, by her mother. I do not know.' She hesitated, then said, 'May I ask why the Green Man seems to disturb you so much?'

It was my turn to be on the defensive.

'Disturb me? No, no! No such thing. As you say, those eyes are very lifelike; the embroidery superb. At a quick glance, it was as if someone were looking up at me. It gave me a bit of shock, that's all.' As I spoke, I laid hold of the quilt and began pulling it off the bed.

'What are you doing?' Mistress Beton demanded indignantly, clawing at my arm with restraining fingers.

I shook myself free.

'I'm stripping the bed,' I answered, 'just to make certain that the diary has not somehow or other become entangled with, or hidden in, the coverings.'

'How could that have happened?' Her tone was furious.

And she was quite right to be angry. I was not even clutching at straws now, but at thin air. I knew very well that I should find nothing, but continued just the same to strip the bed of all its furnishings, even shaking the curtains and climbing on the stool again to inspect the top of the canopy, simply in order to convince myself that I was doing something useful. The truth was that I had no more idea where this diary, so vital to proving Rab Sinclair's innocence, was concealed than I had when I entered the house half an hour and more ago.

I stared in frustration at the pile of bed linen, pillows and feather mattress heaped on the floor. I bent to heave the latter back into its wooden frame, but Maria Beton snapped, 'Leave it! I'll see to it later. When you've gone,' she added pointedly, and led the way downstairs again. She made no effort to return to the solar, but stood in the passageway, one hand on the latch of the street door, a foot tapping impatiently on the flagstones.

However, I made no immediate move to depart.

'Mistress,' I said imploringly, 'can you think of no one else besides your neighbour who entered this house on either Saturday or Sunday last?' A thought occurred to me. 'Did neither you nor Master Sinclair go to church on Sunday?'

But I was doomed to disappointment here as well.

'No.' She did not elaborate and I had no choice but to accept this brusque and unadorned negative. I sighed.

'Then I won't bother you any further, Mistress, except to thank you for your courtesy in receiving me. Meantime, if you do remember anything, or if the diary suddenly comes to light, you may send a message to the castle to any one of the Duke of Albany's servants.' I executed a brief bow. 'I'll relieve you of my presence and go to call on Mistress Callender.'

The housekeeper frowned and gestured angrily.

'Do you really need to bother the goodwife? She can tell you nothing. Nothing! She will not like to be questioned.'

I doubted this. My experience as a chapman had taught me that in general goodwives, bored and lonely by the middle of the day, were only too glad to talk to anyone who was not either a debt or a rent collector. Mistress Callender might, of course, prove to be an exception to the rule, but if that were indeed the case, I should have to rely on my well-practised charm. (I could hear Adela's mocking laughter echoing in my head.) It also struck me that Maria Beton's agitation on behalf of her neighbour was not consonant with her general air of self-containment and indifference to her fellow creatures. I was more than ever determined to call next door.

Mistress Callender was every bit as pleased to see me, and every bit as voluble as I had expected her to be. A little, bird-like woman of indeterminate age – she could have been anything between forty and sixty – with exceedingly bright blue eyes (an ugly, almost kingfisher blue), I was in possession of her life's history within quarter of an hour of entering the house.

She was the widow of a carpet-maker who had left her in comfortable, if not affluent, circumstances, sole owner of this comparatively recently built house close to the castle ward, and with sufficient savings to maintain it as a lady would wish. For she desired to assure me that she was indeed a lady, daughter of a gentleman and gentlewoman as I could probably tell by the fact that she spoke English with a fluency taught her at her mother's knee, and not the broad Scots dialect used by so many of her neighbours.

'For my mother, sir, was an Englishwoman. Only from just over the Border, it is true, but English nevertheless. And she never did hold with the Scots' tongue, even though my dear father would speak it occasionally, to her great distress. I must admit that I do use it myself now and then, but only when forced to.' She smiled, batting surprisingly thick eyelashes at me, suddenly coquettish. 'You, I think, are not from these parts?'

We were by this time seated in her upstairs parlour, for her house was one, like most of the others, with an outside staircase and I thought I had glimpsed a cow and a sheep peering at me from the ground floor casement, but I had been hurried past before I had time to be certain. The parlour was a comfortable chamber with cushions distributed the whole length of a settle pulled up in front of a small, but very welcome, fire burning on the hearth which was set, as modern hearths were, in the wall instead of in the centre of the room. Chimneys were now much in vogue, even here in the wild, barbarian north. The floor was covered not with the usual rushes but with a beautifully woven carpet in vivid greens and reds and yellows, a rare luxury even in the more decadent south and something I had never seen before except once, in a royal palace. I complimented my hostess on it.

She flushed with pleasure and suspended the story of her life to assure me that it was an example of her late husband's work and as fine an example of the carpet-maker's art as you would find anywhere in Scotland or, indeed, in England.

'For my dear Thomas said to me, "Annuciata," he said, "why should we not have the comfort of my trade as well as those whom God, in His wisdom, has seen fit to set over us?" And I agreed with him.'

I nodded vigorously to demonstrate that I, too, was in agreement with the late Master Callender's sentiments; then before

the widow could continue with her narrative, I proceeded to
enlarge on the brief explanation for my presence that I had
been able to give her when she first answered my knock at
her door. The realization, not perfectly understood until then,
that I was working on behalf of no less a personage than the
Duke of Albany – possibly her future king, as I was at pains
to emphasize – finally stemmed Mistress Callender's recital
of her own concerns and made her more than eager to cooper-
ate with anything I wished to know.

Not that she wouldn't have eventually got round to the
murder next door, for it was plainly the most exciting occurrence in her life so far, but from the moment she accepted
that I was an emissary of royalty – even renegade royalty –
she became even more loquacious than before.

'I was the one who found them, you know.' Her voice rose
a little as the full horror of that moment returned to her.
'They were in the kitchen. Aline was lying on her back on
the floor, and just for a moment I thought she'd slipped and
fallen and that Master Sinclair was trying to help her to her
feet. Then I saw the knife in his hand, dripping with blood.
Aline's blood.' Mistress Callender's tone was shrill now and
she had gone rather pale. There was no doubt that the memory
affected her deeply. 'He had stabbed her, right through the
heart.'

One of her hands fluttered towards me. I took and held it
in a sustaining clasp as I was plainly meant to do while
making sympathetic noises.

'It must have been a terrible moment for you. Why had
you gone in there?'

'I saw Aline and her brother return some while earlier and
thought it would be neighbourly to call and welcome her
home. Maria had told me on the Friday that she – Aline –
had gone to visit her aunt at Roslin, accompanied by Master
Buchanan, and would be away two or three nights. So I
waited until I saw her brother leave, and then I . . . I . . .'

I pressed her hand before releasing it. 'I understand,' I
said. 'And after that?'

She shook her head. 'I don't remember really. I think I
screamed and ran into the street . . . and went on screaming.
I recall a lot of people surrounding me, shouting and asking

questions, but I think, after that, I must have fainted, because the next thing I remember is being in a neighbour's house and her husband forcing whisky down my throat.' She shuddered delicately. 'Such a horrid drink.'

'You say that Mistress Beton had told you of Mistress Sinclair's visit to Roslin on the Friday. How . . . How did that come about?'

'I'd gone in there with a recipe for quince jelly that I'd promised Maria. She and I often exchange recipes. She's not quite so good a cook as I am, but she tries.'

I doubted if Mistress Beton would agree with this dictum, but held my peace.

So far everything Mistress Callender had told me agreed with the testimony of both Rab Sinclair and the housekeeper. It was time to probe a little deeper.

'Had you ever had reason to believe,' I asked, 'that Mistress Sinclair had a lover?'

My companion's extraordinary blue eyes opened to their widest extent.

'A lover?' she breathed. 'Aline?'

I nodded. The idea was plainly new to her.

'No, never,' she answered. 'She wouldn't. Not Aline. Why, she adored Robert.' She paused, then added slowly, 'But I would have said that he adored her, as well.'

'So why did he kill her?'

'He . . . He said it was an accident. Of course! I'd forgotten until this moment, but I can remember him shouting it after me as I ran from the kitchen.'

'Yet when you saw him stooping over Mistress Sinclair's body, that wasn't your impression?'

'No. I mean yes. Or do I? I don't know. Sir, you're confusing me.'

'I'm sorry.' I took her hand again and patted it. 'Think back, Mistress. Clear your mind of all I've said to you. Just think of what you saw when you entered the room.'

She stared at me, all coquetry forgotten. I could feel that she was trembling. After a moment or two, however, she answered quietly, 'I thought – I was sure – that he had killed her. But maybe I was wrong. Perhaps it was an accident . . .'

'Why did you think Master Sinclair had killed his wife?'
I insisted. 'You knew them both. You believed that they adored
one another. So why would you think, even for a moment,
that he'd murdered her?' She was silent, mulling over what
I had said. 'Did you,' I went on, 'hear raised voices as you
entered the Sinclairs' house?'

Somewhat to my surprise, she shook her head decidedly.
'No, all was quiet as far as I can recall.' Then, suddenly, she
gave a brief nod. 'Yes, I remember now. It was the expression on Robert's face as he looked down at her that made
me think he'd killed Aline.'

'What sort of expression? Can you describe it?'

Mistress Callender closed her eyes for a second or two,
frowning.

'I'm not sure,' she said at last, withdrawing her hand from
mine and pressing it to her forehead. 'In fact the more I
think about it, the less reason there seems to be for me to
have suspected what I did. I suppose it was simply shock
that prompted my behaviour. And yet . . .'

'Go on,' I urged. 'Try to picture the scene again in your
mind's eye. It's not so long ago, after all.'

Obediently she closed her eyes once more and concentrated hard, but finally gave a little sigh and shook her head.

'No. I'm sorry. But I do assure you, sir, that something at
the time made me take fright. And if you are saying that
Aline had taken a lover that would surely explain any untoward expression of Master Sinclair's that I might have seen.'
The full import of what I had been hinting at suddenly struck
her; and the bird-like features sharpened with curiosity. 'But
who says that Aline had taken a lover? Maria Beton? You
don't want to believe everything she tells you, that's for
certain. It's my opinion that she's in love with Robert Sinclair
herself. I wouldn't put it past her to have tried to poison his
mind against his wife.'

For a moment or two I debated with myself the wisdom
of putting my hostess in full possession of the facts, then
decided against it.

'It was Master Sinclair himself who told me of his suspicions,' I said, 'not Maria Beton. So I ask you again, have
you ever had any reason to think that it could be the case?

Have you ever seen Mistress Sinclair in the company of a younger man? A man who could have been her lover?'

My companion shook her head slowly and, I thought, rather regretfully.

'No. I can't say I have. Indeed, as I told you, I was certain that there was no one for Aline but Robert. Mind you, she could be very discreet; almost secretive in some respects. You never knew what she was really thinking. She was one of those people,' Mistress Callender added shrewdly, 'with whom you imagine that you are having an intimate conversation, only to discover later, when you think back, that you have done all the talking and that she has said very little. Yes . . . Yes, I suppose it is possible that she could have tired of Robert. He is older than she is – or, rather, was. Oh, how terrible to think that she has gone, and in such a dreadful way!'

Deciding that I had prised as much – or as little – from Mistress Callender as I was likely to get, and that she seemed as reluctant to offer me any refreshment as Maria Beton had been, I rose to my feet. I was beginning to utter my thanks, but she ignored them, still absorbed in thoughts of her own.

'Of course,' she began, looking up at me in puzzlement, obviously wondering why I was no longer sitting down, so I resumed my seat. 'Of course,' she went on, 'there hasn't been so much money these past three years. Perhaps Aline resented that. Robert had always been a very generous husband. More than generous some would say. She had grown used to having anything she wished for. Maybe she had become discontented. Maybe she had found a richer, younger man.'

'Why had money become short?' I asked.

'Oh, well –' my hostess lowered her voice conspiratorially – 'Robert Sinclair had been a companion and friend of the Earl of Mar. When Mar was accused of treason and died in Craigmillar Castle . . .' Her voice sank to a whisper and she moved closer to me as though afraid of being overheard, although there was no one else in the room. 'The rumour is that he was murdered on the king's orders because of his involvement with witchcraft. Certainly his brother, my lord Albany, thought he was done to death because he

fled to France, and a number of Mar's servants joined him
there.'

'I know, Mistress,' I said, somewhat impatiently. 'And they
have now all returned with the duke and are at present quar-
tered in the castle' Her mouth formed a little O of surprise.
'So how did the earl's death – or murder – affect Master
Sinclair?'

Once more the kingfisher-blue eyes widened and a bird-
like had clutched at my arm.

'He was forced to compound with the crown for being
Mar's friend. It was a choice between being accused of
treason and clapped in prison or paying an enormous fine.
So, naturally, he chose the latter.'

'Naturally,' I agreed. I remembered something Donald
Seton had said; that Rab Sinclair had not followed Albany
to France because he would not leave his young and lovely
wife. And now he had killed her, accidentally maybe, but
certainly she was dead. So the wheel of fortune turned.
'Would the lack of money really have bothered Mistress
Sinclair?'

Mistress Callender grimaced.

'I wouldn't go so far as to say that there was a lack of
money,' she demurred. 'The Sinclairs have always been a
wealthy family, even the cadet members of the clan. But
there was less to spend, that's for sure. But what Aline's
feelings were on the matter, I have no idea. Nor would she
have given the slightest hint. I've told you, she was not one
who discussed her affairs.'

'Mistress Beton dropped no word in your ear?'

'Alas!' Again came that regretful note. 'She always had
as little to say as Aline. But the setback in their fortunes
might explain . . . might be one reason . . . why Aline took a
lover. If she did.'

'You are certain that you never saw her in the company
of another man?' I persisted. 'You never noticed anyone
entering or leaving next door who might possibly have
fulfilled the role of a lover? There is no one you can
remember seeing who could fit that description? Please think
very carefully. Master Sinclair's life may depend on your
evidence.'

Mistress Callender's thin bosom swelled with importance, rather like a sparrow attempting to emulate a pouter pigeon I couldn't help thinking, and tried not to smile. But after considerable cogitation, she was forced, most reluctantly, to shake her head.

'No, I'm sorry. There's no one. I noticed people calling at the house now and again, of course, but they were tradesmen or friends of Robert. That isn't to say that your information is incorrect. Indeed, how could it be when you got it from Master Sinclair himself? There has to be a reason for him acting as he did. But,' she added with a note of asperity, 'I have better things to do with my time than to spend my days poking my nose into my neighbours' affairs.'

'Of course. Of course,' I murmured soothingly. 'It wasn't my intention to accuse you of any such thing. I just thought that an intelligent woman like yourself might have noticed something that wouldn't perhaps have seemed of any moment to you at the time, but which could, in the light of extra knowledge, assume some significance.' I got to my feet again and now my hostess rose with me. I held out my hand. 'Forgive me for bothering you, Mistress Callender. You have been most forbearing.'

She flushed a delicate pink. (She didn't look to have sufficient blood in her to turn red.)

'No, no!' she disclaimed, once more allowing one of her little hands to be engulfed by mine. 'I'm afraid I have been of no help whatsoever, and of no use to poor Master Sinclair. And if what you have confided in me is indeed true – and if it is, it is most shocking and throws an entirely different light upon events – then I regret exceedingly that I have been unable to assist in any way. What does Maria Beton say? You have questioned her, of course?'

I inclined my head. 'I came directly here from next door. However, I'm sorry to say that Mistress Beton had as little information to impart as your good self. There is one other person I must visit and that is Mistress Sinclair's brother, Master . . .'

'Buchanan,' my companion prompted.

I thanked her, adding, 'I believe he lives somewhere called the Grassmarket. Is that correct?'

'Yes, indeed,' Mistress Callender concurred with a vigorous nod of her head, and proceeded to give me instructions how to get there. 'Any one will tell you which is Master Buchanan's house.'

I thanked her yet again, but as I was turning to leave the room, she laid an anxious hand on my sleeve.

'Sir, what is the news at the castle? I know the English are in the city. I saw the great procession pass by early this morning. I know, too, that the king is a prisoner in Craigmillar Castle and that all his minions were hanged from Lauder Bridge on the order of his uncles. Is it true that Lord Albany is to be crowned in his place? And why was there no resistance? We were all expecting a siege.'

I patted her hand reassuringly.

'I don't believe, Mistress, that you have any cause to be alarmed. My own feeling is that neither side truly has the stomach for a fight. And to the best of my knowledge the Duke of Gloucester, as King Edward's representative and with full regal powers, is, at this very moment, at the negotiating table with the Scottish lords. More than that, I can't tell you, except that it's my opinion the English are as eager to go home as the Scots are to see the back of us. As to what will happen to King James, and, equally, as to my lord Albany replacing him, I have no idea. My own guess, for what it's worth, is that the duke is living in a fool's paradise and that his ambitions will be sacrificed for the surrender of Berwick and a return of the Princess Cicely's dowry.' I saw that this last piece of information puzzled her, but was myself sufficiently confused not to attempt an explanation. I simply added, 'But for the moment, His Grace of Albany is more concerned with proving his old friend, Rab Sinclair, innocent of the charge of murder than with promoting his claim to the crown.'

This reminded me that I had been strictly charged with urgency over this affair by my temporary lord and master as he had matters of his own to attend to. Although exactly what they were, and how they could possibly involve me, I again had no idea. But I did know that if a peace treaty with the Scots were to be hammered out speedily, I wanted to be ready to march south as soon as the English army was on the move. It behoved me, therefore, to try to solve this mystery of the missing diary and Master Sinclair's innocence as quickly as possible.

As Mistress Callender's outer door closed behind me, I realized that it was well into the afternoon, and, moreover that I was extremely thirsty, so I crossed the street and bought a drink from a stall opposite. As pies were also on sale, I had one of those as well, after some altercation with the owner about the English coin I had offered him. He also treated me to a harangue in broad Scots which, although I could understand little of it, left me in no doubt that all Sassenachs were the sons of the Devil and that hanging, drawing and quartering was far too good for them. Restraining my natural impulse to land the unmannerly brute a punch on the nose, I did the next best thing and smiled beatifically, thanking him copiously for his great compliments to the English race. (Mind you, I couldn't really blame him. My fellow countrymen can be arrogant bastards when in the company of foreigners, and the busy messengers riding between the castle and the abbey were running true to form, jostling the natives to one side and shouting at them to get out of the way.)

Suddenly, I found Maria Beton at my elbow. She had seen me from a window and had crossed the street to know what Mistress Callender might have said. She didn't put it into so many words, remarking merely that she had come to buy a pie for her supper, but once the purchase was made, she was in no hurry to leave.

'And what, if anything, did you learn from my neighbour?' she demanded truculently.

There was, however, an underlying note of anxiety in the question, and a tense frown between the eyes, that I found hard to explain. And when I answered that I had learned nothing of significance, she let out a breath almost like a sigh.

'Well, I cannot stand here all day,' she said and prepared to depart. Halfway across the street, she turned and came back. 'If my cousin's diary should come to light, I will immediately send word to the castle. You are returning there now?'

'Yes,' I lied. 'Almost at once.'

She nodded, and I watched her until she had once more disappeared inside the Sinclair house. Then, following Mistress Callender's instructions, I made my way to the Grassmarket to find John Buchanan.

Fifteen

While I had been in the Widow Callender's house, the sky had grown darker, and now I could see black clouds shouldering their way across the hill that rose up behind the abbey at the other end of the town. There was suddenly a sullen look to the afternoon and I noticed people pulling their caps more firmly about their ears, the itinerant street sellers beginning to look for the shelter of nearby doorways. As the last rags of sunlight disappeared, I realized yet again, if anything even more forcibly than before, how far I was from home; how alien this bleak, grey city seemed to me after the soft, rolling hills of my native west country and the small, smudged towns and villages that nestled in their folds. I was once more gripped by panic that I was trapped in some dream from which I could not awaken, and was caught for ever, like a fly in amber, unable to get free.

'Saint Margaret,' I prayed fervently. 'child of Wessex, come to my aid. Saint Dunstan, Saint Patrick, assist me now.'

I kept repeating the words foolishly, and after a while meaninglessly, as I walked blindly through the Lawnmarket, oblivious of the surrounding booths with their bales of chequered cloth, bright among the paler silks and linens, and the stalls where butter and cheese were displayed, until a man barged into me with a muttered oath of annoyance and brought me to my senses. Regardless of passers-by, I stood stock still and took a deep breath.

Gradually, peace and common sense returned. I felt comforted by some inner presence as I recollected that I was not alone, but in the company of several thousand fellow Englishmen, camped in the valley below the city, at the foot of the castle rock. Moreover, my friend (if I dared to think of him as such) and patron, the Duke of Gloucester, was only quarter of a mile distant, perhaps less, in the castle itself. What possible harm could come to me while I had his protection?

And yet I could not quite suppress all uneasiness. I kept remembering the strange warnings I had received from the 'Green Man' that suggested I was in some kind of danger; and from there my thoughts inevitably strayed to the depictions of this weird figure in Master Sinclair's house. Was there any connection, or was it just a coincidence, a part of the same nightmare?

I was growing morbid again. I drew a second deep breath, sent up another short prayer to my three Wessex saints and, with a sense of renewed purpose, strode forward through a maze of little alleys, described to me by Mistress Callender, into the Grassmarket.

It was a busy, thriving place which, again according to my erstwhile hostess, had been granted a royal charter five years previously to hold a weekly market, making it one of the busiest quarters of the city. But slicing through the friendlier, commercial smells of spices and fruit, vegetables and meat, together with the less exotic aromas of the open drains and cess-pits of the crowding houses, was the familiar, but gut-churning stench of rotting corpses. For the Grassmarket was also the place of execution, and the bodies of three felons, in various states of decomposition, were dangling from the gallows; never a pretty sight, but one from which, like most people, I had learned to avert my gaze with practised ease. Only the nostrils remained offended.

It had started to rain by now, not the torrential downpour promised earlier by the gathering clouds, but a steady pitter-pattering on the cobbles that washed away some of the dirt and excrement, yet not hard enough to send the scavenging wild dogs and cats scurrying for shelter.

I stopped at one of the stalls and asked for Master Buchanan's direction. Five minutes or so later, after a good deal of shouting and gesticulating, after sorting out which particular Master Buchanan was meant, and, finally, after being spat at for the bastard Sassenach I so obviously was, I found myself knocking at the door of a solid, two-storey house near the West Port.

My summons was answered by a little maid with a soiled apron over her grey worsted dress and a general air of untidiness that suggested there was no mistress of the establishment, only a bachelor master. I had not enquired whether John Buchanan were married or no, but my guess was proved to be correct when I was at last shown into his presence by the flustered young girl who had failed to understand a word that I was saying. Only my continued shouts of 'Master Buchanan!' had eventually produced the desired result.

The man who rose to greet me in the front, downstairs parlour, from behind a table littered with papers, was clad in funereal black from neck to toe and wore a large and ostentatious mourning ring on one of his fingers. I judged him to be around thirty years of age, blue-eyed, with shoulder-length brown hair; good-looking without being handsome. In short, the sort of man who would be passed in the street every day of the week without exciting a great deal of notice.

'Master Buchanan! Sir!' I bowed, but not too low. 'Do you speak English?'

He raised thin eyebrows. 'Tolerably well. Are you one of our English conquerors?' There was a slight sneer as he said it. I was so patently not someone of any great importance, but, equally obviously, I was one of the hated enemy, so what was I doing there?

I hastened to explain, making my story as brief as clarity would allow for my own sake as well as his. It was the third time I had repeated it that day. He heard me out in a frowning silence that grew more oppressive by the minute and which lasted for some thirty or so seconds after I had finished speaking.

'So!' he said at last. 'My lord Albany's back, is he? And in the company of his country's enemies, the treacherous bastard! And if that's not enough, he wants to prove that murdering brother-in-law of mine innocent of Aline's killing. A secret diary you say? What sort of lying nonsense is this? A secret diary that tells of a secret lover?' He brought his fist slamming down on the table top, making the papers jump, a few sliding over the edge on to the floor. I would have stooped to pick them up, but he yelled at me to let them alone. He was working himself up into a fine lather of rage, spittle flecking his lips. 'Miserable cur!' I wasn't sure whether he was referring to me, Albany or Master Sinclair. Perhaps it was meant for all three of us. Master Buchanan didn't pause to elucidate, raging on, 'My poor sister never had eyes but for one man, and that was her husband. The fool adored him! Worshipped him! And don't tell me it was mutual!' I hadn't been about to utter a word. 'That . . . That . . . That dung-beetle, that piece of horse-shit, that goose-turd never adored or worshipped anyone but himself!'

He was slavering at the mouth now and I began to be afraid that he was having a fit. I pushed him gently back into his chair and looked around for a wine jug. Unable to see one, I went in search of the little maid, running her to earth in the kitchen, and told her to bring some wine and two beakers to the parlour. I realized that I was in need of some refreshment myself.

Master Buchanan was quieter now, slumped forward, one elbow resting on the table and supporting his chin. Tears were coursing down his cheeks and his whole body was racked by sobs. I suddenly felt uncomfortable; an intruder on another person's private grief.

It did strike me, though, that his grief seemed somewhat excessive, and yet what right had I to think so? I knew little of grieving. My father had been killed when I was four years old, following a fall from the nave roof of Wells Cathedral. I had shed a few dutiful tears when my mother died, but her death had touched me no more deeply than had the subsequent death in childbed of my first wife, my daughter Elizabeth's mother, Lillis Walker. I tried to conjure up how I would feel if something were to happen to Adela or one of the children and began to understand in some small measure the agony of loss. Perhaps I was being too severe.

The maid came in with a tarnished silver jug and beakers on an equally tarnished silver tray which she put down on the table so carelessly that some of the wine slopped over, staining one or two of the documents lying scattered around. Even this didn't rouse Master Buchanan to a protest, so I poured and handed him a beaker of wine, at the same time adjuring him to pull himself together.

'Your sorrow undoubtedly does you credit,' I remarked sententiously, 'but it won't help to discover the truth about your sister's death.'

'We know the truth about my sister's death,' he answered in a voice harsh with suppressed anger. 'Rab killed her.'

'But why?' I demanded. 'Have you asked yourself that? Everyone seems to be of the opinion that he adored her. So why would he take a knife to her if that were true? Unless, of course, his explanation of what happened is the correct one.'

John Buchanan said something under his breath. I couldn't quite catch the words but they sounded vicious. His fingers curled around the beaker he was holding, and I thought for a moment that he was going to throw its contents in my face, but he evidently thought better of such a gesture and swallowed the wine in three quick gulps. He replaced the empty beaker on the tray and sat up, wiping his mouth and the rest of his face on the back of his hand.

It had occurred to me, while I was watching him, to wonder if he had had an incestuous relationship with his sister. His name, after all, began with the letter J and it would explain why Aline's lover seemed to have been invisible to both Mistress Callender and Maria Beton, and why no suspicion of infidelity had been aroused in Master Sinclair's mind. What could be more natural than for her to be constantly in the company of her brother? It was not something that I wanted to believe. Like sodomy, incest was a sin punishable by death, but such things were not unknown, and were practised more often than many people imagined. It might also explain other things, like Aline's reluctance to name her lover and Master Buchanan's excessive grief.

But almost immediately, I began to feel ashamed of myself for harbouring any such thoughts. Particularly when he rounded on me with a face like thunder, almost as if he knew what I had been thinking.

'You ask me why Rab killed my sister?' he said. 'I'll tell you if you're really serious about discovering the truth. He killed her and then cooked up this cock-and-bull story of a secret diary and secret lover because he's the one who's playing her false with that housekeeper of theirs. Rab wanted Aline dead, not the other way around.'

There was a moment's sheer, astonished silence on my part before I burst out laughing.

'Mistress Beton?' I gasped. 'No! No, I don't believe it!'

And I didn't believe it. It was not simply that Maria Beton was a plain woman and Rab Sinclair a handsome man. (Well, he would be handsome enough when he was not pinched with fear and grimed from rough handling by his prison guards.) In my time, I have encountered plenty of such mismatched couples where I would have thought it almost impossible for either the man or the woman to have chosen such an unlikely partner. But always the plainer of the two had some obvious attraction; a beautiful voice perhaps, a lovely smile, fascinating eyes or, most potent of all, an indefinable promise of giving pleasure in bed. But as far as I could tell, Maria Beton had none of those attributes. She had struck me as a peculiarly charmless woman.

John Buchanan slapped the arm of his chair.

'You may laugh,' he snapped, 'but I assure you that it's true.'

'Do you have proof?' I asked.

He looked uncomfortable. 'If you mean have I seen them kissing or holding hands or giving any outward signs of affection, then I suppose the answer must be no. But once or twice when I've been visiting Aline, I've caught them whispering together in corners, and breaking off hurriedly – guiltily, more like – as soon as they've become aware of my presence. And not only in the house. On two occasions at least I've seen them from my window here, deep in conversation on the other side of the street.'

I shrugged. I could see nothing extraordinary in a man being caught conversing with his housekeeper. Indeed, it seemed a perfectly normal occurrence, and I suspected that Master Buchanan was reading more into what was an entirely acceptable situation in order to convince himself of his sister's innocence and his brother-in-law's guilt. I therefore decided that no advantage could be gained by pursuing this line of enquiry and abruptly changed the subject, asking, 'When you and Mistress Sinclair returned home on Monday, after visiting your aunt, were you and she alone at any point in the house?'

I thought he would be bound to follow the drift of my questioning and avoid the trap, but he replied angrily, 'Yes. Neither of them were there to greet her, although they knew to expect us. You might have thought that if Rab were as fond of my sister as he professed to be, and as everyone considered him, he would have been waiting to welcome her back after three days deprived of her company. But some time elapsed before he put in an appearance, and longer again before Maria Beton came in. Her excuse was that she'd been in the garden picking herbs for some new dish she was making for supper. Something of that sort. I didn't stop to hear all of their reasons for their absence. I wanted to get home. My nag was tired after the journey and needed his stable. So I exchanged a brief word with Rab and left.' He took a great gulp of air and tears gathered again in the corners of his eyes. 'Not knowing,' he added in a shaking voice, 'that that was the last time I was to see my dear sister alive.'

'I'm sorry,' I said mechanically, but my thoughts were otherwise occupied.

If John Buchanan and Aline Sinclair had indeed had some time alone together in the Sinclair house, could she not have passed the diary to him for safekeeping? It would have been the work of only a few minutes for her to run upstairs – so simple with that indoor staircase – unlock the cupboard and bring it down. If he was already aware of its contents for whatever reason, her lover or her confidant, he could have slipped it beneath his travelling cloak and taken it away with him. I found myself glancing around the room, half expecting to see the diary carelessly dropped in a corner or amidst the welter of papers littering the table.

I breathed deeply and told myself not to be so foolish. If what I suspected was indeed the truth, the foolishly incriminating diary had probably been destroyed by now. But then a niggling doubt raised its unwelcome head. Why would Aline suddenly have taken fright and passed her confession of intent to murder to her brother? She knew nothing of what had happened while she had been away. So what would have been the reason for her sudden panic?

'Why are you staring around like that?' my companion asked aggressively. 'What are you looking for?' I didn't know what to answer and stood there, appearing no doubt more than a little foolish, trying to conjure up a suitable reply. But my companion, who proved to be sharper than I had given him credit for, exclaimed indignantly, 'You're thinking that Aline might have given the diary to me, aren't you? That's what those questions were about. To find out if we were alone; if Aline had time to pass the wretched thing to me?' He jumped up from his chair, bringing his fist crashing down on the table top for a second time. (That right hand of his was taking a lot of unnecessary punishment. He would have some bruises, I reckoned, in the morning.) 'Can't you understand, you great ungainly Sassenach, that there never was, never has been, a diary? I'd stake my life on it! I told you! It's something Rab's thought up to explain his murder of my sister!'

I had to admit to myself that it was a possibility that had begun to nudge at the edges of my own mind, but as yet I could see no alternative reason for Rab Sinclair wanting to kill his wife. The one offered by Master Buchanan I dismissed. I didn't know why – as I've said, I'd known some very strange matings and couplings in my life – but some deep-rooted instinct told me that, in this instance, it was not the case. And I have, to a large extent, learned to trust that instinct. So, if Master Sinclair were lying, I had yet to discover his purpose.

Nevertheless, I had a nagging feeling that I was missing a vital clue; that I had been told something of significance that I had ignored, that had not made the impact on my consciousness that it should have done. But the more I struggled to remember what it was, the more it eluded me.

'Well, say something!' John Buchanan barked. 'Don't just stand there, staring, like a stuffed duck!'

I have been called some names in my time, most of them unrepeatable, but to be likened to a duck (and a stuffed one at that) insulted me beyond measure. I opened my mouth to retaliate in kind, but instead, to my own great surprise, as well as that of my host, I heard myself ask, 'What do you know of the Green Man?'

'What?' Master Buchanan was regarding me in astonishment at a question that seemed to him to be a total irrelevancy. His bewilderment was not to be wondered at. I was confused myself.

'The Green Man,' I repeated feebly.

'The Green Man?'

'Yes.'

His face suffused with colour. He was getting angrier by the minute.

'Is this a joke?' he demanded scathingly. 'And if not, what does the Green Man have to do with my sister and this diary that she is supposed to have written?'

'Nothing really. At least . . .' I hesitated. The thought had come from somewhere and it suddenly occurred to me that God might be giving me a nudge. 'It's just . . . It's just that Mistress Beton told me that the Green Man has a particular significance for the Sinclair family. The coverlet on your sister's bed has an embroidered medallion of the Green Man as its centrepiece; a coverlet made by your great-grandmother or, possibly, great-great-grandmother Sinclair. You are related to your brother-in-law, I believe, by blood as well as marriage?'

John Buchanan had sunk back into his chair, a frown between his brows.

'Yes,' he admitted, still puzzled. 'Both Aline and I are – were . . .' He broke off with a choking sob that half-stifled him for a second or two, but then made an effort to pull himself together and continued, 'I have Sinclair blood in me, yes. So, therefore, did Aline. But what's this nonsense about the Green Man? I know his effigy, of course. It's carved in a great many places.'

I nodded. 'Robert Sinclair even has it carved on a beam-end in the back parlour of his house. Have you never noticed it?'

The frown deepened. 'No, I can't say that I have.'

'Well it's there.'

I decided at this point that I'd had enough of standing up and that if my host wasn't prepared to invite me to sit down, I would find my own seat. So I hooked one leg over the edge of the table and eased my buttocks on top of the litter

of papers, ignoring his indignant protest. I pushed the tray
out of the way, slopping a little more of the wine in the
process.

Master Buchanan furiously mopped up the mess with his
sleeve, eyeing me malevolently as he did so.

Before he could say anything, however, I went on, 'Mistress
Beton also told me that the chapel at this village where your
aunt lives – Roslin is it? – the chapel built forty years ago
by one of your ancestors – is filled with images of the Green
Man.'

'Oh, that place!' he said, his annoyance suddenly evapor-
ating. He shivered. 'It's a very strange building. Very strange
indeed. Do you know it?'

I pointed out politely that I wouldn't be asking about it if
I did.

'I'm a stranger to Scotland,' I said, and was about to add
that that was how I hoped matters would stay; that I never
wanted to come back to this cold northern land with its bleak
hills, its seemingly never-ending vistas of moorland, its dark,
brooding forests and the winds that blustered in from the
wild North Sea. Yet even as I spoke, other pictures crowded
my mind; a grassy hollow clouded with harebells and sweet-
smelling thyme; the long, startled cry of a curlew as the bird
beat its way skyward with a whisper and rush of wings; a
breeze that silvered the heather and rippled the face of a
little black tarn; and, far away in some high glen, a string
of goblin figures as a herdsman took his goats and cattle to
the shelter of his hut for the night, sleeping, curled for
warmth, against their stinking hides. I realized then that it
was a country that could come back to haunt the soul.

'Tell me about this chapel at Roslin,' I invited.

'Why? What has it to do with my sister and that murdering
husband of hers?'

'I'm just curious. My lord Albany was so anxious to turn
aside to visit it on our journey to Edinburgh that it excited
my interest. There's no other reason.'

John Buchanan shrugged like one humouring an idiot.

'It was built about forty years ago,' he said, 'maybe not
so long, by William Sinclair, last Earl of Orkney. In fact, I
think I'm right in saying that it was never finished. Only the

choir and part of the transepts were completed. A lot of the local inhabitants don't like it. Won't go near the place.'

'Why not?'

'It's the carvings. The place is full of them. God alone knows what stonemasons William employed, but whoever they were, they knew how to work stone. They carved it like it was butter. Mind you, some people hold that it's all the work of the Devil. They say that many of the images aren't even Christian. Some are pagan like the Green Man, the ancient symbol of death and rebirth, and he's everywhere you look. My aunt reckons there must be sixty or more carvings of him in the choir alone. Swears she's counted 'em. Mind you, I wouldn't place too much reliance on anything she told me. She's getting on a bit now. Wanders in her mind occasionally. I've also heard it said by those who claim to know about such things that some of the symbols are Judaic. Then there's the great pillar. I've never seen anything like the carving on that. There's a story about it.'

My companion was warming now to his theme, his grief for his sister's death temporarily forgotten. If I'd achieved nothing else, I had at least done that much for him. He went on, 'They say the master mason let his apprentice carve it. Didn't think he'd make much of a fist of it, I suppose. Thought he'd have a laugh at the poor lad's expense and then show him how it ought to be done. He went away for a few days, but when he came back and saw this work of art, he was so jealous that he clubbed the lad on the head with his mallet and killed him.'

'A gruesome little tale,' I commented. 'What happened to the master mason?'

Once more, John Buchanan hunched his shoulders. 'I don't know. And in any case, it's only a story. There are others. My aunt swears the pillar is modelled on one that supported an inner porch of King Solomon's Temple, and that the architect of that temple, Hiram Abif, was also killed by a blow to the head. It was a kind of ritual murder, she says. A blood sacrifice, if you like, to appease the wrath of God.'

There was silence for a moment and I realized that I had strayed a long way from my reason for being there, in that

house in the Grassmarket. Ask a silly question and you get
nothing but a digression; a lot of information which, no
matter how interesting it might be, is of no use at all. If it
had been God who nudged me to ask it, then He was playing
tricks; enjoying a joke at my expense. (I wouldn't put it past
Him.)

I cleared my throat and stood upright again, more papers
floating to the ground as I lifted my leg clear of the table.
I gave one last look around.

'I'm sorry to have intruded on your time, Master
Buchanan,' I said reluctantly. 'And your grief,' I added as an
afterthought.

'If you are indeed acting on the Duke of Albany's orders,
as you say, then I understand that you had no choice. But I
assure you, and you may tell the duke that I said so, there
is no need to look further than my brother-in-law and his
paramour, Maria Beton, for the reason for my sister's death.
All this talk of the discovery of a secret diary with its plans
for Rab's murder and details of a secret lover, is so much
nonsense. Just so many lies. It's something that the pair of
them have concocted together. That diary will never be found,
mark my words.'

'And if it is?'

He made no answer, but shook his head.

There was nothing more I could usefully say or do. Aline
Sinclair had had both the time and opportunity to pass the
diary to her brother on Monday, the day they both returned
from Roslin. But if John Buchanan had it and it was hidden
somewhere in his house, there was no way I could search
for it. If Albany wanted the place ransacked, he would have
to arrange the matter himself.

But there was also the possibility that the diary had been
destroyed. In John Buchanan's shoes, that is what I would
have done. However shocked – or not – he had been by his
sister's revelations, that would have been the sensible course
to follow, even had she not been murdered. And if he had
indeed been her lover, he must have been appalled to realize
that she had committed her thoughts and plans to paper. I
could imagine him cursing the stupidity of womankind.
Perhaps, after all, this case would never be resolved. Rab

Sinclair would be duly executed for his wife's murder and my lord Albany would have to reconcile himself to losing a valued friend.

I said my farewells and left.

Sixteen

It had stopped raining, but the atmosphere was still heavy and overcast. Above the distant crag, the sky was illumined, every now and then, with brief flashes of lightning. The absence of any subsequent clap of thunder suggested that whatever new storm was brewing was as yet some way away, but the effect was unsettling, like waiting for a threatened danger that failed to arrive.

I reckoned that by now the afternoon was almost over. Indeed, judging by my ravenous hunger and the gurgling of my empty belly I guessed it must be nearly suppertime. It was my cue to return to the castle and report such progress as I had made. Which wasn't much. I didn't fool myself that Albany would be pleased. People always expected miracles and instant solutions. They could never understand why it took time and patience to put a picture together, piece by piece.

I directed my footsteps back the way I had come, across the Grassmarket and through the maze of alleys connecting it to the Lawnmarket and so to the long, uphill thoroughfare that was the heart of the city, linking the abbey at one end to the castle at the other. It was not yet dusk, nor would be for some hours, but there was already a sense of traders at least beginning to think of packing up, locking their stalls for the night and sliding away home or to whatever dens of vice and iniquity they were patronizing that particular evening; an end of the day feeling that told me it was probably even later than I had thought.

I was within an easy few paces of my objective – I could see the sentries on guard at the castle gates quite plainly – when I was seized roughly from behind by an arm pinned across my throat and forced back against the nearest wall.

A blast of bad breath, redolent of decaying teeth and garlic, caught me full in the face as my assailant removed his arm from my windpipe and placed his hands on my shoulders, making it impossible for me to move until such time as I recovered my breath. A square, pugnacious face, bristling with a red beard and topped by a thatch of the same-coloured hair, was thrust up against mine, while two extremely blue eyes indicated that their owner was contemplating violence of a very unpleasant kind.

A stream of rapid Scots assaulted my ears and my head was banged against the wall with a brutality that caused everything to go out of focus for several unnerving seconds. A swarm of very angry bees seemed to have taken up residence inside my ears. As another torrent of unintelligible language smote them, I did the only thing possible in the circumstances: I brought up my right knee with all the force of which I was capable and slammed it into those parts which my assailant had possibly been intending to put to good use that evening. (I had noticed on my travels that there was no shortage of brothels in the city.) He gave a yell, dropped his hands and doubled over, clutching the afflicted member. But the screech he set up had attracted the attention of other passers-by who, until then, had presumably thought the assault on me nothing more than a normal, everyday pocket-picking. Now, however, they perceived by the language with which I was berating my attacker that I was English, one of the hated Sassenachs whose uninvited presence was besmirching their streets. Immediately half a dozen stalwart citizens hurried to the aid of one of their own.

I backed up against the wall again, bunched my fists and waited. I wasn't prepared to go down without a fight, but neither did I delude myself that I was in anything but the tightest of tight places, or that I might not get out of it alive. The six men, already joined by others who had crossed the street to see what was going on, were advancing slowly, grins of anticipation lighting their ugly faces. They were enjoying prolonging my agony. My original enemy had been kicked unceremoniously out of the way, as he continued to nurse himself where it hurt and spit expletives at me. They sounded wonderfully venomous; I just wished I knew what they meant.

I shifted my stance against the wall and watched to see who would land the first blow. My guess was that it would come from the big man in the middle, but in the end it was a little runt of a fellow with a broken nose who dodged in under my guard and punched me in the chest. My height stood me in good stead: he was too short to reach any higher and I returned his punch with interest, giving him a bloody nose. It was no hit to boast about, but I had drawn blood and suddenly the grins were wiped from my opponents' lips as the general mood became darker. This was no longer a street brawl but a settlement of accounts with the age-old enemy from across the Border. I felt my stomach muscles tighten and fought down the impulse to retch. I knew now that this was definitely going to be a fight to the death. And there was no doubt in anyone's mind whose death it would be. Mine.

I clenched my fists even tighter and thought fleetingly of Adela and the children. At the same time, I reflected in a detached sort of way how stupid it was to be ending my life in a foreign street in a foreign country and all because of an incident that had blown up out of a clear blue sky (in a manner of speaking) without any rhyme or reason. If I had just allowed the first man take whatever he could find – and he wouldn't have found much: Albany had forgotten to pay me lately – instead of playing the hero, I should not now be facing this hostile crowd and praying for a miracle. I closed my eyes, steeling myself for the next blow . . .

Nothing happened except that a furious voice yelled a string of words amongst which I just managed to make out the duke's name and also those of his half-uncles, Atholl and Buchan; and on opening my eyes again, I saw Donald Seton and Murdo MacGregor pushing their way through my would-be assailants and laying about them with drawn swords. At the sight of naked steel, the mob dispersed hurriedly, if not quietly, most of them exchanging insults (well, I presumed they were insults: they certainly didn't sound like invitations to supper) with my rescuers.

I gasped my thanks as I straightened my clothing, trying to appear more nonchalant than I felt.

'I never thought I should be so glad to see you two,' I admitted somewhat ungraciously.

Murdo gave a sardonic grin but said nothing. Donald, on the other hand, was angrily berating my original assailant who was still huddled on the ground, rocking to and fro, continuing to nurse those parts I had damaged and muttering sullenly in response to this tongue-lashing.

'I don't know who he is,' I said. 'He just came at me out of the blue. A pickpocket, I suppose.'

Donald gave the poor wretch a final kick for good measure and turned to me.

'The fool's name is Jared Lockhart and he's Robert Sinclair's man. He must have learned that you've been making enquiries about his master and decided to warn you off.' He regarded me a little contemptuously. 'Don't you know better than to go about a city like this unarmed? And you an Englishman into the bargain.'

'I've never been issued with any arms,' I pointed out savagely. 'Not even a staff. Blame my lord Albany who's kept me dancing attendance on him like a glorified chamberer.'

They both sniggered at that, but then Donald Seton pulled a long-bladed dagger from his belt and tossed it to me.

'Here! Borrow this!'

Murdo let out a growl of protest, but his companion quelled his objections with a frown.

'Roger can't go around Edinburgh without protection,' he said shortly. 'He could have been killed back there if we hadn't arrived on the scene.' He added something else in Scots to which Murdo shrugged and pulled down the corners of his mouth, but he made no further protest.

We were by now inside the castle precincts and ascending the steep staircase by the Portcullis Gate towards the cluster of buildings on the summit.

'And have you discovered anything to Master Sinclair's advantage?' Donald asked as we paused at the top to catch our breath. Even three fit men like ourselves found the climb tiring. Heaven alone knew how armoured men had coped with it during an assault. (Except that they probably wouldn't have tried. They'd have sent in the lightly clad, expendable foot soldiers to clear their path.)

As I took in the astonishing view from that eagle's eyrie, I shook my head. 'Not as much as my lord duke would no doubt like,' I answered and sniffed. 'Is that supper I can smell? I'm ravenous.'

Donald grinned and clapped me on the back.

'Hungry, eh?' I nodded emphatically. 'I'm afraid you'll have to wait until you've seen the duke. I was told to bring you straight to him as soon as we'd found you. He was getting worried about you, Roger. He'd expected to hear from you sooner, my friend.'

I snorted angrily. Exactly as I had thought! As always, I was being asked to work miracles.

'Take me to him, then,' I said. 'He might as well know the worst as soon as possible. Where is he?'

Donald glanced at Murdo with a lift of his eyebrows. The other man responded with a typical hunching of his shoulders, but at least, and most unusually, he had the courtesy to speak in English for my benefit.

'He was in the Council Chamber when he sent me to fetch you. Maybe he's still there. Try it first. If he isn't, he's probably gone to his quarters.' The squire gave a mirthless smile. 'I understand there's to be a "friendly" banquet tonight to set the seal on whatever agreements have been reached today and to put everyone in a good mood for further negotiations tomorrow.'

Donald drew in his breath sharply through clenched teeth.

'That doesn't augur well for my lord's hopes, then.' Both men fell silent for a moment, their thoughts obviously elsewhere, before Donald continued, 'We'd better go and find him, Roger, and get it over with. We'll try the Council Chamber first.'

We made our way towards a building in the lee of a tower which I had heard referred to as David's Tower, and entered by a thick, iron-studded door into an ante-chamber hung with tapestries depicting scenes in the lives – or so I assumed – of ancient kings. Scenes of mayhem and murder nudged those of pomp and splendour, all glowing with rich reds and yellows, blues and greens, an adornment to any walls in any palace in Europe. I don't know why it surprised me to see them here, in Scotland, except that I had always presumed

it to be a poverty-stricken land with an equally poverty-stricken court. A typically English presumption I suppose. (Nevertheless, it was a poor country, and it had been hit even harder than our own northern shires by the recent months of atrocious weather.)

A second door at the far end of the room stood slightly ajar, and from behind it, Albany's voice could be heard raised in protest.

'He's still here,' Donald Seton muttered in my ear. 'Wait for him to come out and tell him your news. If any,' he added with a mocking grin. 'I'm off to my supper before all the best of the food gets taken. There are a lot of us to be fed, what with the castle's normal inhabitants and all the visiting retainers. And they're a greedy bunch. I'd advise you to come along as soon as you can.'

I thanked him acidly for his concern. He laughed, clapped me on the shoulder a second time and departed, his opening and shutting of the outer door creating a draught that lifted the tapestries, making the woven figures seemingly come alive. It was then that I noticed a young page asleep on a stool in one corner, wearing the blue and murrey livery of the Duke of Gloucester. Prince Richard must also still be in the Council Chamber, and was most likely the person to whom Albany was talking.

I edged a little closer to the open inner door and cautiously eased it a fraction wider with my foot. This gave me a view of the right-hand side of the room as I faced it; part of a table and a row of cushioned chairs and stools ranged alongside, some of the latter partially pushed back as their occupants had left them. Another set of glowing tapestries adorned the walls that I could see, and candlelight spilled across the table top, adding its smoky radiance to the watery daylight seeping in from a window at the far end of the chamber.

As I watched, carefully concealed in the shadow of the half-open door, the Duke of Gloucester walked into view. His thin frame was richly, but not sumptuously dressed; and a light breastplate, although not one he would wear into battle, plainly hinted that the recent meeting was no mere social gathering of neighbouring princes, but a situation that could still flare into open war. All the same, he had lost the careworn frown that had marred his handsome features of late, and the narrow, mobile mouth had a more contented tilt to the corners. But for all that, he had not shed those little nervous tricks of fiddling with the hilt of his dagger, twisting the rings on his fingers or smoothing his left sleeve with the long, sensitive fingers of his right hand. People who knew him well – or who knew people who knew him well, like Timothy Plummer – said he was a poor sleeper, very often troubled by nightmares. And I suppose, given the history of his very nearly thirty years, that was hardly surprising. He had been the prop and stay of his brother's throne for the past two decades, saddled with responsibility from a horrifyingly early age, and with a hatred of his Woodville in-laws that had to be continually suppressed. Given such circumstances, I felt that I would, myself, have grown a little twitchy.

He was speaking to someone on the other side of the table, out of my line of vision, but who, I knew, must be Albany. As far as I could make out, they were alone in the room.

'I have done my best for you, Cousin.' He threw out his arms. 'You know that! You must have heard me, but they won't accept you as king.'

'You and Edward promised—' Albany began hotly in that whining voice that always made him sound like a thwarted child.

'I know what we promised,' my lord Gloucester interrupted. 'But things haven't gone according to plan. There's been no battle, no conquest! We aren't in a position to impose our will. Your brother isn't dead. He's a prisoner, it's true, but he isn't *our* prisoner. And your uncles and the other lords are willing to make peace on honourable terms. But they won't have you as king.'

Albany moved round the top of the table so that I could just see him, illumined by the light from the window. His face was nothing but a pale oval, but I could easily picture its petulant expression.

'Then let's withdraw,' he urged, banging his fist on the back of the nearest chair. 'Let's withdraw on some pretext or another and then lay siege to the place.'

'You think that would be honourable?' Gloucester's tone was mocking. Albany shrugged. The candlelight shimmered

across his satin sleeves, turning the scarlet to plum. Prince
Richard continued, his voice persuasive, almost wheedling,
'You have been offered a great position, Cousin. Lieutenant
General of Scotland.'

'Lieutenant General!' Albany exclaimed scathingly. 'Is that
any substitute for a crown?'

Gloucester made an impatient movement with his arm.
'You heard your countrymen yourself. They refuse to force
your brother's abdication. It's true, I grant you, that many
of them don't like him; don't trust him—'

'But they dislike and mistrust me more, is that it?' Albany
gave a sour laugh.

'They won't dethrone an anointed king.'

'And you agree with them!' The accusation sounded
like a statement, not a question. 'What about your own
Richard II?'

The Duke of Gloucester smiled. 'You choose your example
badly, Alexander. We of the House of York spent decades
fighting for the succession that was rightfully ours. You can't
accuse me of approving of the deposing of a crowned and
God-anointed king.'

'What hypocrisy,' Albany snarled. 'You and Edward were
willing enough to try to depose James by killing him in
battle.'

'That would have been an indication of God's will,'
Gloucester replied sternly. 'But now that God has shown
his will in a different way, it is not for me or any man to
dispute it.'

'What you really mean is that you and your brother are
going to get all you want, all you set out to get – the return
of Cicely's dowry and the surrender of Berwick – without
having to fight for it.' Albany's voice rose shrilly.

'If lives are saved on both sides, what is there to condemn
in that?'

'You think God condones broken promises?'

'Not if they are made under oath, no. But neither Edward
nor I swore to make you King of Scotland. Such a contin-
gency always depended on the outcome of the invasion.'

'You fooled me!'

'No, Cousin.' Gloucester moved restlessly, holding out a

hand to Albany, the rings glittering on his fingers. 'Come, my dear fellow, be friends! Take what has been offered you. A prime position in the government of Scotland. Lieutenant General is a generous offer. Much more than might have been expected in the circumstances, you must agree.'

'And what about my brother, Mar? Is his death to go unavenged?'

Duke Richard put up a hand and brushed aside a lock of hair that had strayed across his forehead. I was struck anew how dark it was – in some lights almost black – and how olive-coloured his skin compared to the king and his other brother, the late Duke of Clarence. They were tall and fair-haired, and in the king's case, blue-eyed (although now I came to picture him, perhaps George had been less of a blond giant than Edward). Nevilles both, whereas Richard favoured his father. Or, at least, so said people who could remember the long-dead Duke of York.

Gloucester spoke wearily, tiring of an argument he must by now have realized he was unlikely to win. 'You have no proof that John was murdered.'

'Of course he was murdered! He was accused of witchcraft. James wouldn't tolerate that.' Albany laughed. 'He's almost as pious as you are, Cousin.'

'You speak as if piety's something to be deplored.'

'Perhaps it is. It depends on your gods.'

'You're close to blasphemy, Alexander. Consider what you're saying, man!'

Albany hesitated for a moment as though he would argue further, but then seemed to think better of it and flung out his hands in a conciliatory gesture.

'Forgive me, Dickon. My disappointment is making me stupid. You're right, of course. I should be grateful that my uncles haven't made one of their conditions that I should be clapped in the dungeons in chains. I don't doubt that there are many of my relatives and enemies who'd like to see me get what they think are my just deserts. Lieutenant General, eh? As you've pointed out, a position of influence.'

My lord Gloucester nodded eagerly, plainly thankful that Albany was prepared to see sense at last.

'And I trust that you will use your influence for good,' he said.

Albany grinned. 'For England's good you mean, Coz.'

They both laughed at that and Duke Richard made a gesture of acknowledgement.

'When do you leave?' Albany asked.

'As soon as all the negotiations have been completed. A day or so I should reckon. Three at the most. I understand that the City Magistrates are undertaking the refund of my niece's dowry. There may be a little haggling with them which may prolong matters a trifle. What of your estates? Are you to get them back intact?'

'Oh, yes. And a full pardon for what is seen as my treasonable behaviour.' Albany's tone had turned bitter again. 'No mention, naturally, that my life was in danger and that was the reason I had to flee the country three years ago.' He started to bite his left thumbnail, a habit he had when disturbed.

It was at this moment that a sudden tickle at the back of my nose caused me to sneeze, and although I tried to suppress it as best I could, the two men heard it and immediately swung round.

'Who's there?' Albany demanded, while my lord Gloucester, not wasting time on words, strode towards the door and pulled it wide open.

'Roger!' he exclaimed without any hesitation, recognizing me at once by my height.

'What are you doing? What do you want?'

I tried to look innocent and breathed heavily as though I had only just arrived instead of having been eavesdropping for the past ten minutes.

'I'm looking for my lord Albany, Your Grace. I was told he might be here.'

'Yes, he's here.' The duke eyed me narrowly, suspicious of my limpid gaze. He hadn't known me for over ten years without coming to the conclusion that I was a devious bastard. His lips twitched as he pulled the door even wider and indicated his cousin, standing behind him. 'I'll leave you to tell him what you have to say.' He spoke with a certain irony, patently glad for an excuse to be free of Albany's company.

But having brushed past me, my lord Gloucester paused and turned back. 'Thank you for all your help on this journey, Roger,' he said courteously, adding, 'And I feel sure that Lord Albany will wish to add his thanks to mine. Also his farewells. In case you haven't already heard –'was there a slightly sarcastic note to his tone? – 'we shall be for the homeward march in a day or so. I expect word any time now that Berwick has surrendered. Your wife and children will be delighted to have you back amongst them, I've no doubt.'

'No doubt at all, Your Grace,' I confirmed.

He looked into my eyes, that always unexpected sense of humour of his lighting his own with laughter.

'Quite so.' He patted my arm and, rousing his sleepy page, crossed the ante-chamber and disappeared through the outer door.

I turned to face Albany.

'What news?' he demanded at once, dispensing with any form of greeting. 'What have you discovered?'

I was tired. I would have appreciated being asked to sit down, but no such invitation was forthcoming. I advanced into the room, the whole of the Council Chamber becoming visible as I did so. There were even more tapestries on the wall so far hidden from my sight, and I could see that they were as beautiful as the rest. Albany saw me looking and gave a short bark of laughter.

'They came with my sister-in-law,' he said 'when she married James, along with the Orkneys and Shetlands, as I told you.' His mood grew impatient again. 'Enough of that! Well, man? What have you found out?'

'I've not discovered the whereabouts of the diary, my lord, if that's what you're hoping.'

He didn't, I noticed, seem unduly cast down by this piece of information. 'That would have been too much to hope for,' he answered brusquely and somewhat surprisingly. 'So what have you found out? You've been gone all day. Surely you must have drawn some conclusions.'

'Not really, my lord.'

His expression became not merely exasperated, but angry. 'I thought – at least, I was told – you had a reputation for solving mysteries. I want this matter cleared up

quickly, Roger. Can't you understand that? I have affairs
of my own to attend to, but I need to see Rab Sinclair
liberated from prison before I can do so. Just tell me where
you've been today, who you've talked to and what they
had to say for themselves . . . Oh, sit down, man!' This as
I swayed suddenly, almost out on my feet with fatigue and
hunger. Albany pulled out a stool and indicated I should
be seated. There was a flagon of wine on a side table,
surrounded by dirty beakers and a few delicate Venetian
glasses. He grabbed one of the former, filled it and thrust
it towards me. 'Here! Drink this!' I wondered with some
distaste who had used it before me. But I could not afford
to be fussy.

The wine steadied me, sending a glow through my veins
and clearing my thoughts. I took a deep breath and began
recounting my day's adventures, repeating the conversations
I had had with Maria Beton, Mistress Callender and John
Buchanan, and adding for good measure the impressions I
had gathered along the way.

I was about to summarize my findings in one or two brief,
but brilliantly acute sentences, when I realized that Albany
was no longer listening. He spoke with suppressed excitement.

'You're right, Roger!' Right? I'd said nothing conclu-
sive. 'It's Rab's brother-in-law, of course! You've proved
that Aline had time to pass the diary to him when she and
Master Buchanan returned from Roslin. She must have
grown uneasy while she was at her aunt's – with good
reason as it turned out: a premonition perhaps, such things
do happen – and decided that it was too great a risk to
keep it in the house any longer. And you're probably
correct in assuming an incestuous relationship between
them.'

'My lord, I'm not assuming—'

Albany ignored me. He was well away now, having gone
from supposition to fact in one short leap.

'Those papers you mentioned on his table! The diary is
among them, I know it. I feel it in my bones.' He leant over
and slapped me on the back. 'Roger, you've solved it!
Tomorrow morning, first thing, I shall send Murdo and

Donald, together with a contingent of the castle guards, to search Master Buchanan's house and mark my words, we shall find what we are looking for. Rab will be free by evening.'

Seventeen

I was appalled.
'My lord, you can't do this!' I was moved to protest
with greater vehemence than I had ever used, either to him
or to anyone in his exalted position. 'This is sheer folly! You
speak as though I have offered you incontrovertible proof of
Master Buchanan's guilt. I haven't. It's a theory, nothing
more; a theory that might prove to be correct, I grant you,
but that's all. I beg you, don't persuade yourself that the
Grassmarket house holds the answer to this puzzle. You are
most likely only storing up disappointment for yourself –
and for Master Sinclair – if you do.'

My voice had risen urgently and I discovered to my horror
that I was actually thumping with my fist on the table. I
broke off and stood nervously awaiting his furious reaction.

Nothing of the sort happened. Albany simply smiled at
me; a smile full of pity and condescension.

'You don't understand, Roger,' he said. 'I have a feeling
about this. As soon as you told me that Aline Sinclair could
have passed the diary to her brother, I knew it was the truth.
Come! You of all people should know what I mean. You have
the "sight". I, too, have these flashes of certainty that amount
almost to glimpses of the future. This is such an occasion.
Oh, I don't boast about my gift.' This was a fact: I couldn't
recall him ever having mentioned it before. He went on, 'But
it's there, waiting to serve me when it's needed.'

I hoped I didn't look as sceptical as I felt.

'My lord,' I said desperately, 'I wish you could disabuse
your mind of this belief that I have, or ever have had, the
"sight" in the way you mean it. I've tried to explain to you
several times in the past that what I get are dreams caused
by my mind working through sleep and reminding me of

facts which my waking self has forgotten. My mother occasionally was gifted with what you are pleased to term the "sight", when she seemed able to foretell the future, but even so it was not often and rarely of things that were important. She didn't foresee my father's death, for instance, when he fell from the ceiling of Wells Cathedral nave. Otherwise, she might have kept him at home that day and prevented it.'

Still smiling, and not at all put out by my insubordinate tone, the duke patted me on the shoulder.

'I can see that you are ignorant of the manner in which the "sight" operates, Roger. It is not given to us for our own benefit, to advance our own designs, but to promote the wishes of the gods.'

'The gods?' I queried nervously, recalling that he had used the same words a short while previously, when the Duke of Gloucester had accused him of blasphemy. 'What gods, my lord?'

He laughed softly and shrugged. Once again the candlelight rippled across the satin of his doublet, this time turning the scarlet to flame. I had the oddest impression that he had suddenly grown taller, that his head was almost touching the ceiling and that there was a strange aureole of light, like green fire, surrounding his whole body. His eyes, too, whose colour I was normally unaware of, were like two chips of emerald between his narrowed lids . . .

Albany was gripping me by the shoulders and forcing me into a chair. He was himself again and I noticed that his eyes were in reality a pale, indeterminate blue. Or were they brown? And why couldn't I be sure?

'What . . . What happened?' I asked.

'My dear fellow, you very nearly fainted,' Albany said and smiled. 'I've been working you too hard. You've been running about the whole day and I daresay you haven't even had your supper yet. Sit here quietly and I'll see that food and drink is brought to you. No one will be returning to the Council Chamber this evening. We've finished our deliberations for the day.' His tone had turned sour once more, reminded of his grievances.

But I was not to be deflected by talk of food and rest, although I was feeling in need of both.

'What gods were you referring to, my lord?'

'Did I say that?' He attempted a look of surprise, as though it was something I had imagined. And indeed I might well have thought so, had I not heard him use the words earlier.

'You did.' I spoke positively, giving him no room for argument.

He wriggled his shoulders uncomfortably and grimaced. 'It was just an expression for Fate or Chance or whatever it is that rules our lives and makes each one of us what we are; that equips us with the gifts life doles out to us.'

'You don't think we owe all that to God?' I was being far bolder than I should have been, but I felt intuitively that Albany would not reprimand me. He appeared uneasy, like a man who had allowed his tongue to run away with him and was now wondering how he could retrieve the situation.

'I think the Almighty may need help now and then, don't you? No! Don't answer me. This is neither the time nor place to enter into a theological discussion. You need that rest and food I promised you, while I must go and sup with my beloved kinfolk and my erstwhile allies.' The bitterness was back in his voice with a vengeance and mixed now with an underlying anger, all the more potent for being carefully suppressed. He paused for a moment, controlling his rampant emotions. When he spoke again, his tone was smooth. 'Do as I bid you. Stay here and I'll have supper sent to you.' Suddenly he smiled as though his mind had been wiped clean of all care and worry in an instant. 'And on that other matter, trust me. You will find, tomorrow, when we ransack Master Buchanan's house that the diary will be found.'

'My lord—' I began, half rising from my seat.

But Albany pushed me down again, his irritation once more floating to the surface.

'I want no further argument, Roger. Believe me when I tell you that I know my premonition is correct. I repeat, trust me!'

He was gone. I heard the outer door of the ante-room close behind him and I was left alone in the empty Council Chamber that still seemed to echo to the sound of his voice. The watery twilight of the August day was seeping through the room, and long shadows inched their way across the rush-strewn floor. A small log fire, which had previously gone unnoticed, smouldered on the hearth; then, with a sudden explosion of noise that made me jump, a tempestuous squall of rain beat against the window. The fire spurted and flared. A bubble of resin burst with a little splutter.

I suddenly felt unutterably weary, my whole body like lead, my mind stupid and confused. There was nothing to be surprised at in this, I told myself. It had been a long day; a very long day. It was only this morning that we had ridden into Edinburgh, although it seemed more like half a week away; only this morning, in the guest chamber at Holy Rood Abbey, that Donald had informed Albany of Rab Sinclair's arrest, a name totally unknown to me then, but now burned into my consciousness with letters of fire; only this morning that I had first set eyes on this castle perched on its great rock, hanging, or so it seemed to me, halfway between heaven and earth. And since then, I had trotted busily around the city, questioning, observing and generally being lied to. Well, someone was lying. He, or maybe she, had to be.

But these things were not really the cause of the lassitude that suddenly held me in an iron grip. There was something more; something that had its roots in my recent conversation with Albany perhaps, or even in his actual presence. But surely that was foolishness. I had never before felt disturbed by his company. I had always known him to be arrogant, self-satisfied, concerned with no one but himself and his own desires. But then he was a prince. What else could one expect of royalty, bred up as they were in conceit and self-importance from the earliest age? And yet, until now, I had found him easy-going enough, although there had always been an invisible line across which one dared not step. But that was so with most people, king or peasant. He was unwise in many ways. Then again, who was not?

There was another burst of rain against the window and a spattering of hail came down the chimney to sizzle and melt among the dying flames on the hearth. Shadows leaped up the walls, then retreated silently, succeeded by an almost eerie stillness. I found myself shivering although I was not conscious of feeling cold. I remained bodily tired, but not sleepy. In fact the earlier confusion of mind was beginning to clear.

I thought once more about the reason given me by Albany for my presence on this expedition; this military invasion that had fractured and splintered apart, descending, as far as he was concerned, into one of those farces played out at fairs to the ribald laughter of the crowds. I had been selected as his protector to guard him from assassination attempts from either ill-wishers within the English camp, who considered it a poor decision to try to enthrone him as King of Scots, or – and this, it seemed, had been Albany's main fear – from one of the late Earl of Mar's adherents who was really in the pay of his brother, King James. And yet, when I looked back over the past weeks, it appeared to me that this fear came and went at his convenience. When it had suited the duke that I should be elsewhere, he had never jibbed at being alone with any one of the five.

All the same, there had been attempts on Albany's life. There was the incident of his horse at Fotheringay Castle when Pegasus had nearly thrown him, and the attempted stabbing at York . . . I was growing confused again, not sure what to think. The rain had decreased to a steady drumming against the oiled panes of the chamber window, like ghostly fingers beating out a tattoo; rhythmic, sleep-inducing. My eyelids began to droop . . .

I glanced up and saw Albany standing in front of me, but as I watched, his head gradually sprouted leaves and branches until it became that of the Green Man. The foliage began to spread, shoots writhing and coiling out of his mouth, filling the room, reaching towards me; then one, longer than the rest, snaked around my neck, tightening its grip, choking me so that I could no longer breathe. My heart was hammering against my ribs as I gasped for air . . .

Someone was shaking me.

'Wake up, Master Chapman! Wake up! You're riding the Night Mare!' It was Davey's voice, half laughing, half concerned. 'What a noise you're making. As if you're being strangled.'

The page was standing by my chair, looking down at me, his hand on my shoulder. On the table was a tray, and I could smell the rich aroma of the stew that had obviously been served up in the servants' hall for supper. There was also a jug and beaker alongside the wooden bowl and spoon and a hunk of bread. Albany had sent my meal as he had promised.

I was sweating profusely. I could feel it coursing down my back underneath my shirt, but at the same time, I felt cold. I passed a hand across my forehead. It came away soaking wet. I sat up straighter in my chair, trying not to look foolish, and gave an awkward laugh.

'Davey! I must have fallen asleep. I was dreaming.'

'It must have been a pretty horrible dream,' my companion condoled. 'Never mind, you're awake now. Here's your supper. My lord said I was to bring it to you. When you've finished, come across to the common hall. Donald's kept you a space and a blanket. Not that I think any of us will get much sleep tonight. Too much snoring. And too much farting,' he added, 'especially after that pottage. It's full of beans, so be warned. By the way, the duke's very pleased with you. I heard him telling Donald and Murdo that you've solved the problem – whatever that is.' He gave me a suddenly impish grin. 'So it's been worthwhile bringing you, after all.'

'Davey,' I began, but stopped. He had no influence with Albany. I doubted if he even knew what was going on. 'No, nothing.' I shook my head as he raised his eyebrows enquiringly. 'I'll be with you when I've eaten this.'

He nodded and left. I drew my chair closer to the table and picked up the spoon, only to find that my hand was trembling. The dream had been too vivid for comfort and was still haunting me. I found myself glancing uneasily around the room as if afraid that the apparition had been real and was lurking somewhere in a corner.

I told myself sternly not to be a fool and started on the rapidly cooling broth.

Davey's prediction about the night ahead proved to be all too accurate.

Goodness knows how many of us there were bedding down in the common hall; fifty perhaps, possibly a great deal more. And of course there is always one rowdy section of any all male gathering; those overgrown schoolboys who want to dice the night away or sit around telling bawdy stories, recounting tales of their sexual prowess (boasting extravagantly about the size of their manly assets) until their hapless listeners fall asleep with boredom and disbelief. And the page had been right about the bean stew, as well. After an hour or so, it was a worry that someone might get out his tinder box and strike a light: there was a good chance, I thought, that the place might go up in flames.

I spent most of what was left of the evening trying to convince Donald and Murdo that Albany's plans for the following morning were likely to prove a grave mistake and should be discouraged.

'I have offered my lord no proof,' I kept reiterating, 'that John Buchanan holds the missing diary, but the –' I nearly said the fool, but checked myself just in time – 'the duke has, for some inexplicable reason, taken it into his head that this is the answer to its mysterious disappearance. For God's sake, one of you must try to drum it into him that nothing will come of this idea.'

Murdo grimaced and laughed. 'He won't listen to us,' he grunted, and Donald agreed with him.

'Once he gets a bee in his bonnet, he won't listen to anyone. Lord Alexander was always the most headstrong of the brothers, everyone says so.' Donald squashed a flea that had hopped out of the floor rushes to bite him and flicked its remains towards James Petrie, who sat with his back propped against the wall, withdrawn as always and unable to understand what we were saying. (The groom, John Tullo, was absent, presumably sleeping in the stables with the horses.) The squire added, with a malevolent grin, 'My lord will make you free of his displeasure when he finds he's disappointed.'

Murdo chuckled. 'He will that.'

'Well, it will do no good getting angry with me. I've warned him.'

I shifted uncomfortably on my patch of floor, wondering if it was worthwhile settling down to sleep with all the noise, the laughter and conversation, going on around us. It suddenly occurred to me that it was a very long time since I had slept on anything other than a mattress, and that from the time of my leaving London, just on two months ago, I had become

used to the best beds on offer. Why, therefore, had I been
so abruptly banished from Albany's company? Had he
nothing to be afraid of any longer?

I put the question to my companions. 'And why aren't
you two on truckle cots in his ante-chamber?'

Murdo guffawed, Donald gave his superior smile and even
Davey giggled. (James Tullo just snored: he had fallen asleep.)

'He's home now, isn't he?' Donald condescended to
answer. 'Not on the march.' He saw I was still puzzled and
said impatiently, 'The duke'll be bedding down with one of
his uncle's whores, lent to him for the occasion. He's been
living like a monk for weeks – not that monks do live like
monks, you can take it from me – and now he's going to
make up for lost time. He wouldn't indulge himself with any
of the camp followers, naturally. Might get a dose of the
pox. As for us –' he nodded at Murdo and the other two –
'he's forbidden us to have too much to do with him for the
moment. It will be remembered in some quarters that we
were Mar's retainers before we escaped to France to join my
lord. All the same, no one, as yet, has insisted that he
dismisses us, nor has there been any suggestion of our arrest.
So the duke has told us to stay near him. We have our uses,
like Davey taking you your supper this evening, and Murdo
and myself accompanying him to Master Buchanan's house
tomorrow. And then, when he becomes king . . .' He broke
off, shrugging.

'Reward time.' Murdo spat into the rushes and his blue
eyes glinted at me from beneath their heavy lids.

'You really believe that he will be made king?' I asked
scornfully. 'Well, I can tell you that he won't.' And I repeated
the conversation between my lord of Gloucester and Albany
that I had overheard in the Council Chamber.

To my astonishment, this revelation was received very
calmly, as though it was something they had known already.
Smiles were exchanged; small, secret, sly smiles suggesting
that they knew something that I didn't. Perhaps they thought
I was making it up to annoy them. But somehow I didn't
think so. Yet what it was they imagined they knew that
could alter a situation already decided upon by both English
and Scots, and at the very heart of the peace negotiations, I had

no idea. Whatever it was, it was a bag of moonshine, but it was no good telling them so. Albany must have managed to convince them that he had some trick up his elegant sleeve and they believed him. I might as well go to sleep.

I lay down, pulled my blanket over me so that it partially covered my face and did just that.

In spite of the discomfort, I must have slept for some hours. When I did at last jerk awake the hall was in darkness, all the candles and wall cressets doused. But the heat was horrendous and the smell even worse. The concentration of bodies, together with the bean stew, had created an atmosphere that was stifling, not to mention the groans and snores that filled the room. After a moment or two, I realized that the heavy weight on my chest was Davey's outflung arm, and also that one of Murdo's feet was resting on the crown of my head. Slowly, I eased myself into a sitting position, returning Davey's arm to him as gently as I could. He murmured a little in his sleep, but did not wake. Murdo also muttered what sounded like a curse as his foot was dislodged, and I thought for a second that he opened his eyes, but then decided that I was mistaken.

By this time, I had also realized that my bladder was at bursting point. I had to get outside or relieve myself where I lay which, judging by some of the odours filling the hall, was the course that many of my companions had already taken. I decided that such embarrassment was not for me and heaved myself upright.

Picking my way between the sprawled bodies was a more difficult task, and as, inevitably, I stood on hands and tripped over feet, I was roundly cursed in both English and Scots. But no one challenged me or showed any inclination to accompany me outside, for which I was truly grateful. They all seemed to be worn out by the rigours of the day, and dog-tired.

The torrential downpour of the previous evening had given way to a gentle drizzle, but if there was a moon, it was hidden behind the wrack of low-flying cloud that veiled the stars. There was a cold wind blowing, tearing at the standard on the top of David's Tower and chilling me to the bone in spite of the fact that it was now the second day of August. I fumbled sleepily with the strings of my codpiece and pissed against the nearest wall, heaving a long sigh of satisfaction as I did so. Then, having straightened my breeches, and feeling hot and clammy in clothes that I had worn all the preceding day, I took a short stroll to where one of several gaps in the curtain wall gave a view into the valley below, where the tents of our army were pitched. I could see a few camp fires starring the darkness and heard, faint and far away, the cries of the sentries on watch, but other than that there was little stirring. The castle guards were out of sight. An owl swooped low over Saint Margaret's chapel, making me start, but reassuring me, also, with the foolish thought that it was a sign from the saint herself that she was indeed looking after me. Then all was quiet again except for the moaning of the wind.

As I made my way back to the common hall, I turned my face up to the fine spray of rain. It was cool and refreshing and I stood for a moment or two, letting it wash over me. I closed my eyes to savour the experience all the better. When I opened them again, it was to find someone looming up in front of me.

My hand flew at once to the haft of the dagger Donald had given me the previous afternoon and which I had failed to return to him. (Indeed, he had not asked for it back and I looked upon it in the light of a loan for the short time now that I and the rest of my countrymen remained in Edinburgh.)

'Who's there?' I demanded. It was too dark to see the man's features, but his lack of stature and slight build made me suspect the truth before he answered.

'Oh, it's you, is it?' grumbled Timothy Plummer. 'I might have guessed. It could only be you, Chapman, traipsing about in the dark and putting the fear of God into honest people.'

'I might well say the same about you,' I retorted, but without heat. It was so good to hear a familiar voice and words spoken in a comfortable southern accent – even if it was that nasal London drawl – that I could almost have embraced him. 'Where have you been hiding yourself since Nottingham?'

'I haven't been hiding myself anywhere,' he snapped. I had obviously ruffled his feathers, which, I have to admit, had partly been my intention. (Baiting Timothy and watching him bridle was one of the great pleasures of my life.) 'I'll remind you, Roger, that I am Spymaster General to my lord of Gloucester and have been at my lord's beck and call throughout the whole of this expedition. And it's not desirable that I should be too visible. My work is often extremely secret.'

'That doesn't explain why you're prowling around in the dead of night,' I said. 'Or does it? Who are you spying on now?'

'More importantly,' he rapped back, 'what are you doing out and about? Why aren't you guarding my lord Albany?'

I laughed. 'The duke has better things to do tonight than allow me to share his bed. My services have been dispensed with for those of a castle whore. His long abstinence on the march has made him randy. I'm in the common hall with the rest of his menie. Even his squires' services have been dispensed with. Well, I suppose he needs some consolation, now that he's not to be king.'

'How do you know that?' The spy's tone was sharp with suspicion. And by the time that I had finished explaining how I came by my knowledge, he was trembling with indignation.

'You could, and should, be severely punished for eavesdropping on my lord's private conversations. If I had my way—'

'Settle down,' I hissed angrily. 'I had been told to report to my lord Albany in connection with a private investigation I've been ordered to undertake for him. That's why I happened to be in the ante-chamber. Neither he nor my lord Gloucester made any move to close the door in spite of the fact that one of Gloucester's pages was also present. True, the boy was asleep, but—'

It was Timothy's turn to interrupt. 'What investigation for Albany?' he demanded.

The rain had suddenly increased as the wind blew more strongly. I put out an imperative hand and drew Timothy towards the shelter of Saint Margaret's Chapel. Once inside, in the musty-smelling darkness, I told him the whole story, including the itinerary of my past twenty-four hours in detail.

It was a relief to be able to unburden myself to someone I knew well, and he listened intently, only interjecting a question or two here and there where my narrative became a little garbled. Somewhat to my surprise, when I had finished, he made no comment, merely lapsing into a thoughtful silence. Finally, when he did speak, it was on another subject altogether.

'Tell me,' he said, 'do these retainers of the Earl of Mar, who have attached themselves to him, realize that Albany will not now become king?'

I nodded. 'I've told them what I overheard. But the strange thing is that they don't seem unduly downcast by the news. In fact they shrug it off as though they think I'm mistaken. And odder, still, Albany himself, although very angry about what he sees as betrayal by his English allies, also behaves as though the game's not played out yet. I find it difficult to understand. I feel he's planning something, but what it could be, I can't imagine. I believe he might have made a move already but for this business of Rab Sinclair.' I shivered as a gust of wind rattled the door behind us and threatened to slam it. I put out a foot to wedge it open. 'At least he seems to be a man loyal to his friends.'

Again, Timothy said nothing, but I could tell by the quality of the silence that he was thinking hard. But eventually he made no comment except, 'We'd better get back to bed. We'll catch our death of cold standing out here.' He made to move away, then swung round and seized me by the shoulders. 'Take care, Roger! Take care!' Then he was gone and the darkness had swallowed him up. I realized that he had still offered no explanation of what he was doing out in the middle of the night, prowling about alone. I felt annoyed that he had prised everything out of me and given away nothing in return. But I suppose that was what made him a good spy.

I went back to bed.

Eighteen

B ut not, immediately, to sleep.
When I returned to the common hall and picked my careful way across the sleeping mass of bodies, it was to discover that Murdo, Donald and Davey were missing. Only James Petrie remained, still propped against the wall and snoring rhythmically. Without compunction, I shook him awake.

'Where are the others?'

He stared at me stupidly for a moment or two, unsure of his surroundings, then slowly shook his head.

I indicated the empty space and, as though I were addressing an idiot, mouthed again, 'Where are they? Donald, Murdo, Davey?'

I was uncertain whether or not he could understand English, but he really wasn't a fool, and the substance of my question was obvious. After a few more seconds of playing dumb, he mumbled something in the broad Scots dialect in which the word 'piss' was clearly recognizable, even if he hadn't mimed the act itself. Then he belched, farted and went back to sleep again. Well, he closed his eyes, although there was something about his bodily posture that suggested tension. I felt sure that he was not as relaxed as he would have me believe.

I lay down and once more pulled my blanket over me, but sleep refused to come. It seemed to me a little unlikely that all three would have gone outside to obey a call of nature together. On the other hand, I knew from sleeping with Adela that if one of us got out of bed to use the chamber-pot, the other would almost inevitably follow suit. And it was the same with the children. If one was disturbed, he or she would very likely wake the other two. I recalled thinking that Murdo had opened his eyes when I went on my own errand, so perhaps I had started a chain of events.

But where were they? The minutes ticked by and still they did not return. What were they doing? Playing the old game of seeing who could aim highest against the wall? Or the comparison game? ('Mine's bigger than yours.') Somehow I hardly thought so, not on a night of wind and rain. And in any case, why hadn't I seen them? I had been detained by Timothy Plummer, so the chances were that we should all have been returning to the hall at about the same time. Yet I had not had even a glimpse of any one of them . . . And that prompted me to wonder once again what the Spymaster General had been doing soft-footing his way around the darkened buildings of this northern acropolis. Had he been expecting some such movement of . . . of what? Conspirators? But who was conspiring with whom? And against whom?

I sat up abruptly, hugging my knees, staring uneasily into the darkness, now rent with groans and moans as the suppertime stew began working on people's guts, giving them bad dreams, mounting them on the Night Mare. I remembered Albany's assurance, frequently repeated, that he would be king, no matter what Fate, in the guise of the Scottish Council and the Duke of Gloucester as King Edward's representative, decided. Why was he so confident? What exactly was he planning?

All my earlier doubts and suspicions regarding his true relationship with the late Earl of Mar's servants began to worry me yet again. Looking back over the past two months, since leaving London, the conviction grew that I had been gulled. Albany's fear that one of the five was in the employ of King James, with instructions to murder him, seemed increasingly threadbare the more I thought seriously about it. Once more I recollected the many occasions on which the duke had been content to dispense with my services, laying himself open, with apparent carelessness, to attack from any one of them.

I recalled the times when his life seemed genuinely to have been under threat and reluctantly arrived at the conclusion that those times could have been staged without much difficulty. The horse nearly throwing him in the courtyard of Fotheringay castle could as easily have been in response to a spur, cruelly applied by the duke himself, as to a cut on its flank delivered by someone else. And then there was the incident at York when an attempt had apparently been made to stab Albany to death in his bed, and only the fact that the duke had been bending over the night-stool, with me in attendance, had prevented a very nasty murder. I remembered how he had retched and retched, but without any resulting vomit. And while Albany had been claiming my attention with his feigned sickness, someone could have entered the room and planted the knife in among the bedclothes. Davey, perhaps? The page, too, had pleaded illness in order to account for his seeming absence.

But all this – what was now assuming the proportions of a certainty in my mind – provoked the question: why? The obvious answer was to convince me that Albany's life really was in danger and to keep me from defecting, either by going directly to the Duke of Gloucester and telling him of my doubts or by simply running away and making my way home to Bristol. But there again, that also raised the question: why? Why was Albany so desperate to keep me by his side? It was possible, I conceded, that he might really have feared assassination by one of his English allies, but I failed to see how my presence provided him with any greater protection than his own retinue could have supplied . . .

The more I thought about it, the more my head began to spin. I felt reasonably certain now that I had been duped and lied to by Albany, but could see no rhyme or reason for it. Why was it so essential that I should accompany him on this invasion of his native country? Our previous acquaintance had been brief. On the first occasion, I had helped him to escape from England to Ireland (from whence he had fled to France and the protection of King Louis) but our relationship had been no more than that of passing strangers. The second time, I had, at his request, been granted a short audience with him at Westminster Palace when he was the guest of King Edward there two years ago – and when, no doubt, past differences reconciled, they had been plotting this present action against the Scots. But, rack my brains as I would, I could come up with no explanation for his urgent request that I should be made his special bodyguard; so urgent, in fact, that it had made me the subject of a royal command.

I became conscious of a dull, throbbing ache behind my eyes to which the airlessness of the hall and my own uneasy thoughts contributed. I glanced around for any kindred soul also unable to sleep and was suddenly aware that neither the two squires nor the page had yet returned. This was far longer than any night-time piss could possibly warrant, and I had started to heave myself to my feet with the intention of going in search of them when I felt someone tap me on the arm. It was James Petrie, awake and leaning forward to offer me a leather flask which he had produced from somewhere about his person.

He grunted a word which could have been interpreted as, 'Drink?' But whatever it was, the message was clear.

I thought of the wind and drizzling rain outside, and after the briefest of hesitations, accepted his offer in the spirit in which it was apparently meant.

'Thanks.' I took a generous swig from the flask only to realize too late that it was the damned 'water of life' that the Scots seemed so keen on. It caught me in the back of the throat and I began to splutter and cough, my eyes streaming with tears, so that I thought I must choke to death there and then. My convulsions were so extreme that several of my neighbours who, until now, had appeared oblivious to any sound, including, I suspected, the Last Trump, woke up and started to throw things at me. Two or three pairs of shoes and a belt, whose buckle scratched my face, all found their mark before I was at last able to breathe freely again. I handed the flask back to James Petrie, who, even in the dark, I could see was shaking with silent laughter. 'I'm going to look for the other three,' I told him huskily and with what dignity I could muster. 'They've been gone too long.' I noticed that I suddenly sounded tipsy.

And that was the last thing I remembered saying . . .

I was standing outside Mistress Callender's house, looking in through one of the open ground floor windows, a sheep and a cow staring back at me. Next, without being aware that I had moved, I was floating effortlessly up the outside staircase, my feet not touching the treads. Mistress Callender was seated on a stool at the top and I could see that she was trying to tell me something. Her lips were moving but I could hear no sound, and in one hand, she held what looked like a bunch of herbs which she kept waving at me. I called out to her to speak louder, but my words, too, drifted away into silence. I touched down on the small stone landing at the top of the flight of steps, but the widow had vanished. I glanced around frantically in an effort to find her, convinced that her message was of vital importance, but she was nowhere to be seen. Instead, I was lying on the bed in Aline Sinclair's bedchamber, the coverlet's Green Man medallion underneath me.

To my horror, I could feel the embroidered tendrils and shoots that wreathed the Green Man's head and coiled in and out of his mouth, begin to come alive, snaking around my limbs and body, holding me in a slowly tightening and ever-more deadly embrace. Living in a port like Bristol, I had heard plenty of sailors' tales of the weird and wonderful creatures to be found in foreign lands; and I recalled one of a snake that could crush a man to death. I'm not sure that I believed the story at the time, but it came back to me now in my dream as the foliage engulfed me.

I yelled, but, as before, could make no sound.

Maria Beton was standing beside the bed, gazing down at me, and beside her was the gaoler's son from the castle, the young boy who had apparently taken her a message from Master Sinclair. In one hand the housekeeper was holding a fruit which, after a moment, I recognized as a quince, and in the other several leaves of parchment tied together with two knots of red ribbon. The missing diary! I sat up, struggling to free myself from the clutches of the Green Man . . .

It was morning. A pale sun lit the windows of the common hall and all around me was the bustle of a new day, men hauling themselves to their feet after an unsatisfactory night's sleep, searching for lost shoes, belts, even tunics that had been discarded due to the heat. I felt like death, as though I had been kicked in the back of the head by a mule. The rags of that hideous dream still hung around me, making me tremble.

'Are you all right, fellow?' someone asked me, and I recognized the livery of one of Lord Rivers's men.

I thanked him and said I was. A lie, but at that moment, all I wanted was to be left alone. In any case, the tardy ones amongst us were being elbowed out of the way by the castle servers who were busy dragging the trestles and boards to the centre of the hall and setting up the tables for breakfast. Kitcheners began to bring in food; great platters of oatcakes and huge bowls of porridge. But the mere thought of eating made me feel queasy again. My one thought was to escape into the fresh air.

I was stamping on my second boot when the night's events suddenly sprang to mind, and I stared around me, ignoring the dizziness that made my head lurch painfully. James Petrie was still there, and Davey, knuckling the sleep from his eyes. But of the two squires there was no sign.

The choice was who to tackle first. In the end, I settled on the page.

'What happened to you three last night?' I demanded. 'Where did you get to?'

Davey opened those great violet-blue eyes of his to their fullest extent.

'What do you mean, where did we get to?' His injured innocence was marvellous to behold. 'We went for a piss, like you.'

'You were gone for ages,' I accused. 'It doesn't take that long to relieve yourselves.'

'How would you know how long we were gone? You were asleep when we got back.'

'Not asleep,' I snarled through gritted teeth. I swung round on James Petrie who recoiled slightly from the expression on my face. 'What was in that damn whisky you gave me?'

He gabbled something, giving a swift, bolt-eyed look at Davey who translated his answer as, 'Nothing! Why should there be? It was just the *usquebaugh*. It was too strong for you.' He added of his own accord and with an impertinent grin, 'You Sassenachs can't stomach it.'

I started to shake my head, but then thought better of it.

'No, it was more than that. I went out like a candle being snuffed, and this morning I feel terrible.'

'Why on earth would Jamie be carrying around a flask of doctored whisky?' Davey was prepared to argue the point, but I cut him short.

'Where are Murdo and Donald?'

'What? Oh . . . . They were up at dawn on my lord's orders to go to search John Buchanan's house in the Grassmarket. They've taken a contingent of soldiers with them to make sure he doesn't resist and that the job's done thoroughly.' At the mention of Buchanan's name there was another fleeting exchange of glances between him and James Petrie. 'Are you going to sit down to breakfast?' Davey continued peevishly. 'If not, would you move? You're blocking my way.'

I could see that there was little point in remaining any longer. Not only would I get no joy out of either the page or James Petrie, but the clatter of knives and spoons and the general chatter of a hundred or more voices was making normal conversation difficult.

'Where's the duke?' I said, but didn't bother to wait for an answer.

I knew that Albany had been lodged in David's Tower, together with the Duke of Gloucester, but my enquiries for him were met by the information that my lord was already up and dressed, in spite of the early hour, and had left the castle some time ago, accompanied by his two body squires. I could guess what that meant: he had gone in person to oversee the ransacking of Master Buchanan's premises. Cursing under my breath, and trying to ignore the fact that I felt like death, I set out after him. I told myself not to be a fool. I could achieve nothing by trying to dissuade Albany from this course of action. And in any case, he would soon discover his mistake when the diary proved not to be among John Buchanan's papers.

But I was wrong.

I had barely left the castle precincts when I met the triumphant party returning, Master Buchanan guarded by several stalwart soldiers, arrested, it seemed, on Albany's say-so for having deliberately suppressed vital evidence. Aline Sinclair's diary, I was told, had been discovered almost at once among the litter of papers on her brother's table.

'And it's all thanks to you, Roger,' Albany said, slapping me on the back. I tried to protest, horrified, but the duke wouldn't have it. 'Yes, yes! Honour where it's due. If you hadn't discovered that Mistress Sinclair had had time to fetch the diary and pass it to her brother on Monday, John Buchanan's involvement might never have occurred to anyone.' He waved the diary at me as he spoke, the pages bound together with their blood-red ribbons. 'This will clear Rab of the charge of murder. I've perused the contents and they're exactly as he described them. The sordid details about Aline and her lover, the different ways they were considering of getting rid of her husband, they're all here. No jury could possibly convict Rab with this evidence to hand. Having read this, when he saw her pick up the knife, of course he thought she was going to kill him.'

I was bemused. It all seemed too pat, too easy. There hadn't even been a real search. The diary had just been lying there, on John Buchanan's table, waiting – practically begging – to be discovered. It didn't make sense. A man who had been entrusted with an incriminating document would surely have taken pains to hide it away, not leave it where any fool could put his hand on it. Nevertheless, I supposed it could be argued that when Aline passed the diary to her brother, neither of them knew that her husband had found and read it. She was simply acting in response to some sort of premonition; that pricking of the thumbs which we all experience sometime or another.

Yet I still felt uneasy. Looking back on yesterday's visit to the house in the Grassmarket, I had no recollection of seeing anything on that table tied with red ribbons. It would have leaped to my eye: it was, after all, what I was looking for. I couldn't have avoided noticing it. Could I?

By this time, we were back in the castle ward and beginning the ascent to the rock's summit.

'The rest of the morning's your own,' Albany told me, 'until after dinner. I must visit Rab to tell him the good news and also put this –' he waved the diary – 'in the hands of the City Magistrates. But when dinner's over, come and find me. We have work to do.'

It was no good asking him, what work. The duke was already gone in a flurry of self-importance, leaving me with Murdo and Donald to watch John Buchanan being marched away. He caught my eye and gave me a filthy look. But he was frightened, too. I felt a surge of guilt and wanted to assure him that his arrest was none of my doing. I turned my back.

I needed to think, but the two squires showed a sudden and unexpected desire for my company, almost, I thought, as if they had been set to guard me; an obviously nonsensical notion.

'What does the duke want me for this afternoon?' I asked. 'Do you know?'

Donald hesitated, as though unsure whether to answer me or not, but Murdo said bluntly, 'He wants us all to ride with him to Roslin to . . . to worship at the chapel there and . . .'

'And give thanks for our safe return to Scotland after all these years,' Donald supplied when his companion's voice faltered. 'It's some few miles to the south of Edinburgh. Not far, but I think my lord plans to stay the night. He has a small hunting lodge on the edge of the village.'

I frowned. 'Why would he want my company? I'm not a returning exile like the rest of you. My services can well be dispensed with. And will be in a few days' time when the negotiations are completed and I return to England.'

'Oh, the duke regards you as quite one of the family now,' Murdo replied smoothly. 'He would be disappointed if you weren't present at his thanksgiving.'

'Albany regards you lot as his family?' I asked in disbelief.

'In the loosest sense of the word,' Donald intervened hastily. 'You're not a fool Roger. You know what Murdo means.'

'All five of you?' I persisted. 'All of the late Earl of Mar's servants?'

'Why not? We've been with him some years now, first in France and then in England.'

'I'll tell you why not,' I said angrily, suddenly standing still and forcing them to turn and face me. 'Are you unaware that Albany made a special petition to King Edward to have me as a bodyguard because he was afraid that one of you five was an assassin in the pay of King James?'

There was a momentary silence during which I could almost feel Donald and Murdo exercising all their self-will not to glance at one another. Then the former gave an awkward laugh.

'No, no! You're mistaken, Roger. What my lord feared was an assassin among his English allies. He knew that there were some who violently disapproved of King Edward's plan to make him King of Scotland.'

'That, too,' I agreed. 'But take my word for it that he suspected one of you, as well. The reason he asked for my services was because he knew me and knew also that he could trust me. At least,' I added, 'that was what I was given to understand.'

Murdo grinned, visibly relaxing and throwing a friendly arm about Donald's shoulders.

'It would seem that my lord has by now discovered his mistake. Nothing's happened to him, has it? He's realized that he can trust us, after all.'

'There were at least two attempts on Albany's life,' I suggested, and waited for their reactions.

'Perpetrated by the English, undoubtedly,' Donald said, without even the flicker of an eyelid to hint that he might be lying.

Or was he simply being truthful? How could I tell? So I returned to my first bone of contention.

'None of this explains my lord's desire for me to accompany you all to this place – what's it called again?'

'Roslin.' It was Murdo who spoke this time. 'And we've told you already. The duke regards you as one of his intimate servitors. One of us. One of the "family". And until you . . . go home again, you will be expected to obey him. I feel certain His Grace of Gloucester will say so.'

I also thought this entirely possible, Prince Richard being a man of his word. I could see no way to get out of this unwanted expedition, and could only pray that a very few more days would bring Anglo-Scottish deliberations to a satisfactory conclusion.

'Look, I need to go for a shit,' I said. I had to shake these two off. 'There's no need for you to accompany me. I know where the latrines are.' And I moved purposefully away. Thankfully, they made no move to follow me.

'We'll see you at dinner in the hall,' Donald shouted after me.

It had occurred to me to quiz them on the morning's doings in the Grassmarket, but common sense told me that I should get no useful information out of either one of them. They had been taken to John Buchanan's house to search for the missing evidence, and they had found it. That was probably all they knew. Or wanted to know if it came to that. But I still found it hard to believe that it could have been discovered so pat, just as though it had been placed on the table for all the world to see. There was something that I was missing; something that my dream of the previous night had tried to tell me, but which I was too tired, or too stupid, to see.

I passed the latrines without a second glance: my bowels were not bothering me for the moment. Instead, I made my way to Saint Margaret's Chapel and went inside. Fresh candles had been lit in the candlesticks on the altar, illuminating the effigy in its niche and showing up the fact that it badly needed repainting. The yellow and blue robe was dingy, spotted here and there with mould, and the gold of the halo tarnished. But I doubted that this was out of disrespect for the saint, ancestress of both the English and Scottish royal lines, but because money was not in plentiful supply at a court where its king had lavished so much of its hard-come-by wealth on his numerous favourites. But that was over now with King James in captivity and his minions dead, hanged from the Lauder Bridge like common felons.

I had the chapel to myself and went down on my knees in front of the altar, but feeling at something of a loss. Although paying lip service to them as a good Christian should, secretly I had little direct contact with the saints, preferring to talk straight to God. (I could never see the point of communicating with the middle-men and – women. And how could I be sure that my messages got passed on?) But this morning, as on my first visit, I appealed for Margaret's help in her capacity as a descendant of the Wessex kings, direct in line from Alfred the Great and from Cerdic, first self-appointed ruler of the West Saxons. But it was only after I had also had a swift word with my fellow west-countrymen, Saint Dunstan and Saint Patrick, that it occurred to me to wonder exactly what it was that I was praying for. Help, obviously; but why? What was it that was troubling me?

For something was trouble me, even though both my missions seemed to be successfully accomplished. I had seen Albany safe to Scotland; and my brief investigation into the facts surrounding Master Sinclair's arrest had culminated – although no particular thanks to me – in the production of the necessary evidence to assure his acquittal on the charge of murder. Self-defence would be his plea, and would undoubtedly be accepted. So why was I bothering the saints?

Well, for a start, there was a growing feeling that Albany had used me as a cat's-paw, not once, but twice, yet without any evidence or any solid reasons to bolster the conviction. Secondly, the arrest of John Buchanan particularly worried me.

I got up from my knees, then sat down on the dusty floor, propping my back against the nearest stretch of wall, trying to sort my thoughts. I fixed my gaze on the figure of the saint, but after a disturbed night, drowsiness overcame me. The painted face became at first a blur, but then gradually assumed the living features of the woman. She held out both hands, one holding a bunch of herbs and the other a fruit, a quince as had been offered to me in my dream by Maria Beton . . . I jerked awake, straightening my back with a suddenness that jarred my spine.

Quince jelly! Recipes!

What was the point of Maria Beton and Mistress Callender exchanging recipes if the former could neither read nor write? Yet both had mentioned the fact, so why the lie? Why the pretence that the housekeeper was illiterate? I recalled the gaoler's son leaving the Sinclair house as I approached it the previous day. Had he been sent by her master to warn her of my impending visit and of the role she must play? I had to be convinced that she could not have known the contents of the diary because she could not read them . . .

Another thought occurred to me like a flash of lightning across a summer sky. She could also have written the diary. For whatever reason Rab Sinclair had murdered his wife, for whatever reason he had wanted her dead, he had to have a story that would exonerate him in the eyes of the law. My guess was that the killing had been unpremeditated, and Mistress Callender's inopportune arrival had caught him literally red-handed. The story of the diary was concocted hastily between Rab and Mistress Beton, but she had needed time to write it. And after that, it had to be searched for and dramatically found. But where?

I had been used to supply them with the answer.

Nineteen

I had been used! I had been used! The four words kept thumping around in my head, like a refrain beaten out by drums. The questions followed.

What had been the point of this elaborate charade in which I had been an innocent player? Answer: to establish the fact that Rab Sinclair had never planned to murder his wife because she had meant to kill him, and that her death had been an accident as a result of Rab defending himself.

Did Albany know the truth, and had he been complicit in the plot to clear his friend's name? Answer: it seemed probable because of the way he had latched on to the possibility of 'finding' the supposedly missing diary in the possession of John Buchanan. And if I hadn't mentioned Aline Sinclair's brother or the fact that she might have had an opportunity to pass him the diary? Who then would have become the focus of suspicion? Mistress Callender? I felt certain that Albany would have seized on something in my report which could be used for his purpose. He must have visited Master Sinclair in his cell before he took me to see him; a visit during which he learned what Rab and the housekeeper were planning.

So why was I brought in? Answer: to add greater credence to the whole sordid affair. I have no idea how the two conspirators originally intended the damning evidence of the diary to be discovered. But Albany must have seen at once that the intervention of a disinterested outsider, particularly one who was already known to no less a personage than the Duke of Gloucester as a solver of mysteries, would carry great weight with Master Sinclair's prosecutors, and almost certainly result in his being acquitted.

That, however, led to the biggest question of all: why

would a royal duke risk an already tarnished reputation by trying to save a murderer from the gallows? And to this I had no answer. I racked my brains, sitting there in the dim light of Saint Margaret's Chapel, but could think of no good or adequate reason. And after a while, I realized that there was no alternative to tackling the duke himself, especially if an innocent man were not to be accused of suppressing vital evidence which would 'prove' that the killer had been the intended victim.

I hauled myself to my feet, brushing my breeches free of dust from the chapel floor, and stood for a minute or two in seeming contemplation of the saint's effigy, but in reality wondering if it would not be wiser to take my story to Prince Richard and ask him to demand an explanation of his cousin. He would listen to me, I felt sure of that, nor would he dismiss my tale without investigation. (He hated injustice of any kind as much as I did.) But he was a very busy man and, by now, would be locked in another session of negotiations with the Scots, hammering out the final details of a deal that would see Berwick returned permanently to the English, and at least part of the Princess Cicely's dowry refunded to swell King Edward's depleted coffers. No; I couldn't trouble him. I should have to demand an explanation of Albany myself. Reluctantly, I made for the chapel door.

There was a strong smell of fish in the air, reminding me that it was Friday and that dinner would undoubtedly be fish stew. The thought made me retch again, prompting fresh memories of the past night's events and causing me to wonder anew what had been in the drink James Petrie had given me. Had there really been anything sinister, or was it simply that my stomach could not tolerate the *usquebaugh?* In the end, I decided that it must be the latter. It seemed highly unlikely that the body-servant would be carrying a flask of drugged whisky in his pocket. For what reason? As for the apparently prolonged absence of the two squires and Davey, perhaps there again I had been mistaken. Maybe it had been a shorter time than I had thought it.

'You're looking green about the gills, Roger,' said a familiar

voice, and Timothy Plummer, an official-looking expression
on his face and an official-looking bundle of documents in
his hands, came up behind me. 'What's the matter, man?
Don't you feel well? And why are you wandering about like
this? Haven't you anything useful to do? I'm sure you could
set your hand to something.'

'I'm riding with my lord to Roslin after dinner,' I snapped.
'Until then, I've been told the time's my own.'

'Roslin, eh?' The Spymaster General eyed me up and down.
'Well, don't let the duke keep you away too long. My lord
Gloucester has given me a strong hint that business may well
be concluded today, so we shall probably be on the road
back to Berwick very shortly. And from there, the levies will
be dispersed. We can all go home.'

I groaned with relief and immediately began to feel better.
Perhaps when I had tackled Albany on the matter of Rab
Sinclair, I would also find the courage to tell him that I
refused to accompany him to Roslin. I was no longer his
unpaid servant. (Although, in truth, I had been promised a
substantial purse by the Crown when this affair was over, in
addition to my initial payment.)

As Timothy was about to move away, I asked, 'Where is
Albany? Do you know?'

'In council, of course, with the rest of 'em. Today, he's
sealing a bargain with the Scottish Chancellor that restores
to him all his former estates in return for renouncing his
claim to the throne and recognizing James as king.
Although he's obviously not proposing to spend much time
on the business, if he's riding to Roslin this afternoon.'
Timothy shrugged. 'But I suspect the deal has already been
struck outside the Council Chamber. This morning's business just makes it official . . . Now, now, this won't do! I
must be on my way.' He puffed up his skinny chest importantly in a manner I had grown to know well over the many
years since I had first rescued him from the importunate
attentions of a London pieman, and, with a brief nod, was
gone.

I was just wondering what to do next when I heard myself
hailed for a second time.

'Roger!' It was Davey, just rounding the corner of a nearby

building and heading for David's Tower. 'You know we're riding to Roslin after dinner? My lord has informed you?'

'Yes.' I noticed suddenly, and with a quickening of my heart beats, what it was he was carrying in his hands. I recognized the knots of red ribbon. 'Is that . . . ?' I began, then stopped.

The page grinned and nodded. 'The famous diary? Yes. I've been told to stand guard over it in my lord's chamber until he's free to take it to the City Magistrates. I've strict instructions not to let it out of my sight.'

'Do you think I might just glance at it?' I asked. 'Just out of curiosity. Just to see what it is I've been looking for. A peek, nothing more.'

Davey hesitated for a moment, then conceded, 'I don't see why not. It seems only fair, after all. But for you, it wouldn't have been discovered, or so I gather. Here.' He put the diary into my hands. 'But be quick. And I'm not moving from this spot until I get it back again.'

There was not a lot to read; both sides of three or four sheets of parchment covered with a spidery writing that was none too easy to decipher, largely because of the fatly looped 'g's and 'j's. The letter 'h', too, was curiously formed. But once my eyes had grown accustomed to these idiosyncrasies of style, the words leaped up at me, off the page; the intimate details of making love with the unnamed lover, referred to merely as 'J', and, after that, a list of possible ways to do away with Rab Sinclair, which method would prove to be easiest and which would attract the least suspicion.

I returned the diary to Davey, who received it back with a sigh of relief.

'Shocking, isn't it?' he said. 'It makes my blood run cold. Well, no one could convict Master Sinclair after reading this. I wonder who "J" is, and if they'll catch him.' He lowered his voice. 'The duke reckons it's Master Buchanan. Incest,' he hissed.

He was plainly disappointed by my lack of reaction to this hideous revelation and, clutching his precious burden, made off, leaving me to my own reflections.

There was something wrong with the diary in my estimation, mainly with the descriptions of love-making, which were both prurient and innocent at one and the same time. My feeling on reading them had been that they were written by someone whose imagination was not matched by experience. Maria Beton?

I glanced up at the pale sun, struggling to be seen through another swarm of black clouds hurrying in from the west, and judged from its position that I had perhaps half an hour or so until ten o'clock and dinner (although I had noticed that the Scots tended to eat somewhat later than we did at home). There was time, I decided, for what I had to do.

I left the castle almost without challenge. The sentries had presumably grown used to the frantic comings and goings of the past twenty-four hours and although one of them stopped me, he seemed satisfied with my mumbled, 'On the Duke of Gloucester's business.' If he understood nothing else, he recognized the name of the King of England's brother.

It was only a short walk to Mistress Callender's house, where I was lucky to find her in, as she answered my knock in her outdoor cap and shawl and with a basket on one arm. She looked astonished to see me.

'Oh, my dear sir! What a surprise. But please come in. Come in!' Her features sharpened with curiosity. 'Has something happened?'

No word, then, of Master Buchanan's arrest had yet reached her. I decided to leave her in ignorance: she would no doubt find out soon enough and I had no wish to be drawn into sharing my doubts and suspicions with her.

'Mistress Callender,' I said, giving her my best smile (the one that always makes my dear wife ask if I have indigestion), 'I've come to beg a favour of you.' She flushed with pleasure and fluttered her eyelids. 'May I see one of the recipes given to you by your neighbour, Mistress Beton?'

She looked astonished, as I suppose was only natural. Whatever reason she had anticipated for my visit, it certainly wasn't this.

'A–A recipe?' she fluttered. 'Why . . . why yes, of course. Which particular one d–did you want?'

Ah! Now which one did I want? I had to think quickly,

but nothing came immediately to mind. Then I remembered the bunch of herbs held out by the saint in my dream.

'Herb broth?' I suggested tentatively. 'I'm sure Mistress Beton mentioned something about herb broth.' I hoped I sounded convincing. I've never been an especially good liar.

'Herb broth . . . Herb broth . . . Now, let me see . . .' The widow put down her basket. 'Yes, I believe there is a recipe for herb broth. It's a favourite of yours, sir?'

'Of my wife's. And Mistress Beton assured me it was a particularly good one.'

'Yes, I think it is. I'll have to go down to my kitchen behind the – er – front parlour,' she murmured, obviously hoping that I had somehow failed to notice her animals in the lower room. 'I shan't be a moment or two.'

She was as good as her word, and was breathing heavily when she returned as though she had been hurrying. 'And now, sir,' she pleaded as she handed me a piece of paper, 'do please tell me what has been happening since your visit yesterday. I went to the Grassmarket very early this morning, and there seemed to me to be a lot of activity around Master Buchanan's house.'

But I was listening to her with only half an ear and was not really aware of what she had been saying until I was almost back at the castle. Instead, I was staring at the piece of paper I held in my hand – the cheap, flimsy stuff that is made from old bits of rag – on which was written a recipe for herb broth. At least, I suppose that's what it was because the sense of the words eluded me. My eyes were fixed on the looped 'g's and 'j's and the oddly formed letter 'h's. Whoever had written the recipe had also written the diary.

'Mistress Callender,' I interrupted without even realizing that I was doing so, 'are you certain that Mistress Beton wrote this recipe?'

She broke off, startled, staring at me wide-eyed, rather like her own sheep. 'Of course. Who else could have written it?'

'Mistress Sinclair?' I suggested.

She gave a high-pitched, tittering laugh. 'Oh my goodness, no! Aline was hopeless at cooking. I'm not even sure she knew how to. Recipes meant nothing to her. And if she had, she wouldn't have used a cheap scrap of paper like that. There was always plenty of the finest parchment in the house. Master Sinclair wouldn't have used anything else, and he was always writing letters.'

'Do you know who to?' It was, on reflection, a stupid question, but it got a far better answer than it deserved.

'Well, I did hear a rumour once—' Mistress Callender lowered her voice to a confidential whisper – 'that he belongs to some ancient cult or another. Don't ask me what! And I must stress that it was only the most insubstantial of rumours. Although it wouldn't surprise me in the least. Men,' she added scornfully, 'never grow up. They always want to be little boys and have secrets from their mothers and sisters and daughters and wives. Especially their wives.' Her contempt was beautiful to behold and made me wonder about the doings of the late carpet-maker.

'And you think Master Sinclair was a person of some importance in this . . . this society? Or whatever it was. He wrote letters to . . .'

'I think nothing!' The widow flushed with indignation. 'I mind my own business. I told you, what I heard was the barest of rumours. I can't even recall who mentioned it. But I know I didn't give it much credence. And now, perhaps, you'll have the kindness to answer a few of my questions . . .'

I waved the paper at her, unheeding. 'So this is definitely Maria Beton's writing? I was told she couldn't read.'

'What nonsense! Who told you that? Of course she can read. And write as well, as you can see. And now maybe you'll . . .'

I leaned forward and planted a resounding kiss on one thin cheek, and while she was still gawping at me in amazement, I asked, 'Can I keep this?' I held up the recipe.

She made no reply, merely blushing fierily, so I took this as an affirmative and made my escape, clutching the piece of paper tightly in my hand.

In the lower ward of the castle, passed by the sentries with a nod of recognition, I slowed my pace, trying to determine what next I should do. It was obvious now that the diary was a forgery written, perhaps overnight, by Maria Beton.

It had to be brought to somebody's attention, but to whose? Albany's would seem to be the answer except for the what now amounted to conviction that he was a party to the plot. I saw no way in which I could exonerate him. His actions of the previous evening and this morning, his determination to pin the blame on John Buchanan, all pointed to his complicity. I should have to find someone else to whom to present my case. The Duke of Gloucester again suggested himself as the obvious choice, but once more I hesitated to bother him over a matter that was beyond his brief as an Englishman and an outsider. I needed a Scot, someone of standing; Atholl or Buchan perhaps, one of Albany's and King James's half-uncles. But how to come at them was the difficulty. I should have to find somebody willing to introduce me.

Who? That was the question. I thought it unlikely that anyone in the Scottish camp would be willing to worry them at this critical juncture in the negotiations with what they would undoubtedly see as the triviality of an unknown man wrongly accused of concealing evidence. No one below a certain rank would contemplate it for a second; and who did I know, apart from Albany himself, of any standing at the Scottish court? With a sigh of frustration, I folded the recipe and put it into the pouch at my belt. If no alternative occurred to me before we left Scotland, I must enlist the support of my lord of Gloucester whose dislike of injustice, as I have just said, equalled mine. He might be able to do something.

I had by this time reached the summit of the rock. The smell of fish was stronger than ever and activity had increased as the dinner hour approached. I was suddenly gripped by both my arms, and there were Donald and Murdo, one on either side of me, rather, I could not help reflecting, like two gaolers escorting a prisoner. The thought made me uneasy.

'Dinnertime,' Murdo announced jovially (not a word I normally associated with the dour MacGregor).

'Look out for Davey,' Donald reminded him. 'We might as well sit together. My lord wants us all assembled in the lower ward as soon as the meal is over. Horses will be waiting for us. He wants to set forward for Roslin before noon.'

'Why the hurry?' Murdo grumbled, reverting to his customary

sullen tone. 'It's no more than seven or eight miles, if that.'

'I'm not questioning my lord's decisions,' his friend chuckled good-humouredly. 'You're welcome to if you like.'

There was the usual jostling and shoving to get into the common hall, accompanied by the even more usual exchange of insults between the different liveries, and between English and Scots. But eventually everyone found a seat, however cramped, and the servers began bringing round the food. Davey had arrived before us and had managed, against all the odds, to save places for the rest of us, including not only James Petrie, but also John Tullo, of whom I had seen comparatively little during our recent odyssey. Not that I had missed him. He smelled strongly of horses and his protuberant brown eyes seemed to bore right through me in the most disconcerting fashion. A taciturn man, he said almost nothing and in any case, responded only to remarks in the Scots tongue. His English, like James Petrie's, was confined to a few words merely. (I couldn't help wondering now and then how these two had survived in France.)

As soon as I had satisfied my initial hunger with a bowlful of surprisingly excellent fish stew, I turned to Donald and asked if he knew what had happened to John Buchanan.

He shrugged. 'In prison, I should imagine, awaiting charges. My lord was hoping to get the diary to the City Magistrates as soon as this morning's session of the Great Council finished. He should have time. He's excused himself from attending today's second meeting.'

It was on the tip of my tongue to tell both Murdo and Donald – and Davey, too, of course – what I had discovered, but an interruption by the servers, collecting dirty bowls and slapping dishes of oatcakes on the table in front of us, made me think twice, and then the moment was lost. They were laughing and talking together in that Scots vernacular from which I was firmly excluded, although, judging by the way their eyes covertly flicked towards me every now and again, I had a feeling that I might be the subject under discussion.

The meal (washed down by small beer) at last over, Donald again demonstrated an unwanted comradeship by linking one of his arms firmly in mine. Murdo, also, was once more my friend, stationing himself on my other side and somehow remaining there as we forced a passage to the door. Nor did he show any inclination to move away when we reached the open air, only falling behind as we descended to the lower ward and then reclaiming his former position with a tenacity that roused my previous misgivings. I recalled my boast to Timothy Plummer that I would hold myself excused from accompanying Albany to Roslin, but now that the moment had arrived, for some reason, could not bring myself to do so. The horses, ready saddled and waiting, seemed to clinch the fact that I was to make one of the party, whatever my own wishes in the matter.

The duke did not keep us waiting for more than ten minutes or so, saluting us in his friendliest fashion, speaking to everyone by name, but, I thought, avoiding my eyes when he addressed a word of greeting to me. It also occurred to me that Donald and Murdo, together with Davey, moved, as if by some prearranged agreement, to hem him in, rather to prevent me getting too close than for any more sinister reason. I considered again breaking free of the group and announcing my refusal to go with them, but before the intention was more than half-formed, John Tullo and James Petrie closed in alongside me, their horses forcing my own mount forward as we passed the sentries and left the castle behind.

Murdo had been right. It was no great distance to Roslin, but riding at a quick trot that occasionally broke into a gallop, still made for an uncomfortable journey as far as I was concerned. Although I seemed to have spent half my life in the saddle these past two months, the pace had been slower and I had been mounted on a more sober beast than the mettlesome one I had now been given. I am, at best, an indifferent horseman, a fact known by now to all Albany's henchmen, and it crossed my mind to wonder if John Tullo had been instructed to provide me with one of the friskier animals in Albany's stable in order to discomfit me.

Here and there, the main tracks had been rendered impassable by the rain of the preceding night and we were forced to take lesser trails winding through woodland, where delicate veils of foliage let in pallid gleams of sun; then bursting out again on to wild sweeps of moorland, lying seemingly empty and unpopulated for mile after desolate mile. Wraiths of early morning mist still clung to the dew-soaked grass in unexpected hollows and crevices that once or twice almost brought me down, and only the steadying hand of one of my companions on my bridle saved horse and rider from imminent disaster. Once, I heard the groom's voice raised in exasperation and someone else sniggered, but I set my teeth and held on like grim death. I would not give them the pleasure of seeing me thrown.

It was past midday when we finally arrived at our destination, and the light, now pale gold, struck the tops of the trees surrounding what I presumed to be Albany's hunting lodge. As far as I could see at first glance, this was nothing more than a twin-storey building of the same grey stone that was widely used for construction purposes in this Border area. It had, as well, a thatched roof, further indication, had I needed one, of the impoverished state of the Scottish court compared with the opulence of the English palaces. True, there was luxury enough in Edinburgh Castle's royal apartments, the little I had seen of them, but there was a Spartan quality to the outbuildings and the town in general that found an echo only in England's northern shires and had nothing to do with the easier living of the south.

Within, the lodge was dank and empty, and I remembered that, of course, Albany had been exiled for the past three years. It seemed no one else had used it in all that time: it had been left to rot on the edge of the village. Which said, I suppose, much for the honesty of the villagers who had neither stolen the thatch nor broken down the door to pilfer what was inside.

Not, I thought, glancing around me once the shutters had been opened, that there was much to tempt a casual thief, not unless he were in need of benches and table or plain tallow candles in pewter holders. Albany, too, seemed somewhat put out by the bareness of the place, and remarked to Donald that he regretted stripping the walls of all their hangings before leaving for France.

'Well, I did reach there eventually,' he added, glancing at me and grinning conspiratorially.

I was in no mood, however, to respond, nor did I make any attempt to join in the general bustle of preparation which kept the others busy. Food and wine had been brought in pannier baskets and had to be carried indoors. John Tullo brought in wood from somewhere to pile it on the old-fashioned central hearth, where it was finally coaxed into a blaze, a welcome contrast to the dull August day outside. If Albany noticed my sullen defiance, he made no mention of it, and even did me the honour of waving me to the seat at his right hand when, at last, he called us all to the table where wine and an array of carved wooden beakers had been set out.

'First, we'll slake our thirst,' he said, 'before we make our pilgrimage to the church. I don't doubt the ride has given us all dry throats. I'll request you to do the honours, Murdo.'

'Can I ask what we're doing here?' I demanded, suddenly finding both courage and voice.

Albany raised his eyebrows slightly at the bluntness of the question and the lack of his title to decorate it, but made no comment.

'Patience, Roger,' he said, smiling. 'All will soon be revealed.' He pushed one of the overflowing beakers towards me. (Murdo had poured out with a generous hand.) 'Drink, now.' He broke into a laugh. 'It will cure you of the sullens.'

'Before I do, my lord,' I said, dragging the piece of rag-paper from my pouch, 'I want you to look at this.'

The duke took it, puzzled, then glanced up for enlightenment. 'It appears to be a recipe for something.'

I nodded. 'A recipe for herb broth that I obtained from Mistress Callender, Master Sinclair's next-door neighbour. A recipe written by Maria Beton who, according to your friend cannot read, let alone write. Moreover,' I continued relentlessly before Albany had time to think up a reply, 'you will find that the writing is identical to that of Aline Sinclair's supposed diary. She didn't have a secret lover, nor was she planning to murder her husband. It is a highly ingenious plot to cover the fact that it was Master Sinclair who killed his wife, deliberately and in cold blood.'

There was a long silence. No one around the table moved. Albany himself sat staring at the piece of paper as if turned to stone, his face expressionless. Finally, after what seemed an age, he shifted in his chair, expelling his pent-up breath and turning his gaze in my direction.

'So . . . Well, this must certainly be looked into, without delay, as soon as we return to Edinburgh. Meantime—' he raised his beaker – 'drink up. A toast, gentlemen! To Roger's ability to uncover the truth!'

Flattered – fool that I was – I lifted my beaker and, being thirsty, swallowed half the contents in almost one gulp.

Twenty

There were lights everywhere.

At first, they were simply a golden glow, spreading inside my eyelids, adding to the confusion of mind as I struggled to recognize where I was and what had happened to me. My body felt like lead and, for the second time, I felt as though a mule had kicked me in the back of my head. I tried to lift my arms, only to discover that something was preventing movement, but at that point I wasn't particularly worried as I teetered once more towards the edge of sleep. Unconsciousness seemed eminently desirable, and I let my body go slack, greeting oblivion like a welcome friend . . .

Then, suddenly, I was wide awake, my heart pounding in unison with my throbbing head as I realized that I was bound upright to some sort of pillar by several coils of rope – ankles, calves, thighs, waist and chest – my arms pulled behind me around the pillar and my wrists lashed together in a very painful fashion.

I opened my eyes and it was then that I saw the lights; what seemed like a myriad candles illuminating the interior of one of the most extraordinary buildings I have ever seen. Everywhere I looked was a riot, an abundance of imagery. Dragons, imps, angels, what appeared to be Judaic and Arabic symbols cheek by jowl, fruit, flowers, sea-serpents, not painted but carved from stone. Heaven knows who were the masons who had done such work; I have never seen anything in the whole of my life to equal it, not even in some of the greatest churches. They had used the stone as if it were clay to be moulded at will to the greater glory of God.

But as I continued to stare around me, I began to wonder uneasily if the glory was indeed to God. In whichever direction I looked, a head of the Green Man met my eyes, an

abundance of foliage spilling out of his mouth. The chapel –
for I had guessed by this time that I was inside the chapel built
by the Sinclairs forty years earlier – was lit by six windows
on either side, and every one was surrounded by mouldings
of this ancient spirit of renewal and replenishment as he spewed
his bounty on to the earth beneath. But there were others,
everywhere . . .

The sudden awareness of acute physical discomfort
dispersed my awe and amazement. The pillar to which I
was bound was also a marvel of the stonemason's art,
being not only ribbed, but also carved with great swathes
of vegetation that spiralled around it, standing proud and
digging into my shoulders, back and legs or any other part
of my anatomy they happened to touch. As the drug with
which my drink had been laced wore off, the pain grew
increasingly intense. I struggled to free myself, knowing
full well that it was impossible, whilst my bolting senses
told me that I was in an exceedingly dangerous predicament. Not to overstate the matter, I was probably going
to be killed.

But why? And who were my potential killers?

The second question was easily answered. It had to be
Albany and his bunch of henchmen. They had brought me
here, to Roslin, but their motive was still obscure. All the
same, a nasty suspicion was beginning to form at the back
of my mind as I recalled someone – exactly who I could not
now remember – telling me that this pillar was thought to
be modelled on one that had supported an inner porch of
King Solomon's Temple and, in the same breath, had
mentioned the slaying of Hiram Abif, the architect, as a ritual
sacrifice. And hadn't the apprentice who built this pillar also
been killed by a blow to the head?

I closed my eyes against the lights and tried to rid myself
of the images of death swirling inside my brain. Why would
Albany want me dead? What for? He had always claimed
me as a friend. Indeed, I had been a friend to him in the
past, a fact he seemed to have acknowledged with becoming
gratitude for one in so exalted a position. But there, of course,
was the rub. 'Put not your trust in princes' was a maxim I
fervently believed in, yet on this occasion I had let myself

ignore it; not completely, it was true, but I had been sufficiently careless to overlook certain warning signs. And, as a result, here I was, in a situation of extreme peril from which, I felt sure, I would be lucky to escape alive.

I tried, unsuccessfully, to lift my back away from the swag of stone foliage that was cutting me between the shoulder blades. My feet and hands were starting to go numb, while a lesser, but more humiliating discomfort began to occupy my mind. My bladder was full to bursting point with the quantity of drink I had taken, and the urge to relieve myself where I stood was overwhelming. But that would be assumed by my captors to be an indication of fear – quite rightly as it happened – and I wasn't prepared to give them that satisfaction. I gritted my teeth and attempted to give my thoughts a different direction.

That wasn't difficult. Where on earth were Albany and the rest? Why didn't they come and put me out of my misery, at least if it was only to tell me what they intended, and what this charade was all about?

The thought had hardly formed before I heard the chapel door creak open. The candle flames tore sideways in the draught, then steadied as the door was closed again. There was the soft pad of booted feet across the flagstones and they stood before me; six men, their features concealed behind masks of the Green Man.

I knew them at once, of course: there had been no other attempt at disguise. Their height, their girth, the shape of their hands and feet, above all, their clothes, still mud-spattered from our morning's ride, all proclaimed their identity. A sudden surge of anger replaced, if only for a moment, my fear.

'You might as well take off those damned comic masks,' I snarled. 'If you think I can't recognize you, you're very much mistaken.' I let the fury take hold of me. 'If you knew how crass, how stupid you all look . . .' I let the sentence hang as terror once more rendered me silent.

Somewhat to my surprise, Albany complied, letting the mask swing from his fingers by its ties. John Tullo would have followed suit, but Davey's hand shot out and clutched the groom's wrist, preventing him.

The duke smiled sadly at me.

'Roger, I'm sorry about this. I had hoped it wouldn't be necessary. And if all had gone to plan, it wouldn't have been. If my brother's army had been defeated in battle by the Sassenachs and Edinburgh conquered by force of arms, James taken prisoner or, even better, killed, then, by now, I would have been accepted as King of Scotland. Unfortunately –' he shrugged – 'these plans were thwarted by my uncles' totally unlooked-for decision to rid the country of James's gaggle of disreputable favourites at Lauder Bridge. Oh, don't think I blame them! It was retribution well deserved and long overdue. But the moment, from my point of view, could not have been more ill-chosen. My brother is a prisoner, but not of the English. And one of my countrymen's conditions – indeed, the chief one – for a peaceful settlement is his restoration to his throne.'

'So?' I croaked.

He smiled again with even greater regret. 'So, I must look for non-human aid in order to achieve my ambition. I must sacrifice to the Green Man, symbol of change and renewal.'

'Sacrifice?' I could barely get the word out. My lips felt so stiff they would barely function.

The duke nodded. 'Just as Mithras cut the throat of the bull, just as Christ gave his own life on the Cross, so all gods need blood before they can bring about change. The Green Man also.'

'He's n – not a god,' I managed to stutter. 'He's nothing but a symbol of fertility.'

The rest of the little group made a hissing sound and I saw hands move to dagger hilts. Donald and Murdo took a step nearer, but Albany flung out his arms.

'No!' he cried imperatively. 'Remember, he must be killed with his own knife or the sacrifice is invalid.'

The two squires fell back, but I could hear their heavy breathing and sense the blood-lust that was now consuming each and every one of the six.

It was like a dream – a nightmare! I couldn't really believe that this sort of nonsense was happening in the modern world. This was the fifteenth century. Surely no one had faith in the pagan rituals of our distant ancestors any more? Not in western

Europe, anyway. What happened in distant, heathen lands, beyond the perimeters of the Christian world, far beyond Muscovy and the realms of Prester John, that was anybody's guess. But this was Scotland and the year was 1482.

Who was I trying to fool? Witchcraft and sorcery were still practised in every remote village and hamlet in England. Hadn't I seen the signs and symbols often enough on my travels, but chosen to ignore them, even going so far, on occasions, as to pretend to myself that I had misinterpreted them? And if in England, why not in Scotland, a country even less civilized than its neighbour? And I suddenly recollected that the Earl of Mar, amongst whose servants Donald, Murdo, Davey and the other two were numbered, had been accused of sorcery. Wrongly, many claimed, but now I felt certain it had been the truth.

Anger again possessed me. I glared at Albany.

'Is this what you brought me from England for?' I demanded, finding my voice and almost shouting at him. 'Is this why you particularly asked King Edward for me to accompany you? All that talk about wanting me for a bodyguard because you feared for your life, of trusting me when you could trust nobody else, was just one great lie?' I drew a deep breath and rapped out, 'Answer me!'

Albany threw out his hands. 'Roger, my friend –' the hypocrisy of that word made me want to spit – 'if anyone else would have done, you must believe me when I say that only desperation would have induced me to put your life at risk. Three years ago, you helped me when I was a friendless outlaw from my brother's court. I appreciate that more than you will ever know.'

'This a strange way to show your appreciation,' I snarled. 'And why me?'

Again he spread his hands.

'But isn't it obvious?' His voice was now soft, persuasive, almost soothing. As he went on talking, I found myself beginning to relax in spite of the stone swags pressing into my back and the loss of feeling in my hands and feet. After a little while, my senses began to swim and the candle flames grew in size, dazzling me with their brightness. 'You are one of us,' he was saying. 'You have the "sight". You are a part of that world of the Elf Queen beneath the Eildon Hills; a part of the Lord of the Wild Hunt's kingdom beneath Glastonbury Tor. You are at one with Thomas the Rhymer and the monk Collen who bearded Gwyn ap Nud in his lair. Your blood will be spilt to make me king and your name will never be forgotten by us, the Brotherhood of the Green Man. You will be remembered and honoured by us for generations to come. I shall . . .'

I don't know what caused it – perhaps I shifted my position and all the agony of my bound limbs returned in a rush – but suddenly I was back in the real world, the candle flames no more than that, the men before me just fools dressed up in stupid masks that wouldn't scare a schoolboy on All Hallows' Night, and Albany spouting enough ill-informed nonsense to make a cat laugh. The trouble being, of course, that there was no cat and I was feeling very far from laughing.

My expression must have altered, for Albany sensed at once that the trance-like state into which I was being lulled had lost its magic. The spell was broken. He turned furiously to the others, a command hovering on his lips, so I instinctively played for time. I don't know what I hoped to gain from a few extra minutes of life, but while I still had breath, there might yet be a gleam of hope.

'Tell me why Mistress Sinclair had to die,' I yelled. 'Tell me the truth!' Having, for the moment, diverted their attention, I moderated my tone. 'And don't pretend she plotted her husband's murder with some mysterious lover. I've proved to my own satisfaction that that was a lie; a clever plot thought up by your friend, Rab Sinclair, and his housekeeper – something that you knew all along, my lord duke!' I put as much contempt as, in the circumstances, I could muster into the last three words.

Albany, however, was indifferent to what I, or anyone else for that matter, thought of him. I could see it in the arrogant set of his head and shoulders and the scorn in his voice as he answered me.

'Aline had to die. She had discovered Rab's involvement with the cult of the Green Man during her recent visit here, to her aunt. Exactly how, Rab didn't know. Perhaps something her aunt had said, or a chance remark from a stranger. Maybe she had had her suspicions for some while and had at last received confirmation of them.' He shrugged. 'Who knows? And, frankly, my dear Roger, who cares? The unfortunate fact is that Aline was a pious little soul with, like so many of her sort, a mind closed against all other forms of worship. Christianity breeds such people and, unhappily, the Church fosters and encourages their narrow-mindedness. Now we –' he turned and made a sweeping gesture that embraced his coterie of followers – 'we tolerate men of all religions, faiths and creeds.'

'You call human sacrifice toleration?'

Albany frowned, pained.

'Not human sacrifice, Roger,' he protested. 'The shedding of blood for renewal of the spirit or, as in this case, to bring about needful change. It is my destiny to be King of Scotland. Scotland needs me.'

'You're mad,' I said with conviction, but I knew, even as I spoke, that no one would ever be able to prove it. In all respects but one, he was as sane as I was, and furthermore he was a prince of the royal blood, related by his descent from John of Gaunt to most of the reigning houses of Europe. Whatever he did, he would be protected. How he would explain my disappearance, I wasn't sure. There was a good chance that the Duke of Gloucester would eventually notice my absence and enquire after me, but by that time it would probably be too late to discover my remains and, in any case, Albany would head them off with some specious explanation. I might on occasions have my uses, but when all was said and done, I was nothing more than a common peasant, not to be weighed in the balance against someone of noble birth.

Albany moved again. I shouted desperately, 'I've told you, I do not have the sight! I have dreams, that's all, and none that foretell the future. Good God! Do you think I would have come with you today if I had known in advance what you had planned for me?'

'On your own admission, your mother had the sight. That's good enough.' The duke turned again to the group behind him who had stood in near silence all this while.

'Come, it's time! Because the sight comes to Roger through the female line, it must be the woman amongst us who does the deed.' He smiled at Davey. 'My dear Eloise, yours is the honour.'

Eloise? The page was really a woman?

I had always thought Davey a somewhat effeminate lad, but had never questioned his sex. Now, however, that Albany had revealed the truth, it was so obvious, in the way she moved, in her voice, in the softness of her skin, in the lustre of those violet-blue eyes. (A pretty boy, I remembered thinking when I first met her.) I cursed that I had not realized the fact for myself. A woman disguised as a man would have alerted me, if not necessarily to my own danger, at least to all not being as it should be.

Albany laughed at what must have been my shocked expression.

'Eloise was my late brother's mistress,' he explained. 'She stayed with the others after his death and came to France to serve me. She preferred to pass as a boy, so we disguised her as my page. She may well stay a boy, even when I am king. She likes it . . . But we are wasting time.' The duke was suddenly serious. He glanced over his shoulder at the slim, straight figure standing behind him, the face hidden by the grotesque Green Man mask so that I had no means of knowing what Davey – or Eloise as I must now try to think of her – was feeling. 'Don't be afraid, my dear. Take his knife from his belt and stab him cleanly through the heart, as Murdo has shown you.'

The girl nodded.

'Saint Margaret,' I prayed fervently, 'help me! You are my countrywoman. You are of the royal house of Wessex. Aid me now in this moment of my greatest danger. Saint Dunstan! Child of Somerset, Abbot of Glastonbury, Archbishop of Canterbury, intercede for the life of a fellow Englishman.'

The words went babbling stupidly through my head, without making any sense, as I saw the slight figure advance resolutely towards me. I believe that at that point my mind was completely numb with terror. I tried desperately to think of Adela and my children, my home, but images of them wouldn't come. All I could see was a great pit of darkness opening up at my feet . . .

'Wait!' No one was more surprised to hear my voice, loud, strong and authoritative than me. For a brief moment, I even wondered who it was that had spoken and why my would-be killer had stopped dead in her tracks.

'Go on!' urged Albany. 'Eloise, go on! Let's get this over with. The sooner he's dead, the sooner the gods will move to have me accepted as king.'

'Wait,' I shouted again, and looked at Albany, the only one who had removed his mask. It was easier to address a human face. 'You say I must be killed with my own knife. Is that part of the ritual?'

'Well, what of it?'

'This is not my knife.' I jerked my head, the only free part of me, downwards to the weapon tucked in my belt.

'What do you mean?' Albany was growing angry. He suspected a trick.

'This is Donald's knife,' I said. 'He lent it to me yesterday when I was attacked in the street. Murdo was present. He can confirm it.'

The duke swore violently and swung round on one of the two taller figures at his side.

'Is this true?' he demanded. The green mask dipped in acknowledgement, calling forth another colourful string of curses that might, in different circumstances, have provoked my admiration. Albany spun back to me. 'Where's your own knife?' he yelled. 'The one you use for meat?'

'I left it behind. I noticed at dinner that it's grown blunt and needs sharpening. I thought Donald wouldn't mind if I used his for a while. He didn't seem in any hurry to have it back.'

'You fool!' the duke screamed at his unfortunate squire. 'You stupid, feckless, unthinking idiot!'

'What are we to do?' asked the familiar voice of 'Davey'. Knowing the truth, I wondered how I could ever have thought it the voice of a man.

'Be quiet and let me think.' Albany was chewing his knuckles in frustration. After what seemed to me to be the longest few moments of my life, he said, 'The apprentice who built this pillar was killed by a blow to the head. We'll use the same method. Find something one of you. Quickly!

We still have to dispose of his body, and that will take time. I must be back in Edinburgh by this evening.'

'And how will you explain my absence?' I asked.

Albany grunted. 'Nothing easier. You gave us the slip. You deserted, as you've been wanting to do for weeks now, and are probably making your own way back to England.' He shrugged. 'If, that is, anyone cares where you've gone.'

'His Grace of Gloucester will care,' I said, hoping to God and all the saints that I was right.

The duke slowly shook his head. 'I've already prepared my cousin's mind, these few days past, for the idea that you're ripe for desertion. In any case, I don't think the notion was new to him. He's a fair man and realizes that you've fulfilled the purpose you were hired for. So he won't send after you or trouble his head with where you've gone until he needs your services again, which may be many months ahead. Perhaps longer.' He rounded furiously on his henchmen. 'Why are you standing there like so many dolts? Don't pretend you can't understand English! Find a bludgeon of some sort. Anything so long as it's heavy enough to kill him with a single blow. And pray to Mother Earth that the blood spilt thus, rather than with his own cold steel, is acceptable enough to secure her and her consort's intervention to make me king.'

Someone moved – I guessed from the size and shape of him that it was the groom, John Tullo – and left the chapel to search for a suitable instrument of death. My death! The truth seemed to strike me afresh.

I strained frantically against my bonds, but I could have saved myself the effort. I was bound too tightly.

Albany shook his head.

'Don't struggle, Roger,' he said reproachfully. 'Accept death as a stepping-stone to the world of the hollow hills, where you will live and feast forever, rejoicing in the knowledge that you have given Scotland her greatest king; greater even than Robert le Brus. For surely I shall have bigger and better triumphs than Bannockburn.'

'And . . . And this was why you asked for me to accompany you to Scotland?' I stuttered. 'To use me as a human sacrifice if you didn't become king?' Even now, I couldn't really believe it. Surely I would suddenly wake up and find that it was all a dream.

Albany nodded. 'I suspected treachery on the part of the English. Or at least let us just say that I judged it wise to take precautions. I remembered from our first encounter, someone – maybe yourself – telling me that you were thought to have the sight, so I knew you to be one of us.'

'I'm not one of you!' I shouted, hoarse now with desperation. 'You're mad, all of you! Heretics! Blasphemers!'

I heard again the intake of breath, like the hiss of a snake. The mood was turning ugly. Uglier, I should say; for what could be nastier or more terrifying than a man who believed that the ritual killing of a fellow human being could win him his heart's desire? And yet . . . And yet . . . Wasn't the spilling of blood at the heart of most religious beliefs? Christianity, Judaism, Mithraism . . .

'And all those apparent attempts on your life were false?' I croaked.

'To keep you from absconding,' the duke agreed. 'To prevent you from suspecting the truth. And in the end, of course, you proved to be worth your weight in gold, worth all the effort to keep you by my side, when it came to assisting my friend, Rab Sinclair. A pity that you stumbled on the truth, but it really doesn't matter, does it? No one will ever hear it from you now.' He turned petulantly to look about him. 'Where's that fool gone? What's taking him so long? Surely by this time he could have found a good, stout branch that would do the job?'

'Perhaps your groom doesn't approve of what you plan to do,' I said, although I had little hope of that. I had just felt a draught as the chapel door opened once more. Nevertheless, I went on, 'Perhaps he's the one of your followers – the man in the Green Man mask – who kept trying to warn me that my life was in danger; who kept urging me to watch my back.'

Albany looked as though I'd struck him. He went red and began to breathe heavily.

'If I thought that—' he was beginning.

'He wasn't the man who warned you, Roger,' said a familiar voice, as Timothy Plummer emerged out of the candlelit shadows. 'I did.' He turned and beckoned, and half a dozen foot-soldiers – big, brawny fellows with a no-nonsense look about them – marched in, two of them holding the struggling John Tullo, minus his mask, between them. He added, pointing at Albany and his followers, 'Arrest these men.'

Do I need to tell you that, in the short, sharp skirmish that followed, Albany somehow mysteriously vanished? Was allowed to vanish, you can be sure of that. It was no part of Timothy's brief to arrest the King of Scotland's brother so that he could publicly be accused of witchcraft and sorcery. These things were better dealt with in the dark, as the Earl of Mar's death had been. But the other five were arrested and taken back to Edinburgh under armed guard. I was cut free of the so-called apprentice's pillar, and a sorry state I was in for a couple of days afterwards as I recuperated in the castle under Timothy's watchful eye. He proved to be a surprisingly good nurse.

'What made you suspicious of Albany's real intentions?' was one of the first questions I asked him.

He snorted indignantly. 'For heaven's sweet sake, Roger, I'm a spy! I know all sorts of things about people that I daresay I shouldn't. I knew, for instance, that that bevy of beauties who had fled to France to join him, had been deeply implicated in the charges of sorcery that had been levied – although never, of course, proved – against Mar. I knew, too of Albany's deep interest in the cult of the Green Man. It was he who requested – no, insisted – on the masque of the Green Man and Mother Earth at Fotheringay. That was where I stole one of the mummers' masks and wore it when I tried to warn you.'

Deeply grateful as I was for my eleventh-hour rescue, I couldn't help asking bitterly, 'Why, in God's Name, didn't you just come out and tell me, man to man, what you suspected?'

'Because,' he snapped back, 'I didn't really know what it was that I did suspect. Only that you might be in some sort of danger. Which you wouldn't have been if things had gone according to plan and Albany crowned King of Scotland. I didn't want you rampaging off home, or storming off to confront Albany, or, worse still, my lord of Gloucester, all on the strength of my unfounded suspicions. I repeat, unfounded. I should have been in the shit up to my neck.'

I agreed he had a point. 'And what will happen to Albany? The others must be for the fire or the hangman's noose.'

Once again, Timothy snorted. 'That one will dig his own grave without any help from me. Meanwhile—' he clapped me on the shoulder – 'news has come that the citadel at Berwick has surrendered. We're for the homeward march, my lad, the day after tomorrow. Negotiations here are completed.'

And so we were. But before I shook the dust of Edinburgh and its castle off my feet, I went to give thanks and homage to my fellow west countrywoman, that descendant of the kings of Wessex, Saint Margaret of Scotland.